JEFF PANTANELLA

THE CHAOS GATE

BOOK ONE IN THE
EVER HERO SAGA

Copyright © 2020 by Jeff Pantanella
All rights reserved.

ISBN 978-1-7356025-0-9

No part of this publication may be reproduced, stored or transmitted in any form or by any means, electronic, mechanical, photocopying, recording, scanning, or otherwise without written permission from the publisher. It is illegal to copy this book, post it to a website, or distribute it by any other means without permission.
Jeff Pantanella asserts the moral right to be identified as the author of this work.

First Printing, 2020
Ever Hero Productions
Yorba Linda, CA 92886
United States of America
www.everheroproductions.com

Cover Design by Jeff Pantanella
Author Photo by Asia Yen Productions and Design
Edited by Maureen Neuman

ALSO BY JEFF PANTANELLA
THE EVER HERO SAGA

NOVELLA: SEKKA
ORIGIN STORY
AVAILABLE NOW

BOOK ONE: THE CHAOS GATE
AVAILABLE NOW

BOOK TWO: THE FOE WARS
AVAILABLE NOW

BOOK THREE: THE DIVINE FIST
AVAILABLE NOW

BOOK FOUR: THE FORGOTTEN GODS
AVAILABLE NOW

BOOK FIVE: KAZUMI, DEMON SPIRIT
AVAILABLE NOW

BOOK SIX: KAZUMI, WICKED FOX
AVAILABLE NOW

BOOK SEVEN: KAZUMI, VAMPIRE HUNTER
AVAILABLE NOW

BOOK EIGHT: EDEN
COMING SOON

YOUR FREE NOVELLA IS WAITING

Vast legions of demons and fiends grovel at her feet, but it is not enough; gods must tremble.

The archdevil, Sekka simmers with discontent. Bled dry by interminable warfare, bitter infighting, and bloody confrontations with formidable foes, she aches for more power. Souls are the currency of the Abyss, and she is in woefully short supply. An opportunistic encounter with an old nemesis offers her a chance to overthrow the reigning monarchs of the Abyss, but in doing so, she sets in motion events that will drag the Three Realms of devils, angels, and mortals into a war to end all wars.

She turns her predatory gaze to the Mortal Realm, searching for the young and naïve, Ever Hero; the one person she needs to fulfill her destiny and the one person who can stop her, unless she claims him before he comes into his power.

However, it would appear the archdevil is not alone in this grand game of conquest. Those possessing god-level powers in the Abyss and Seven Heavens are gathering their forces, preparing to use Sekka's ambition to their own advantage.

One simple rule applies: YOU DON'T GET POWER. YOU TAKE IT.

CLICK HERE to get your FREE eBook novella of Sekka's rise to power in the Abyss or type: https://BookHip.com/FTRLPW into your browser window

This one is for P

ACKNOWLEDGMENTS

There are too many people to thank for helping me see this work to completion. First and foremost to my mom, for the encouragement to keep going and then my favorite witches, Manna D, Jennifer V, and Sunny L, for the inspiration they provided.

DRAMATIS PERSONAE

The Divine of the Seven Heavens
    The Immortal Mother, creator of the Three Worlds
    Illyria, ninth daughter of the Immortal Mother
    Aetenos Sommai, 'The Divine Fist', 'The Great Monk', mortal who ascended to the rank of demigod

The Wicked of the Abyss
    Azrollorza, Supreme Devil, one of the 'Great Three', ruler of Mazzagratur, Sea of Terror, the fifth Layer in the Abyss
    Morrdilliax, Supreme Devil, one of the 'Great Three', ruler of Torremor, Plain of Infinite Decay, the sixth Layer in the Abyss
    Xerthotha, 'The Chaos Devil', Supreme Devil, one of the 'Great Three', ruler of Stomoxys, The Land of Eternal Strife, the seventh Layer in the Abyss
    Sekka, 'The Ice Queen', 'Mistress Sekka', reigning archdevil of Gathos, the seventh Circle, on the Land of Sorrow, the third Layer of the Abyss

Lord Oziax, 'The Soul Breaker', greater demon, general of Sekka's Frost Legions on Gathos

Sess'thra, greater demon, succubus, infiltrator, commander of Sekka's agents in the Mortal Realm

Daxzulz Thrum, 'Dax', doppelganger assassin, agent of Sekka, commanded by Sess'thra

Khalkoroth, 'The Pale Demon', shadow demon, agent of Sekka, commanded by Sess'thra

Chedipe, demon witch, Sekka's chief tormentor

Zizphander, 'The Red Devil of Naraka, archnemesis of Sekka, reigning archdevil of Naraka, the eighth Circle, on Purgio, the first Layer of the Abyss

Monastery of Ordu, one of the Four Orders of Light, Kingdom of Baroqia

Kasai Ch'ou, junior monk of the Brotherhood of Ordu

Daku, junior monk of the Brotherhood of Ordu

Master Choejor, 12th rank, master monk of Ordu, one of the 'Three Master Monks of Ordu'

Master Dorje, 12th rank, master monk of Ordu, one of the 'Three Master Monks of Ordu'

Master Kunchen, 12th rank, master monk of Ordu, one of the 'Three Master Monks of Ordu'

Ninziz-zida, 'The Fire Serpent', sentient three sectioned staff

Forest Folk, Kingdom of Baroqia

Desdemonia Mishi, wood witch

Gauldumor, earth elemental, protector of Desdemonia Mishi

Pallo Katan, Kibo Gensai warrior, brother to Veers 'Run-Run' Katan

Veers Katan, 'Run-Run', Kibo Gensai warrior, brother to Pallo Katan

House Conrad and Allies, Kingdom of Baroqia
    Mortimer Conrad, King of Baroqia
    Duke Manda, ruler of House Manda, loyal to King Conrad
    Lord Fritta, ruler of House Fritta, loyal to King Conrad
    Baron Rokig, ruler of House Rokig, loyal to King Conrad
    Lord Jolla, ruler of House Jolla, loyal to King Conrad

House Shiverrig
    Duke Gerun Shiverrig, 'The War Duke', Duke of Gethem
    Archvashim Malachi, advisor to Duke Shiverrig

Rachlach Fortress, Kingdom of Trosk
    Maugris Hennerstrum, 'The Mad One,' banished sorcerer

"The Heavens spin right. The Hells spin left. Each in opposition to the other. Each searching for advantage. The Mortal Realm is forever pulled and squeezed in the middle. In all things, the Great Balance must remain."

~The Prophetess Miko Nuna

"A thousand wicks can be lit from the flame of a single candle, and the fire of the originator will not be lessened. Each new candle will add their flame to light ten thousand candles, and so on, creating an infinite sea of light. This is the Boundless."

~The First of Aetenos, Gen Moll

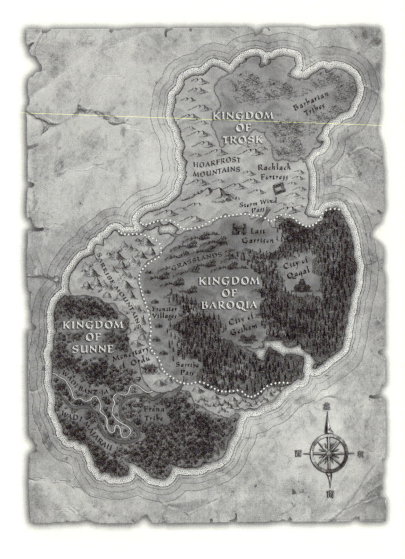

PROLOGUE

"Hold! Hold!" a senior officer cried into the din of ferocious roars and wailing cries. His breath frosted before his face. Irrelevant whether his soldiers heard him, whether they wanted to comply; the battle had turned to a rout. Sekka's Frost Legion hammered the last remnants of the human army sent to halt her advance.

Sekka chuckled at the futility of the officer's command. "You should have sent more men, foolish monk. It won't be long now," she crowed.

The sky was ablaze with the crimson hue of a setting sun, reaching long blood-red fingers over the battleground. Despite the fire in the sky, there was no warmth. A cold wind blew through pockets of fighting, biting as deeply as the claws, teeth, and horns of her troops. The air reeked with the stench of open flesh and spilled viscera.

Sekka stretched her arms to the sky and flung her head back, full of joy. She twirled once, hugging herself, "Glorious!" The sobs of the wounded replaced the clang of swords and shields.

At the center of the battlefield, knights in once-shining armor moved like dwindling beacons of hope, their swords gleaming with enchantments meant to pierce the hideous hides of her demons. Even so, too few remained.

"A foul gift from those miserable do-gooders," Sekka cursed, raising her black-on-black eyes to the red sky, scanning for any indication *they* would interfere. A cruel smile curled the corners of her mouth. "Just clouds."

She brought her attention back to the battle, relishing its fury and inevitability. Despite the knights' valor, Sekka's Frost Legion was an unstoppable force impervious to fear or pain, bred on her home world of Gathos for the conquest of this realm. Scanning the field with a predator's interest, she spotted a human forming a last stand. Demon death ash formed miniature clouds, swirling over his head.

"Ah, there you are," Sekka purred. She had chosen a mortal form—sleek, sexual, and dangerous; fitting for conquest in this realm. Dressed in form-fitting war gear embossed with the eight-pointed Wheel of Chaos, she appeared the perfect image of a dread warlord. Her delicate hands, at odds with the lethal dark magic they summoned, flickered with shadowy tendrils, weaving a tapestry of malevolence. "At last the titans meet."

Others saw the lone warrior, too, and moved in frantic clusters, desperate to reach the tiny island of hope which stood against the storming sea of destruction. "The knights have rallied to their hero, wonderful," she observed. "More souls for the pits."

She moved gracefully through the battlefield, taking pleasure in ending life, in whichever foul way she deemed most enjoyable, until she finally reached the warrior.

"You will not win this day, devil," her opponent said before tucking his segmented staff under the crutch of his arm in order to dispatch a horned monster, using a palm-heel strike to its head. She was impressed by how easily he pulverized the demon's skull, turning the brain matter inside to pulp. The demon sat back on it haunches, eyes locked in a befuddled stare before bits and pieces of its flesh decomposed to ash, adding to the whirlwind circling above the warrior.

"Oh, I think I will. Look around. You're all that's left. It's over. This realm is mine. Quite frankly, I'm disappointed. This was the best you could bring to bear?" Sekka mocked, her eyes glinting with a dark mirth.

The warrior stood grounded in the packed snow and trampled grass. His calm demeanor a stark contrast to the surrounding carnage. Clad in simple, weathered cobalt robes, he spun the three-sectioned staff with an ease into an aggressive, attacking posture, belying his humble appearance. Sekka knew of the legendary staff, unassuming at first glance, it carried within it a powerful adversary. A blue flame rippled along its three sections as if the inhabitant within bided; impatient to be released.

"Ninziz-zida has been waiting for you," the monk said.

Sekka sneered, eyeing the staff with revulsion. "Is there anything you possess that wasn't stolen?"

"I—"

Sekka didn't wait for his explanation, striking in a blur of movement, launching shards of darkness that screamed through the air like malevolent spirits. The monk deftly maneuvered, his staff spinning in seamless arcs, each action a precise counter to the devil's magical assault. The staff's blue flame intensified, burning beyond the sticks, coiling into the fiery form above the monk.

Gritting her teeth, Sekka set her feet apart, preparing for the final battle—the real fight that would determine whether she dominated the Mortal Realm or if she would be cast back to the Abyss to suffer the torment of her disappointed benefactors.

The blue flames hissed at her, twisting through a transformation into an ancient fire elemental dragon. Sekka felt as if she stood before a volcano's fury, the heat from the dragon scolded her skin and crisped her hair. Blinded by the brightness of the serpent's flame, Sekka instinctively shielded her eyes. It was a mistake. The dragon and monk attacked as one, pummeling her with blows and bites. Her human form was weak and could not withstand such punishment for long.

Growling through a guttural curse, Sekka shifted into her true form. Her human facade melted away, revealing a horrific infernal creature, towering and fearsome. Four curling horns began to frame her head, and four hooked teeth protruded menacingly from her mouth. Floating above her head, a crown of bones materialized, adorned with glowing sigils of power that pulsed ominously from the gems at its base. Her body expanded, becoming immense and robust, her muscles hardening and rippling as if challenging magical restraints that sought to contain her.

Coarse, white fur sprouted and blanketed her back, each strand thick and wild. Her arms thickened. Claws grew from her fingers, gleaming from the light of the dragon's flame, each one capable of tearing through stone and flesh alike. Her legs, now avian in structure, ended in feet with raptor-like talons, ready to tear and rend anything in their path.

The dragon and monk continued their assault as she contorted and struggled, her chest heaved, her form swelling with raw, demonic power. Sekka lashed out blindly, hoping to gouge either foe. Innate chaos magic seeped from her pours. She would need to rely on it more that brute strength against her adversaries.

The monk, agile and serene, danced between the swipes

of her claws, his staff a blur of motion, striking with the force of a tempest. Each hit from the fire dragon seared her flesh, but she was relentless, her dark magic weaving a shield of shadow and despair, absorbing the fiery onslaught and striking back with tendrils of pure darkness.

She shouted out another curse, this one directed at the mortality of the monk. Through squinted eyes, she saw him doubled over, vomiting blood. Ninziz-zida roared. The fire dragon reared up, sucking in a large draught of air, her eyes glaring at Sekka.

"Chanta-thriz-hor," Sekka chanted, summoning a protective aegis around her as the dragon spewed a thick stream of lava, making the air shimmer from its heat.

Sekka renewed her attack, aware that if the staff fell from the monk's hands, the fire dragon would lose its connection to the material world and be snuffed out. Lashing out with her claws and biting fiercely, she engaged in a brutal exchange with the fire dragon before unleashing a barrage of spells aimed to disable and disorient the monk. Anything to get him to drop the damned staff.

While the monk evaded most of her onslaught, one in every ten of Sekka's spells found its mark. She saw him stumble on unsure legs as a bolt of death energy grazed his thigh. She summoned lesser demons to her aid, each one a horrific nightmare of gnashing teeth and icy death. The monk fought through them all, but she could see it—almost taste it—he was slowing down.

She lunged forward, seizing the staff, and wrenching it from his grasp. The searing pain that raced up her arm, causing her flesh to melt off the bones of her hand, was a small price to pay for triumph. The fire dragon emitted a piercing shriek before it dissolved, its life essence being reabsorbed into the staff.

Sekka thrust the staff behind her. She sought the monk's eyes. "You see it now, don't you? My time has come."

The weakened monk leaped with a spinning high kick directed at her head. She grabbed his leg mid-flight and hurled him across the field. This day would see the end of the Great Monk, Aetenos, and mark the beginning of her rule in the Mortal Realm. *Oh, the delight!* she thought, stomping to where the monk lay on his back. "Perhaps a more delicate shape to savor my victory," she said, transforming back to the form of a wicked human queen. "They will look upon my beauty and despair."

And then, the clarion call of her doom pealed, ringing in her ears like ten thousand church bells. Her eyes shot skyward. From the billowing, crimson clouds, the Heavenly Host descended, a radiant legion of angels whose presence alone commanded awe. Their wings, vast and resplendent, shimmered with celestial light, casting beams that cut through the gathering dusk.

The Frost Legion awaited on the muted, snow-covered plains below, their grotesque forms and icy auras stark against the long shadows of the setting sun. As the angels approached, a profound silence fell, broken only by the soft whisper of feathered wings against the air.

Sekka found herself transfixed by the sudden and disastrous shift in events until a second clarion call pealed across the sky. Another legion! And then a third and fourth broke through the cloud cover. They were not here to stop her; they had come to annihilate her.

With an otherworldly grace and power that seemed to bend the very fabric of reality, the angels engaged the demons. The contrast was absolute: where the demons were harsh and brutal, the angels moved with a precision and elegance. Their weapons, forged from divine essence of righteous might, burned with holy fire.

The battle, though fierce, was one-sided. The Heavenly Host wielded powers that transcended the physical realm, commanding forces of light and purity that unraveled the demonic beings with each touch. Her Frost Legion was dismantled with a decisive and methodical efficiency.

With a final, concerted effort that seemed to draw on the very essence of the heavens, the angels unleashed a torrent of radiant energy that swept across the battlefield. As the light receded, Sekka's Frost Legion was no more, erased from existence but for the ash of their memory.

Sekka dropped to her knees, broken and defeated. In retrospect, perhaps she had been a tad overconfident, changing back to her mortal form after defeating the monk and his fire serpent. She was weakened in this form, bruised and swollen from her earlier entanglement—not that it mattered now. Nothing could stand against what hovered beneath the clouds. Victory had been within her grasp, but now her armies were gone, obliterated unfairly. The angels had no right to interfere, and yet they had.

She sneered as the ashes of her dead warriors floated past her face. Clenching her fists in frustration, she tallied the mortal soul energy she had spent to create her armies. The Gathos reserves were depleted now; she was vulnerable to attack, yet it wasn't the Heavenly Host that worried her for no angel would dare tread into the Abyss. The denizens of the Lower Planes could smell weakness and would race to claim what was hers.

She raised her pale face, and through clumps of matted, white hair, she vaguely saw the last remaining angels vanishing through a portal that illuminated the sky like a second sun. The bulk of the Heavenly Host had already departed, having finished their work here.

"Fly back to your precious Elysian; you thrice-damned little birds," she cursed. "I will have my revenge!"

She licked her dry, blue lips, with a pasty tongue. Everything hurt. Her innate healing powers worked tirelessly to repair the damage the staff had caused. Nonetheless, through cracked and sore lips a wicked smile crossed her bruised face. The fools had let her live, and there was still a chance she could gain a permanent foothold in the Mortal Realm, considering the agents she had previously scattered throughout this realm. Her succubus, Sess'thra, would find her another suitable host and then she would rebuild. The thought of harvesting so many souls gave her renewed strength. Sekka tried to rise. "As long as I draw breath…"

Then *he* stepped forward; his robed silhouette backlit by the distant sun. Light gleamed off his partially bald head. She envisioned him smiling, with a kind, worry-free expression, as if he possessed the secret to eternal contentment. One of the Great Three save her, how she hated him.

He held one arm comfortably behind his back. In the other was the three-sectioned staff she had torn from his grasp. The burn of its kiss still sizzled the rejoining flesh of her hand. Ninziz-zida remained confined within the sticks—for now.

As he drew closer, she saw his dull, cobalt blue robes were in tatters. Bloody, burgundy stains had soaked into its threads. She cracked a weak smirk, remembering the blows which had struck true.

"Aetenos," Sekka snarled. "It's not like you to gloat."

"I am here to do what must be done. I wish it was otherwise," he replied with a strained politeness.

He studied her, shaking his head with a sadness she found arrogant. The physical pain she felt was nothing compared to his pity. She cursed his soul a thousand times for interfering in her plans—centuries in the making yet destroyed in a blink of an eye. How had he contacted the Trueborn? There were protocols that must be followed!

"Your trespass into the Mortal Realm has ended. The laws of the Immortal Mother must never be broken. The Great Balance must remain," he schooled.

"You cannot beat me alone," Sekka scoffed.

"In this, you are correct, nor is it my destiny to do so, in this lifetime or the next. Yet, we remain connected through them all like the overlapping threads of an everlasting tapestry."

"This is not the end."

"There is no end, only a formless continuation of the spirit through the Boundless."

She hated his riddles. "Get on with it, monk."

"As you wish, devil."

Ninziz-zida blazed to life from the staff in Aetenos' hands, and Sekka's end came swiftly.

CENTURIES LATER...

1

KASAI

Brother Kasai raced down the polished stone corridors of Zazen Hall. His topknot of braided, black hair whipped like an angry viper behind his head. Light from rows of beeswax candles gleamed off the rest of his shiny scalp. He did his best to run silently, but his loose brown robes billowed like sheets in the wind. He was sure the noise could wake the dead.

The young monk had removed his sandals at the entrance to the Hall, as was customary. His wool socks slipped on the smooth stone, making running down the concourse difficult, and he was late to morning meditation ... again. Why he couldn't finish his dawn chores on time as the rest of his Brothers was a mystery to him. Master Dorje would not be pleased.

With a bit of luck, the doors to the Meditation Hall would be open, Kasai hoped. As he slid around the last corner, he watched the strip of light between the tall red doors narrow and disappear as they closed with a soft click. A sigh of disappointment escaped his lips. "I'm not even that late." He gripped the door ring and pulled slowly. "Quiet as a mouse now. Not a sound." The dry hinges refused to listen, and with an agonizingly slow creak, they shattered the silence of the room. Kasai scrunched his shoulders, grimacing as he slowly pushed the door open.

Peering into the dimly lit room, he spied all forty-three monks, ranging from child to young adult, heads down, sitting in quiet contemplation. Each had been brought to the monastery as a youngster by a Traveling Master, just like Kasai. The monastery offered orphaned and abandoned children a home and family when they otherwise would have none. Even so, their life was not easy. The monks were deprived of many comforts, but it was safe and a place they could call home.

Each monk chose to wear their hair in a formal topknot style or to shave their head clean. They sat in rows depicting age groups, older students to the front with the younger initiates in the rear. Legs were tucked under their knees, tan, sleeveless shirts gathered into dark brown leggings above the slippery, off-white socks. Some wore loose rusty-orange robes that billowed in the mountain winds and did nothing to curtail the cold. Others had removed their outer robes, folding them neatly on the floor before them. A few scattered candles threw a feeble glow upon their still bodies.

Master Dorje, one of the Three Masters of Ordu, was seated upon a raised platform, draped in simple blue robes. His head was upright, but his face remained in shadow. Interrupting his teaching, Master Dorje turned his smooth head towards Kasai, keeping his eyes closed.

"Stay shut. Stay shut," Kasai silently pleaded, squeezing through the narrowest gap the door would allow.

Master Dorje's eyes flashed open, acknowledging Kasai with a cold stare and disapproving frown. *This is going to be a bad day*, Kasai thought.

"Please have a seat, Brother Kasai. We have been waiting

for you," Master Dorje instructed. The tone of his voice was neutral. This was another bad sign.

Nothing to do about it now. Kasai shuffled across the room to his zabuton, a somewhat safe three rows from Master Dorje's platform. He plopped down on his small, square mat and joined the rest of his Brothers in meditation.

Master Dorje continued his lesson, "All things are contained within the Boundless, yet the Boundless remains invisible to eyes that are blind, ears that are deaf, and hands unable to touch. The mountain filled with stones and the trees that grow in its earth is part of the Boundless. The water that flows in a stream, the air the blows with the wind, and the fire that burns, but lights our way are all the same. When you are one with the Boundless, you will see, hear, and feel the vibrations of their essence."

"You make more noise than a raccoon caught in the pantry. I heard you coming as far away as the dormitories," Brother Daku whispered from Kasai's right side.

Daku was a year older than Kasai. His muscular body could have been sculpted from stone. His face was sharp and angular in the same way. He looked like a living granite statue in a king's courtyard. "Master Dorje will not go lightly on you this time."

"I know. I know," Kasai sighed. "Who was assigned to oil the door hinges this month?"

"Me," Daku snickered.

"Thanks, *friend*." Kasai shut his almond-shaped eyes and concentrated on Master Dorje's lesson.

The Master continued, "Through the Boundless, you will share the gift of understanding with all things, for all things are alive with vibration. Their thoughts will be your thoughts, their actions, your actions, their energy shall be your energy. In return, you shall give all of yourself. This is the Openness. It is a bond of truth.

"When you free yourself from misery, from hate and revenge, you will be ready to embrace the Boundless. Do not fear the unknown, for within the unknown is the seed for growth."

The Master remained silent for a time. He breathed out slowly. Kasai heard the platform boards creak. *Oh, please let him leave without another word*, Kasai hoped.

"Contemplate what you have learned today, for it will help you in the future. Tomorrow, the Test of Pillars await the senior initiates."

Kasai cracked open his eyes, watching Master Dorje pad to the door leading to his private chamber. His pace was agonizingly slow. "Lucky, lucky, lucky," Kasai whispered with each of the Master's steps.

Master Dorje stopped at the door. "Brother Kasai, I shall have a word with you in my chamber when you have finished."

Kasai slumped on his zabuton. "I'm sunk." The old monk was known for his stringent punishments and Kasai hoped he would not be forced to choose between two impossible tasks again. That was a special torture. Once, he had to choose between balancing on one leg for a day and night or sitting naked in the snow until the morning sun was overhead. He now hated the cold with an extraordinary passion.

"Why must I always be late?" he lamented, shaking his head.

Two hours later, a bell chimed three times, signaling the end of morning meditation. Kasai got up and walked with heavy steps to Master Dorje's private chamber. Before he could reach the door, Daku hurried over to him.

"I don't want to hear it, Daku," Kasai said as the bigger Brother slung his heavy arm over Kasai's shoulder. Standing at least two hand's width taller than most of the Brothers at the monastery, Daku relished the view from above, particularly when it came to Kasai.

"Cheer up, Little Brother, this was only the third time you were late this month," Daku jested. He rarely, if ever, used the title "Brother" with any of the monks of the order. "I don't think that warrants anything too severe."

"Really?" Kasai said, hopefully.

"No, not really. You'll pull midnight watch for sure this time. Just think of it, you, alone on the North Ridge. The heavens are full of stars. The cold wind is blowing, but there's no fire to warm you. *Brrrrr.* I hope you have properly mastered the deeper fire xindu forms."

"You know I haven't," Kasai sighed.

"And only the calls of the vargru to keep you company," Daku added. "You'll know when they're close because their howling shifts to maniacal laughter and then stops abruptly."

"That's not true," Kasai said, his voice cracking with a hint of fear. "The vargru keep to the lower forests."

"If you say so," Daku chuckled. "I'll be with Jia'mu and Ri'sonu in the courtyard. Meet us after."

Daku left the meditation hall with the rest of the monks. Kasai turned to the side door. "This always happens to me. Why am I so unlucky?" He sighed once more as he grabbed the handle.

A short time later, Kasai entered the outside courtyard. He dragged his feet and wore the expression of a man resigned to a harsh fate. Brothers Jia'mu, Ri'sonu, and Daku joined him.

"Will it be an extra hour or two of sweeping the outer steps, or did Master Dorje go hard on you?" Jia'mu teased. He was roughly the same age as Kasai, though the Masters discouraged discussing a person's age in numbers. The Masters said it was a self-defeating idea used to count the days left in life, rather than the accomplishments that lay ahead.

Jia'mu was small and round, built like a cannon shot, which earned him the name Cannonball from his friends. His shaved head and puffy cheeks gave him the appearance of having a second, smaller ball, precariously balanced on his rounded shoulders. Not even Daku could move Cannonball from the center circle once he crouched in a static basket position.

Kasai tried, unsuccessfully, to smile. "Master Dorje fully expressed his disapproval with me for being late. I was granted a month's worth of midnight sentry duty on the North Ridge," Kasai reported.

Jia'mu and Ri'sonu grimaced and moaned.

"I knew it!" Daku's dark eyes flashed with excitement. He pointed his finger at Kasai. "It's not more than you deserve."

"Be thankful it's still early autumn, and you didn't draw winter duty," Ri'sonu said. "I'd hate to be out all night in the middle of December."

Ri'sonu wrapped his long arms around his thin body. His frame was the opposite of Jia'mu. He was just a few fingers shorter than Daku but skinny as a reed. His body could move like a length of rope, which made him difficult to hit in a fight.

"I didn't say guard duty started tonight." Kasai's shoulders slumped.

"Oh no," Ri'sonu cringed.

Daku laughed. "Serves you right, Kasai. You're always late. Knowing you, you'll be late for your own funeral."

"Speaking of funerals, we face the pillar test tomorrow. I didn't think it would be this soon. I'm not ready. What if it's a cloudy day tomorrow? We won't be able to see where we're going," Cannonball theorized, biting on a well-chewed fingernail. Ri'sonu nodded in agreement.

Daku scoffed at their nervous reactions.

"Finally, we are given a true test. I'm eager to pit my xindu energy against something real. I'm tired of practicing lame tricks over-and-over again. Hot hands, cold hands. Hot feet, cold feet. None of this is like fighting in the real world. I'm ready for a challenge!"

Daku was in a boastful mood today. *When was he not?* Kasai wondered.

Cannonball wasn't as confident. "I overheard two of the senior monks saying to Brother Maru that if you fail here, you won't be able to ascend to the higher ranks." He craned his head towards the clouds. "How far up do you think they go?"

"The pillar test is not meant to be completed by initiates. It was designed to help open us to the Boundless," Ri'sonu informed. He hid his hesitation behind a more scholarly approach. "Master Kunchen posted a scroll of who shall go tomorrow. We are the first four to attempt the challenge."

"I thought it wouldn't happen for another season after we had more training," Kasai said.

Ri'sonu and Cannonball stared uncertainly at each other.

"What a bunch of worriers. I'll race you all to the finish," Daku said. "And I'll win, no question."

"It's not a competition," Kasai said.

"Yes, it is. It always is," Daku said with a twisted smile. He turned to walk towards the sparring grounds. "I need to practice a new, low-kick combination. One of you come with me."

Kasai and Ri'sonu shook their heads. But Cannonball fell in step behind Daku.

"Don't go, Cannonball," Kasai said. "You'll regret it."

"I need to practice, too," Cannonball acknowledged.

"Let him go. He's a glutton for punishment when it comes to Daku," Ri'sonu said. "I'm convinced Cannonball reasons the more he lets Daku beat him up, the better friends they will be."

"That's messed up," Kasai said, wondering how often he though the same of himself.

The next morning, the young monks assembled around Master Choejor at the steps of the first pillars. He stood with his arms behind his back, hands clasped beneath his blue robe. His long mustache and wiry beard flowed in a smooth breeze.

Master Choejor's sightless, milk-colored eyes idly gazed at four lines of pillars; each one shaped from white marble quarried along the lower Sarribe hills. Their smooth surfaces glistened with dew. Four stones rested on the ground, starting the first step of an upward climb.

Master Choejor raised his voice to the group, "Brother Kasai, Brother Daku, Brother Jia'mu and Brother Ri'sonu. Step forward. Place your feet on the stone before you. Then you must step to the top of the first pillar, and then the next and next. Let the Boundless guide you, and your path will be clear."

Kasai looked to his right. Ri'sonu and Cannonball had taken their places on the first stones. Cannonball's fat face was filled with worry. He rubbed his left thigh. Brother Daku had not been kind in the sparring circle.

Kasai looked to the pillars before him. Each column rose slightly higher than the previous one. The long line ran parallel to the bend in the hillside and out of sight. Kasai wondered why he had never really noticed them before, or their height.

"Kasai, why are you waiting? Keep up!" Daku said. He had already leaped to the fifth column, which was now at least as tall as a grown man.

Kasai took the first two column steps. Easy. The sun was out, and the path of column tops before him was clear. Although each new column was higher in elevation, it was the same distance from the last one. Soon he was leaping from one column to the next, gaining on Daku.

"This isn't much of a test. I could probably do this blindfolded," Kasai boasted to himself. He could hear Ri'sonu and Cannonball behind him. Neither had difficulty leaping from one column to the next on their designated route.

The pillars mirrored the twisting natural rock formations that populated the area. Kasai rather enjoyed the exercise until the position of the posts became erratic. Up and down they went or jerked out of line. A gust of wind caught Kasai unaware and pushed him to one side. He almost slipped off the top before regaining his balance. "That was close."

Beads of sweat formed on his forehead. "Be mindful of the wind!" Kasai called out to his Brothers.

"I am the wind!" Daku sang. He was at least ten pillars ahead of the others. "Kasai, why so slow? Did you stop for morning tea and a biscuit?"

"Show off!" Cannonball yelled.

"Reckless is more like it," Ri'sonu declared. He was starting to huff.

"I never knew these pillars to be so high," Cannonball complained. "What do the Masters think we will accomplish? What happens if we fall?"

"Keep advancing. Don't give in to fear," Kasai reassured. He wished he could believe his own words. The winds picked up, and with it came a clinging mist. The line of pillars became obscured.

Kasai leaped to the next pillar. This time he skid a heart-stopping inch over the top's slick surface. The entire column shook slightly under his feet, casting subtle vibrations that echoed into the air.

"I can't see anything through the fog," Cannonball said. "I'm getting dizzy. I'm sure to fall."

"Jia'mu, be calm. Breath. Remember your training. Feel the Boundless," Kasai said. He hoped it would reassure Cannonball. Although, when he searched for a connection to the Boundless, all he felt was the cold, wet air.

"I'm climbing down. This is madness," Cannonball said with determined certainty. "Kasai, where are you?"

"Stay on your path. Trust yourself and keep moving forward. You will make it," Kasai called out.

The pillars before Kasai became ghostly silhouettes. *If Daku can do it, so can I*, he reasoned. He leaped to the next pillar and his sandaled feet slid out from under him. He landed on his back, legs dangling in the air. Instinctively, he locked his outstretched hands on the column's shaft. The surface of the stone was slick. Kasai found it challenging to keep his hands in one place. His eyes went wide, staring into white nothingness as his heart pounded in his chest.

"Concentrate on the air around you," Master Choejor called out from somewhere below. "Feel the movement of the moisture in the air. Feel its spirit. Let it define the form of the pillars. Trust your inner sight to guide your next step and leap!"

"But Master, if we fall…" Cannonball said. His voice was like a distant echo to Kasai now.

"Do not let the fear of the unknown prevent you from seeing the truth," Master Choejor said. "Believe in the path Aetenos has set for you. He will guide you. But you must open your eyes and see."

"I cannot see anything!" Cannonball's voice was shaky and small.

"If you cannot see with your eyes open, close them and embrace the Boundless," Master Choejor said.

"I'm afraid!"

"Afraid or not afraid, the outcome is the same. You must jump." Master Choejor's voice drifted into the wind.

Kasai had hardened his body through countless hours of physical training over the years at Ordu. Exposed to harsh weather conditions of the open mountain, he thought he was prepared for anything, yet somehow, this was worse than he could have imagined. The air was cold and biting, draining his strength as he rested on the pillar. Fear invaded his thoughts, causing his muscles trembled.

"Remember your training," Kasai said to the sky. He surrendered to the impossible situation he was in and let the fear fade. He forced his mind to become quiet and relaxed. Somehow, he needed to help Cannonball. Kasai could sense the conflict raging in his friend's thoughts.

"Brother! Calm your mind. Relax!" Kasai shouted from his back.

But as usual, Cannonball refused to listen to good advice. He jumped impulsively to the next column but never landed on its top. Kasai heard a desperate yell falling until the white mist consumed it.

"Cannonball fell!" Ri'sonu shouted. Kasai could tell Ri'sonu was close to breaking.

Master Choejor's calm voice returned. "Do not let the darkness consume you with fear. All is not as it appears in the physical world. Follow the path of Light set by Aetenos. See it. Reach out to it, and it will take your hand."

"I don't see any hands!" Ri'sonu said.

"Ri'sonu, calm down," Kasai called out.

"Kasai, I can't see a thing! Where are you?"

"I am here, Brother. Follow Master Choejor's instructions."

Kasai gathered his strength, curling himself to a sitting position before attempting to stand. Breathe in, breathe out.

Kasai twisted his head to the right to where Ri'sonu was trapped. "Concentrate on my voice," Kasai said.

"No. Forget it. I'm done. I'm climbing down. There is no shame in being safe. Climb down with me."

"Ri'sonu, steel your mind and calm your heart. You must move forward."

"No way. I'm not crazy like you and Daku. I have nothing to prove!"

Kasai heard Ri'sonu struggle to lower himself over the edge of the pillar.

"Ri'sonu! Don't do it! The columns are too slick." But it was too late. Ri'sonu's scream echoed throughout the pillars as he fell.

Kasai felt sick to his stomach. What sort of fatal test was this? Climb down and fall. Move forward and fall. Where was Daku? How had he escaped this fate?

Suddenly, Kasai was seized by panic, his breath trapped in his chest. After a moment, he released a deep exhale and regained his composure. "Ok, I can do this."

Exhaling deeply again, he finally felt calm. He balanced on his left leg so he could slip off his right sandal. Kasai tossed it into the mist along with the wet sock he peeled off his foot. The stone was cold and wet on his barefoot, the tactile sensation was reassuring.

Kasi removed his other sandal and sock in the same manner. Now he could press his toes into the stone surface. "If I am to meet my end, then I shall do it moving forward."

Kasai was ready. He leaped for the next pillar but came up short. He just managed to catch the edge of the surface with his toes. Luckily, his momentum carried him forward enough to regain his balance.

Kasai's heart leaped to his throat. His entire body trembled no matter how hard he tried to keep himself calm. He scanned the air in front of him but could barely see the next pillar.

"I must not fear this test. Aetenos shall guide me," Kasai mumbled, wishing the words held more meaning to him.

The air shifted, and the mist blew in his face, blinding him. It was cold, silent, and suffocating. His temples throbbed like thunder at the sides of his head. His breath was quick.

Standing as still as he could, Kasai closed his eyes and forced himself to be calm. He wanted to believe that Aetenos would guide him, but what proof did he have? The Great Monk did not guide the path of his Brothers. How could he let them fall? These initiates were his monks. They represented the living symbols of the man who achieved enlightenment and rose to defeat evil at the height of its power.

And where was the guiding light of Aetenos when he was six years old. His Pa was a true believer in Aetenos, but still, he abandoned Kasai and his Ma to the Darkness. It was why he was here and not still living in the village. He ached for the comfort of his Ma now. She had died that fateful day, but he still felt the loss as if just witnessing it.

Kasai drew a deep breath and exhaled. He would not rely on an absent figurehead to save him. He had done that once when he was six, and it had cost him so much.

"I'm climbing down. Maybe I'll have better luck than Ri'sonu. This is crazy. The Boundless is not real. I don't want to die."

"Trust me, my son." A soft voice came entered his thoughts.

"Father?" Kasai said into the mist.

"I will guide you." Again, the voice was sent through his thoughts. It was like a familiar memory.

Kasai shook his head. "You cannot be my father. He wouldn't be here now. He would be somewhere safe."

"Believe in me, and I will guide you."

"I can do this on my own."

"Then, you shall fall."

"No, I won't." Kasai leaped for the next pillar, landing on the surface but promptly skidding over the side. His head struck something hard. Stars flashed before his eyes, and then he was the air.

Kasai's vision cleared to a dull blur. Somehow, he was alive, feeling like his brain was pushing against his eyeballs. The rough texture of hemp rope crisscrossing his body made his skin raw. Soft voices below him grew louder.

Kasai crawled to the edge of the safety net and lowered himself down to the solid ground. Daku was the first to greet him. "Did you enjoy your little nap?"

"How long have I been up there?" Kasai asked, trying to rub away the stiffness in his arms and legs.

"Who cares? I was the last to fall. I nearly made it to the end!"

Kasai looked dubiously at his friend. Although he had lost sight and sound of Daku, he doubted his friend could have lasted much longer than he did. But what did it matter? The pillars were impossible for anyone to complete.

Kasai realized the point of the lesson was to be exposed to the impossible and contemplate what it was not. Kasai had wished he had known about the safety nets earlier. But then his attempt to reach the Boundless would have been insincere. He needed to learn to trust the unknown.

"Come on, let's watch the next group. They don't know about the nets either. I bet nobody gets even close to my record." Daku said as he ran ahead.

"I'm sure they won't, Brother." Kasai continued rubbing his arms. He was simply happy to be alive.

2

SEKKA

The Arch Devil approached the prison door from a long corridor festooned with the bones of her enemies. It was a menagerie of sorts, dedicated to the souls used to feed her powerful and still growing empire; a dominion that had been brought dangerously close to the brink of disaster by a single man. It had taken long centuries it had taken to rebuild her strength ... all because of *him*.

She reflected momentarily on her prisoner, the one being who had thwarted her plans of conquest in the Mortal Realm. She wasn't even sure how he had managed to gain access to her homeworld of Gathos after her fall. It was said nothing could travel between the Three Realms since the Immortal Mother had created the Amaranthine Barrier. And she should know, she had tried and failed many times to return to the land of mortals after she had been banished.

"It's an intriguing riddle to be solved for another time," she said and tapped the ornate box she held in her hand. "This time will be different, now that I have the proper means to lay the foundation for my return."

She inserted her key into the well-worn lock of the

dented, filthy cell door, pushing it through the lock's tumblers. It settled into place, the heavy *thunk* echoing through the depths of the lonely passage. The door swung open and flooded the prison cell with cold light. The prisoner released a painful gasp, but his head remained heavy on his chest.

She saw him as she had left him, a trophy hanging from the wall. His wrists were shackled and spread wide by chains hammered into the stone wall behind him. He turned his head to shield his one remaining eye from the blinding light.

He was not a handsome man, and worse to look at now that his face was swollen and bruised. He was bald except for a graying topknot growing from the back of his head, its braided ends frayed, tangled, and twisted.

She wore a luxurious, ice-blue gown that opened at her navel, plunging to her waistline like the wavy kris tucked in her sash. Her shapely neck rose from a fountain of white sable clasped at her throat. The bottom ruffles of the gown swished upon the thin layer of fresh blood which coated the floor. She left a trail of crimson snakes in her wake.

She wore it as if the Three Kingdoms of Hanna already bowed down to her as their beloved monarch, eager to pay homage to her with their very souls. And that was precisely what she intended. She moved as if part of a breeze towards a small table in the corner. It was cluttered with instruments of torture.

"This mess just won't do," she said, shaking her head. She brushed the iron pinchers and sharp-edged tools aside, casting them unceremoniously to the stone floor in a cacophonous clatter.

She gently placed the box down on the table's surface. Her black nails tapped out a simple rhythm over its top. She wore gaudy rings covered in precious stones on her fingers. The facets caught the light and created a dazzling kaleidoscope of color against the walls, though the onyx stone on her left index finger refused to join the celebration of light. The stone greedily devoured the light rather than reflect it with its sisters.

The angles of her face sat high on her long, serpentine neck. She looked him over with dark, iris-less eyes. He was helpless.

His abused body shivered underneath the tatters of his once cobalt-blue robes, now soiled and faded. She thought the sharp lines of his ruined face agreed handsomely with the cracked backdrop of the masonry from which he hung.

She swept towards him, wearing a devilish grin of satisfaction, stopping intimately close to his body to breathe in a deep draught of his intoxicating stench.

She had been thrown a morsel of luck, and she intended to exploit it to the fullness of its measure. She had longed for this moment for over a thousand years. He would serve as the leverage she needed to defeat her rivals. And, he had practically shown up on her doorstep. Oh, this was rich.

She glided forward into the cramped cell. An intricate, alabaster headdress rested on her head, blending gracefully with her white mane of long hair. The fiendish crown was made of hundreds of human bones and revealed the truth of her nature. Tiny skulls of infants dangled down her back and mingled with the long strands of her stark hair. Her headpiece clattered and knocked as the smaller pieces spun with her movements and clashed together.

Her thick, indigo lips parted ever so slightly as her excitement grew. She imagined the suffering he would endure when he discovered the full magnitude of her intentions. It was a just punishment for interfering with her plans of conquest so many years ago.

Today was the day of reckoning. Her gaze swept over his stretched and suspended body, which somehow still managed to resist the harsh lashes and probing cuts of her chief tormentor, the demon witch, Chedipe.

She lowered her head and raised playfully seductive eyes towards her unlikely benefactor. Her mocking interest was as a cruel reminder of her duplicitous nature. She gripped his chin with slender fingers and forced him to look back at her. "Aetenos, my dear. Why such a dour face? Are you not happy to see me again?" she chuckled mockingly. "Perhaps my flavor of hospitality is not to your liking?"

She moved even closer to his body and dropped her hand to glide along his quivering flesh. "I'm surprised you haven't called your winged playmates to rescue you. Snap, snap, and here they come, ready to save the day." She sneered at him. "But not this time and not here; Gathos is where angels come to die."

Aetenos twisted his neck away from her and whispered out her name in a sorrowful sigh, "Sekka."

A wicked smile played across her over-sized mouth. She dragged her fingers across his tormented flesh, angling pointed nails into the dark burgundy welts already covering his body. New lines of bright red beaded on his skin.

She glanced down at the three small beasts at her feet. The creatures feasted on the dripping life fluid of her prisoner. She kicked one to the side, and it became animated with excitement as if her action was an acknowledgment of tenderness. The others howled back at her in earnest.

"I am hoping they sing a song of joyful despair to the innocents you have failed. Alas, who can understand such beasts? Nonetheless, I am forever grateful to you for coming to my home as you did. I assure you, if I were allowed to go to you on my own accord, I would have been at your doorstep ages ago. But such fanciful ideas are no longer the way of things, and sadly, one must accept the rules of the game as they change."

She took a step backward, admiring Chedipe's work. "I imagine your journey here was arduous and fraught with peril, yes? Now tell me, truthfully, you missed me, didn't you? We have such history together, do we not? Did true love finally bring you running to my door, or was it simply the desire to lay with one not so innocent of the flesh?"

"I would never," Aetenos said.

"Oh, do stop with all this self-righteous dignity. The heavenly shine of your soul has dimmed. I can see that clearly enough."

Aetenos showed little spark of life. His body hung deflated like a condemned and forsaken man.

"Come now. You look disheartened. Tsk, tsk, what did you expect, a parade?"

Her brows furrowed, and she glared intensely at the monk. "You cheated when you called the angels for help and cost me centuries of accumulated mortal soul energy! I should have rivaled the power of the Great Three by now, but no, you had to interfere. You left me weak on Gathos. Do you have any idea how much favor I needed to call due … just to survive?"

Sekka brought her hands down to the edges of her open gown and traced the exposed parts of her breasts with her two small fingers. Her black nails traveled down to her midsection, leaving razor-thin lines of blue malice in her translucent skin. "But survive I did."

She giggled. "How bitter I must sound. But one must play their part, and I do so love mine. Isn't that what you preach, 'All things in their natural way' or some such nonsense?"

Sekka played absentmindedly with the blood that bubbled up from the cuts. It was one of her favorite pastimes. She drew a blue line across his cracked lips, then licked her fingers clean, one-by-one. She savored every drop. Her wounds closed immediately, leaving no trace of the incision.

She grabbed his flaccid cock, squeezing it until he moaned. Her eyes widened with anticipation as his meat filled with blood. "You cannot fool me. You thought to break me again, but I did not see Ninziz-zida in your hands when you arrived. Has the Fire Serpent abandoned you as well, or did you think to use this righteous scepter instead of the fiery sticks?" Sekka shook his member. "Did you hope to turn me to the Light? Was that your plan?"

Sekka laughed. "Or better yet, did you wish to possess me like one of your mind slaves? I hear you are known for choosing an unsuspecting mortal to carry out your whim, all in the name of…"

She observed his reaction. "Not so easy, silly monk. I wouldn't dare speak *Her* name here. Names are so important, are they not?" Sekka warily glanced upwards and waited. Nothing. She gave Aetenos a knowing wink. "There, you see. Nothing to fear."

She brought one hand to her mouth. Her long fingers danced over her lips. "I wonder, could it be that you are here because you no longer hold favor with the little birds in their pristine halls and cloudless skies?" Sekka squeezed his thick member again, her nails digging into the flesh. "I hate little birds."

Then she released him. She swished away as if twirled by an invisible dance partner.

"But the reasons why you are here and how you skirted the Amaranthine Barrier carry little importance to me at the moment. What matters to me now is that you *are* here, and I can use you.

"My dear Aetenos, you have been as much a thorn in my side, much like that irritating Red Devil. But now, like him, you are pitiful and weak. My trap is closing over you both. Be assured, you will not beat me a second time."

Aetenos raised his head. "I am bound by way of the Immortal Mother. Her sight of all things flows quick...as the monsoon. You...have been...exposed, like all things...under the sun." His breath wheezed out of his mouth. "You cannot hide...from her eyes," he said in a shaky voice. "But...I did not come for...you."

She laughed. "Oh, but you did. You came straight to my door. You were driven here by madness with the hopes of being a hero once more. Slay the dragon, save the despairing, helpless maiden, and all that nonsense. If you succeeded, you could regain the respect of your winged friends. Maybe the little birds might even take you back. Ah, but now the dragon has you by the balls, and the maiden has vanished. Found another plaything, has she?"

"I know...Illyria is here. Prisoner...through trickery," he said. "I am here to free her...from your prison of lies."

Sekka could see he barely had the strength to speak.

"Yes, your passionate devotion to that *angel* is admirable, if not misplaced. Illyria is here and has become a favorite plaything to many of the dark lords of Gathos. Much to her liking, I might add."

"Lies...Illyria remains...pure."

"And you remain delusional to the end. But we have other matters to discuss."

He raised his head slowly. "You will get nothing from me. You cannot hide...behind this glamour...vile creature." His head dropped to his chest again. Drool laced with blood bubbled at his lips. "I know what you are."

"Vile? I chose this attire just for you. Don't you like my appearance? Tempting, is it not?" She traced the heavily embroidered silk lace and stroked the white ermine at its edge.

She gave Aetenos a dramatic pout. "I'd like our time together to be enjoyable. I simply thought this form would be more pleasing to you," Sekka said with an impish smile. Her tone was seductive.

She grabbed his chin again. "Look at me! Do I not entice you? There are other, more aggressive forms I can take if you like. You've seen them before."

Her fingers teased down his stomach again and traced his exposed manhood. She cradled its length gently in her palm. "I see the angels didn't squeeze all mortal desire from you during your transformation."

"The Boundless…is my truth. It will save me…from your temptations…" He shook his head. His voice was barely a whisper. "It is…my truth."

"I will tell you what is true, monk. Me! I am the truth!" The fury in her voice magnified in the small chamber. "I am the cold in the air, and I am the frost on the ground. The deep power of Gathos is mine! The flames of the Red Devil will not have this land!"

Aetenos smiled. "Zizphander approaches…once more, but…in strength. The gameboard…grows broader."

She finally heard the quiet confidence in his voice that she so despised.

"You know nothing!" Her black eyes blazed with hatred, and she clenched her jaw.

How could he know? Her body shook with rage causing the skulls and bones of her headdress to thrash together. She stopped at the table and marshaled her emotions.

"But enough of this seriousness. Your hallowed serenity is all I desire, my dear. And so, I have brought you this gift in appreciation for our time together. I crafted it specifically for you and your unique nature."

Sekka opened the lavish box and took out a small, finely detailed amulet. The jeweled piece was attached to an intricately woven chain. Carved upon each link were hundreds of hard-edged symbols. Her face was close to his when she placed it around his neck. She lightly caressed his cheeks with both hands and kissed him hard against the lips. Then she pushed his head away.

His arms stretched to take on the weight of the amulet. Its small size belied its burden. The charm began to glow a putrid green as it throbbed against his bare chest like a second heart.

Sekka stepped back, appreciating the beautiful work of her craftsmanship. "It's perfect, just as I had hoped."

She shut the lid of the box, closing it with a click. She then moved towards the chamber door. Sekka stopped at the entrance and glanced back at Aetenos.

"You cannot fathom the boon you have given me by coming here. And for that, I am grateful. The legions of Gathos shall sacrifice uncounted mortal souls on temples raised in your honor. Your name will be worshiped throughout eternity."

Sekka slammed the heavy door shut. She leaned her back against its cold metal. Her smile came quickly as the Great Monk began to chant. The typical melodic tones and overlapping harmonies were replaced by sound patterns of pleading desperation. It was music to her ears.

There was just one more piece to connect. When it fell into place, she would ascend higher than any Arch Devil in the timeless history of the Abyss. Her nemesis, the Red Devil, Zizphander, would become an afterthought.

"That's it. Call to your mind-slave. Raise the next Ever Hero and seal the fate of the Mortal Realm into everlasting doom."

Sekka left the monk to his work; she had much to prepare.

3

SHIVERRIG

Volkerrum Keep was an ancient castle. It was built long ago on the backs of the conquered after the invasion of the warlord, Baroq Shiverrig from the East. The castle was the first of its kind to be built in the untamed wilderness.

Within a generation, the families of the invading warriors flowed beyond the Keep's walls and settled closer to the sea. The port city of Gethem was established and served as the entryway into untapped trade opportunities with the homeland across the sea.

Volkerrum Keep had been the seat of power for the Kingdom of Baroqia and the home of House Shiverrig for countless generations. War banners of deep-rose and purple hung from ceiling rafters within the Keep's Great Hall. The heavy cloth fluttered in a lazy dance from heat billowing from the blazing fire against the wall.

Duke Gerun Shiverrig, the last scion of the Shiverrig bloodline and heir to a usurped throne, sat at a long table and brooded over unpleasant news. He raised his eyes to King Mortimer Conrad's court messenger. The young boy's face showed a hint of impatience, which further infuriated Duke Shiverrig. *Again, Mortimer sinks his jackal's teeth into my flesh. The man means to bleed me dry*, Duke Shiverrig thought.

"Your answer, my lord?" the messenger said. The boy possessed the same arrogance as the king. He spoke as if he commanded a hundred knights at his back.

"No." The answer was more of a growl than a word.

"My pardon, my lord. What?"

"I said, no!"

Duke Shiverrig pounded his oversized fist on the massive, oak table. The force of the blow shook the clay jugs filled with dry wine from the plains of Western Baroqia. Exotic fruit wobbled in their shallow bowls, freeing an orange to drop from its stack and roll across the table. Duke Shiverrig eyed it menacingly then swatted it across the room.

Shadows from the fire rippled across his smooth scalp. His anger took on the fiery aspect of the blaze. The short whiskers that made up his dark, trimmed beard stood out like the raised hackles of a beast.

"I will not be dictated to by that fool, Mortimer Conrad, and his council of dimwitted sycophants. I refuse to acknowledge him as the rightful King of Baroqia!" Duke Shiverrig said.

He stood abruptly. His legs tangled with the chair until he kicked it away as if he was an angry mule. He was a colossal man and moved like an apex predator. Shiverrig circled the young messenger whose eyes were now wide with fear.

"For twenty-two years, I have endured this imposter who poses like a king on my father's stolen throne. And now, he looks to weaken my family's House even further by stealing more men."

"Yes, my lord." The boy bowed in acquiescence. He was trembling when he rose. "I mean, the king wishes to have you formally acknowledge the demands of his letter, Sir."

Duke Shiverrig stopped his rampage. He turned to the tall stone columns that supported the rafters.

"Malachi, come out where I can see you. This is your responsibility. You are supposed to be managing this!"

Archvashim Malachi stepped out of the shadows in burgundy robes with copper trim. Malachi was a tall man. He was narrow at the shoulders with angular features and penetrating eyes. He bowed in silence before Duke Shiverrig.

"I am here, my lord. It would seem impolite not to reply in some way to King Conrad's letter. Ideally, he will wish to know that you have complied with his command."

Duke Shiverrig's eyes grew wide with amazement. "I know that!"

He twisted back to the messenger. The quickness of his movement belied his considerable bulk. He looked for something to break. The messenger would do.

"A symbol of my obedience is needed, yes?" His slate-grey eyes narrowed on the messenger like a lion eying a rabbit. Duke Shiverrig pulled the long knife from the belt at his waist and watched the messenger's complexion pale. The boy took a few steps backward.

"A simple word of acknowledgment will do, my lord," the messenger stuttered.

"My lord," Malachi spoke in soothing tones, "Perhaps this is not the ideal message to send at this time."

"It is a message that is long overdue, Malachi," Duke Shiverrig said. He looked over the messenger's body with hungry eyes. "I'll carve it into the lad's flesh."

Malachi moved passed Duke Shiverrig like a specter. He laid a bony hand on the messenger's shoulder.

"Please inform King Conrad that Duke Gerun Shiverrig, the one hundred and fifteenth lord bearing the Shiverrig crest, is willing to do his duty to the realm. House Shiverrig will send more troops to patrol the borderlands. The Knights of Gethem will end the rash of brigand attacks against the frontier villages. See to the notary in the front chambers. He will affix the Duke's seal to the King's Letter, along with my blessing."

"Thank you, Archvashim Malachi," the messenger said. He quickly bowed, then scurried out of the room.

"Malachi, you overstep your usefulness once again," Duke Shiverrig said. His flash temper had abated but simmered just under the surface of control. "I have no intention of sending the Knights of Gethem to protect peasants in frontier villages. MY men will not be used to bolster the king's weak position in the outer territories. Let him send his reserves from Qaqal."

"The king is testing you. But there is a greater prize to be had here than rebuking the king's wishes. In time you will convert more of the kingdom's people to your cause than mere peasants," Malachi said in a conspirator's tone. The Archvashim rounded the large table and poured two glasses of wine from one of the clay jugs. "Come, let us sit and talk."

Duke Shiverrig remained standing. His burly arms folded across his chest. His stance was as immovable as his opinion of the king. "So, you still advocate an alliance with those meddling monks, or do you have some new scheme for me to ponder?"

Malachi took a sip from his glass and considered the bouquet. "There are many possibilities to consider but let us speak of the monks today. You must seek either an alliance with the monks of the Four Orders or their destruction. Each outcome would serve you well. Faith is an exquisite weapon when wielded with artful hands. Many subjects of the realm still pray for the return of Aetenos. He became a demigod, after all, or so say the true believers." Malachi rolled his eyes at the lunacy that any man could ascend to godhood.

"His monks represent the undefinable connection to the divine in human form. That is a powerful tool to be manipulated. Most people need to believe there is something more waiting for them after their time in this world is over."

"Yet, you have cast your die with Mor, the embodiment of change, chaos, and creation. He is the antithesis of the stability and lawfulness that Aetenos offers his followers. Why would you give your support to those who oppose your prophet?"

"The masses are easily swayed," answered Malachi. "There is a fine line between truth and heresy. Influence, not power, control the ideas that take shape on either side of that line. The song of Aetenos has been silent for hundreds of years. The convenient story says he has fully ascended and will never return to the Mortal Realm, which makes the monks the last embodiment of his legacy to this land. Win over the monks and slowly have your influence become their influence."

The Duke shook his head doubtfully. "No easy feat. Those stubborn monks are set in their ways. They will not turn. And who knows how many still exist outside of the Temple of Illumination? The locations of their remote monasteries remain hidden, though I suspect their sanctuaries were abandoned long ago. But if we could apply political pressure on the Temple and change the mindset from the top down…"

Malachi sipped his wine before answering. "Yes, that would seem to be the solution. Unfortunately, Grandmaster Marmo Nysulu remains shackled to tradition. As we have seen time and again, he is steadfast in his unwillingness to become associated with any political affiliations whatsoever. Eventually, he will need to be removed."

Malachi smiled at the thought and continued, "For now, the prudent strategy is to stay the course. Let the despair of the land prove Aetenos has fled this world. The last blight was not so long ago that people have forgotten hardship. Let the monks become reminders of Aetenos' betrayal of the people's trust. Cast the blame for the difficulties throughout the land on them. Nobody wants to see the hard times return, and when they do, the people will need someone to blame.

"Either way, you are in control of the levers of influence. They will join you, or they will be replaced."

"The spoils of the chaos you are advocating is taking longer to enjoy than you anticipated. As it is, I am depleting my power base by supporting Conrad's demands for more troops. This will only get worse." Duke Shiverrig reached for the glass of wine Malachi had poured for him. He drank deeply from the cup as if it was water. He hardly appreciated the vintage. His grandfather once said, 'Wine was a fancy drink for fancy men.'

"No, I think we go for the head of the beast and work our way down. Nysulu must have a vulnerability, something we can exploit."

"He is the Grandmaster of the Seventh Heaven. One does not ascend to such an elevated rank without amassing certain powers. To say he is vulnerable would be a mistake. But he has been the spiritual leader of the monks of the Four Orders for many decades. No matter how noble the heart, ambition stirs the desires of those who wait impatiently in line for their turn to rule."

Duke Shiverrig tapped the rim of the wine glass with his index finger. "I do not want to disrupt the machinations of the Temple. The last thing I need is a martyrdom here in Gethem. Conrad would not hesitate to use that against me. We shall work to sway Nysulu to our cause, rather than remove him outright."

"As luck would have it, Grandmaster Nysulu has deigned to come down from his lofty tower and is eager to bend your ear to his needs. He shall arrive at Volkerrum Keep upon the morrow. We shall see then if he is willing to listen to reason or not," Malachi said, wearing a fox's smile.

The Duke looked suspiciously at his Archvashim. He knew better than to take anything Malachi said at face-value. His Archvashim was a cunning and deceptive man with a head for politics. There was always a hidden twist to every plot Malachi hatched.

"How convenient," Shiverrig deadpanned.

The corridor walls leading to the Grand Hall of Volkerrum Keep were lined with stone sculptures of House Shiverrig's legendary heroes. The figures displayed a decisive victory over a beaten and broken foe and presented a powerful icon during the rise of the Kingdom Baroqia.

Each stone progeny was twice the size of an ordinary man. The figures had been carved masterfully from a single block of Phrygian marble. The artisans used the purple and rose veins found naturally in the rock to form the appearance of a circulatory system around the stone bodies. House Shiverrig had long ago associated their rule with the enduring qualities of the rock and took the colors for their banners and shields.

The Shiverrig family crest was proudly displayed on the heroes' shields and armored plates. Centered in the shield, a mastiff appeared ready to slip its stone confines to tear out the viewer's throat, its snarling muzzle showing that it would give no quarter, nor let go with its long, slavering fangs. The statues were also meant to be a stark reminder of House Shiverrig's dominance over any who challenged their rule. The message was clear. Defy us at your own risk.

The first statues wore artifacts of the warlord's power and absolute rule, and the latter figures were graced with majestic crowns, except for the last one. The stone icon of Gareth Shiverrig, Gerun's father, wore no such article of office. The bitter taste of Mortimer Conrad's ascension over his father's was ever present in Gerun's mouth. Between each sculpture hung a thick, purple banner with rose trim—colors meant for royalty and rule and another unpleasant reminder to Gerun's current station.

Duke Shiverrig waited the next petitioner, impatient in his majestic chair. Tapping his fingers slowly on the arm, he scanned the room looking for threats; a habit learned from the murder of his father.

An immense tapestry hung the length of the wall behind him. The finely crafted artwork depicted scenes of his paternal ancestors commanding the Five Armies of the realm to victory. It was the backdrop he preferred when addressing the citizen of Gethem or nobles from neighboring cities.

Two men stood to either side of Duke Shiverrig. On his left was Archvashim Malachi who bent slightly to speak in Shiverrig's ear.

"They will be along shortly."

Duke Shiverrig gave a gruff nod.

Malachi wore his religious robes of high office for the meeting with Grandmaster Nysulu. The cloth was bruised purple and flaunted gold trim around the wrists and neckline. A medallion inlaid with a faceted ruby hung heavy at his neck. The jewelry reflected a myriad of red hues whenever the Archvashim moved. The Shiverrig crest was proudly displayed on the upper left side of Malachi's robe. The emblem of Mor was embroidered on the right side. The design was a haphazard pattern to symbolize the constant change of chaos.

A famed Knight of Gethem stood at attention to Duke Shiverrig's right. He was encased in light armor with formal purple tabard hanging low over his steel plate. He stood silent and tall. The studded mace at his hip was well worn and easily accessible if needed. The knight's hands repeatedly flexed into fists at his sides.

A page appeared at the entered the entrance of the Great Hall to announce the arrival of Marmo Nysulu, the Revered Grandmaster of the Seventh Heaven, along with two of his senior monks. Duke Shiverrig bade them forward with a wave of his hand. He waited for what felt like an eternity for them to approach.

"As if time stood still for the righteous. They move slower than crawling stones," Shiverrig said under his breath.

"Quite so," Malachi said. "Pride goeth before the fall."

The Grandmaster and his attendants stopped at the foot of the dais, looking up at the Duke in unison, while Duke Shiverrig eased back in his chair. He appraised Nysulu with a tight smile. The man was old. He looked frail enough to be toppled by a strong wind.

"My Lord Duke Shiverrig, we are honored to be accepted into your home and to share this time with you. We have urgent matters to discuss," Grandmaster Nysulu said.

"A good day to you, Old Father," Duke Shiverrig said. "Please proceed."

Nysulu gathered his thoughts. Everything he did was frustratingly slow. Finally, he cleared his throat and spoke. "Horrendous reports continue to arrive at the Temple of Illumination. Barbarian raiders have come down from the Hoarfrost Mountains and sacked many of the frontier villages. Brigands roam unchecked across the grasslands. Even the streets of your fair city have become infected by a great madness. Gethem has turned sour."

Shiverrig shrugged as if the news was commonplace.

"It has always fallen to House Shiverrig to be the shield of the land," Nysulu said. His tone was patronizing.

"I am aware of the responsibilities bestowed to my

House," Duke Shiverrig said. Anger laced his voice at being reprimanded in such a way. "Of course, there is some unrest in the outer provinces. That is to be expected during the harvest months."

"I fear we are being plagued by something far worse than typical unrest. Seven villages containing small monasteries devoted to the teaching of Aetenos have been destroyed. The farmhouses have been put to the torch, and the livestock of the village butchered and left to rot in the smoking embers."

"I am sorry to hear this, Old Father," Shiverrig said. His fingers rolled on the armrest of his chair. "The frontier villagers are not for the meek. Those who live there know the risks."

"The villagers were left crucified on tall posts surrounding the halls of prayer. Each post has a plaque nailed to the top of the cross with the words 'False Believer' written in blood.

"Yet, in other villages, the ravens have been deprived of their feast. The villagers have vanished; yet all of their possessions remain in place. This is not the work of commonplace bandits. You must send troops to protect the souls of the innocents."

Duke Shiverrig's ire grew. His opinion of Grandmaster Nysulu changed. The man was just another version of King Conrad. Only Nysulu disguised his desire to take from House Shiverrig behind the glamour of spiritual guidance.

"As I have said, the wilderness is a dangerous place, and I cannot run to the rescue of every remote hamlet when a roving band of brigands comes calling. The king has taken great care to thin my already depleted armed ranks. I have no more to give." Shiverrig shrugged his shoulders.

"These people have chosen to live outside the protection of my city walls. They pay little in tax to Volkerrum Keep's coffers, and therefore, I'm less inclined to help. Perhaps you could send a gaggle of monks to each village and pray for their wellbeing."

"My Lord Duke, brigands pay no heed to the faith of others or care of the taxes paid to coffers," Grandmaster Nysulu said. "These people need you. The Knights of Gethem must ride."

Malachi subtly cleared his throat in disagreement causing the Grandmaster to raise a curious eyebrow.

"This is the work of the Followers of Mor!" a senior monk exclaimed. "They are attempting to drive the faithful of Aetenos from the land of Baroqia. King Conrad has decreed that all faiths are welcome in the realm."

"You have no proof of this, monk. The Followers of Mor are not butchers. This is an outrageous accusation," Malachi said. He glared at the Grandmaster. "You should know better."

The Grandmaster nodded to Malachi. "This is true. My aid misspoke. At this time, there is no conclusive evidence to the contrary. For now, we will assume these atrocities are what they appear to be. I apologize for the slight to your prophet, Archvashim Malachi." The Grandmaster's tone was respectful yet carried the weight of a man with a heavy burden.

The Grandmaster returned his attention to Duke Shiverrig. "The City of Gethem is in chaos. Have you not seen this with your own eyes? When has a son of House Shiverrig allowed such lawlessness in the streets of Gethem?"

Duke Shiverrig straightened in his chair. His anger rose. Who was this feeble monk to dare criticize him and his family's honor? He felt Malachi's bony fingers press into his shoulder. It was enough of a gesture to remind Shiverrig of the strategy behind this meeting.

"Yes, the unrest does appear to be a bit more pronounced of late. Perhaps some of it is caused by these unorthodox cults of the prophet, Mor. I don't know. Their ideas of constant change are not to my taste. I appreciate order.

"But, as your man says, all religions and faiths are welcome, per the king," Duke Shiverrig said. "I suggest you take your grievances to the King's Council in Qaqal."

"You are honor-bound to at least investigate the evil infecting the lands under your stewardship. You must report your findings to the highest authority so that a solution can be found." Nysulu's demeanor remained calm, though his words were like arrows into Duke Shiverrig's pride.

"Highest of authority, indeed. By that, you mean King Conrad," Duke Shiverrig said with a slight smirk. "This is unlikely to happen. Conrad can reconnoiter with his men, or you can send one of your traveling monks to the borderlands."

"The monks of the Four Orders will wait to see how we can best assist the king's decision."

Duke Shiverrig leaned forward. "There is another solution. Help me take command of the Five Armies. I assure you I would end the malady afflicting the land in short order. I'm sure the spiritual blessing of the Reverend Grandmaster Nysulu and the backing of the Temple of Illumination would go far in the ears of the King's Council."

The Grandmaster closed his eyes. Duke Shiverrig heard a slight sigh escape the Grandmaster's lips. Duke Shiverrig knew his message had been received. He waited patiently for the Grandmaster's answer. The crackle and pop of the fire burning against the wall filled the room. The Grandmaster finally shook his head.

"You know I cannot. The officials at the Temple are not to influence politics or side with any noble house or cause. We are the living spirit and faith of Aetenos. We are not political pawns to be used to outmaneuver rivals."

Duke Shiverrig eased back into his chair. He wasn't

surprised by Nysulu's obvious answer. "Indeed, we all have our paths to walk. You see, Old Father, I have already mobilized a contingent of my forces to the northern border. My men may already be shedding their blood defending the land. And just earlier, your king asked for more. But where are the other armies? There is but a token host mustering at Qaqal. Where are Duke Rokig's, Lord Fritta's, or Lord Manda's men?"

The Duke continued with an irritated voice. "Truly, I am doing everything in my power to assist the paper crown, even at the expense of the stability of my fair Gethem, as you have so kindly pointed out.

"And why are my forces spread thin across Baroqia while King Conrad keeps his men safely in Qaqal? Why indeed, I wonder. Why does King Conrad not deal with these brigands himself? Perhaps there is a deeper reason."

"Which would be?" Nysulu looked perplexed.

"Due to the lack of support and decisive action from the crown, my thoughts cannot help but stray to thinking King Conrad is under the yoke of the Mad One in the North."

"Impossible!" Nysulu's second aid barked. The younger monk placed his foot on the first step of the dais. The knight at Duke Shiverrig's side held his mace ready to strike.

The Grandmaster gave a sideways glance at his aid. The monk immediately bowed low. "Forgive me, Grandmaster. I apologize for my emotional outburst and lack of control." Nysulu accepted his apology with a nod. The Grandmaster then looked at the Duke Shiverrig and his knight.

"Lower your weapon, Sir Marchan. Let us remain cordial in the presence of our esteemed guest," Duke Shiverrig added. He was curious about what would happen if the conversation escalated to violence. Just how fast could the old monk move?

The Grandmaster nodded his appreciation as Sir

Marchan begrudgingly lowered his mace. "Duke Shiverrig, you are considered the Champion of Baroqia, and as such, you must accept your role as the servant of the king."

"Yes, yes," Duke Shiverrig spat, his voice was razor-sharp. "All the symbolism and none of the authority. Command of the Five Armies should be mine and mine alone. I fear our dear king will bestow that honor to his incompetent son, Dane, or perhaps that imbecile Baron Rokig.

"Yet, the Knights of Gethem account for more than a third of the might of the Five Armies. These are my loyal men. Again, if I had the support of the Temple, we could correct what is now wrong in the realm."

Grandmaster Nysulu listened politely. His manner was peaceful when he spoke. "Now is not the time to revisit family rivalries or hurt pride. Times have changed. Let the past stay where it belongs. You have authority in your city, yet we see the faithful of Aetenos being unjustly persecuted. The public squares in the Temple District are full of crucifixions. How can you turn a blind eye? All faiths and spiritual ways must be given equal measure. That is the great balance we all bow to."

"Thieves, witches and the treasonous are dealt with according to the law. Faith is irrelevant," Duke Shiverrig said. "I will not tolerate disloyalty or betrayal. This is well known."

Shiverrig's eyes challenged Nysulu. But Nysulu would not rise to the bait. The Grandmaster remained calm and composed.

Malachi boldly stepped in front of the Duke, his voice that of a hissing snake. "Aetenos the Bright has passed into darkness. He is known as Aetenos the Abandoner in many corners of the realm. When the people have fully embraced the Change of Mor, they will want for naught and will be delivered from this depravity. There shall be a great cleansing, and the faithful will be rewarded."

The Grandmaster's countenance softened as he looked at Malachi. His words were coated with pity. "You seek to control the people through deception and distraction. You court the weak-minded and take advantage of their fears. To do so upsets the Great Balance and darkens the light of those you touch. I fear your prophet Mor is but a pawn to the Great Manipulator."

Malachi sneered. "Such are the words of the self-righteous!" He turned to Duke Shiverrig. "You see, my lord? It is worse than you expected. Not only has Aetenos abandoned the people, but his servants that remain have mouths filled with lies."

Duke Shiverrig worried at the sudden level of passion emanating from his Archvashim. Malachi's voice held too much excitement. This wasn't the approach he had expected or wanted from his advisor. Rather than building a bridge of common ground with the Grandmaster and the Temple of Illumination, Malachi was pushing the monks away. At this rate, they would never unify under his banner.

Duke Shiverrig motioned to the page at the far entrance of the Great Hall.

"Who's next?"

Thankfully, the Grandmaster understood at once that his time was over. He bowed low.

"I apologize for being abrupt, Old Father, but there are many that would have the ear of their Duke this day. Let me think more about what you have said. We shall speak again."

"Thank you for the time you have given us, Duke Shiverrig. Follow and be guided by the Light."

Another page came to ferry the monks away from the dais. Duke Shiverrig barely acknowledged the good wishes of the Grandmaster. *Malachi, you damn fool*, he thought. He was tempted to cancel the remaining audiences. His mind raced with appropriate punishments for his Archvashim. *I should have you flogged for such an outburst or rip that viper's tongue out of your throat.* Malachi had some explaining to do.

"I question your tact," Duke Shiverrig said. He pointed a gnarled finger at Malachi as the Archvashim entered the library. "You did more damage than good."

Malachi poured himself a goblet of wine and sat at the large oak table at the center of the room. The walls were lined with old tomes, bound in leather. Iron candelabras stood upright, holding candles of various lengths. Their flames danced upon oiled wicks. The hot wax dripped from the candelabra's iron arms, creating miniature stalactites.

"If I had played to the sensibilities of the old man, he would have immediately seen through that act. I told you; he will not sway from tradition.

"To borrow a simple idea of those fervent monks, when faced against an immovable object, one must flow like water around it. Simply put, there are other avenues to reach your goal. Your path to the throne requires a broader view of our world and the other realms connected to it."

"Don't bore me with your stories of divine intervention. Influence be damned. Steel is the real power that creates empires and brings lesser men to their knees," Duke Shiverrig said.

"With all due respect, my lord. Grandmaster Nysulu is no lesser man. You will need something special to move him," Malachi said.

"No doubt you have a lever in mind."

"Naturally, I would be of little use to you otherwise."

"Get on with it then," Shiverrig growled impatiently.

"There are alliances to be made that will unite the Three Kingdoms under one rule. I have recently contacted one who will be a great asset to you. She is the lever that will move Nysulu, one way, or the other.

"More politics," Duke Shiverrig grumbled. He yearned for the truth of battle, not more of Malachi's schemes. He understood what a properly placed sword could do to bone, blood, and muscle. Politics were for weak men that tricked and schemed behind each other's backs. He took the dagger from his belt and thrust it into the table. "I grow tired of waiting."

Malachi took a long draught of wine from his goblet. "Soon, everything will change. Of course, there will be a price to pay, but when is there not—for greatness?"

"Malachi, you sound as if you wish for me to make a deal with the devil."

A mischievous smile crept up the corners of Malachi's mouth. "Interesting choice of words."

4

SEKKA

Sekka brooded as she walked along the ice passageway that led to her bath chamber. Word from her spies was that the Red Devil was on the move again. Zizphander had invaded the territory of one of her weaker allies, a devil based in the outer planes that provided her with early warnings of the movements of her enemies, of which there were many. In all of her years, she had never known a more tenacious devil than Zizphander. Well, except for herself, of course.

Soon, she would be called upon to send more troops from her Frost Legion to support her ally's war effort. The plea for help was nothing new. But it was best to be cautious rather than rash. Lord Oziax, First General of her armies, was sent to survey the actual damage. It was wise to keep a watchful eye on her allies and their so-called needs.

The outskirt of Gathos was a spawning ground for ambitious demons and the occasional lesser devil. Every *thing* in the Abyss desired more power. It was a greedy addiction that was never satiated. Therefore, whenever she discovered one of her minions had become too influential, she would send Lord Oziax to ensure the new demon lord knew his place.

Typically, a tithe would be levied, and a new warlord would rise in the ranks of her Frost Legion. On rare occasions, Oziax brought back the demon lord's head. There were those in the Abyss that simply did not understand their place.

She reflected on the numerous carcasses of demons and devils collected over the centuries and frozen within the walls of the corridor. Each of them had thought to betray her or steal what was hers. *Such fools*, she thought. One day, that pest Zizphander would become an addition to her macabre museum. Seka smiled, thinking of his permanent installation.

She entered the changing room, moving over to her jewelry counter where she removed her ornamental headdress and set it upon a polished skull of a lesser demon—the tiny skulls and bones clattering as they settled into place. She still remembered the beast's name, for names were so important in the Abyss.

Beside it, a row of bone tiaras, crowns, headpieces and necklaces, all placed neatly on the skulls of defeated foes. She picked up a favorite small crown made of upright canine teeth; each one ripped from the mouth of an insubordinate demon.

Sekka saw herself reflected in the smooth surface of the ice walls of the chamber. She was glorious. She enjoyed being in the form of a mortal human and appreciated the sleek, sensual curves of her body. She was fascinated by the graceful way her arms and legs flowed as she walked.

She saved her demonic body for bloodier work. Even after all the centuries of her existence, she still relished the expression of horror her captives wore as she changed her shape before their awestruck eyes.

Her quick ascendancy had created bitter jealously among

the minions of Hell, with mortal and divine enemies soon to follow. Chief among them was now the Red Devil, Zizphander. He was the only force strong enough to challenge her reign on Gathos.

I have defeated him before and will do so again, she thought, but her confidence was thin. Somehow, Zizphander was able to move his horde of fire demons across the Abyss unseen until the moment he struck. Taken by surprise, her allies would crumble before the overwhelming force of his war machine.

"I must have more soul energy—and soon," Sekka mattered as she undid her formal gown and let it fall to the floor. She stepped out of the encircling material, kicking it to the corner for a servant to pick up. From the row of softly simmering gowns, she picked a sheer robe, donning it as she once again ruminated on opening a Chaos Gate to the Mortal Realm. She'd have the means to crush any that opponent; Zizphander would be the first to perish, this time for good.

The Immortal Mother had made access to the Mortal Realm limited or near impossible since Sekka's last invasion. Only a small, cumbersome portal could be opened for a short period of time. *Oh*, she thought longingly, *a Chaos Gate*. It was the one thing that could potentially bypass the magic wards of the Amaranthine Barrier. The endeavor had a high likelihood of failure and would kill the witches and warlocks used during the spell casting. Damn the Immortal Mother and her rules!

Sekka imagined the soul energy she could harvest with such a diabolical portal. It would be limitless! She fantasized about the day when one of the Great Three would elevate her status in exchange for eternal access to the Mortal Realm. Which Supreme Devil would it be, Xerthotha or Azrollorza, she mused? She didn't think the third, Morrdilliax, with his myriad personalities, could ever stop debating with himself long enough to grant her wish.

No, it would be either Xerthotha or Azrollorza. She would stand with one of them as an equal in the High Pantheon of Hell, a Supreme Devil in her own right. Ascension was the real prize. A functioning and permanent Chaos Gate would ensure she would receive her greatest desire.

Sekka quickened her step. Her diaphanous gown was made from the skin of mortals. Humans had such thin skin, and so soft. She had left it open in the front and tied it off at her waist. It was more of an afterthought. Maybe she would wear it next time she visited her captive guest.

She chuckled at the absurdity of the joke as if an Arch Devil of the Ice Planes of Hell could seduce one so pure as the Great Monk. Yet, the myriad temptations of the Abyss eventually corrupted the souls of all men. A demigod of the Seven Heavens was no different.

The sides of the gown fluttered against her skin. The material tickled her breasts and sent sensations of delight up her spine. Sekka reveled in the juxtaposition of containing her immense power in such a vulnerable shell. She also loved the accessories, especially her human eyes. Gateway to the soul, they said. Ha! If the mortals only knew the truth of it.

Why she had never thought to spend more time in such a form was lost to her. She thrilled at the variety of new sensations her body experienced since the arrival of Aetenos to Gathos so many years ago. The Great Monk remained hard and steadfast in his resistance to her charms. Eventually, that would change as she introduced the second part of her masterful plan.

The humans must think he is dead by now. But of course, time moves differently in the Abyss, she mused. She pushed open the door to her bath chamber. The room was dimly lit by sconces emanating a blueish glow around the base of the walls. A circular tub full of slush was sunk into the middle of the floor. Two dozen humans hung from great hooks above the tub. They resembled beasts swinging in a slaughterhouse.

Sekka watched with a pleasant appreciation as their life fluid streamed out of their bodies to fill her bath. Their moans resonated off the cold walls and filled the chamber with an eerie melody. It was music to her ears.

Sekka looked up at them with contempt. Humans were blind and dumb to the hidden power they each possessed. The true essence of the soul remained a mystery to them. Yet, it determined their actions and was the spark that enabled them to think, to feel, and to evolve.

She shook her head as she thought of how badly they misused such a gift on mundane endeavors. No matter. They served as an excellent fuel for her dark machinations.

This group was all that was left from Lord Oziax's last visit to her slave pits. The stockade would need to be replenished. She knew she was desperately low on reserves. Fighting the wars of others for future favor had helped her ascend quickly, but it came with a cost. She was starved continuously for more soul energy to replenish the ranks of her armies.

The only way to increase her allotment of souls in the Abyss was to gain more territory. But Zizphander was consuming the lands of her allies faster than she could conquer or steal more. Again, she thought of the power she could wield by maintaining an active Chaos Gate. Even before the Amaranthine Barrier, the portal was inconceivable to create. The unique components needed for its birth were not to be found in the Abyss.

She chuckled to herself. That foolish monk had given her the first rare component with his arrival on Gathos. It was only a matter of time before he unwittingly provided her with the second piece. Aetenos would be the doom of the

Mortal Realm. Ah, her revenge became sweeter by the moment.

Sekka disrobed and descended into the red slush with a satisfied smile. Her skin became taut as the refreshing cold wrapped around her flesh. The soothing properties of the bath relaxed her muscles as she waded deeper into the pool. The warm blood of the dying slaves showered over her head. It matted her hair in red clumps. A deep sigh eased from her lips as she smeared blood over her cheeks and mouth. The pain of her slaves was delicious.

Her mind drifted towards the pleasurable scenarios of pain she intended to inflict on Zizphander. She would take her time and savor the victory. She grew excited when she envisioned turning all of his lands of fire to ice.

Sekka heard the clatter of heavy armor approaching the bath chamber. Her mood soured. General Oziax had returned early from his mission. That much was clear, but she hadn't expected his return for days. *Could this not wait until I called for him?*

Something was very wrong. Sekka could hear it in his quickened footsteps as well as the heavy knock on the chamber door.

"My Queen, I bring dire news."

Sekka scowled and rose from her bath.

"Enter Lord Oziax."

The great demon lord bowed low upon entering the chamber. He wore his mortal form, as was her command while in her inner sanctum.

General Oziax appeared as a tall, well-built man. He wore pure white armor the texture of a seashell covered in barnacles, with ocean-blue accents gleamed along the seams of the ancient plate. He held his helm in his hand. The fell blade Eishorror was sheathed in its scabbard at his hip.

"You had best have a good reason for disturbing my

respite. What news do you bring that requires such a dramatic entrance?" Sekka said.

General Oziax brushed long, white strands of hair from his face and tucked them behind his mortal ears. "My apologies, my Queen. I thought you would want to hear my report as soon as possible. Zizphander has taken another of the wild frost lands that border Gathos. It has been turned into molten slag."

"Yes, that seems to be his agenda of late. What about it? Annihilating a frontier realm, even one neighboring Gathos seems hardly worth the effort. What does he hope to gain? There is no strategic significance in holding unformed lands that dissolve with the whims of chaos. There is no soul reward to exploit, and the inhabitants are a scattering of undisciplined war-bands. Let Lord Auzdioz worry about controlling his stewardship of those shapeless lands."

"My Queen, everything is gone. Buried under cooling magma."

"And soon, Lord Auzdioz will regroup. He will spread his seed and fertilize another uncharted land as he had done for countless millennia. That is his role in the Abyss. Why worry if Zizphander wastes his resources in such a way?" She played with the viscous strands of blood that stretched down from the bodies above her head. Zizphander was trying to taunt her, nothing more. She wouldn't be distracted by such things.

"Lord Auzdioz has been obliterated. His infernal essence has been utterly destroyed, never to be reformed."

"Well, now, that is something." Lord Oziax now had her full attention. "Zizphander does not possess such power to remove one such as Lord Auzdioz from the Abyss permanently. He must have a patron shadow. But who?"

"I know not, my Queen. Many have openly shown their

resentment of your triumphs." Oziax snarled. "But I will find out."

"Time has quickened for us," Sekka said. She raised herself out of the bath. She scoffed at the robe offered to her late by Lord Oziax. She was in no mood for his inability to understand mortal formalities.

"Have Chedipe send word to my minions on the Mortal Plane. Sess'thra is to go to the Northern Kingdom. There she will find the Sorcerer Maugris. She will know what to do. Then, the assassin Dax will introduce himself to one of the monks at the Temple of Illumination in Gethem."

"And the prisoner? Has there been any progress?" Lord Oziax said.

The Arch Devil had already left the chamber. A trail of red footprints followed her down the corridor. "The Great Monk will break. In the meantime, I shall lay out my plans for the invasion of the Three Kingdoms of Hanna."

5

KASAI

Kasai sat motionless on his square mat in the dimly lit meditation hall. His eyes were closed while he breathed slowly through his nose. The distant screech of a broad-winged crest eagle. He envisioned the majestic bird soaring on thermal drafts in a cloudless sky. The whisper of a light breeze rippled through the pine needles and oak leaves in the lower ravine, miles below the monastery buildings. He reprimanded himself for being so easily distracted. A wandering mind was a weak-mind, and that was a dangerous thing. He returned to concentrating on the flow of his breathing.

He sat in the half-light of the room with his Brothers. Each monk focused on observing the sensation of air passing over their upper lip, through their nostrils, and then out again. All other aches and pains, no matter how severe or uncomfortable, were dismissed. The exercise was designed to reduce the noise within one's conscious mind and reveal to the monk the possibilities of the subconscious world. The monks maintained their concentration for long hours each day. Master Dorje spoke silently from the shadows of the raised dais in the front of the Hall.

"The Order of Ordu has always followed the teachings of the Pillars of Light, set by the First Monk, Gen Moll, the founder of the Four Orders of Aetenos. We join our spirit to the life force held within each being. We share in its peace and harmonize together to become one. It is a sacred gift from the Boundless. Only when you have achieved complete selflessness of heart, mind, and body, will you come to know the full power of the Boundless.

"Be wary of the Path of Ease, for this is the path of the common man. He will walk it as the accepted and proper way. He will believe it is the only truth that exists. He will believe and accept only what is known to be possible. His mind then enters a trap of containment and stagnation.

"You must erase what is possible from your mind. Only then will you see the infinite paths of not yet conceived realities. These are the paths you will walk as a Master Monk of Ordu. This is the Boundless."

Kasai heard a whisper and then soft laughter from the row behind him. His mind snapped back to the reality of the room. Painful pinpricks raced through his crossed legs. A dull ache in his lower back made itself known. How long had they been sitting, he wondered?

Brother Jarescu was at it again with his ill-timed wit. "But how will the Boundless get us girls?" He was one of the older monks. Daku referred to him as Flapping Gums.

Like many of the monks living at Ordu, Jarescu had been brought to the monastery by a Traveling Master. He was a mix between the dark-haired jungle dwellers of Sunne and the light-skinned, horse farmers of the great grass plains of Northern Baroqia. He had a broad frame yet delicate facial features and hands. His cheekbones sat high on his face and emphasized the upward slant of his almond-shaped eyes.

Jarescu continued, "Let me introduce you to the Boundless, my dear. It will set you free of those clothes."

Kasai heard more quiet laughter from behind. He worried that Master Dorje might think it was him interrupting the lesson. Just what he needed, more attention from the Master Monk.

Luckily, Master Dorje chose to ignore the slight disturbance of his pupils. "The Four Orders were built upon this premise. It is the Way of Aetenos. This is your path, young initiates."

Jarescu was relentless now that he had his audience. "I think I'll develop a different Way. I'll call it the Way of Jarescu. My path will combine the ancient powers of Rest, Relaxation, and Sleep. My arse is killing me."

Daku sat to the right of Kasai. Kasai could feel the tension stirring in his friend. Daku's breathing had changed from steady and calm to short, quick breaths.

"Concentrate, Brother," Kasai whispered while keeping his own eyes closed. "I can feel the heat from your fire xindu from where I sit. Release your water xindu. Let it soothe you."

Kasai heard Daku's breathing increase in tempo. "Stay with Master Dorje's words."

"That's right, Master Dorje, I'll travel straight to dreamland, I will," Jarescu continued, eliciting more quiet laughter from the younger monks. Kasai cracked his eyes. Master Dorje's eyes were open and looking straight at him. Kasai immediately closed his eyes.

Master Dorje continued with emphasis. "Meditation strengthens the mind. It provides a true path for the flesh to follow. But beware, the Path of Ease will ensnare the undisciplined mind. You must always be mindful of distraction for the unfocused mind is susceptible to the temptations of the Deep Dark.

"You will learn to channel the wonders of the Boundless through diligent training and meditation. Harness your passion and control its direction. Otherwise, you will lose your way and become a lost soul. This is suffering. This is the Emptiness.

"Meditate on my words. Contemplate the Boundless," Master Dorje said.

Kasai heard Master Dorje shuffle out of the room. The rapid breathing of Daku continued and echoed in his ears.

"Calm your breathing, Brother, and be at peace," Kasai whispered.

"I can manage without your instruction," Daku said tersely. His words came between clenched teeth. A moment later, Kasai felt the air move swiftly across his right side. Daku spoke in a low, menacing tone to the row behind him.

"You have upset my meditation with your distractions, Jarescu. Apparently, the meaning of Master Dorje's lesson is outside the realm of your understanding," Daku said.

Jarescu stared back defiantly. "Lighten up, Daku. You could benefit from a good laugh."

A few of the monks to his right and left chuckled under their breath. That's it, thought Kasai. Jarescu is a dead man. Kasai turned his head just enough to see Daku entirely reversed on his mat, staring intently at Jarescu.

Daku leaned forward, closer to Jarescu's face. "And since today's lesson was lost upon you, I am willing to bring special attention to your spiritual well-being during the tournament today."

The smile dropped from Jarescu's slender lips. Daku pointed his finger into the Jarescu's chest, almost pushing him over. "That's right, Jarescu, you see it now, don't you? Your lesson begins in the sparring circles. And at that time, *Brother*, I will take my time explaining Master Dorje's words to you. Until then, keep your mouth shut." Daku turned back around and closed his eyes.

"Why did you threaten him like that?" Kasai whispered. "He is your Brother."

Daku scoffed at the familial reference. "I am tenderizing the meat before the tournament. Plus, I just don't like him."

"You don't like anyone."

"Mostly."

Kasai shook his head. Daku was headed down a dangerous road. He pushed the boundaries of what was needed to achieve a goal, and what was overkill. Kasai's thoughts drifted back to Master Dorje's lesson. Somewhere there was an answer.

An early morning mist lingered when the monks emptied from the meditation hall into the central courtyard. The colors of their training garb resembled Autumn's seasonal bounty of falling leaves. The warm sun reflected off the monks' yellow shirts and bright-orange leggings as they practiced the secret fighting techniques known only to the Four Orders of Aetenos.

Twenty of the younger monks took the center of the square. They placed themselves in an equally spaced pattern before bowing to the senior monk who led them through the drill. Their lean, muscular bodies moved in unison, sometimes as a flash of lightning from Heaven, while at other times stiff and static like the granite of the deepest earth.

Kasai removed his outer robe. His forearms were covered in tattoos. The markings were runes of power he had received from past achievements. The symbols granted him limited abilities when he mentally engaged their stored energy.

Kasai knelt over a bucket filled with gravel. A similar

bucket to his right was filled with sand, then one with rice and the last one with dried beans. Daku joined him but took the one to the left. It was filled with iron shot.

"If they had a final bucket of sharp glass, you would take it if I took the iron first," Kasai said to his friend.

"Yup."

Daku cocked his arm back and thrust his hand into bits of iron like a spade. "Feels good."

Kasai rolled his eyes. "Show off." He jabbed his hand into his bucket of gravel. He twisted his entire arm at the shoulder with each blow. Daku picked up the pace of his strikes. Kasai followed. It was a race to the bottom.

"Touched!" Daku said. He pulled his hand out and held up his bloody fingertips. Kasai was only about a third of the way through the gravel in his bucket.

"One of these days I will beat you," Kasai said. He didn't care who won, but he knew Daku did.

"No, Kasai, you won't."

The Three Masters of Ordu came into the square to observe the progress of the initiates. They were dressed in long, multi-layered robes of sky-blue with indigo pants and white sashes. Master Dorje's face was round and smooth as polished stone. He stood in between Master Choejor and Master Kunchen. He was built like a glacial boulder with short legs and a barrel-shaped chest.

Master Dorje was a foot shorter than Master Choejor, and half that again of Master Kunchen. He wore a wide-brimmed hat made of straw, the crown of which ended in a point. He nodded in agreement as Master Kunchen pointed out a young monk performing a particularly challenging punch-kick-punch combination.

Master Kunchen wore a similar wide-brimmed hat. The thin leather strap holding it in place disappeared beneath his long, wispy beard. His keen eyes carried the heritage of

Sunne, raised upwards at the corners, but were an uncanny blue. His flowing hair had aged to a soft grey.

Master Choejor stepped forward to address the monks. He stroked his long mustache and beard in contemplation while the sun warmed his smooth, hatless head. Master Choejor's hair always reminded Kasai of unblemished snow.

Master Choejor clapped his hands once. The monks stopped their training and jogged to form a circle around the Masters. They bowed and waited patiently for instruction.

Master Choejor stroked his long beard again. "You shall now be paired with your opposite. Choose one to attack and one to protect. You shall learn your weakness by observing the strength of your partner. The winner will lead the rest on a mission outside the monastery walls. Let the tournament begin."

Kasai felt a firm hand on his shoulder from behind. He didn't need to turn around to know who it was.

"Let's go, Kasai. It's you and me."

Daku's body was built for strength and power. He fought like an enraged bull. Daku always took an aggressive approach when sparring. Strike first and hard, and before your opponent can respond, charge forward and strike again.

Kasai was smaller than most of the Brothers his age, especially Daku. He was a smart fighter who took a defensive approach against his opponents. Kasai was patient. When the moment was right, he unleashed quick and accurate counter strikes. The two friends made a formidable fighting team.

Daku surveyed the other monks with contempt. "We both know how this will play out. I'll take the role of striker. You protect my weak side. We are assured of victory."

"Not this time, Brother. I'm faster," Kasai said as the two friends received matching red arm sashes from a young initiate.

"Your opinion is noted and dismissed as irrelevant. I

mean to win. You go too easy." Daku searched the other monks being paired with their partners. "Where is Jarescu? Ah, there he is over there."

Kasai saw Jarescu being matched with Brother Shiro.

"This will easier than I thought. I won't even need you to defeat them both."

"Daku, why must you make enemies of your Brothers? It won't always be me protecting your back. One day you will need to rely on one of them, perhaps with your life."

"Doubtful. But I'm glad you have accepted your role without much fuss today. Let's go. We are being called to the first circle."

Individually, Kasai and Daku were formidable opponents. When they were paired together, they had no rivals. Much of their friendship was based on outdoing the other's most recent accomplishments.

The competition began. The monks fought in pairs as Master Choejor dictated. The winners advanced, while the defeated moved to the side. Eventually, two pairs remained. Jarescu and Shiro stepped into the center circle. An unfortunate fate for the two monks.

"I'm impressed you dared to remain in the competition this long, Jarescu. I had thought you would intentionally remove yourself early, rather than face me in the later rounds," Daku said. He prowled around Jarescu and Shiro like a hungry predator. "I wonder, did you tell Shiro of the punishment that awaited you? Did he know I would have to go through him to get to you?"

"So much talk, talk, talk. I think he's scared, Jarescu," Shiro said. He had a slight Sunnese accent, which accentuated the vowels of each word. Shiro had mixed blood and was the offspring of foothill nomads that travels between Sunne and Baroqia.

Daku glared at Shiro. "Poor, poor Shiro."

Shiro accepted a blue arm sash and tied a second to Jarescu's bicep. Shiro was a scrappy and wiry fighter with long limbs and wore his hair in a topknot like Kasai. Today it was pulled and wound in a ball on the back of his head.

"You're lucky to be paired with Kasai. Without him, you would be lost. He's the only reason you have made it this far," Jarescu said. He stretched out his limbs, then unleashed a furious punching combination into the air.

Jarescu continued to bait Daku as the other monks gathered around the center circle.

"And Daku, as you can see by our Brother's smiles, they know it too."

Kasai was impressed with Jarescu's confidence, though it was misplaced. Kasai knew Daku was growing angrier with each insult. He would not hold back.

The four monks entered the center circle. They formally bowed to each other and then to the Masters. Some of the monks began to cheer on their favorites. Kasai stretched and rolled through different martial forms. Daku just stared at Jarescu.

"Stay with the strategy. It has worked well today," Kasai said. "Jarescu will eventually strike with a Mountain Wind Kick. He always does," Kasai said. He shook out his arms and legs. "This leaves him vulnerable, and Shiro is usually out of position for a proper defense. If you are patient, we will have them with ease."

Kasai looked at his friend with worried eyes. He knew Daku's judgment faltered when his anger took him. His fire xindu would rise to uncontrollable levels, and he would lose himself to blind rage. All the monks had a difficult life before coming to the monastery. Daku had it worse than most.

"Don't let his words distract you. Stay with the strategy," Kasai said. He moved in front of Daku and once more became a whirlwind of defensive postures. Each movement overlapped the last to prevent an opponent from gaining a positional advantage. He was ready.

Daku needed only to wait. It was the key to their success as a team. Eventually, their opponents would make a mistake. Then the two friends would pounce in tandem like waves upon the sand.

"Change of plans, Kasai, this one has a painful lesson to learn," Daku said. He jumped ahead of Kasai and unleashed a brutal kick with a shimmering, red glow trailed behind his spinning leg. His foot whipped around and connected with Shiro's midsection.

The move was completely unexpected. Shiro crumbled to the dirt of the circle, gasping for air. In the next instant, Daku was driving Jarescu back to the edge of the ring.

"You dare use xindu energy on a Brother?" Jarescu cried out. He shuffled backward in a mixture of confusion and fear. "What kind of monster are you?"

"The kind who wins," Daku said. He shoved Jarescu back a step, then twisted around and hit him with a kick to the chest. A strike to a nerve cluster in Jarescu's right arm left it dead below the elbow.

Jarescu looked expectantly at Kasai. "Do something!"

Kasai stood as dumbfounded as the rest of his Brothers. Jarescu was a skilled fighter, but he was outmatched. Daku was relentless. Even if Jarescu had a second defensive partner, the outcome would have been the same.

Jarescu took a vicious kick to the side of the face and dropped to one knee. His mouth was red from blood. "Enough. I yield."

Daku chopped down to the left side of Jarescu's neck. The beaten monk dropped to the ground with a thud. The fight was over for Jarescu, but not for Daku. He kneeled beside Jarescu and grabbed him by the shirt. Daku lifted Jarescu enough so he could speak clearly in his ear.

"Remember this moment, Jarescu. It will help strengthen your mind and keep it aligned during meditation. I expect your full attention during Master Dorje's next lesson."

Daku curled his fist into a tight ball. He smiled as he punched Jarescu in the face. Jarescu's nose shattered. Daku released Jarescu's shirt, dropping unceremoniously to the ground.

The central square was deathly quiet. Kasai was stunned.

Daku stood up. Darkness fell across his face when he stepped over Jarescu. "Easy."

Shiro found his strength and crawled over to his fallen partner. He raised his fists in a valiant defense. Two monks ran into the circle to collect Jarescu before Daku could do more harm. They lifted his body off the ground and carried him in the direction of the infirmary. Shiro followed behind. His eyes never left Daku. The monks surrounding the circle began talking and shouting at once.

Master Choejor clapped his hands together, and order was restored. The wall of monks reformed around the sparring circle. Kasai wondered why the Masters had not stepped in and disqualified them. Was this another lesson?

"Brother Daku, please return to the circle. You and Brother Kasai have earned the right to continue. In this contest, you shall face your ally and your weakness. Thus, you shall expose your truth and find inner balance," Master Choejor said.

Kasai looked squarely at Daku. "Was that necessary? Jarescu could have easily been removed, and Shiro was no treat. You and I both knew their blind spots."

Daku took the blue arm sash handed to him. "You were there, Kasai. You heard him. He needed to be taught a lesson."

"But not by you. That is for the Masters to decide. There are rules."

"Your rules, not mine."

"What?"

"Leaders blaze new trails for others to follow. That's always been your problem, Kasai. You refuse to take the first step; therefore, you will always be a follower. Not me. I intend to win now too. That is why I will be commanding the Brothers tomorrow and not you, my friend."

The two were a dynamic pair when fighting as a unit. Daku excelled at throwing lethal offensive strikes, while Kasai masterfully countered every attack from their opponents. But now it was a contest of opposing styles. Kasai moved with exceptional agility. His fighting style was based on making his opponent miss, rather than seeking to strike a critical blow.

Daku had less finesse. He used aggression and strength to overwhelm his opponents.

"Begin!" Master Choejor said.

Daku was on him before Kasai finished his bow. Daku spun using the same strike that left Shiro doubled over in pain. His attack was aggressive and quick.

Kasai snapped his body backward. "Really?"

Daku was caught off guard and spun full circle. His leg hung overextended in the air just long enough for Kasai to step forward and grab it. For the briefest moment, Kasai had Daku at his mercy.

The match could have been decided then with one blow, but Kasai released Daku without delivering a successful strike. Sounds of disappointment rose from the crowd.

"See? You are not able to do what is necessary to win," Daku said. He regained his balance.

"Brother, these bouts mean nothing to me. Everyone knows you strike first. It leaves your defense vulnerable."

"Always the honorable one and forever second. Trust me. The real world doesn't follow your rules."

Daku lunged at him. Kasai moved to the side with fluid

grace. He found the perfect defensive posture to deflect Daku's attack, then diverted the power of the strike away from his body.

Daku's growled with frustration. Kasai sent a barrage of harmless yet distracting jabs to Daku's face. Daku swatted them all away, grabbed Kasai by the shirt, and knee-kicked Kasai in the chest. That one hurt.

"So, the little mouse can be hit after all," Daku said. He gloated as if he had already won.

Kasai threw a jab that got through Daku's defense. He snapped his fist when he hit Daku's nose. It wasn't a powerful blow, but it stung. Daku cursed and staggered backward. He fell to one knee with his eyes covered.

Kasai lowered his guard. He worried that he had broken his friend's nose. He had not meant to harm Daku, just push him back.

"Daku?"

Daku narrowed his watering eyes, then swept Kasai's leg with a locking kick. Kasai lost his footing and fell to the ground. Daku delivered a critical blow to Kasai's face that snapped his head to the dirt.

"That's it. I win!" Daku exclaimed.

"I see a bit of trickery is fair game now," Kasai said. He raised himself to his knees. He shook the dizziness from his head.

Daku was already up and brushing the dirt dust from his pants. "I told you, the world is an unfair place. You are not ready for it."

The Three Masters gathered together in the center circle. "Brother Daku, you have demonstrated your ability to triumph over your weakness," Master Dorje said. "Tomorrow, you shall lead your Brothers outside the monastery walls."

"Thank you, Master Dorje. I am grateful to pass this

honorable challenge. I will lead the expedition with honor," Daku said. He bowed excitedly in front of Master Dorje. His Brothers did not share his enthusiasm.

"Brother Kasai, to my side," Master Choejor said. The elder monk was already walking in the opposite direction.

"Yes, Master Choejor?"

"Son, I may not have the use of these eyes, but I am not blind. Nor is the true sight robbed from Master Dorje or Master Kunchen. Might you tell me what stayed your hand during the last fight?"

"It is important for Daku to be chosen to lead. I don't care as much."

"This is certain, but is Brother Daku to be the leader because he is most worthy of leading or most needy?"

"Master, I'm not a leader. Daku is right. I am not ready for such responsibility. I will only let down those who follow me."

"Those are Brother Daku's words. Why are you content to be the shadow of his mountain? I sense a deeper conflict, young one. We will discuss it later. Now, bring me to lunch. I was told we would each have a bite of honey cake today. I mean to get mine before Master Dorje tries to convince me there wasn't enough for everyone again.

6

SHIVERRIG

The city of Qaqal, also known as the City of Spires, served as the capital city of the Kingdom of Baroqia. The throne had been moved from Gethem twenty-six years past when House Conrad claimed control of the kingdom from House Shiverrig.

The king's castle was an architectural masterpiece composed of a thick bundle of towers and tall spires, inspired by the mighty pines that rose in the forests of central Baroqia. The spires were made from multi-colored granite, quarried from the low hills of the Sarribe Mountains in the southwest, and the Hoarfrost Mountains in the northeast. Long poles sprouted from the sides of the lower towers that circled the central spire. Hanging from each was a pennant depicting a pouncing white griffon against a sky of blue.

The Great Houses of Baroqia gathered each year in King's Hall to hear their ruler's new policy decrees and to voice their grievances. Most of the nobles used the time to solidify side pacts with other Houses in hopes of weakening the political position of their rivals.

King's Hall was an immense room, which could comfortably seat a thousand persons with more standing room to the sides. At regular intervals, twelve ivory columns stood witness to the achievements and treachery both playing out within the confines; lit by long, delicate sconces affixed to the columns. Above the capitals, a cathedral ceiling inlaid with a mosaic of blue and white tiles resembled the heavenly skies over the tall spires of Qaqal.

The flickering light from the torches lightly lapped against white marble icons and carved images of the Immortal Mother and her scions. The divine figures looked down upon the limestone floor of the extravagant hall, judging all who crossed beneath them.

At the far end of the Hall sat the marble throne. A chestnut rug ran down from its base then split at the floor to encircle the entire hall. Blue banners adorned with proud white griffons hung heavy from the walls. An illuminated painting was placed beneath each banner illustrating a heroic deed of King Mortimer Conrad or his father before him. *All lies*, thought Duke Shiverrig as he and his retainers bullied their way into the hall.

Thick, stained-glass windows depicting angelic victories over the denizens of darkness were bracketed by drapes colored the same blue as the banners. The curtains had been adorned with impressive needlework of pouncing griffons, outlined with jewels. It was false evidence of House Conrad's delusional claim to power. The history of Baroqia was being rewritten while the scions of the real heroes still lived.

A magnificent throne made from a solid block of creamy-white marble sat at the end of the Hall. The sides were covered in decorative etchings. Two large statues of knights in full plate stood sentry behind the king. The head of a screeching griffon was fixed at the end of each armrest. The heads were made from a single, flawless stone of blue and purple tanzanite.

The crown was too big on King Conrad's head. It sloped forward so that its weight wrinkled his brow. His elaborate robes draped loosely over effeminate, narrow shoulders covering his weak knees and diminutive boots. He looked like a tiny man in an oversized dress. His displeasure at being made to wait was written across his doughy face.

Let the lesser man wait, thought Shiverrig, *he sits on a borrowed throne.*

Below the throne was the King's Table. Four similar, but far less ornate seats sat on a lower tier. Three of those seats were now occupied by the ruling member of a Great House.

Baron Rokig occupied the first seat to the right of the throne. He had a lean, sickly-looking face; high eyebrows with a bulbous nose above narrow lips. His hair was mousy-brown and slick, as if coated with the leftover grease from cooked bacon. Shiverrig never understood how a man of his nature had risen so high in the king's esteem. But then again, conniving men had a taste for one another.

Rokig had a troublesome feel about him. The man was a plague in his pompous, knightly half-armor and airs of importance. None of his influence had been earned in battle, as was proper to Shiverrig's way of thinking. The baron was a leech of other men's greatness and a whisperer of falsehoods. Shiverrig despised the man.

To Rokig's left, Duke Manda relaxed in his chair. He claimed the self-appointed title of High Merchant of the Realm. His family's wealth was second only to House Conrad's. Manda was a tall man with a penchant for the stylish trends of the day, no matter how obscure. Shiverrig took him for a flashy peacock who's only useful trait was his ability to fund war campaigns.

Duke Manda had a pretty face, well-formed nose, and

angular lips. He covered it all in a delicate powder, with pastel eye shadow and rose-colored blush. His clothing was no less sensational than his face. He wore deep green ceremonial robes layered over thin ivory cloth, with topaz earrings and rings and an orange handkerchief. Shiverrig's ire rose from just looking at the man.

Lord Fritta sat primly in his chair across the landing, hands folded quietly in his lap, legs stretched out casually, crossed at the ankles. He was an older man with dark set eyes, who held his tongue until he could make an informed opinion. Shiverrig liked the man and appreciated his reserved quality.

Fritta wore an unadorned doublet and traditional breeches with high leather riding boots. A long scar rode across the side of his square face and dropped beneath his jawline. Fritta's attention remained sharp and focused.

Fritta's ancestors had a privileged history of fighting side-by-side with House Shiverrig during the founding of the kingdom. Shiverrig would not call the man friend, but he did have his respect, which was worth more in Shiverrig's eyes than some foolish notion of friendship.

Respect—and the brotherhood of combat—were the bridges that connected Shiverrig to other men. He knew what pushed a man's resolve and loyalty to the limit. Shiverrig valued a man's mettle under pressure, when blades were wet, and the screams of agony pierced the air.

Shiverrig eyed each of the men as he took his seat. Lord Fritta gave him a brisk nod. Duke Manda was aloof to Shiverrig's arrival; he was preoccupied with preening for the crowd of nobles. King Conrad sat on comfortable pillows of blue and white, adorned with emblazoned tips of darker blue. *He is a soft man*, thought Shiverrig. *He's always been soft.*

Rokig glared at Shiverrig from his chair across the platform. His pale skin reflected a tinge of blue. "You strike at the king's displeasure with your lack of punctuality, Duke Shiverrig."

Shiverrig stood. He addressed the king with a short bow. "My apologies to the king and lords present. I was busy doing nothing and forgot," Shiverrig responded without much sincerity.

Laughter echoed through the Hall, followed by excited murmurs. Many of the nobles from the Great Houses came solely to hear the strained discourse between Conrad and Shiverrig. They stood in a wide semi-circle set back twenty paces from the throne. There was standing room only today.

"You shall not mock this court with your insolence, Duke Shiverrig," King Conrad said. "The Crown relieves you of one thousand gold diras for your tardiness. And levies the same each year for a two-year tax period."

Baron Rokig called for the seneschal. "Make a note and draw documents."

"It's always about the money. Fine, fine. Shall we begin?" Shiverrig waved the proceeds forward. The Hall was called to order.

"Bring forth the first petitioner," King Conrad called out.

A commoner rose from the back of the room. He raised a copper baton. He was ushered to the edge of the throne area.

Shiverrig stood just as the petitioner was about to address the king. "Stop," Shiverrig commanded. The petitioner froze. Shiverrig scanned the faces of the nobles present.

"It is well known that House Conrad holds title on much of the lands outside Qaqal. Paper barons with familial and political ties have been installed to govern these lands. In so doing, King Conrad manipulates political opinion. Bit by bit, the Great Houses lose their voice to the underlying Conrad dictatorship."

Shiverrig's face reddened as his voice rose. "Weak decisions, nay, dangerous decisions are made without proper consideration or vote from the Greater and Lower Houses, allowing Conrad's predatory edicts to become the law of the land."

He watched the reaction of the nobles, seeing familiar heads nodding in agreement, while others continued with private conversations, paying him and his message no mind. There were too many of the latter.

Shiverrig was an influential and highly respected military leader. His strategic victories against invading barbarians from the northern Kingdom of Trosk were well known. His bravery in battle was unquestioned. However, his prowess on the battlefield did not carry over into the superficial politics of court.

Here, men changed their allegiance without thought or conscious in exchange for land, titles, and future favors. They forsook historic allegiances to the Great Houses that tamed the land. Traitors to bonds of loyalty infuriated him. Their honor was worthless.

Shiverrig continued, "Lesser men gain influence based on favorable political opinion, or due to duplicitous and underhanded betrayals of solemn pledges that have endured for generations. Most of you have bought your way into lordships!"

The floor erupted with shouts of denial from many of the nobles. Some shook angry fists at Shiverrig. *I have their attention now*, he thought.

"No longer do great champions rule ... rather, the one who controls the Great Houses," he paused to check the eyes of the crowd upon him before staring down Conrad's gaze, "and does so through political blackmail."

Again, he surveyed the crowd to see if they were making the connection. "Perhaps this is nothing new to the *uncivilized* world outside the Kingdom of Baroqia," he paused, gathering the attention of the nobles, "perhaps it will become commonplace here as well." Shiverrig flicked his eyes to Conrad before roving the crowd again; he thought it better to let that point fester in the minds of the ambitious and the fearful.

If his Great House could be stripped of power, it could just as easily happen to others. Still, he needed to ensure they understood. "We have created a weakness of rule with the safety of the realm at stake. Our decision-makers are compromised to those who hold ill-favors over their heads."

Shiverrig looked to those who had taken oaths of allegiance to his family. Their nods of agreement stoked his aggressive nature.

"House Shiverrig was hamstrung not so long ago from regaining succession over the new administration. I call to the Lesser Houses to band together with me now. Our collective influence will rid House Conrad's stranglehold on the realm."

Shiverrig stood with legs apart, hands curled into fists at his hips.

Into the rustling of shifting fabric and murmurings in the bright chamber, a voice arose, "Duke Shiverrig, we have respectfully entertained this argument of yours on numerous occasions in the past. Must you continue to bore us with this same diatribe again and again? The law is set for the betterment of the realm. If you have nothing of value to present to this council, please let another take the floor. If you wish to persist, I will think your words bear the mark of treason, and you will be dealt with accordingly," King Conrad said. The condescending manner in which the king spoke infuriated Shiverrig. Was this all just a game to the man?

Shiverrig's temper flared. "I will not be silenced. I am the head of a Great House of Baroqia, and a member of the King's Table. I have the right to speak my mind." He turned to the king. "Or are you afraid the illusion of your rule will vanish?"

Sound stopped as everyone waited for a response from the king. When none came, the floor erupted in shouts of outrage. Nobles stood, some moved forward, brandishing fists or pointing accusatory fingers. Shiverrig waved his arm to settle the crowd. "It is imperative that the nobles listen to reason. I have confirmed reports that a vast horde of barbarian raiders have massed at the northern side of Stormwind Pass. It is time to mount a pre-emptive strike against the North. Hear my words, fellow nobles, and be concerned. An invasion from the sorcerer, Maugris, is inevitable!"

Shiverrig noted many of the wealthy land barons with vast farming estates shook their heads in dismay. Their harvests would immediately be appropriated if a war was declared. Their annual profits would disappear. Shiverrig watched them closely. It would only take the slightest shake of their heads, and Conrad would decree that war was not the answer.

"What you suggest will create an immediate declaration of war from the North. I will not move forward based on information gathered from frightened peasants," King Conrad said. He shrugged his shoulders. "These are rumors at best and not immediate concerns."

"These reports are from my Borderland Rangers! The markers of a full-scale invasion are clear. Anyone with an iota of military experience would recognize the imminent danger to our kingdom. I have detailed accounts of massive movements of war machines and the strategic positioning of troops along the southern side of the Hoarfrost Mountains."

Shiverrig turned to the nobles. "You see? The decisions of a coward forsake the safety of Baroqia. We need leadership capable of protecting the realm. Now is the time to cripple the advance of the North, not with words and diplomacy, but with the strength of arms. We must root out Maugris in his mountain stronghold. If House Conrad does not have the strength of resolve to do what is necessary to protect the realm, I move for a vote of new rule!"

The hall erupted in a second upheaval of outrage and cheers. Shiverrig assumed the Lesser nobles attached to House Conrad would fear the change for it would jeopardize their highly coveted positions, while those aligned with House Shiverrig would consider how they might profit from a new regime.

Shiverrig remained standing as chaos ensued below him. The guards did not come to remove him for his outburst, and he was not surprised. Conrad was a coward and did not have Shiverrig blood running through his veins, for if any man spoke in such a way in Volkerrum Keep, they would be cut down without hesitation.

"Sir, you have been given leniency due to the historical debt owed to House Shiverrig. However, if you disrespect the Crown again, I will have you barred from King's Hall. You will be stripped of all lands and titles. Duke or not, you shall respect my authority! Am I clear?" King Conrad shouted over the din of the hall.

He was such a weak and feeble man.

The malicious smile of a viper before it struck, played over Shiverrig's face. "Please excuse me, Highness." He let the bitterness fade from his voice. "I am impassioned by the safety of our realm. I look at current events through a different lens. I see dark times ahead."

Shiverrig half turned so the rest of the hall could hear. "I have expressed numerous times my willingness to take command of the Five Armies of Baroqia. I will bring the fight to the sorcerer before he has time to marshal his barbarian forces."

The king shook his head. He was weary and sat back in his cushioned throne.

"Command of the Five Armies is not your concern, Duke Shiverrig. Contrary to your personal belief, I am well equipped to handle our military engagements.

"Our strategy is a defensive one, which revolves around open communication and negotiations. We need accurate reports from credible sources. Ill-educated border folk posing as rangers of the forest will not do. If you have reconnaissance reports to share, I suggest you hand them over immediately.

"And, I will remind you that if needed, you will add the Knights of Gethem to the host of the King's Army here is Qaqal. You will advise when and if called upon, but ultimate leadership will fall to others."

Shiverrig played his last card. "Mortimer Conrad, you have the military prowess of a child playing in the mud. I will not take orders from a lesser commander, especially one who hails from the bloodline of a traitorous house! You may hold sway over the realm for now, but I will not be pushed aside like a stray dog!"

The hall erupted into madness. Political allies loyal to the king jumped to his defense. A call for war sounded from those sided with House Shiverrig. A noble was shoved to the floor. Small scuffles broke out in the middle of the hall. The royal bodyguards moved into position around the king. Their weapons were drawn and pointed at Shiverrig.

His eyes narrowed, daring the guards to move first. As expected, they did nothing. Instead, they shuffled the king around the throne and to safety. Shiverrig stomped down the short steps from the landing of the King's Table to the hall floor. He and his contingent of followers shoved their way out of King's Hall.

Shiverrig left Qaqal pleased with the outcome of the day's

events. He was sure there would be no disciplinary action from the Crown. War was pending, and the king knew it.

Although Conrad was a weak man, he was politically savvy enough to understand he still needed House Shiverrig and its knights when war was declared. The nobles of the Great Houses trusted House Shiverrig to save them in times of need. At least that much had not changed.

"Now, the true hearts of the nobles are known," Shiverrig commented. His outburst and harsh remarks of the king had revealed the allegiances of the nobles who had not yet publicly sided with any Great House. *They will return to the embrace of Shiverrig rule once war engulfs the land*, he thought.

Volkerrum Keep was a cold, indomitable place. Shiverrig liked it that way. He had no time for fancy balls or grand dinner parties to entertain his fellow nobles. Let Conrad waste valuable time and money on such worthless endeavors. Shiverrig stared into the fire warming the room. Today was a decision-making day.

His two mastiffs lay at his feet before the fire. They growled low when the Archvashim entered the room. Malachi's calculating expression paled at the sight of the dogs. He was wary of the beasts.

"Your methods begin to foster results, my Duke. The unrest is growing at a steady rate. The death of the Port Deputy at Parne, as well as the disappearance of another shipping baron, can only be good for us," Malachi disclosed with a soft voice. He shifted his way between the dogs to sit in the chair opposite the Duke. As he eased into the seat, one dog growled, the other snapped at his foot. Malachi yelped, quickly vacating the chair, opting for a position behind it.

Shiverrig watched the scene unfold, a smirk playing at the

corners of his mouth as he noted Malachi's discomfort. "Please, continue when you're ready," he jibbed.

"Yes, thank you, my lord. Once the Northern Raiders attack, the economic stability of Baroqia will collapse. The nobles will realize the threat from the North is real, and the king will be forced to declare war. And as you know…," Malachi effused, "wars have always been good for House Shiverrig."

"There will be no raids if I pivot from this course," Shiverrig mused, staring into the fire. "Gethem bears the brunt of the unrest you are so fond of escalating. Conrad will use this to his advantage. He will declare me incompetent and unable to govern Gethem effectively. He will say such a liege-lord could never succeed him to rule the whole kingdom or be entrusted with its military."

Shiverrig's eyes bore into Malachi. "I'm taking a big risk. Your plan had better work."

Malachi met his gaze, light from the fire playing across his face. "Profit is what controls the actions of the nobles in Qaqal. And a secure king equates to secure profits. The coffers of Great and Lesser Houses alike have swollen due to King Conrad's favors and appointments. Therefore, the nobles will continue to invest their support with the current holder of the crown.

"But trust me, the moment their coin is threatened, their opinions will change. We find ourselves in a time when allegiances shift according to the winds of opportunity."

"It is your clever allegiances that trouble me most. Are you sure I can trust the Maugris to fulfill his part?"

"I believe he will. He has much to gain with this coup. He will see it through to the end. His delegates await you in the reception room. They are comfortable with food and wine."

Shiverrig rose. Mastiffs at his heel, he paced across the floor toward the study door. The larger dog turned, snarled at Malachi and woofed, causing the Archvashim to jump. Shiverrig dropped his hand to pat the mastiff's shoulder. "Good boy," he praised.

Duke Shiverrig paused at the door leading to the reception room. How could *this* be the only viable option to reclaim the throne? How had his Great House lost so much strength in so few years? It was inconceivable that he was courting with a madman as his last resort.

If he was having second thoughts, now was the time to alter his course of his actions. He could just walk away and have his men dispose of Maugris' delegates. He looked to the coat-of-arms above the door and the snarling dog against crossed swords. The Shiverrig name represented power and might across the Three Kingdoms.

"If I do nothing, King Conrad will bleed House Shiverrig of wealth, power, and influence. The legacy of my House will end with me," he acknowledged.

He had laid out his pieces like a chess master; Conrad had taken each token offered. While the fool thought he was gaining the upper hand, the endgame would soon begin, the trap beckoned. The king had been warned.

What happened next was his own doing. Shiverrig's hands were clean. "No, I will not back down now. Maugris need only fulfill his role and House of Shiverrig will rise to prominence again."

Shiverrig pulled on the wrought-iron handles of the reception room doors, scanning the room for threats. The Northerners congregated in the far corner; their conversation interrupted as they turned to observe him. Between them, a long table had been set with food and refreshments. Bowls of assorted fruits were placed between platters of glazed ham and honied carrots, though the food remained untouched, and the wine goblets unfilled.

One of the delegation members separated from the group, walking toward Shiverrig. He shimmered in the light. Shiverrig assumed the optical effect was because of the man's obscure clothing. It appeared to be made from something he couldn't identify, some kind of exotic skin, reptilian perhaps. Or was it the man himself that was shifting?

Uneasy with the individual moving forward, Shiverrig's already dubious opinion deepened. The remainder of the party—three oddly shaped men huddled in the far shadows of the room—were flanked by two larger men still wearing traveling furs.

Taking command of the room, Shiverrig opened his arms wide. "Gentlemen, Gethem welcomes you. Volkerrum Keep is at your service. I am Duke Gerun Shiverrig."

The three figures moved as one into a twisted heap of gangly flesh. Shiverrig was repulsed at the sight of the wretches but stood fast; it would be unfitting to cringe. Somehow, he had been placed in a position of service to these frail men with boney arms and gooey smiles. War made for strange bedfellows.

The three who were one came to him in a morbidly fascinating embrace of interlocking elbows and shuffling feet. They stooped forward and addressed the duke in unison. Shiverrig shook the hand that was offered to him. The slick surface of the palm felt like wet, rotting leaves. He surreptitiously wiped his hand on his trousers.

Shiverrig watched slick drool slip freely from their oversized mouths as they forced smiles to their puffy faces. Their breath reeked of old eggs. The gorge rose in his throat, and he forced it back down. His instinct was to kill this abomination, but he reminded himself that the needs of the people outweighed his own. The kingdom would be strong once more. He would set things right.

Their heads were shaved to an unusually high hairline. A tattoo of red ink was painted across their eyes. Shiverrig thought it resembled a mask. How appropriate, he thought, thieves at my door with smiling faces and hidden daggers.

He tracked the two men who approached as shadows behind the three wretches. They moved faster than the steps they took. They were physically wrong as if their bodies had been stuffed into human skin a size too small. The skin was stretched thin across their faces and hands. They stopped to either side of the three. These must be the enforcers intended to intimidate me, he thought. Curious.

"Lord Maugris is well, I hope?" Shiverrig said to his guests.

"We are The Three. We are here to ensure the will of Maugris the Infinite is carried out to his exact specifications. The timetables must be adhered to and under no circumstances altered." The Three spoke at the same time. The sound of their voices blended into a preternatural whine.

"I see, straight to the point. Well then, if I deliver my part of the alliance, what guarantee do I have that Maugris will keep his promise?" Shiverrig said. "My men are equipped and ready to move as soon as I…"

"See that they are, Duke Shiverrig. Failure to do so will be punishable by death." The Three gloated in one sick smirk. "Maugris the Infinite has no use for petty titles over these rural lands. Soon he shall command all of the Three Kingdoms of Hanna, and then the world beyond. His promise to you will stand."

Shiverrig looked squarely at the three odd men. They were lying. Maugris needed him. Otherwise, these three cripples would not be here claiming a victory that was, at best, a distant dream. He watched their drool fall on his floor. His desire to inflict pain upon them rose.

Possibly they had a layer of magical protection, perhaps not. Maugris was that arrogant to think the threat of his retaliation would be enough to stay Shiverrig's hand. The enforcers were another matter. They moved to positions behind him.

Two clicks alerted Shiverrig that the bodyguards had unsheathed hidden blades. Shiverrig's body relaxed into a defensive posture. He would strike fast if they continued. The shambling mound of human flesh in front of him would die first.

"Gentlemen, please. We are one in this endeavor. There is no cause for threats," the shimmering man said. He moved fluidly between Shiverrig and The Three. "Duke Shiverrig, let me introduce myself. I am Dax, Emissary of the North and Master of Secrets to Mistress Sekka."

Shiverrig took stock of the man. "Assassin then."

Dax nodded and gave a dramatic bow, hand sweeping to the side as he bent. Shiverrig looked upon his co-conspirators and calmed; what had he expected, a tea party with lads and ladies from the court? He opened his arms wide and bellowed out a hearty laugh.

"It is a strange time indeed. Come, my friends, let us eat and drink together while we discuss the future of the Three Kingdoms." He gestured to the table. The Three partially returned his sentiment. They presented queer smiles that revealed blackened teeth; huddling close and shuffling back to the corner shadows as if the food and drink were anathema to their tastes.

"Duke Shiverrig, let us discuss matters in a more civilized exchange. My lord Maugris is confident you will honor your pledge of men to his cause. Though today, he has a small request to ask of your great and influential, House," Dax said.

"Go on," said Shiverrig. He was unmoved by this false mockingbird's lip service.

"My lord would like the exact locations of the monasteries of Ordu, Symmetu, Harmonu, and Metho. This information would be sincerely appreciated." Dax held up his hand before Shiverrig could speak. "And well rewarded."

"What could Maugris want with a bunch of reclusive monks? He turned from the Light years ago," Shiverrig challenged. He moved around the table of food and wine to create some space between him and the two enforcers. "Aetenos has fled this world. Maugris has nothing to fear from an old wife's tale."

"Maugris the Infinite fears nothing! The Light betrayed him," The Three said from the shadows. Six eyes caught the light of the fire and blazed at Shiverrig.

"Old scores must be settled," Dax said. He shrugged. He then meandered to the table and perused the bowl of fruit.

Shiverrig heard the lie beneath the innocent remark. The prophecy of Aetenos' return and the rise of a new Ever Hero was alive and well through the frontier villages to the hamlets outside Gethem.

Shiverrig thought the lot of it was a bunch of nonsense. However, Maugris wanted anyone who might claim to be the avatar of Aetenos, dead. And those would be the monks of the Four Orders. It mattered little to Shiverrig. The monks were meddlesome and best left to their secret sanctuaries. Plus, he had no use for would-be saviors.

"Unfortunately, the Temple of Illumination owes no favors to House Shiverrig. If my studies serve me, only the Grandmaster of the Temple knows the locations of those monasteries," Shiverrig said. "But I will lend some resources to assist in this endeavor if it helps build a bond of trust between us."

Dax bowed deeply. "My lord Maugris gives you thanks. All shall be as foretold. The Time of Change is near."

"Indeed," said Shiverrig. His tone became serious. "Listen to me, I want real assurances that your lord will uphold his agreement." He looked again at the three miserable wretches huddled together. "Perhaps a show of his current strength. Remove House Conrad from the throne. I do not care how."

Dax ignored Shiverrig's obvious ruse to divulge Maugris' strength of arms or depth of infiltration into the King's Court. "At the appropriate time, you shall gather your armies and bring them North. There you will join under Maugris' banner. Your combined strength shall prevail over whatever strength King Conrad can muster."

"Combined strength? The Mad One has no standing army, or you would not be here. The barbarians he has collected number just over a thousand and the northern tribes do not mix well. Even if he doubled or tripled that number, they will do nothing against the might of the Five Armies.

"You want the knights, archers, and foot soldiers of Gethem to be his army. The blood of my men would be shed for his revenge, and I have no desire to declare myself a Rogue House."

"Mistress Sekka comes. She will provide Maugris with a power not seen in these lands for an age. Her legions brought forth from the realm of Gathos shall bolster your armies. Together you shall destroy all that oppose you."

Shiverrig looked at Dax in disbelief. "Are you insane? The last thing I want is Sekka to return to these lands. And you say she intends to bring her legions from Gathos to the Mortal Realm? The answer is no!"

"Duke Shiverrig, perhaps if you looked at the bigger picture and saw how this will all be to your benefit, you would have a change of heart."

"You must take me for a fool. Creatures from the Abyss cannot cross the Amaranthine Barrier. What you claim is impossible. If it were true, there would be demons walking the lands today."

"You'd be surprised," Dax said with a sly smile. "And nothing lasts forever."

"Let's say, against my better judgment, I believe you. Somehow, Sekka and her legions arrive on mortal soil. King Conrad is defeated, and Maugris has his revenge. What happens next? It seems unlikely the demons will simply return to the Abyss. I think they decide to stay. And why would I want that to happen?"

"The Mistress or I should say Maugris, needs great commanders to lead his armies. Exceptional men such as yourself, who know this land and its people. I can see no reason why you, Duke Shiverrig, would not become the supreme warlord of these forces when they arrive."

Dax picked through the fruit and snapped a grape from its bunch and popped it into his mouth. "Quite delicious."

Shiverrig scowled. "I can easily hold the Kingdom of Baroqia with command of the Five Armies. I do not need a horde of demons laying waste to the lands after the fighting is done."

"Yes, of course. I would not keep them here either. Disgusting creatures, really."

He ate another grape and its juices squirted over his lips. "Afterwards, take them where you will. There are other lands outside the boundaries of the Three Kingdoms to conquer."

Shiverrig rubbed his jaw and brooded.

"What does Sekka want in return for her … gift? There's always a price." He spoke calmly, though his stomach was churning. Was Maugris foolish enough to summon Sekka of Gathos back into the Mortal Realm? Could he do it?

"You are a wise man, Duke Shiverrig, it is true, there is

always an exchange of one type of currency or another for such matters. Sekka demands a small tribute of human slaves for each season. Cull a frontier village here or there along the border fringes. Nothing more. They will hardly be missed." Dax held his forefinger close to his thumb as he spoke the word 'small,' opening his hand wide and waving it nonchalantly as he spoke further.

A hole of uncertainty opened in Shiverrig's gut. He could manipulate Maugris to do his bidding and over time, have him removed. Sekka was something completely different. He felt control slipping through his fingers.

"To what end? What would the villagers be used for?" he questioned, agitated.

"Frankly, I am surprised at your hesitancy. What choice do you have but to accept the helping hand of the Mistress? By my account, the king will not see House Shiverrig survive his rule." Dax tossed another grape in his mouth, savoring the sweet juice. "And more so, what do a few peasants matter, once you sit the throne of Baroqia?"

7

SEKKA

Sekka entered Aetenos' cell. She observed her prisoner with a surgeon's eye. He hung limp against the cold, unforgiving wall.

"You've seen better days, I'm sure," she said with a light chuckle.

Time in her dungeon had the desired effect on the old monk. The chains no longer rattled from feeble attempts at escape. Urns at his feet chugged out smoke laced with a unique blend of toxins. She intended to break his spirit along with his mind, but the mind was always first. She wouldn't want the demigod's thoughts to clear and have him call his winged friends again.

She was so close. He was almost ready. She broke into a wide grin as her human toes curled on the ice floor. "My dear monk, your fight has been a valiant one. I'm impressed it has lasted this long. But alas, there is no escape. You will die here on Gathos."

Dried blood and dark bruises covered Aetenos' body. All but a few tattered scraps of his cobalt-blue robes had been torn away. His lips wobbled slowly, swollen and parched. Sekka leaned in close. "You ... shall ... not ... win."

"Is that so?" Sekka said. She carefully moved the amulet that hung from his neck to the side. She spread the first two fingers of her other hand and dragged her sharp nails down the monk's exposed chest, starting at the base of his neck and ending just above his navel. She sliced a final stroke across the top where she began.

"I find your grasp of current events amusing."

Aetenos flinched in pain. Sekka gave him a wink. She took hold of the loose skin at the top and gave it a slight tug to make sure she had his attention.

"Ready?" She started to pull.

She tore the strip of skin from the monk's flesh. His unusual resistance to pain had evaporated years ago. His scream echoed through the dungeon halls.

"Why are you still here, I wonder?" Sekka mused. She let go of the loose skin. She tapped him on the forehead with two bloodied fingernails, then pushed his head up, forcing him to look at her. "Where are the faithful servants of Aetenos? You somehow managed to find your way to my doorstep. Did you forget to leave a trail of crumbs for them to follow?"

Sekka made playful designs on the monk's chest with the blood that came from his flayed skin. "Have all of the sheep in your flock lost their way? Eaten by wolves in your absence?" she taunted. "Where is your Ever Hero? Isn't his job to rescue you or some such thing?"

"No more ... Ever Heroes."

"You didn't make more before you came to my home? Tsk, tsk, such a shame. Did you know that your little stunt of breaching the Amaranthine Barrier has provided me with a way to travel back to the Mortal Realm?"

Aetenos opened his one good eye, swollen as it was.

"Once there, I shall renew the harvest of precious souls you have protected for ages. Would you like to hear what really tickles me with joy? My way will be initialed by one of your Chosen. Do you remember the one? His big spell gone bad, then shunned by the Light, and forced into exile?"

"Maugris..." Aetenos' head dropped to his chest. Gibberish spewed from his mouth. The amulet was feeding on what little remained of his sanity.

"Yes, Maugris. Isn't that just grand?" She giggled in mirth, drunk on her delight. Her eyes blazed with anticipation. "The Mortal Realm shall be mine! But there are things we must discuss first." She whispered in his ear with the voice of an angel, soft and comforting and filled with innocence.

"Aetenos, my love, are you there? I need you." Sekka waited in silence. She watched as Aetenos' broken mind finally recognized the sound of the voice.

"Illyria?" Aetenos whispered. His head rolled to the side to better see her from his remaining eye. "Where are you?"

"Yes! Yes, my love. I'm here. I'm here to save you," Sekka said. She projected her voice outside the chamber. "But the door to your cell is locked."

Aetenos' raised his head for a moment. He looked straight ahead as if seeing an imaginary door. He struggled to speak but managed only a whisper. "I am here ... in chains."

"Someone comes, my love. I will return."

Aetenos shook his head slightly as if to clear it. "Illyria ... is here," he whispered. "...was not mistaken." A single tear ran down his grimy face. "Save her ... but how?"

He pulled weakly against the shackles holding him in place. The chains mocked his efforts with clangs of their permanence.

"Find a way," he muttered softly. "All ... depends ... on me. No, no, no ... not on me." His head sunk to his chest. "No ... longer ... my ... time. I am ... done. Time... Which time is this? Always ... a mystery... Time." He pulled against the chains again and sighed deeply.

"Ever Hero ... one chance ... save a world."

"Yes, yes, reveal to me your avatar," Sekka whispered in his ear.

She cast an illusion upon herself. Her hair turned golden blonde and her eyes the blue of a cloudless sky. She called out to Aetenos in the voice of the angel, Illyria.

"Aetenos?"

The sound of a turning key released the latch locking the door. Aetenos still looked straight ahead. Sekka acted the part of a lithe figure dashing into the room.

"Oh, Aetenos. What have they done to you!" Sekka's illusion of Illyria burst into tears. "How you have suffered. It's all my fault."

He lowered his gaze at her. His smile was slow and sincere. "Dear Illyria ... have joy..."

"We must get you down from there. Where are the keys?"

"No keys ... Sekka only ... spells of power..." Aetenos said.

"I shall steal the secret from her as I stole the keys for the door. I shall be silent and quick as a needle in the darkness."

"No, no. Must not... Flee, flee ... evil place." His head fell forward. She was losing him.

"Oh no, not yet, my dear monk, not when we are so close."

Sekka grabbed a small vial from a nearby table. The elixir was used to revive him during more intimate sessions with sharper tools. Sekka forced the foul liquid between his lips.

"My love, if I cannot set you free, you must call your Chosen."

Aetenos could only slightly raise his head. He murmured through cracked lips, "Chosen ... my Chosen, where are they?" He seemed perplexed. "Can't remember ... where ... I put them."

"You must find them. Call them with your song." Sekka noticed he had regained a portion of his vigor. The elixir was working.

"Song ... no more, cannot ... sing." He moved his head slowly in denial.

Sekka patiently kept him focused on her goal. "Concentrate and remember. Names, I must have their names," Sekka moved around Aetenos. Her agents in the Mortal Realm had provided her with the identities of potential candidates. Maybe one of them would be the next Ever Hero.

"Nysulu," she said. The name curled around her tongue.

A faint smile crossed Aetenos' face when he recognized the name. "We ... raced through the jungles of Sunne."

"Yes, Nysulu. Who else, my love?

"Master Monks ... fifteen ... Master Dorje, Master Aika... Those two ... always competing ... who could hold ... breath the longest. Such shades of purple ... wonderful ... yes, so much purple." He sighed, and his head lolled to his chest. "Playful monks ... miss them. Master Aika ... loved pasta ... no sauce, only butter and cheese."

Sekka licked her lips, anticipating a savory feast. These were the foremost followers of the demigod. Undoubtedly one of them would be transformed into the next Ever Hero.

"How will you choose? Will it be one of the Fifteen Masters? Grandmaster Nysulu?" Sekka became eager with the prospect of finally discovering the final component of her grand scheme. "Who shall be your Ever Hero?"

"Ever Hero? No, no ... too soon. Not yet ... not ready. No hero ... shall rise. All is lost." He fell back into his private delirium.

"My love, you must bring forth the savior. You must!"

"Very tired. Tired ... and weak. My time gone, passed ...

all alone, so alone. Wanted you ... be with you." He gasped for breath. "So very tired."

"We will travel beyond the realms of the Three Heavenly Rings and visit all of the Seven Heavens. But you must do this one last small thing to keep the Great Balance. You must let the Ever Hero rise."

Aetenos tried to lift his head but couldn't. He breathed out a ragged sigh.

"Tell me who is the next Ever Hero. Give me a name. The Grandmaster?"

"Nysulu? No ... no ... nor Masters" Aetenos was fading in and out of consciousness.

"Not the Grandmaster nor the Fifteen Masters? An acolyte? From which of the Four Orders?" Sekka pressed.

"My song ... no longer heard. Too many ... bright lights ... now dark." His words drifted in the air. Aetenos moved his head, but then stopped and tilted it to one side. "Maybe one ... in a sky filled with stone ... will listen."

"Stop playing your games. Who shall hear? Who is listening? A name. I must have a name!" Sekka was losing her patience.

"Names ... yes ... names. He will be called the Mountain Climber ... Pillar Dancer ... The Divine Fist... Happy you ... are ... here. Must ... sleep ... so very tired. Watch over me." He gasped for another breath. His body shuddered. Then he was still.

Sekka looked at Aetenos in disbelief. She had thought she would finally have her answer. But no. More riddles. Could he see through her glamour all this time? Was he playing her for a fool?

The paradox of this puzzle was profound. She would like nothing better than to eliminate Aetenos and everyone connected to him, especially his meddlesome monks. But she could not touch them until she knew who would be chosen to be the next Ever Hero.

At least now she knew who the next Ever Hero would not be. Grandmaster Nysulu and the Fifteen Masters would be removed first. That was a delightful thought. But she must warn her minions already in the Mortal Realm that no other monk was to be harmed. When she had the individual she needed, then they would all die.

Sekka left his cell. There was nothing more she would get from him today. She went to the chamber that housed her scrying pool. Reflected light rippled across the inner walls of the small room and bathed the ice queen in an eerie glow.

Sekka dipped her fingers into the thin layer of slush sitting at the surface of the bowl. The spell of divination was a mere command.

"Show me." Blurred images in the slush coalesced and became clear. She watched events unfold across familiar regions it the Abyss. A wave of fire moved towards Gathos. It was distant now, but its destination was obvious. She curled her lips in anger, and deep shadows lined her face from the light of the bowl. Time was mocking her.

"Get me Oziax!" Sekka yelled. Her anger seethed in her cold heart.

Lord Oziax raced to the chamber. Sekka could hear his footsteps stomping as he approached. "Make no mistake, that beast will never sneak up on anyone," she said into the bowl of slush.

"My Queen. What is your wish?" Oziax bowed before entering the chamber.

"Zizphander vexes me."

"He is nothing."

"I should have destroyed the Red Devil the last time he thought to flex his might." She lamented. "But now he marches with impunity across the Abyss. Has he truly grown that powerful?"

"Impossible! Allow me to unleash the Frost Legions. I shall crush this pretender and bring you his head to mount on the gates of Furia Keep. We shall avenge the loss of Lord Auzdioz," Oziax said.

Lord Oziax's rage was equal to her own when it came to matters concerning the Zizphander. Oziax was a demon lord of the highest order, and the perceived loss to a lesser devil such as Zizphander during their first encounter was a dark blemish on his ruthless legacy. But now it seemed Zizphander's power, and his station had grown considerably.

"Lord Auzdioz means nothing to me. He was an annoyance at best."

Sekka looked back to her scrying pool. Why would it not reveal to her the answers that eluded her? "He must have a shadow patron. He must. No matter, I have pushed him back before with less, and now that I have the Great Monk, well, things will be different. Gathos shall remain a realm of ice and frost."

"My Queen, I implore you, let me empty the garrisons of Furia Keep. His horde is not but fire fiends and lesser demons. I will crush him."

Sekka turned away from the scrying pool in disgust. She would not lose everything she had accomplished, especially now that she was very close to solidifying her eminence in the Abyss.

"Zizphander grows in strength claiming whatever soul energy he can from the demon lords he vanquishes," Sekka said. She tapped her fingers together. "All of our forces may truly be needed to defeat him. But now is not the time for hasty decisions. A full engagement with Zizphander would leave Gathos open to attack. I can think of several greater devils waiting for their chance to strike."

She turned back to Oziax. "The time is almost ripe for the next Ever Hero to arise. I can hear it in the mumblings of that old fool chained to the wall. Precise planning and cunning shall prevail over brute force, my handsome beast."

The scrying pool rippled with new energy. Sekka skimmed her hand over the frigid water. "Ah, Sess'thra reports. The sorcerer, Maugris, has been swayed. He blindly assumes that by summoning me to the Mortal Realm he will also forever bind me to his will. Such hubris! Though I will become his slave, for a time, the shackles of his will should not be hard to break."

She chuckled with sinister glee. "It will not be long now."

"The Amaranthine Barrier has yet to be tested by one of your ancient blood. This is a dangerous plan," Oziax said.

"And I am a dangerous devil," Sekka replied.

8

KASAI

The morning air carried the first chill of the season. Twenty-three monks gathered in the central square. They wore sleepy faces and rubbed the soreness out of their stiff limbs.

Masters Dorje and Choejor spoke quietly in the pebbled courtyard, while Master Kunchen surveyed the faces of the assembled monks. All had participated in yesterday's tournament. Many were bruised and bandaged, but all stood at attention, awaiting his instructions.

Kasai saw Jarescu in the mix. The under part of his eyes was colored purple, and his nose was covered in white bandages.

"I know how that feels," Kasai sighed. The left side of Kasai's face was just as swollen and bruised. It was tender to the touch. But the real pain came from the fact that his Brothers knew he had thrown the fight with Daku.

"They just don't understand him," Kasai said to himself.

Kasai remembered arriving at the monastery alone and afraid. He was six years old. A week earlier, he had witnessed the death of his mother to unspeakable things. His father had abandoned them both when their need was most dire. Still, everyone at the monastery had a tale of hardship, or else they wouldn't be there. Kasai had never felt so sad and hollow inside.

He stood in the middle of this same courtyard. He was surrounded by monks of all ages doing their morning exercise. He wasn't sure what he was supposed to do. All he could see was orange, orange, and more orange. He started to cry when another young boy sided up to him.

"Just do it like this," the boy said. He showed Kasai the proper movements for each exercise. Kasai followed the boy's lead.

"I'm Daku," the boy said. He had a black eye and a puffy lip. But that didn't seem to bother him at all.

"I'm...Kasai Ch'ou."

"Don't worry, kid. I know how it feels. Stick with me. I'll watch your back," Daku said. He narrowed his eyes as he looked at the other monks. "You can't trust them."

The presence of Daku in his life filled the void left by the loss of his parents. Daku was like an older brother, and best friend rolled into one. No matter what Daku did, Kasai would defend him. He was a loyal friend.

Kasai gently touched the bruise on his face. It stung. "Or my Brothers are right, and I'm an idiot."

Kasai heard Master Kunchen clear his throat. The rest of the monks stopped talking.

"Brother Daku, please step forward," Master Kunchen said. "The Sunrise Bridge on the fifth cliff of Montouse Peak requires attention. You will lead your Brothers to the bridge, repair it, and return to the monastery before nightfall. You are the captain of this expedition. The decisions are yours to make. The successful completion of this assignment and the safety of your Brothers falls to you."

"Thank you, Master Kunchen. I will not fail," Brother

Daku said. He bowed low to each Master, then turned to the monks behind him. "Gather your tools. Our mission is to repair the Sunrise Bridge and return before the fall of night. We shall not fail in either of these two objectives."

The group passed the main gates of the monastery and moved down into the wooded area of the mountain. Daku took the lead, as was his honor and right. Kasai followed next in line, then Jia'mu and Ri'sonu. The rest of the monks trailed behind in a winding but orderly line along a path through the woods.

"You know, leading an expedition like this is crucial to attaining the rank of Master. I bet I'll be the youngest Master Monk at Ordu," Daku said. He talked as if nature itself was listening to his every word.

"I'd put my money on Kasai," Cannonball said. "Masters Dorje and Choejor watch him. They talk."

"Only because he is always late to meditation," countered Daku.

"I've been at the Monastery for almost all my life. I wonder what the outside world is like now?" Ri'sonu said. He grabbed a dead twig overhanging the path. It snapped from its branch. "The Masters talk about the past and the future, but never about what is happening now." He tossed the stick casually into a patch of ferns.

"I'm sure it's all the same. Crops are planted in the Spring and harvested in the Fall. The rainy season comes and goes. Sunshine warms the valley in Summer, and snow blankets the land in Winter," Kasai said.

The day was warming. The air was fresh but had the taste of oncoming rain. Kasai took a glance through the trees. The bits of sky he could see was blue and cloudless. Nothing to worry about, he thought.

"How very poetic," Daku said. "There is more to life than what you read in books, Kasai. It's not all about falling leaves and soaring eagles." He moved his arms in grand gestures mimicking the way Kasai spoke.

"Oh, here we go again. Daku is going to school us on the merits of a powerful punch and a swift kick," Cannonball said.

"I'm talking about women. But I don't expect you to know much about them."

"Ok Brother Smooth," Ri'sonu said.

"All hail, Brother Smooth, Master Monk and lover of women," added Cannonball.

Kasai could not suppress a chuckle. Brother Smooth. That was perfect because Daku was anything but smooth. He was rough around every edge.

"That's right. I knew plenty of women before I came to this dismal place."

"There's no doubt," Cannonball said.

Kasai looked back at Ri'sonu. He was rolling his eyes in disbelief and whistled the sound of a rock being thrown in the air.

"Tell them, Kasai. He knows I'm telling the truth. Plus, I'm the Captain. You have to listen to what I say."

"Come on, you two, knock it off. Leave Captain Smooth alone," Kasai said.

Ri'sonu and Cannonball burst into laughter. Daku only scowled. Kasai had a feeling he would pay for that playful jab later.

The monks followed the path through the thick woods. Kasai always liked this time of year, especially when he could walk outside the monastery walls. The trees were just starting to change color. It reminded him of younger days when he raced through the forest surrounding his small village.

"I wonder if this is what it is like to be a Traveling Monk," Ri'sonu said. "Where do you think they send us when we are ready to leave the monastery? We are closer to the Kingdom of Sunne, and all its jungles, and bugs, and hidden things.

"Yet, history says the Kingdom of Baroqia is typically most in need of guidance. Prideful and ambitious family clans raise their swords first and find reasons later. It is a land of war."

Ri'sonu was a natural worrier and never stopped calculating his odds of success or failure.

"I don't think it matters where they send us. We must help where we can and protect those in need. Everything is the same in the eyes of the Boundless," Kasai said.

"Ugh, you sound more like Master Choejor every day," Ri'sonu said.

"Untrue." Kasai gave Ri'sonu a friendly shove.

"Hey!" Ri'sonu said. He rubbed his shoulder.

"The first thing I'm going to do is find myself a real woman," Daku said, steering the conversation back to him.

"Like you would know what to do if you found one," Cannonball quickly to chime in.

"I'm very experienced," Daku said. He raised a thumb to his chest.

"Ya, right. You were what seven, maybe eight when you arrived at Ordu?" Cannonball said.

"Ten. I was ten. That's plenty old enough."

"I found an old scroll in the library that said laying with a woman will keep you from the Boundless. That's why we are kept way up in the mountains, away from them, where it is safe," Ri'sonu said. "But that can't be true. Can it?"

"The Priestesses of Aetenos are cloistered in temples in all the major cities," Kasai said. "I'm sure exposure to women does not hinder one from reaching the Boundless. We are here at Ordu because this is where we must be."

"Master Kasai has all the answers today," Daku said. He kicked a rock on the path, sending it hard into a larger rock off to the side. "Please tell us, Great Master, where will your first stop be once you are freed from our monastery's hallowed walls? The city of Gethem is closest to us in Baroqia. There you will find the Temple of Illumination, as well as many dimly lit brothels. I'm sure Qaqal will have more action. There's a reason it's called the City of Spires. Which will it be? Meditation for your mind or pleasure for your body?"

"I hadn't thought about it," Kasai said, which, of course, was a lie. He had thought about it a lot. He wondered what it would feel like to receive a kiss from a girl. But not one from his mother, or an awkward kiss from an overly friendly neighbor. He meant a real kiss, on the lips, from someone he liked. Was there some kind of ritual or courtship that happened first? Did one kiss in public? Did one ask first? He had no idea. He had seen his parents kiss before, but they were married. Must you be married first? It all seemed very confusing and frustrating.

He fantasized about living in a small village by a wide river. He was older in the vision, like how he remembered his father. He had a small home of his own, in a clearing surrounded by tall pine trees. The fishing from the river was plentiful, and a vegetable garden provided in the Spring and Summer months.

A woman stood as a silhouette in the doorway of his small home. She had long, dark hair that flowed gracefully down her back. Lazy grey smoke rose from the chimney. He could smell carrot and potato stew simmering over the fire.

It was a quiet life and filled with happiness. The image shifted abruptly. The smoke turned black as night and poured out of the doorway and windows. Tongues of fire leaped from the rooftop. He raced to the house, but the woman was gone, consumed by the darkness. The dream shattered.

"Ahh!" Kasai said abruptly.

"Kasai? You ok?" Ri'sonu said.

"What? Yes, of course." Kasai shook himself back to the present.

He wasn't sure kissing girls even mattered. His life was devoted to the Monastery of Ordu. It was better that way. "I would probably meditate."

"Ha! I knew it! Kasai, the stupid monk," Daku said. "Never willing to take a chance."

"Yes, that's me."

Kasai remained quiet for a time. He walked with his Brothers but stopped listening to their conversation. He vaguely heard Daku ramble on about the spiral kick he had mastered. Kasai was relieved. He didn't like talking about himself so much. He was happy Daku had enough to say for both of them.

Daku called a halt to the group. The path had snaked towards the edge of the cliff. Over the side, and six thousand feet below was the Sunrise Bridge. It was a sheer drop.

"Ok, this is the spot. This should be an easy climb. I don't want anyone falling behind," Daku said.

The monks had been trained to find minute imperfections along smooth surfaces. The skill allowed them to scale what appeared to be unscalable. They moved with the precision and ease of rock spiders, scampering over the polished rock.

One by one, they slipped over the edge and climbed down the cliff wall. The descent was relatively easy. The sun was high and provided plenty of light to see the big jugs of rock ideal for hand and footholds.

The work to repair the bridge was not complicated. To his credit, Daku managed the repairs efficiently, though most of the work was more physical toil rather than anything requiring finesse. He organized the monks into smaller groups, each with a particular task. Old and rotted wood was replaced with new planks. A more durable rope was added to the underside of the bridge to allow for more weight. The work was completed within a few hours.

Daku was pleased, mostly with himself. The quick completion of the repair work would ensure he returned to the monastery well before nightfall. An accommodation would follow, and a new tattoo of power added to his arm.

"Gather your things. We're going back," Daku said. He grabbed a thick protrusion of rock above his head and started to climb.

"No rest for the weary, so the saying goes," Kasai said. He started his ascent and quickly caught up to Daku. Kasai noticed the air tasted wet. He glanced over his shoulder to see dark, angry clouds rumbling in the distance. They were coming closer.

"A storm is coming," Kasai said.

"Yes, of course. What of it?" Daku said.

"We won't beat it to the top. We must take the route of the Winding Snake. Today is the first scaling test for some of the younger Brothers. When those clouds burst, it will not go easy for them."

"That route is too long. We will not make it back to the monastery before dark. They will be fine," Daku countered.

"Just for once, could you think of someone other than yourself?"

"You sound like fat Jia'mu. If the Boundless holds such a trial for the young ones, so be it. They must learn the world is not always sunshine and warm breezes. Master Kunchen said return before nightfall." Daku turned to the horizon. "The skies will hold."

Kasai watched the progress of his Brothers. They were keeping pace. A feeling of pride came over him. He knew they were all just as sore as he was from the previous day's tournament, but all pushed on without complaint. He was proud to be part of such an honorable brotherhood.

Kasai saw that two of the youngest Brothers had fallen behind. Their movements were slow and overly cautious. They were preoccupied with the coming storm.

"Brothers make haste. We do not want you caught on the mountainside with this weather!"

Kasai watched the progress of the storm clouds with dismay. They rolled and tumbled in massive, gray waves. Bright sheets of heat lightning flashed within the billowing darkness.

The wind kicked up. Kasai shielded his eyes from the dust and debris. A light spattering of rain covered the mountain. A low rumble of thunder rolled over the mountain. The storm came fast; rain fell hard in fat drops.

"Daku, the rope. It's time," Kasai said.

Daku's face darkened in the dimming light. "Afraid of a little water, Kasai? The jugs are big and meaty along this pitch."

"The younglings, Brother." Kasai pointed below. The two young monks were well behind the main group.

"Stop worrying. This section is basic climbing." Daku grabbed a big jug with one hand and hung like a monkey from a branch. The wind turned him one way, and then the other.

Kasai watched the younger monks struggle. "The fear is upon them. It will steal their strength."

Daku shook his head. "They will make it. Stop mothering them." He continued climbing.

Kasai knew the role of the leader was everything to Daku. He had no desire to take it away from his friend. But Daku was blind to the greater need of the group. He was following the assignment to its defined conclusion, regardless of the safety of his Brothers. Flexibility through circumstance created the foundation of leadership. Not this.

Daku held tight to a different lesson, one he learned in the rough alleys of the coastal city of Ottoloto before he arrived at Ordu. The strong survive, and the weak perish. There was no middle ground.

Daku glared back at Kasai as if hearing his thoughts. Did he think this was a challenge to his authority? Daku's eyes bore into Kasai for a moment more, then he smiled, albeit reluctantly. "Fine. The rope then if it will stay your worrisome nagging."

Daku took the coiled rope from his back. He secured one end around his waist and lowered the rest. "Listen up! I am lowering a rope. Attach it to your sash and then let the remainder fall to the next. Be quick."

The monks worked efficiently, and soon the last Brother had tied off.

"Happy now, Old Mother?" Daku said.

"I will be when we crest the plateau. I'll wait until the younglings catch up. I'll tie on last."

Daku just peered upward. He grabbed another handhold and resumed his climb. "Just hurry up."

Kasai wedged his torso into a wall crevasse at his back. It was a useful technique to rest his arms and legs. One by one, his Brothers climbed past. Each acknowledged him with a thankful nod.

Kasai looked out into the horizon. A silver-blue light illuminated the air and everything it touched. The trees far below looked like miniature toys rather than the soaring pines of the forest. It was beautiful to behold, even with the rain and oppressive gloom of the storm clouds overhead.

"It is a beautiful land. One worthy of protection."

Kasai heard the words in his head. It was the same voice

that spoke to him during his trial on the Pillars. Was it his conscience speaking to him, or was this something else?

"Not just an idiot monk, but a crazy one too," he chuckled.

"Let's go, you two. I'm getting soaked," Kasai called down to his Brothers. They were just below the lip of a nearby outcropping. The rope was taut and rubbed over the rock's sharp edge.

Two hands reached over the lip seeking purchase. Then two more followed. The hands grabbed ahold of meaty jugs, and Kasai breathed a sigh of relief. This was the last challenge the younglings would face alone today. The rest of his Brothers were already waiting at the next pitch. The rope was only so long.

"I'll tie off with these two. We'll catch up," Kasai yelled. He dislodged his body from the fissure and took the coiled rope from his back.

The first youngling to climb onto the narrow rock shelf was Brother Maru. Kasai liked him. He was a thinker and always had curious questions for the Masters. Kasai smiled, not that the Masters ever straightforwardly answered anything.

Maru knelt to give his fellow Brother a hand up onto the ledge. It was Brother Hondo. Kasai didn't know him as well, but that didn't matter. They were his Brothers at the monastery, and Kasai considered them part of his family now.

The younglings looked up at Kasai with faces filled with gratitude. and waved the two monks to him. "Didn't I say I was getting wet?"

"Coming, Brother Kasai," Maru said.

"Be quick!" The voice boomed in his head.

The mountain shuddered. A sharp slab popped from the cliff wall and shattered above Kasai's head. He wedged himself back into the crevasse just as a large boulder flew past his face, followed by a shower of smaller rocks. The boulder clipped the ledge holding Maru and Hondo.

The young monk's eyes grew wide as the ledge collapsed beneath them. The safety rope snapped. Kasai watched everything fall away in shimmering slow-motion.

He instinctively locked his legs into the crevasse and thrust the rest of his body towards his Brothers. His hands darted out, but he was too far away. He missed both by a long shot. Kasai watched in horror as Maru and Hondo dropped with the rest of the ledge.

"Daku! Stop!" Kasai yelled out. "Brothers have fallen!"

"What?" Daku said.

"We lost Maru and Hondo. We must climb down and see if they are still alive," Kasai shouted above the noise of the pelting rain and boisterous wind. The storm was getting worse by the moment.

Kasai somehow remembered a childhood story of Aetenos braving the fury of a mountain to rescue the chicks of the rare Crest Eagle. When he first heard the story, Kasai envisioned himself being that brave. Now that it was his reality, he wondered at his foolish childhood desires.

"Kasai, we must continue," Daku cried out. "We are wasting time! Nighttime will be upon us soon."

"I'll go," Kasai yelled back to the group.

"You'll do no such thing!" Daku barked back. "Continue climbing. They're gone. Don't be a hero."

Water ran down his face. His robes were heavy on his back. Maybe Daku was right. *There's no sense risking my neck if they are already dead.*

Kasai immediately regretted the thought. What if Maru and Hondo were alive but hurt? One did not remain connected to the Boundless by forsaking those who trusted in you or needed you.

"Courage," the voice spoke softly. *"They live."*

"I am not my father's son," he said into the rain, unsure as to why. Was he hoping for confirmation? The voice in his head remained silent.

Kasai shot his voice above the wind. "Daku, take the group back. I will fetch the fallen. Go!" His voice was filled with command.

"We'll all climb down search together. Hold there." Kasai recognized Jarescu's voice.

"Leave him," Daku yelled above the howling winds. "One life, or three, is not balanced with the lives of twenty. We climb to the monastery. Now!"

"They are our Brothers!" Jarescu shouted back. "We cannot leave them to the storm."

"Must I teach you another lesson, Jarescu? Master Kunchen decreed I am captain, not you, and not Kasai. He disobeyed my direct order. He made the group weak. He must live with that shame."

"He's your friend! Does that mean nothing to you?"

"Continue climbing, Jarescu. I won't repeat myself." Daku hoisted himself up to another handhold and resumed his climb.

Kasai heard every word. "That's just great," Kasai said.

He scanned the area where he had last seen the younglings. There! He saw a speck of orange on a ledge below. Kasai went fast. He practically fell, rather than climbed from one handhold to the next.

Maru was flat on his back. He was still alive, at least Kasai thought so. The rope connecting Maru to Hondo was snagged on a rock higher up on the wall. It was all that kept Hondo from falling to his death. Kasai lowered himself to the ledge.

Maru had a large lump on his forehead, and his face was cut and bleeding. Hondo remained suspended in air only by the grace of the rope. He moaned in pain each time his body swayed into the unforgiving mountainside.

"There are better ways to get attention," Kasai said. The brevity in his voice was not seen in his eyes.

Kasai grabbed the rope and pulled Hondo onto the ledge. Hondo's leg was broken. He would not be able to climb on his own.

"Faith in me," the voice said.

The fury of the storm was directly overhead. Rain fell in cutting sheets of pelting water. Small waterfalls drained the excess to the distant ground below. Kasai absentmindedly stood to relax his legs. A gust of wind almost pushed him off the ledge. His stomach lurched. "Not smart," he said.

A flash of lightning lit the entire valley. A thunderous BOOM followed. The cliff wall shook, sending more rocks tumbling past them. It seemed as if the mountain was purposely trying to shake the three monks from its skin, like unwanted pests.

Chapter 9 SHIVERRIG

Shiverrig marched down a roughhewn stone corridor in Volkerrum Keep. Many of the torches were unlit. Though he knew his way, his irritation flared at the lack of proper lighting. 'A man should know every inch of the Keep he holds,' his late father had schooled him in younger days.

"Malachi, do you mean for me to go blind? Fix this. I want more light."

"Of course, my Duke." Malachi hurried to catch up. He cleared his throat. "I have news concerning the king's plans."

"Don't provoke me. I know what he's doing. The Royal Army sits in Qaqal."

"My associates from Rachlach Fortress have informed me that the king has opened talks of peace with Maugris."

"The fool has long enjoyed the sound of his own voice," Shiverrig said. "These talks will bear no fruit. The man is out of his depth."

"The threads of the great tapestry of life are woven together in minute detail. Look too closely, and one is driven mad by the complexity. Look from afar, and the secrets of the realms are revealed. The Lord of Change has provided an opportunity to seize power. All who follow the false light of Aetenos shall fall in ruin," Malachi said. Malachi's devotion to the prophet, Mor, bordered on fanatical.

Shiverrig worried at the ease in which his typically level-headed Archvashim could spin into fits of religious fervor. He couldn't care less about this man, Mor, who deemed himself the liaison to higher powers. Shiverrig had no time for delusional misfits with fairytale visions of the supernatural. Sword and shield, blood and honor, these were the things of value to the Duke.

"Calm yourself, Malachi. There is much work to do. I want the spiritual support from the Temple of Illumination. The transition of power will be easier for the people to accept when the deity of favor is on our side, and for most of Baroqia's nobles, that still means Aetenos."

"If Grandmaster Nysulu does not comply, he must be removed," Malachi said matter-of-factly.

"But not before we know if he will join us or not. I'd have him on our side rather than dead," Shiverrig said.

"The time of Aetenos is at its end. His flock will fade or be slaughtered. It is all the same in the eyes of Mor. Grandmaster Nysulu will be consumed by the fire of the purge like all non-believers!"

Shiverrig stopped fast. He grabbed Malachi by the shoulder and spun the slight man to face him. "I care not which demigod, god, or shining spirit holds sway over the hearts of the people of Baroqia. Faith and devotion to absent deities is a weakness that can be exploited. No more, no less.

"You may dismiss Aetenos and his followers as no longer relevant, but the Grandmaster of the Seventh Heaven is not to be dealt with lightly. The old man is odd, but I won't underestimate him. I'm not enough of a fool to think he is as feeble as he looks.

"Do not let your fanatical obsession cloud your judgment. I will not be denied my birthright to the throne of Baroqia."

Malachi's shifty eyes gleamed in the half-light of the sputtering torches. "My Duke, I have given the challenge of the Grandmaster considerable thought. I believe I have found an interesting solution. *She* will appreciate the endeavor of converting him to your cause."

"Be mindful of your steps, Malachi. I'm growing weary of the dubious company you keep of late. I don't trust *her*."

Malachi gave a short bow to Shiverrig. "Yes, my Lord."

"Now, what do you know of the monk, Eto Vyliche? Can he be moved to support my cause?"

Malachi nodded his agreement. "Yes, Eto Vyliche is a good choice to replace Nysulu. He is a favored disciple of Mor."

"Mor? Interesting. How can the Temple allow this?" Shiverrig was genuinely surprised.

"All worships are welcome at the Temple of Illumination. The absurdity of having two opposing forces under one roof is beyond me," Malachi scoffed. "But such are the mysteries of Nysulu."

"Will he follow?" Shiverrig said.

"All men conform to the desires of others until their mutual goals become unaligned. Eto Vyliche is ambitious. He grows impatient to bring the Way of Mor to the masses. That is his lever. Pull it, and you shall pull him along with you."

Shiverrig pondered Malachi's assessment for a moment.

"My preference is to keep Nysulu in place but do what must be done to ensure Vyliche is with us as well. Invite the Grandmaster back to the Keep. I want to see if we can pull his levers first."

A page escorted the Grandmaster Nysulu and his young attendant into a large, but private audience chamber. Two of Shiverrig's guards remained at the door. Waves of heat billowed into the room from a fire blazing in a grand hearth along the wall.

"The Keep has no shortage of heat," Nysulu murmured.

"If you please, my lord. There are refreshments," the page said. He directed the monks to a large table set for a feast. Candles burned brightly above platters filled with roasted meats and colorful fruits from across Baroqia. Pitchers filled with dark wine were placed evenly between the trays on the table.

"The Duke shall be along momentarily." The page bowed and left the room.

Servants stationed at the walls came forward and pulled back plush seats for the monks.

"I shall stand, thank you," the Grandmaster said. He and his attendant remained standing.

Shiverrig and Malachi entered the room from the east door. A small figure walked with them. The figure was cloaked in the deep purple and rose colors of House Shiverrig and remained a shadow amongst shadows.

"Gentlemen, my apologies for keeping you waiting," Shiverrig said. "I've been busy with the mobilization of troops… at the king's pleasure. Please be seated and refresh yourselves."

The monks remained standing. It was to be a faceoff then, thought Shiverrig. He calmed his rising irritation. The Grandmaster was playing a losing game.

"Duke Shiverrig, we have returned at your request. I hope

that you are ready to assume your role as protector of the land. It is time to purge Gethem of its current sorrow," Nysulu said. The Grandmaster's voice was soft but direct.

"Yes, thank you for coming on such short notice. We have much to discuss. I'd like you to reconsider your position on my request to assume control of the Five Armies. The support of the Temple of Illumination will sway the favor of the lords and force King Conrad to return military leadership to House Shiverrig.

"My promise in return shall be to rid the land of this unfortunate plague of depravity. And then we can begin to rebuild this great realm of ours. I'm sure the construction of more monasteries would be beneficial to your followers."

The Grandmaster became thoughtful. Shiverrig was sure the old man was working through new locations where he spread the word of Aetenos to the far reaches of the realm.

"And when you once more control the full military might of the kingdom, what then? Where does the ambition of Duke Gerund Shiverrig end?"

He's a clever old man, Shiverrig thought.

"I meant only to extend the reach of the Temple's message to the people of Baroqia, perhaps even beyond our borders," Shiverrig said. "But of course, there are other endeavors one might consider. Many nobles agree a stronger Baroqia would be a welcome change to our status in the Three Kingdoms. Borders could be extended, and we could establish more favorable trade agreements with the southern Kingdom of Sunne. The vast jungles hold many natural resources that would benefit Baroqia's growth.

"My armies would march on Rachlach Fortress and eliminate the threat from Maugris in the north. I see prosperity for Baroqia. Let King Conrad sit on his throne. He will reap the rewards of my toils. This is familiar territory for him. I only wish for the security of the people of our realm."

The Grandmaster listened intently, then slowly shook his head. "No, Duke Shiverrig. Your grand words do not mirror the flow of your movements. I sense a taint within the air that surrounds you. It is much fouler than the smell of charred flesh and decaying corpses littering the squares. The sweet perfume of Gethem has changed to a maleficent odor.

"I fear something wicked has taken hold of this city. And now I see its roots have been allowed to grow deep." Nysulu's eyes shifted to the hooded figure then back at Shiverrig.

"You are mistaken," Shiverrig said.

"We both know I am not. Duke Shiverrig, you must never be allowed to command the Five Armies, even in the king's name. You will use the fear of a northern invasion to create a defensive barrier around Qaqal. Your control over the Great Houses would grow by leveraging military protection to the outer estates. It is a short step from there to a coup for the throne. For that is your ultimate goal, is it not? To supplant the king, and assume the throne for yourself?" Nysulu looked questioningly at the Duke.

Shiverrig clapped his hands together in applause. "I'll never understand how you monks do that clever trick, truth-saying do you call it? But yes, to your point, I will have the Temple's support in this matter. I will not ask again."

"I see things are worse than I originally suspected. The Temple of Illumination does not involve itself with matters of politics. Our position remains unchanged. However, your path will thrust the Great Houses into civil war, causing the deaths of thousands. This, we cannot condone. The Temple will no longer remain silent."

Shiverrig was about to speak, but he held his tongue. He could see the Grandmaster had made his decision.

"For the way of the world is through change. Those who cannot or will not alter their ways must be removed. So says the prophet, Mor," Malachi quoted.

The Grandmaster ignored Malachi's threat. His eyes were locked on Shiverrig. He spoke as a father would a wayward son, "I do not understand, Gerun. Your family has sired many of Baroqia's greatest heroes. How did one of their brightest stars fall so deep into darkness?"

This was the moment. Once he stepped forward down this path, there was no turning back. Was he sure? Shiverrig paused to collect his thoughts. His answer was clear in his head; Baroqia must be strong.

"I am sorry to hear you will not listen to reason, Old Father. But I will not sit idle and watch the kingdom of my forefathers crumble to dust." He nodded to Malachi.

"It is time we introduced our guest," Malachi said with glee. "May I present Sess'thra, from the frozen court of Sekka, the Arch Devil of Gathos."

Sess'thra removed her hooded and let the cloak fall to the ground. A lithe and supple body stepped out of the purple puddle of cloth. Her naked body glistened in the firelight. Her thin, almond-shaped eyes tapered upwards at their sides.

A feral smell emanated from her demonic pores as a long, serpentine tail grew from her backside. It swayed with a feline twitch.

"Finally," Sess'thra purred. She lunged forward at the young aid at the Grandmaster's side. Her hand shot out and tore through his throat. Sess'thra vaulted over Nysulu. A thick braid of jet-black hair uncoiled down her back. An eerie innocence filled her laughter as she landed softly across the room.

Nysulu flashed into action. Gone was any resemblance of a tired, old man content to spend his remaining days in quiet meditation. The Grandmaster of the Seventh Heaven spun to face the demon. He crouched in a defensive posture as an aura of blue radiance formed around his body.

Shiverrig felt the air in the room change. The hairs on his

arms rose off his skin. A burst of energy rippled past him that felt like a wave of electricity. It rattled the contents of the table and knocked over the empty wine goblets.

The Grandmaster held one hand out straight against the demon's advance. His other hand was curled at his side in a fist, ready to strike. Both glowed white-hot. Shiverrig watched the Grandmaster with fascination. He had heard of the mystical martial arts of the monks of the Four Orders, but he had never seen one of them in action. Real combat was the most accurate measure of a man.

Sess'thra wore a wolfish grin. She approached the Grandmaster with the ease of a streetwalker. She oozed with seduction as her slight hips swayed with each step. "So, this is the pride of Aetenos," Sess'thra mocked. Her magenta-hued eyes sparkled with intensity as they caught the white light burning from Nysulu's hands.

"I know not how you came so far without being detected, demon, but I see you now," Nysulu said.

Sess'thra brought her slender index finger to her lips and kissed the onyx ring upon it. She then wagged the finger side-to-side. "My Mistress Sekka provides."

Sess'thra ran towards the Grandmaster in a blurring, zig-zagged course. Nysulu held his position. He brought his clenched fist up to mirror his outstretched palm just before she crashed into him. A force of air slammed into the demon. Sess'thra was tossed across the floor. She tumbled into a roll and rose like an indignant cat.

"You have doomed yourself, Duke Shiverrig," Nysulu said, keeping his eyes fixed upon the demon. His manner was completely calm, almost peaceful.

"Join us!" Malachi yelled, "Join the new power of the Three Kingdoms. The Change of Mor is upon you! Decide!"

No answer came from the Grandmaster. Sess'thra sauntered towards the monk again. She wiped away a touch of blood from her nose with the back of her hand. She raised her eyebrow and gave Nysulu a bit of a smirk. The air shimmered behind her, and Shiverrig watched in amazement as bat-like wings sprouted from her back. They were the color of a moonless night and unfurled like a virgin fern. She took to the air.

Nysulu followed her movement as she flew above him. His arms slowly moved through different defensive gestures in anticipation of her next attack. It came quickly. Sess'thra dove towards him like a bird of prey. She shrieked as talons sprouted from her fingers. Her thinly shaped eyes grew wide with excitement.

Nysulu braced himself. He manipulated the air to form a white barrier between him and the demon. Sess'thra barked out a word of power that made Shiverrig wince.

The shield above Nysulu wavered just enough for the demon to slice through it. She plowed into Nysulu. The momentum of her impact carried both of them to the floor, though the Grandmaster rolled with fluid ease.

They grappled together in a climatic embrace. Nysulu masterfully blocked each of the furious strikes from her hands and feet. They missed his flesh and succeeded in only tattering his robes.

Nysulu struck back, but Sess'thra's leathery wings shielded her from his counter punches. Sess'thra strikes were wild. They grazed his skin, but she couldn't land a decisive blow. The Grandmaster's face and hands became lined with razor-thin scratches.

Somehow, Nysulu managed to get his feet under the demon. He braced himself against the floor and thrust his legs upwards. Sess'thra was blasted into the air with such force that she broke through one of the overhead rafters, spraying splinters of wood through a cloud of dust. Once the air clears, Sess'thra leered down at the old man.

Nysulu raised himself from the floor. His robes were torn, even shredded in some places, but he seemed intact. The Grandmaster was a formidable opponent. Shiverrig was right not to have underestimated his abilities.

"Your dark minion will not prevail here, Shiverrig," Nysulu warned. The man seemed unphased by the attack.

"You are already dead, monk!" Sess'thra hissed, "You have been kissed by my Mistress' nectar at least a dozen times."

Nysulu brought his hands to his face and examined the numerous welts and claw marks. He chuckled and shook his head. "You thought to defeat me with a little poison? Toxins of any kind shall not affect me," Nysulu said. "Now, let us finish this."

The Grandmaster assumed a sturdy pose. His arms circled as he breathed out deeply. Sess'thra remained in the rafters, watching, waiting.

A drop of blood oozed from Nysulu's nose, followed by a red gush that streamed down his face. The welts covering his body swelled like giant worms under his skin. White puss wept from the open scratch wounds on his hands. His arms dropped to his sides as if all strength had fled.

Somehow, the Grandmaster remained standing. The calm expression on his face never changed, yet his body trembled with exertion.

Sess'thra floated down from the rafters and stood confidently next to the monk. She leaned in close to the side of Nysulu's face. Her smooth cheek brushed against his weathered skin as she whispered in his ear. "As I said, my Mistress provides."

Shiverrig approached the Grandmaster. Malachi was by his side like a faithful dog. "This does not have to be the end, Old Father. The time has come to choose," Shiverrig said. Nysulu's eyes were filled with sadness and disappointment.

"Can he speak?" Shiverrig asked the demon.

"Let's see," Sess'thra purred before thrusting her clawed hand deep into the Grandmaster's chest. Nysulu's mouth opened wide, but only emitted a slight wheeze. She yanked her arm from his body and the Grandmaster of the Seven Heavens fell dead to the floor.

"No. He cannot," Sess'thra confirmed.

She swiveled her eyes to meet Shiverrig's, cocking her head to the side, smugly daring him to say or do anything. Shiverrig was tempted to throttle the little bitch. Instead, he grabbed a fistful of Malachi's robes and pulled his Archvashim close.

"The demon was not to kill the old man! He would have been a useful prisoner if he could not be swayed."

"You knew as well as I, the Grandmaster had made his decision before entering the keep," Malachi said, "It was a false hope he would be swayed."

Shiverrig was furious. He thrust Malachi away. Sess'thra's bloodlust had created a massive setback to his plans. He motioned to the guards at the main door. "Remove this mess and have the bodies burned. Tell no one."

Shiverrig would worry about the explanation for the Grandmaster's disappearance later. Malachi would come up with something plausible, he hoped. Shiverrig was under no delusions that the temple monks would believe him. "Fucking hell!" he yelled out into the room.

Malachi, oblivious to Shiverrig's rage, moved closer to Sess'thra. "You truly are a wondrous sight. Your perfect precision is a marvel. Your sanguine and seductive movements have enchanted me. Perhaps we can share more of your otherworldly delights in private, my lovely succubus."

Malachi ran his hand along her shoulder. His fingers traced her collar bone, then moved down towards the divide between her breasts. She looked at him, tenderly with a smile that was coaxing and dangerous at once. One of her sharp incisors peaked out over her bottom lip and bit down at its corner. Malachi's hopes broadened. He licked his dry lips.

His hand reached for her right breast. A quick flash of steel rose from Sess'thra's waist. Malachi's hand was sliced off at his wrist. It landed with a slap against the stone floor. A small dagger, hitherto unseen, glistened with dark blood.

"Touch me again, worm, and you shall lose the other," Sess'thra said.

Malachi's piercing shriek bounced against the walls of the room. He dropped to his knees. His remaining hand alternated between holding his bleeding stump and trying to pick up his lost appendage.

"Was that necessary, demon?" Shiverrig said through frustrated teeth. Malachi still had his uses. "I don't want him dead."

Sess'thra's lascivious smile was the only answer she gave before licking the knife clean. "Be thankful. My Mistress did not bless the dagger as well."

Shiverrig turned to face the fire burning in the hearth. He sighed. This was a frustration he did not need. His mind shifted through possible contingency plans. His wartime mind took over. First, stop the immediate bleeding. "Get him to the healers; perhaps something can be saved."

Shiverrig turned back to the fire. He nodded to himself. "It's time to move my plans to the next level. I will need Vyliche if I am to move on House Conrad."

Although unwelcome so soon, today's mess was not entirely unexpected. It just shifted a few new pieces into play as others were removed. Shiverrig tried to console himself to no avail. His pieces were now scattering in a foreign wind.

Sometimes, it's better just to embrace the chaos, he thought as he walked toward the door. Stopping, he looked over his shoulder at Sess'thra. "Demon, a word with you. Tell me more about Sekka."

9

KASAI

Two oddly shaped bodies stumbled toward the main gate of the Monastery of Ordu. One was the size of a young boy and walked with a hitched step. The other was a monstrosity with a massive upper torso, two heads, and what appeared to be multiple arms and legs. Both were silhouetted by the sun. The warning gong was struck four times.

One of the wall sentries pointed to the approaching figures. "There, do you see that?"

A second shouted from the wall to the monks gathered in the courtyard. "It's Brother Kasai! He's with Brothers Maru and Hondo. The younglings look hurt. Bring help!"

Kasai was relieved to see the gates open and Brothers rushing out to meet them. His back and legs ached from carrying Hondo. Maru kept pace at his side and offered whatever support he could.

Kasai heard faint cheering coming from the monks overhead as he stumbled through the gateway into the safety of Ordu. Hands grabbed his robe to keep him upright. His

Brothers gently took Hondo from his back and laid him on the ground.

Kasai put his arm around Maru's shoulder and guided him to a nearby bench.

"We're home now. No more worry," Kasai encouraged. He closed his eyes and exhaled. His back was stiff from fatigue. His legs trembled as if chilled from being out in the snow too long.

Monks raced towards them with stretchers. Maru and Hondo were carted off to the infirmary. Brother Nabu offered Kasai a cup of water from a nearby rain barrel. Kasai drank down its fill. His mouth was already dry when he handed the empty cup back.

"Another, please."

"Should I bring you the entire barrel next time?" Nabu said as he handed a fresh cup to Kasai. "You certainly deserve it. Daku said you fell with the younglings. He told everyone you were lost. I am glad to see you are all in one piece."

A frowned stole across Kasai's face for just a moment, and then he forced a smile. "Happy to be in one piece, Brother," Kasai replied. He gulped down the second cup of cold rainwater. Water never tasted so good. He leaned back on the bench.

"I see you still carry the weight of the brotherhood on your shoulders," Nabu said.

"I'm tired."

"Uh oh, here comes Brother Manno. He's wearing the white robes this month."

"Ugh. Hide me," Kasai said halfheartedly.

Manno had pulled the duty of Master's Messenger. He bowed respectfully, but his face was all business. "Brother Kasai, the Masters would like a word with you. They wait for you in the Chamber of Reflection."

"All of them?" Kasai asked.

"I'm afraid so," Manno said.

"Looks like you are not done yet," Nabu said.

Kasai's spirit fell. What would it be now? A full season of midnight watch on the North Ridge? Various punishments rifled through his head, none of them pleasant. His legs hurt. His back hurt. He was tired, hungry, and just wanted to sleep.

Kasai reluctantly rose. He headed for the Chamber of Reflection. Daku must have said something about disobeying his direct orders. He was sure to receive a severe reprimand by Master Dorje. Daku would never let him live this down.

Kasai entered the hall containing the Chamber of Reflection. He walked hesitantly down a long wooden corridor. The walls of the hallway were covered with ancient scrolls. Each one was filled with colorful images depicting the great deeds and sacrifices of legendary monks from Ordu.

Gen Moll was given the first scroll as was his due. He had the honor of being the first Ever Hero of Aetenos. He was shown fighting against demons from the Abyss. His holy sword Azurn blazed bright red. Next to Gen Moll was Aetenos, who wielded Ninziz-zida. The weapon's segments spun in a blue swirl of fire.

Kasai felt a profound appreciation for the history of Ordu. His trial on the mountain had shown him some of the reality of those feats. Maybe he would one day have a scroll made in his honor. He shook his head. Who was he kidding? He was no hero. He was just a stupid monk.

Kasai arrived at the door to the Chamber of Reflection. The door was already open. Beeswax candles cast a dim, orange glow through the room. The delicate smell of sweet honey and aged wood filled the space. The Three Masters of Ordu waited inside.

Kasai took a deep breath and gathered his thoughts. He knew they would ask him to explain his conduct on the mountain. Daku had earned the right to command. That was the rule. He should not have gone against his captain's orders, but he couldn't forsake the younglings.

"Brother Kasai, it will be difficult to talk if you remain outside. Please come in," Master Kunchen said from inside the chamber.

"Yes, Master." Kasai hurried into the room.

"We are happy to see you have returned to Ordu. I hope your overnight stay on the mountain was a pleasant one?" His eyes crinkled and sparkled with amusement.

Kasai bowed to each Master before he spoke. "Yes, Master Kunchen, we were humbled by the hospitality of the great mountain. She graciously provided us with a small nook to take shelter against the rains. I secured Brother Hondo's leg with a basic rock splint. But I fear it will need to be reset. When the rains ceased, we scaled the wall as one. Brother Maru is quite skilled when he puts his mind to it." Kasai smiled. He remembered where he was and why and made his face blank.

"Tell me, did you discover your path to the Boundless?" Master Choejor said. He traced a design in the air that only his blind eyes could see. Then he blew it forward.

Kasai thought he saw the soft glow of candlelight on the Master's body grow brighter. He rubbed his eyes. When he opened them, a faint blue image floated in the air towards him. It was the same design the Master had drawn in the air. I'm so tired, he thought. I'm starting to see things. Kasai rubbed his eyes again for good measure.

"The Boundless did not fully reveal itself to me, Master Choejor, but it provided what was necessary when it was needed most." Kasai bowed respectfully after answering the question.

"Know that the Boundless interacts with us all as individuals. It is a path that you will travel alone, for the Boundless accepts us as ourselves in total as we are added to its whole.

But you must have faith if you wish to succeed," said Master Choejor.

"Faith in a wandering demigod that has vanished from the lands, or an unseen goddess, who has created a world of misery and suffering, Master?" Kasai immediately regretting what he said. He would receive a double dose of punishment for sure.

"No, nothing so dramatic as that. You must have faith in yourself. No otherworldly being controls our actions or determines our fate. They merely point us in a direction based on influence. We do the rest."

"Brother Kasai," said Master Dorje in a stern voice. "We have discussed at length your actions on the mountain and their consequences."

"Yes, Master Dorje. I understand," said Kasai. He bowed once more and stood straight. He was ready to accept whatever punishment the Masters saw fit to give him for disobeying Daku's orders.

Master Dorje continued, "On the morrow, you shall receive the mark of Oh-hur, a shield against the outer elements. It will ward you for a time against the frigid cold of the deepest lake, and the fiery embrace of the burning pyre. Also, we will mark you with Mizzen, to fill the hearts of those around you with the courage you possess. As you are strong of will, so shall you inspire the will of others. That is all. You may take your rest."

Kasai was stunned. He stood dumbfounded for long moments.

"Brother Kasai?" Master Dorje said.

Kasai humbly bowed before each of the Masters and left the Chamber of Reflection. He wondered if he had heard correctly. Instead of receiving a reprimand, he was being rewarded. He would figure it out after he had rested. He was exhausted.

Kasai opened his eyes to a room filled with sunlight. It was already the following morning when he rose from his cot. The Masters had let him sleep throughout the day and night. He was famished. Kasai realized he had missed dawn chores and morning meditation. Maybe he could still get a bite of warm bread to eat before calisthenics and sparring.

Kasai left his small room and went outside. He saw Daku across the courtyard.

"Daku, wait!" he shouted.

Daku turned fast. His face was an angry mask of betrayal. "Leave me be! I want nothing to do with you. You have ruined my honor. The Masters look at me as something broken."

"Let me explain," Kasai implored.

Daku grabbed Kasai's forearm and held it up to his face. "When you get branded with Oh-hur and Mizzen later today, remember that you stole them from me."

"Brother. It wasn't like that."

Daku stepped uncomfortably close to Kasai. "How could I have been so blind? I have always carried you during the tournaments. I see now you've always been jealous." Daku squeezed Kasai's forearm. He had a grip as secure as a steel trap.

"You meant to humiliate me and undermine my authority. You and the two younglings were in it together. And Jarescu and Shiro as well!" Spittle flew from Daku's mouth. His face was bright red.

"You all wanted me to fail. But I won't! Now that I know of your betrayal, I will be prepared next time. I will show you what it means to betray me."

Kasai broke away from Daku's handhold. "Brother, none of what you say is true. I did not mean for the Masters to strip you of leadership. I said nothing of what happened. They already knew."

"Of course, they knew! Everyone here is a rat. Except for Kasai. He's a hero."

"I'm no hero, Brother."

"No, you're not. And stop calling me that. I am not your *Brother*. You are just like the rest. You have betrayed our friendship. We're finished." Daku marched away.

"Daku, wait!" Kasai wished he could think of something to say that would quench the fire xindu burning through his friend. Daku was caught up in a wild passion, and it would be best to wait until he was calm and at peace. Kasai strolled to kitchens. He wondered if he had lost his best friend.

Kasai left the refectory with a roll of bread dipped in honey. The earlier scuffle with Daku had mostly been forgotten. Kasai had no control over his Brother's emotions and therefore decided to let go of his guilt. The two friends had tenuous moments in the past. Eventually, they would find common ground together.

The mountain air was clean and crisp from the early autumn rains. The sky was the color of everlasting blue, and morning dew glistened in the yard. Kasai heard small mountain birds chirping their happiness at the start of a new day.

He sighed with contentment. He enjoyed the simple routine of his days. He was well-suited to a structured and ordered life, notwithstanding his consistent tardiness. But who among his Brothers was perfect?

The Way of Ordu challenged his mind in the same way his body worked through handholds and kicks. It required complete focus, dedication, and practice.

The monks of the Four Orders spent their lives seeking to perfect the execution of each unique doctrine of their particular Order. The Order of Ordu focused on the understanding and use of xindu energy.

The Masters continuously pushed the monks to develop their inner connection to the elemental forces of water, fire, earth, air, and spirit. In this way, they learned to manipulate the vibrations of energy flowing through their bodies. Mastery demanded deep concentration. When done correctly, a monk could achieve miraculous feats. This was the Way of Ordu.

"When you master the ability to control the depth of your concentration, you will understand the boundaries of self and non-self. This is the key to understanding the Boundless," Master Choejor had said.

Kasai was a diligent student. He excelled at the intellectual understanding of the xindu mysteries. Unfortunately, he lagged behind his Brothers when using the strange gift in his daily life. He was told xindu energy was the primordial force that gave life to the world, and mastering one's internal energy was a part of the Boundless. It was a big part.

That didn't matter to Kasai. It seemed unnatural to him. Using xindu energy felt like wielding some kind of dark magic. He didn't trust it.

"That's probably why the Boundless seems so very far away from me," Kasai said as he walked to the central square. He kicked a pebble in the courtyard. At least the bread was good.

He entered the central square just as his Brothers moved into the sparring circles to fight against one another. Some were lone defenders against multiple attackers, while others faced only a single adversary. The Masters watched and instructed. The monks changed positions when each match reached its conclusion.

"Brother Ori. Let's match up," Kasai said.

"Sure," Ori said.

They bowed once and then began. Within a few exchanges, Ori was on his back. Kasai reached down to help his Brother up. "Your strike combinations are becoming more fluid, Ori. It looks like you have been doing some extra practicing with the new technique." Kasai gave his Ori a friendly pat on the back.

"I need all the practice I can get. These advanced techniques are getting more difficult to perform," Ori said. "Yet, you make it look so easy."

"You need only let go of what you think you must do and focus on what fills its place."

"Has Master Choejor taught you to speak in riddles as well?"

"Do I really sound like him?" Both young monks paused a moment to reflect and then laughed. They resumed their positions opposite one another, bowed, and began again.

"I heard the Masters are looking for the next Capu to the junior Brothers," Ori said. "You would be perfect."

"I know. They asked before we left to repair the Dawn Bridge. I respectfully declined."

"You declined the Masters?" Ori was stunned. "Why? You are one of the best fighters at Ordu. The Brothers look up to you. You're a natural leader. Let's face it, Kasai, you already talk like one of them." They both laughed again.

"I think Daku is more interested in taking on the responsibilities of being Capu," Kasai said. "He is better suited for that role."

"Are you crazy? Daku? He left you, Hondo, and Maru on the mountain to die. Who does that to their Brothers?"

"Daku was only looking out for the safety of the group." Kasai brushed some ground debris from his shirt. He looked over to where Daku was sparring with another Brother. The fight had its typical outcome with Daku dominating his opponent with ease.

"Why must you always defend him? How did he earn such loyalty from you?"

"You don't understand him. His life before Ordu was harder than most of us. He'll change," Kasai said hopefully. "You'll see."

"We've all had bad weather in our past, Brother. For most of us, being here was the best option."

"Yes, we've all been through something," Kasai thought about his younger days. Darker days.

"Kasai, you owe it to us younger monks to be Capu. If nothing else, you would prevent Daku from breaking our backs."

"Ori, I think I would only let you down. I can best serve the brotherhood by following rather than leading. The ego leads. The servant follows, and through his service, more are helped. I am content with my role."

"So, you leave us to the whims of that bully? Watch him now. You'll see." Ori pointed back to where Daku was sparring. A new match had started.

Daku stepped into the sparring circle. He faced off against four junior Brothers. They immediately circled him. Each sought a weakness they could exploit. But as a whole, they took on different attack styles to prevent Daku from mounting a proper defense.

Daku rotated counter to their movements. He assessed each of his adversaries, then launched himself at Brother Lo. He was small, about the same height as Kasai.

Daku grabbed a handful of Lo's loose shirt and brought up his knee hard. It connected with Lo's midsection. Brother Meeri rushed him. Daku smoothly pivoted to his right and sent his heel to Meeri's jaw. Lo and Meeri were done. They dropped to the dusty ground at the same time.

Kasai could see the fear in the body language of the two remaining Brothers. Daku was in his element. He reveled in having power over others. Kasai saw Brother Jonah and Brother Nico contemplated their next moves carefully.

Daku took advantage of their hesitation and launched into the air with a spinning-hammer kick. His heel slammed down on Nico's shoulder. The young monk cried out in pain. The force of the blow must have shattered his collarbone. Daku spun in the opposite direction and delivered a second kick to Nico's handsome face. His nose exploded with blood, and he crumbled to the ground. Daku left him crying in the dirt.

Brother Jonah did his best to shore up his defense. Daku threw a flurry of punches at him, which eventually broke down Jonah's guard. Three quick strikes to the face and Johan was on his knees. Daku had systematically incapacitated four junior Brothers with ease. His form was perfect, and his swiftness of movement was astonishing.

"Daku strikes to hurt, not to disarm," Ori said.

"He wins because he instills fear in his opponents. Those four are better fighters against anyone else." Kasai watched as Daku celebrated his victory. He felt ashamed for his friend's exuberance.

"I'm the best! I'm the best!" Daku pumped his fist in the air. He looked around to see if anyone else had watched his match.

Kasai and Ori edged closer to where the Three Masters stood. They had watched the bout with great interest. Kasai knew he shouldn't eavesdrop. His curiosity got the better of him, and he listened anyway.

"Bitterness and loneliness fill the young man's heart. The bad memories of his youth fuel his fire xindu to dangerous levels. He must learn to control his rage, or he will become a problem," Master Dorje commented.

"The walls protecting his garden go high. They shield the seeds of his fear with resentment. The flowers he grows will be ill-formed if we cannot help him," Master Choejor added.

"Too great is his unwillingness to embrace in the Boundless. The Openness is closed to him. He refuses to share equally of himself with the world around him. Never formless is this one. He remains Daku at all times," Master Kunchen noted.

"The best, the best. Hmm, what is best? What is worst? Perhaps they are the same with our young monk? He hides much of himself in secret places. Maybe he has found a different path to the Boundless, unique only to him," Master Choejor said. "Let us present Brother Daku with the light of a different target. We will see what we can retrieve from the shadows of his anger."

The blind Master walked to the sparring circle where Daku stood victorious. Master Choejor bowed deferentially to the young monk. "You may use any weapon of your choice, Brother Daku. I shall rely solely on the Boundless and use what is offered."

Kasai and Ori looked at each other with apparent surprise. Masters did not spar with the junior or even senior monks. It would be as if a champion knight chose to joust against a horseless peasant.

Kasai could imagine what Daku was thinking. He would be eager to pit his skill against Master Choejor. Defeating a Master in one-on-one combat would ensure he regained his honor.

"It would be dishonorable to use a weapon against you, Master Choejor, when you have none," Daku said.

Kasai shook his head in disbelief. That was a mistake.

"As you wish," Master Choejor said. "Let us begin."

The two monks faced each other and bowed. Daku conclusively demonstrated a series of complex movements that conveyed the different offensive styles he had already mastered. He was ready.

Master Choejor remained calm and still. Daku's leg flashed low. He sought to sweep the Master's legs from under him. Master Choejor was a blur of motion. Daku spun in a complete circle. He stopped where he had started but was left off-balance. Daku crouched as best he could. He scanned for the Master.

Master Choejor tapped Daku on the back of his shoulder and sent him to the ground in obvious pain. Daku looked up in astonishment. Master Choejor simply smiled and patiently waited for Daku to recover.

Daku grimaced as he surged to his feet. He rolled his shoulder and did his best to relax the muscles before striking out with a powerful punch of his own. Master Choejor pivoted to the side, and Daku's strike found empty air. Master Choejor touched Daku's outstretched arm with two fingers to the deltoid. Daku's arm fell limp at his side.

Daku attacked with a reverse kick and found himself on the ground again. He scurried forward to grapple with Master Choejor. Daku's good hand shot out to grab the Master's pant leg but missed.

Daku was angry and frustrated. Some of the Brothers snickered under their breath. They were enjoying the payback. Daku leaped to his feet and scowled at the crowd. He launched into a furious and undisciplined attack.

"Don't lose yourself to your fury. You must control your fire xindu as you do all things passing through you," Master Choejor said. His words were calm and soothing.

"I am strongest with my fire xindu blazing!" Daku punched out again and followed with a leaping kick. The Master defected both blows with his outstretched hand.

Daku kicked a second time. Master Choejor grabbed the

foot and twisted it around. Daku twirled in the air before he hit the ground hard.

"Guide your passion, young one. Be at peace with your xindu, or you are lost."

"I am not lost, Master!" Daku spat dirt from his mouth. He managed to stand, barely. With great effort, he raised the arm that Master Choejor had paralyzed earlier. "I can still fight." Kasai could see the focus was lost from Daku's eyes. His upper body swayed on weak legs.

"No, this match has reached its conclusion," Master Choejor said.

Brother Daku collapsed back to the ground. He could hear his Brothers mock him. "Stop laughing," he said.

"There is a lesson here, my son. Have you discovered it?"

Daku looked up at Master Choejor. Exasperation was written across his face. "As you say, Master, I must learn to control my fire xindu energy."

"That is partially correct, but the higher truth of the xindu mysteries still eludes you. Xindu energy fuels much more than merely your martial prowess. It will influence the creation or the destruction of your higher purpose.

"When you silence your passion, you will see the many options available to you on your path of life, instead of running blindly down the one you currently travel. What else have you learned?"

"I hoped I was your equal, but I was wrong. You are stronger, faster, and more skilled than me."

"No, that is not the lesson of today. This is not where you stumbled. Your eyes are open but are still blind to the higher world around you. You fail to grasp the totality of the Boundless, and so you remain a crude weapon."

Master Choejor walked a few steps in contemplation, then continued. "You maintain boundaries where there are none. You are Daku at all times. You hold tight to this identity, but it serves only to prevent you from Openness. You must learn to let go of the self if you are to be one with the Boundless. Contemplate Openness during your meditations, my young monk. Tomorrow is another day to grow."

"I will do as you say, Master. I am humbled by your skill and thankful for your wisdom." Daku bowed low to Master Choejor.

The lunchtime bell chimed in the background, and the monks made their way to the refectory. Kasai watched his friend intently. Daku was not known to exhibit humility or acceptance of defeat so readily. Perhaps this was a new beginning for his friend.

Unfortunately, when Daku rose, there was bitterness written across his face. Nothing had changed. Perhaps it never would.

But something Master Choejor had said to Daku resonated with Kasai. 'You maintain boundaries where there are none.' Kasai knew the same could be said for him. But something inside him was working to bring down those walls.

It started when he faced the Trial of Pillars and became more pronounced on the mountainside. It was as if a small space had opened in his mind. Or maybe it was there before, but he had never noticed. Kasai hoped it meant he was taking his first steps to become one with the Boundless. The voice in his head spoke to him frequently, but more often than not, it whispered twisted words Kasai did not understand. That was worrisome.

He said nothing about it to Maru or Hondo when they were sequestered on the mountainside together. He hid it again from the Masters in the Chamber of Reflection as well. He was unsure of what it meant. He feared if he expressed himself to the Masters, they would fill him with more riddles. No, this was something he needed to figure out for himself. But how? Kasai had a stupid idea. He walked in the direction of the pillars.

"I must not fear this test. If what I hear is truly my connection to the Boundless, I shall hear it again," Kasai said. "Either that or I am going as mad as the voice in my head."

He closed his mind from the noise of conflicting thoughts. He would be calm and let the fear subside. He was eager to see the higher world of the Boundless.

Kasai removed his sandals. He placed them neatly to the side of the first pillar. The first step was just as easy to take as before. The stone felt cold and hard against his bare feet. Kasai stepped to the next pillar and the next.

"This isn't too bad," he said.

He took the pillars at a run, and soon he was high above the ground. Then the air temperature suddenly dropped. The pillars became shrouded in mist, and a claustrophobic fear crept up his spine. He didn't want to take the next leap. "Just be calm. The voice will come."

The winds picked up, and the pillar swayed gracefully under him. No reassuring message came to mind. The voice was silent. What was he doing here? He had purposely put himself in a dangerous situation, thinking he was special. He wasn't touched by something special. That hard truth pounded in his head like a hammer against a dense stone.

He swiveled around. Maybe he could go back. He saw only swirling mists. The pillar top behind him was lost from sight. "Can't go that way."

A quick gust of air pushed him close to the edge of the pillar. He stumbled while trying to maintain his balance. His back foot slid off the top. His body dropped first to one knee and then over the side.

His hand shot out and grabbed the crest of the pillar. He quickly wrapped his thumb over his fingers to solidify the grip. Kasai dangled in the white air bumping against the post.

It was a long way down, even with the safety nets. Wait, were they up? He had forgotten to check. His heart thumped in his chest, and the sweat of fear covered his body.

"Where are you when I need you?" Kasai said into the empty air. "Have you abandoned me as well?"

"*Trust,*" came the voice in a whisper. "*Calm. Concentrate.*"

Kasai listened to the message echoing in his thoughts, and he calmed his fear. He concentrated his efforts on regaining purchase on the pillar top. Once there, Kasai sat with his legs hooked around the column for support. He recited mantras to relax his body and mind. Eventually, his breathing came slow and even. He could feel the relaxed rhythm of his chest expanding with air and then deflating as he released it.

"*Look.*"

Kasai fixed his sight to a point in space where he suspected the next pillar to be. He stared intently at the same spot as moments stretched into minutes. Something was happening. He could see small particles of moisture floating in the air before his eyes. He felt each tiny droplet as it touched his skin. Kasai held his hand in front of his face. He could barely see it through the thick mist.

He focused more intently on the particles of moisture that separated from the air. They swirled around his hand in a shimmering, blue haze. The moisture moved passed his hand as a river flowed around boulders impeding its course. The flow was hardly discernable, but it was there. Kasai saw a map of what was and what was not.

"What dark magic is this?" He lost his focus. The impenetrable air returned to blanket his sight, and his hand disappeared from view.

"*Safe,*" the voice said.

Kasai sighed. "Ok. Ok."

Hesitantly, he sought the division between the water and the air. What else was out there? Where was the sun? The clouds? The birds? Kasai's heartbeat slowed. His mind became silent. His breathing was even.

"Show me the river that flows. Where are the rocks that are not the river?" Kasai saw trails of swirling blue flow around a long line of shadowy shapes. He saw the next pillar. It was so close he would barely need to jump.

Kasai leaped and landed squarely on its top. He jumped again, and again. It was as easy as walking in broad strides. The pillars finally descended. He cleared the mist layer and eventually stepped from the last pillar onto soft grass.

He felt each blade of grass underfoot. His toes dug into the soil. It felt warm even though the grass was cool. The mist was gone, but he could still see the currents of moisture flowing around whatever he saw.

Kasai suddenly became anxious. He had completed what should not have been able to be accomplished. He turned back to see the marble pillars winding up into the air behind him. A giddy feeling of unease filled his gut. He didn't know if he was going to cheer or vomit. "What have I done?"

"An interesting question," responded a voice approaching from across the lawn.

Kasai turned to see Master Choejor walking towards him. He saw a wisp of yellow flash over the Master's head. It was reminiscent of what Kasai saw when he was in the Chamber of Reflection with the Three Masters. He focused his attention on the color, and it blossomed into a golden glow around his teacher. Kasai bowed to Master Choejor.

"You have passed the Trial of Pillars, my son," Master Choejor said. "An impossible challenge for one of your level of training. This is a curious thing. But for now, I am wondering what led you to such a bold endeavor when the safety nets were not in place?"

Because I'm an idiot, Kasai thought.

"Master, please forgive my rashness. I'm not sure how to explain my actions. But it was something I had to do."

"Indulge me an attempt," Master Choejor said. He stroked his beard and mustache, which he was fond of doing.

"Master, there has been a voice with me since my first attempt ascending the pillars. I heard it again on the mountain. Maybe I've heard it for many years, but just not a clear. It says little but directs my thoughts and actions."

"Interesting. One would welcome such a helpful guide, yet you sound distraught."

"At first, I thought I was getting closer to understanding the Boundless. But now I am worried fell magic has befallen me. The voice guides me and shows me things I shouldn't know. That no one should know."

"Ah, perhaps you hear the Song of Aetenos."

"I thought that was only a myth. Something created to bolster the legend of the Great Monk."

"This does not surprise me," Master Choejor said. "Brother Kasai, you have always excelled in your studies of Aetenos, but a deeper belief in our patron seems to be missing. When you first arrived at Ordu, you could recite many of the stories before they were told to you."

"My father told me stories of Aetenos when I was very young before..." Kasai became silent.

"Before coming to the Monastery?"

"Yes, Master."

"Please, sit with me a moment."

Kasai sat down next to Master Choejor. They both looked to the majestic vista of the mountain range. The sky was clear and blue. Kasai wondered what had happened to the mist surrounding the pillars. Was it all just something he created in his head?

"There is great hesitancy in your actions. It was evident in the tournament bout against Brother Daku, and it is even more profound in acceptance of the xindu mysteries. Your overall spiritual progression is slow."

"I trust you and the other Masters, of course. I think I trust in the Boundless, though at times it seems very far from me."

"And what of Aetenos, my son? How does he fit into your understanding of all that is around you?"

"I'm not sure, Master. Things were much simpler when I was a little boy. The people of my small village followed his Light. He was our guide, and my father was a devoted follower. Everyone looked up to him. He was a hero.

But then, the dark things came. I was abandoned when I needed him most. How could that happen, Master? How could he allow so much misery to fall upon his faithful? Where was the hero when he was needed most?"

"Are you referring to Aetenos or your father, Brother Kasai?"

Kasai did not respond. He had often searched for answers to that question. The connection between Aetenos and his father always ended in the same way, a dead end.

It appeared Master Choejor had read his thoughts. "For each of us, the answer to such questions remain hidden until we are ready to accept the truth."

"But isn't Aetenos supposed to be the protector of his faithful?"

"Yes, of course. At times Aetenos himself is the divine hammer that smites the darkness. Other times he is the forge unto which his avatars are created. The souls of his Chosen become tempered through his trials. The process can be brutal. But eventually, the mettle in their hearts becomes unbreakable. They are his Ever Heroes."

Kasai thought about what Master Choejor said, then realized he was frowning. Kasai searched the expansive sky surrounding the snowcapped mountains for answers to unasked questions. He spotted a lone Crest Eagle climbing for warmer air drafts as it used its strength to gain altitude and then soared with outstretched wings atop the air streams. Its bright-orange feathers were golden in the yellow sunlight.

The eagle cried out as it snatched a smaller bird out of the sky. "The Crest Eagle is with us," Master Choejor said. "Perhaps the great bird is here now to help you along in your pensive journey?"

"Perhaps, Master."

"Brother Kasai, are you familiar with the legend of the Fire Serpent?"

"You speak of the great artifact, Ninziz-zida. I know that it is a three-section staff."

"Yes, that's right. But do you know of the unique characteristics of the weapon?"

"Some stories say Aetenos created Ninziz-zida during the Frost War against the devil, Sekka. But it was lost. Other stories tell how Aetenos gave Ninziz-zida to Gen Moll before he ascended to the Seven Heavens.

"I have read that the Fire Serpent is a bane against evil. It has traveled through the centuries wielded by heroes of old seeking to destroy the minions from the Deep Dark. Other texts say that Ninziz-zida is a damned thing with a mind of its own. It seeks to possess the soul of its wielder and make him or her its slave.

"You have studied the scrolls well," Master Choejor said. "And do you have thoughts of your own concerning the Fire Serpent? Would you welcome the opportunity to wield her in battle?"

"Me? Certainly not. I am not worthy of any weapon forged by Aetenos." Kasai was amused at the idea. "No, no, no. I am not a hero. Leave that weapon to the likes of Daku."

"You believe Brother Daku to be a more likely candidate for Ninziz-zida?"

"Well, he certainly has a great desire for battle and a healthy supply of fire xindu. Perhaps he could control the Fire Serpent and not become possessed by the staff."

"Interesting that you would say such a thing. There is no doubt the Fire Serpent commands respect. However, she seeks to belong to something greater than herself. She is incomplete without a greater power to wield her."

"The other Masters and I have noticed your proficiency in the use of the mundane sanjiegun, a weapon of similar size and design to the Fire Serpent. There has been a debate on introducing you to Ninziz-zida. The weapon chooses its own, mind you."

"I am unworthy, Master. Surely there is another more qualified." Kasai wasn't sure how or why this was being discussed. He was no champion to wield such a weapon, and he did not want to be one. Kasai was content to be a simple monk. He changed the subject. "You keep referring to Ninziz-zida as a 'she,' Master. Why?"

Master Choejor remained silent for a moment then spoke. "We shall talk more of this later. For now, you must remember, one must seek to be whole, not perfect. Now, news of your accomplishment will travel fast. Do not think these blind eyes were the only ones to see such foolishness. You had best prepare your answers for the questions to come." Master Choejor gave Kasai a tender smile.

"Thank you for your wise counsel, Master Choejor. I shall meditate on the mysteries of Aetenos and his relationship to us all. And prepare for a lot of unwanted attention." Kasai returned Master Choejor's smile and somehow knew the elderly monk felt it.

Kasai excused himself and walked away in silence. Yes, he recited the mantras of Aetenos with the rest of his Brothers, but he did not fully accept the message of hope they conveyed. How could he? While he was sequestered in the safety of Ordu, the nightmares of the real world preyed upon the weak.

Periodically, Traveling Monks returned to Ordu to discuss the events happening throughout the Three Kingdoms. The lands outside the monastery walls could be a cruel place.

"This is precisely why the message of Aetenos was so important. All things have their balance. We must act as the counterweight to the darker side of the human spirit. We must become the beacon of light which reveals the path of goodness within all of us," Master Kunchen had said.

Daku had a different philosophy. "The strong fist prevails over the tender heart." He only believed in the power of his own hands and not the ramblings of a crazed monk, long dead. Daku was always at odds with everyone.

Kasai wondered if he could make a difference in the real world. It all seemed so far away. He just wanted to belong somewhere, as he did in his small village. He wanted to have a home and be at peace. Life at Ordu was something he could believe in and protect. "This is where I belong. Ordu is my home now." Yet for all Ordu had to offer, Kasai still felt empty inside. Something was missing. He wished he had more faith, but sadly, it did not come to him as effortlessly as it did for the others. Master Choejor was right. He was incomplete.

There was fear in his heart that traveled with him like a second shadow. He feared being left behind and alone. He feared to fail those who counted on him to keep them safe, just like his father had done. No, he would not be the one who ran from danger. He would not follow in his father's footsteps. He would be different. He vowed then to protect those he loved. That would be his truth.

10

SEKKA

Sekka was the epitome of beauty and seduction in her human form. Tall, curvaceous, and slender she radiated a glamour that stirred desire in all who beheld her. She had been known to stir many a man to do impossibly wicked things. The female slaves she devoured could not help but be drawn to her womanhood before they met their fates. She was the dark side of desire. She was strength. She was chaos.

The witches and warlocks in her coven were drawn to her power. They craved even a morsel of the magic she possessed. Those lucky enough to win her favor would experience a touch of deep magic normally reserved for those born of devilish blood. It would destroy them over time, but they willingly accepted the gift. Anything for more power, even if it was fleeting.

Sekka was something far different in her abyssal form. A monstrous nightmare to behold, she had a body that was dense and formidable. Coarse, white fur blanketed her back in thick clumps. Four curling horns framed her head, and a crown of bones embedded with onyx stones at its base hovered above her head as smoky sigils of power rose through its center. Four hooked teeth jutted from her full mouth, which gnashed together in delight when she tore the souls from her human slaves.

She squatted at the center of an inverted cone-shaped pit. The walls of the hole were slick with ice. Human soul-slaves below frantically attempted to scurry over one another like rats fleeing a flooded hollow. Winds howling across the Wastelands of Thresh added to the sweet melody of their suffering.

Ending in great talons, her avian legs could grasp five grown men at once and rip them to shreds. Even lowered on her legs as she was, she towered ten feet above the pit's floor. The steaming blood and innards of the dead covered her chest and stomach like a thick apron of red and brown sludge.

Her black-within-black eyes scanned the delicious banquet before her. A hundred human slaves desperately climbed the slick sides of the outwardly sloping pit, tearing savagely at one another. The slaves pulled back the heads of their fellows by yanking handfuls of hair, eyeballs were gouged out, and necks throttled mercilessly. They climbed higher and higher, using each other to build a ladder to freedom.

This was how she played with her toys. Escape the pit and live, that was the game. Slaves already on the slippery floor dashed about like mice. They battled each other to gain purchase on the highest rung of the human ladder. None cared that the cost of their freedom was the souls of their brethren.

The longer the game played out, the more soul-slaves would be devoured, causing the height of the human ladders to decrease so that reaching the top became an impossible task. When the slaves realized their route of escape was gone, the ladders would break apart and those who could still move, would scurry like mice seeking another way to freedom, but there was none. It was then that they looked up at her, wide-eyed with absolute terror and remorse. She savored those moments the most.

Sekka spun on her haunches and spotted her next victim, a slave who had the misfortune of being pushed too close to her grasp. Plucking him off the ground, she gazed deeply into his eyes as a lover would before a kiss. The slave screamed in terror when she raised him over her head. Opening her mouth, she lowered him in to the waist. She held his horror-stricken gaze as her tongue coiled around his midsection, drawing him in deeper. Warm blood sprayed across her face when her teeth chomped down on another tasty treat.

Sekka caught the telltale scent of another blizzard sweeping down from the crater peak of the sleeping volcano that had given birth to the ice realm of Gathos. The Dead Giant, as it was named, remained dormant. She swallowed the last bits of the slave, before licking the blood from her mouth. It was a good day on Gathos.

A quick jerk pulled Sekka's mind to a prison within a black, silver sphere. And then she felt another, more urgent this time with command. "Finally," she exulted. "Maugris, you, wonderful fool!" A smile widened across her face as her conscious mind was dragged to the Mortal Realm.

If Maugris was strong enough, he would pull the corporeal aspect of her being through the Amaranthine Barrier as well. But if she was wrong about Maugris, or her intended path through the Barrier, she would suffer the pain of a thousand deaths.

Sekka's astral eyes adjusted to the atmosphere of the black, silver sphere. She recognized the residual energy left by the use of dark magic. The sticky mist clung to the surface of the spherical chamber like rogue strands of spider silk adrift in the wind. She could almost taste the suffering lingering in the metaphysical air.

Sekka felt the weight of heavy stone surrounding the chamber. She assumed the space had been delved deep within the roots of a mountain. It was a perfect prison with no visible entrances or doorways and one last precaution against *She* that was to be summoned. Maugris was clever.

In truth, she was powerless to make the journey on her own. The Immortal Mother's blasted Amaranthine Barrier now prevented any unauthorized crossings between realms. She supposed she was as much to blame for the Barrier as any ambitious devil who stole souls from the Mortal Realm.

The Immortal Mother had placed strict rules on the worlds she created. The Great Balance must remain constant amongst the different realms. That was the first and most revered law. Sekka's last invasion to the Mortal Realm had tipped the scales and disrupted that precious balance enough to call the angels to war. If they had just stayed put in their clouds, she would have been victorious. But things did not always go as planned.

Upon the smooth inner surface of the chamber's dark metal were laid thousands of intricate runes, each one representing another binding layer of to keep her captive. Interlaced with those symbols were other wards against infernal attack. Pure silver chains crisscrossed the center and wove together to form the strands of a shimmering web.

The links of the chains contained similar runes to those inscribed on the surface walls. As the strands of silver came together towards the center of the sphere, they formed a three-dimensional outline of a multi-pointed star. A perfect trap to collect an Arch Devil from the Abyss.

Twenty-five warlocks, clad in heavy robes hovered in the open space surrounding her summoned spirit. Their placement corresponded to the open areas of the three-dimensional star. Their breath clouded in the frigid air as they chanted ancient words. The sounds twisted and coiled like snakes from their mouths.

A bound slaves shimmered into reality in front of each warlock. The captives trembled uncontrollably from fear and the shock of the cold. The warlocks took black-bladed daggers from their sleeves and, as one, plunged them deep into the abdomens of the slaves. Blood sprayed against the silver chains. The excess dripped to the bottom of the chamber.

The moans of the dying echoed off the black-silver walls. *Pain was such a lovely bonding component*, thought Sekka. It was a nice touch to welcome her return to the Mortal Realm.

Maugris hovered at the top of the chamber as his shifty eyes scanned the placement of his warlocks and accepted everything was in order. She ignored the insult of a mere mortal having control over her for any amount of time. She assured herself it was only temporary, a minor discomfort.

Maugris' breath frosted the air before his face as the words of the final spell spilled from his mouth. Sekka focused her wicked mind on the transference from one plane of existence to another. She absorbed every syllable and gesture as Maugris' cast the binding spell. She searched for where his spell craft faltered, for she had no doubt she would unravel the spell at a later time. The magic of mortals was thin.

Sekka's essence shifted towards him.

Maugris wore heavy robes, lined with dense fur to protect him from the sub-zero temperature of the chamber. Dark-maroon and bright-orange sigils of protection radiated from his robes. The symbols revolved in a slow circle around him. Eventually, each one fluttered out of sight when its protective enchantment was secured. *How quaint*, Sekka thought.

A blood-ruby pendant hung at Maugris' neck, pulsing like a heart as it joined with the magic flowing through the chamber. He had prepared well for this confrontation, yet she still scoffed at his trinkets and false confidence.

Sekka searched for the mental flame of the sorcerer. It was like finding a mote of sawdust in the sand. *Mortals were such insignificant beings outside of the energy of their souls*, she thought with contempt. She poured her consciousness into the endeavor. There! She found him. She squirmed in glee. He was nothing compared to her.

Sekka plunged herself into Maugris like the sharp barb of a scorpion. Her preternatural awareness flooded into his thoughts. She felt his entire being gasp at her arrival.

This was his first test. Sekka would use the surprise of her overwhelming presence to gain control over him. The wards around him flared brighter. She snuffed the lesser ones out without much of a thought. Maugris staggered. She must be careful. If he lost control, the spell would unravel before it took hold. If he were unable to bring her corporeal form into the Mortal Realm, then her scheme would be delayed. She couldn't start over. She needed more souls now!

She knew Maugris had never confronted such raw power as hers. What mortal had? He fought against her will like a desperate man caught in a riptide. The more he struggled, the more she dragged him out to sea. The two engaged in a precarious tug-of-war. If she pulled too hard, she would break him, and the connection would be lost. If she gave in too readily to the summons, she would have a difficult time breaking the spell later. Time worked against her as Zizphander approached her now defenseless Gathos.

She felt Maugris' strength decline. The final summoning spell had siphoned away too much of his magical strength.

He had underestimated the resources needed to control one of her might.

If Maugris proved to be too weak to enable her to crossover, then it would end badly for him. The Amaranthine Barrier would devour him along with the dark magic he used to conduct the spell. She thought of Aetenos wasting away in her dungeon. *How had he been granted access to the Abyss when all others of his kind were denied?* The riddle still plagued her.

Sekka eased off the drowning assault and withdrew direct contact with his essence. Instead, she flowed through his mind like a cerebral fog. She caressed his memories and absorbed his desires. She sucked at his mortal coil and gently probed him for weaknesses. She showed him visions of ultimate power. He could be a god. Just surrender.

His foolish pride refused her. Rather than succumb to her will, he would end his own life. Sekka watched in frustration as Maugris' body shriveled beneath his heavy robes. He was too weak.

He had lost control of the dark magic, and now it was feasting on him. His eyes grew wide and wild. He was desperate for more energy, and the connection faltered. He called to the other warlocks in the room for support.

"Lend me your strength! I am losing her!" he yelled.

Sekka saw no help forthcoming. Interesting. She would use this information against him in the future if there were a future for the failing mage.

Somehow, Maugris regained enough of his composure to tap the blood-ruby pendant on his chest. His eyes sought the nearest warlock hovering beneath him. The pendant flared bright red as its vampiric magic drank the life force of the unsuspecting warlock.

The wrinkles smoothed on Maugris' skin. His face became full once more. The empty husk of the dead warlock dropped out of sight. It landed with a thud and light splash in the bowels of the chamber.

Maugris sent the pendant's magic to the next warlock, and then the next. The warlocks were consumed in rapid succession. Good, thought Sekka, very good. Her smile broadened as she watched each warlock disappear. He was back in control of the dark magic, and he enforced his will upon the spell of binding.

"Sekka! Arch Devil of Gathos and Queen of the Frost Plane, I, Maugris the Infinite, bind you to me. Do my bidding, and ten thousand and one soul-slaves shall be yours to devour. I make this pact with you. Come Sekka! Come to your new master!" Maugris cried out in a voice magnified by the stolen energy he had consumed.

A horrific wail flooded into the chamber, causing blood to erupt from Maugris' ears. Streams of red flowed freely out of his nostrils. The chamber shuddered. Then the chains vibrated as if shaken in the hands of giants. A pinprick of light appeared in the center of the star prison. It grew in size and shape. First as a globe and then as something with the distinct form of a massive horror.

The preternatural wail grew louder in the chamber. The sweat covering Maugris' body turned to frost. He churned out heavy white breaths into the stale air.

Sekka's abyssal form joined with her consciousness and materialized at the center of the star prison. Her raptor talons flashed out to tear and rend. Her chest heaved, and her breasts swelled as she became entangled in the silver chains.

Hard muscles rippled against the magical bonds surrounding her. She could hear the sizzle of her flesh as the touch of the wards burned into her skin. Sekka shrieked in pain.

The soul-slave she brought forth from her orgy on Gathos dissolved in her clawed hand. She maliciously glared at Maugris for depriving her of such a savory meal. She played the part of the bound slave perfectly.

The silver chains were pulled tight like a fisherman's net, and wrapped around her writhing body, locking her in place. Sapphire-blue runes shimmered off the chains then vanished into the air. She howled in rage. The spell of binding was complete. It held her in its magical grip. But the battle was far from over.

Sekka's onyx eyes smiled at him with an otherworldly intelligence. She marveled at her cleverness. She had succeeded in passing through the Amaranthine Barrier. Now she could exert more power. She reapplied pressure on Maugris' mind and squeezed his thoughts together into mush. He buckled but did not break.

She tested his resolve with pleasures rather than pain. "Lower your guard, mortal. I shall make you king of all you see. Release me, and I shall grant your every last desire. Yours shall be the seed that sires' legions made for conquest."

"I saw you … in a vision. Now you are…here before me. You are…mine…to command," Maugris stuttered. His words came slowly, but they gave him confidence. "Enough with your torments."

Sekka howled. She could not harm Maugris. Not yet. The magic placed upon the chains was too deep. Pacts had to be honored. She must do as he bid.

+**What is it you wish of me, mortal?**+ Sekka spoke directly into Maugris' mind. He shuddered.

"You shall be my instrument of despair upon the Lands of Hanna," Maugris said aloud. "The bindings placed upon you shall force you to obey my commands."

+**Failure to provide the soul-slaves promised to bind me will be your undoing, little mage.**+

Sekka fought once more against the invisible chains that bound her. While her body convulsed in pain from the binding, she continued to probe his mind. She sought areas of weakness she might exploit in the future.

"A vision, you say?" Sekka purred in a sensual voice as her bestial form changed into the more subtle curves of a human woman. "Tell me more."

Sekka lounged across her divan like a feline leisurely basking in the warmth of the sun. Ironically, her chamber was cold and dark. Precious items from the Three Kingdoms filled the room. Maugris' minions had brought her thick bear fur, skinned from the northern grizzlies of Trosk. There were exquisite, wooded chairs hewn from a single block of Baroqia's mighty redwood trees in the corner. Hanging on the walls were rare silk tapestries of vibrant color and detail. Sekka suspected they were stolen from the jungle tribes of Sunne. It all bored her.

She decided to redecorate her room with the mutilated bodies of the playthings Maugris had gifted her. "These witches and warlocks shall serve as you cabal," he had said. Their skill and ability were laughable. Most she took as sex slaves, but their uses were limited. She draped their skins over the priceless chairs from Baroqia. Their blood cast a rosy reflection throughout the room.

Her thoughts lurched to the image of Maugris. He had *summoned* her. The compulsion placed upon her still held, but barely. Soon, she would have it unraveled, and his trivial magic would no longer have sway over her.

A fresh batch of apprentices had arrived. Sekka studied them through black-on-black eyes. They observed the flayed skins of their predecessors, and an uneasiness passed through the group. Their breath frosted the air as they patiently waited for her to command them. The men and women before her were frail; weak magicians at best, but such were the shortcomings of all mortals.

They dressed in the garb of witches and warlocks. Sekka saw them only as costumed children playing with silly wands and staffs. They were mere sycophants who posed at being bold wielders of magic yet, knew nothing of the dark arts. All sought her favor for a chance to drink from the fountain of deep magic that flowed through her. They would get nothing from her.

She smiled pleasantly at them. She would let Lord Oziax play with them for a day, once he arrived. Then they would understand power. But, for now, they were distractions to alleviate her boredom. She was sure she could find a use for them eventually.

She rose like a serpent from her repose, causing her sheer robe to flow down over her shapely legs like a slow waterfall. Seduction radiated from her as she approached the first apprentice. He trembled in anticipation. Did he fear her or desire her? It mattered not. Both were acceptable forms of supplication to the Arch Devil.

As much as she relished the physical strength of her abyssal body, she did savor the subtlety of her human form. Her senses appreciated things differently. Perhaps it was due to the frailty of this body? Humans cherished life more since it could be ripped away at a moment's notice. That was why the human soul was such valuable currency in both the Abyss and the Seven Heavens.

It was the soul where the real power of mortals existed, and sadly for them, they wouldn't realize it until after their death. Such was the great paradox of all things set forth by the Immortal Mother.

Her flock of neophytes fluttered around her like black butterflies. They followed in her wake as she left her grisly chamber. Sekka casually led them down a long flight of stairs en route to the central keep. She occasionally stopped to lay her hands on the sigils of warding and binding that were carved into the stone. It was an irrelevant precaution Maugris had added to his fortress.

The sigils held no sway over her, not anymore. She snuffed each one out as she meandered through Rachlach Fortress. She knew the sigils would be back in place when she returned down the same corridor. It was just something to pass the time. Once she had broken the foundation spell, all secondary and tertiary spells would fail as well.

Sekka eventually came to another room filled with stacked books and unrolled scrolls. Maugris was there grumbling to himself. He paced before twelve bound slaves lined against a wall. Sekka assumed they were borderland peasants. Villagers who chose a piss-poor existence along the fringes of Baroqia.

Maugris' hands were clasped behind his bent back as he walked. He mumbled gibberish to himself between swift intakes of breath. He turned towards the slaves.

"Be honored, for you have been chosen. Your souls will fuel the otherworldly gifts provided by my concubine and slave. A higher purpose awaits you."

He turned away as if distracted by another conversation before he returned to mumbling in broken sentences. Then he raised his hands in a proclamation. "By my will shall a new age be delivered to the Three Kingdoms! And vengeance shall know my name!"

The twelve slaves were on their knees. Tight, razor-sharp chords crisscrossed their bodies. Each breath saw the chords dig deeper into their flesh. Purple elixirs were force-fed to the slaves by small gnome-like creatures. It was a special brew Sekka had taught to Maugris that kept the slaves alive.

Sekka remained at the entrance, unimpressed.

Maugris saw her and turned away, irritated by her lack of

urgency to his summons. "You are *finally* here. It is time. I must have the Frost Legions of Gathos. I command you to open a portal." He refused to look at her.

He wore layers of furs to fend off the cold that seeped through the stones of his tower. He moved to a desk cluttered with bound scrolls. He hunched over a massive book opened at a marked spot. He carefully scanned the brittle pages of the ancient tome.

Maugris pointed over his shoulder at the twelve slaves bound against the far wall. "Those there, use them as you must to open the portal."

Sekka shook her head, no. It was the same demand he had made countless times.

"You would bring forth a legion of demons with no commander to lead them? Are you mad? Lord Oziax must come first."

"I will lead them," Maugris said with confidence. "I do not trust you, or your white-maned demon."

"Lord Oziax has been the General of my Frost Legion for millennia. Only by his presence and force of will can the armies of Gathos be controlled. Without him, the greater demons and fiends would revert to their vicious and chaotic nature. The weaker spawn would be butchered without a second thought. Might I remind you of the hatred and rivalry all demonkind have for one another?"

"I am aware of the feuds of demons and devils alike. All those mad creatures, eternally scurrying up the layers of ascendency until they are brought low by overwhelming power."

"Quite so," she said.

He looked straight into her black-on-black eyes. "It seems Zizphander has been busy during your absence. The Red Devil moves through the Abyss uncontested. He leaves the realms of his rivals covered in molten slag. Now there is an

Arch Devil worthy of the title. Perhaps he intends to finish what was once started so long ago. What would happen, I wonder if he rekindled the fires of the Dead Giant?"

"You dare!"

"There are many in the Abyss who gladly divulge information for the proper payment. I have watched your struggle against the Red Devil for quite some time."

Sekka kept a calm expression, though she internally seethed with fury. She knew he was testing her to see if what he said was true. She would give him no such satisfaction, nor would she reveal her predicament in the Lower Planes. She would have her day with him. This fool Maugris knew nothing of the depths of deception and pain a true Arch Devil could conceive.

Maugris strode from behind the table. "No, your pet Oziax shall not have sole reign over the demonic army you will provide me. You are a cunning devil, but that was never part of my plan. I will turn my attention to other lands when the Three Kingdoms of Hanna are mine. Perhaps I shall also rule the wastelands you call home.

"And when that time comes, I will need a queen to rule at my side. If you are worthy, I may grant you such favor."

The cold sparkle in her black eyes betrayed knowledge of a different outcome. She decided then that merely ripping his soul from his body and dining on his tender memories would not be enough punishment for his insolence. She would reserve a special place for him in the coldest pit of Gathos. Maugris would suffer for ages uncounted. But for now, she would wait. He still had a role to play.

"Maugris, why must you tease me such? You know I am already your captive. Your will is my command. But you would be wise to heed my advice. Lord Oziax shall obey you, as I must."

"Do not press your agenda, devil. I demand you open me

a portal. Bring forth the means to destroy my enemies. I grow tired of your excuses and delays!"

"With what raw material? Do you think the soul energy of a few slaves to be enough to bridge the gap between realms? But no matter, the Amaranthine Barrier prevents such a portal from opening for any length of time."

"Do not mock my intelligence. Use your infernal magic to compensate."

"Certain divine rules must be obeyed, even for one as mighty as me. However, there is another way. Bring me the Ever Hero of this age. Then you will know the power of the Abyss."

Maugris brought his hand up to massage his forehead. His eyes squinted closed. "The Ever Heroes of Aetenos are a myth. They are little stories created over the centuries by weak-minded commoners and the monks who control them.

"Even if the Ever Hero were real, he would be a pale comparison to the demigod himself. What use could a fragment of the divine possibly be to help you breach the Barrier?" Maugris looked hard into her eyes. His eyes shifted back and forth as if the solution to a complex equation was within his grasp. "Unless…"

He shook his head, dismissing the idea. "Bah, it matters not. Aetenos has not walked these lands in many, many years. He has forsaken this realm. His religion is dead. His faithful are scattered and lost."

Maugris smiled as if he had won a significant victory. He staggered to a large map hanging on the wall. He tried to hide his discomfort. Her relentless mind-probing left him weary and weak.

He traced his fingers over the Sarribe Mountain range in the Southern Province of Baroqia. "Everything is happening according to my will. By now, that vainglorious Duke Shiverrig has discovered the locations of the monasteries. There will be no one to stop me once those troublesome monks of the Four Orders have been eradicated."

"No! You must not harm the monks!" Sekka demanded. "They are part of unwinding the riddle of the Ever Hero. The Masters may perish, but the younger acolytes must survive. They are needed."

Maugris turned back to Sekka. His eyes flared like that of a starved animal protecting a morsel of food. "Enough! I do not wish to hear any more nonsense of Ever Heroes. The monks will die." His eyes grew dark. "You are mine to control. Now open the portal."

"Yes, I am bound by you, yet you can only receive a fraction of my power. Now, if a Chaos Gate were to be opened…"

"Do you take me for a fool? A living Chaos Gate would mean the end of this realm."

"Obviously, you misunderstand the intricacies of a Chaos Gate and the rules of deep magic."

"Enlighten me," Maugris said.

"A Chaos Gate only allows passage to those deemed worthy by its creator. Yes, others may pass, but the cost is significant. But more importantly, those who pass through would be leashed to the will of the creator of the Gate." Sekka doubted if that were true. But never ruin a good story with the truth.

"Yes, and?"

Sekka wondered how one of such dull intellect possessed the magical strength to have summoned her from Gathos. "My dear Maugris, if the forger of the portal happened to be under the control of a powerful sorcerer, well, then who would control the horde?" She gave a mental tug at the strings of his desire for conquest.

"A Chaos Gate would allow for the entirety of the Frost Legion to bypass the Amaranthine Barrier."

She had him.

He shook his finger at Sekka as if he was the brunt of a playful joke. "You have your worth, devil. A simple portal will not do when a Chaos Gate provides all I need."

Sekka crossed her arms over her chest. "If there is no Ever Hero, then there is no Chaos Gate. As I have said, I must have the raw material to create the bridge. Only the soul of one fused with the essence of the divine can provide the required building blocks." She spoke to him as if he were a petulant child. "And unless you are hiding Aetenos somewhere in your dreary fortress, I will need the next best thing."

Maugris' demeanor shifted again. "How can one such as you be so blind? The Ever Hero is a myth. I was a Chosen of Aetenos at one time. I had power. Real power. Then the demigod betrayed me. If there were to be an Ever Hero of this time, it would have been me!

"When the Time of Fire and Famine came to Baroqia, the crown looked to me to quell land's fury with my art. I crafted a spell to tame the wild Elemenati magic infecting the land. It was a brilliant work of creative genius. My spell would save the realm and ensure my legacy as the greatest mage in the history of Baroqia. But something went wrong.

"I had made sure every nuance was accounted for and in place." Maugris looked past Sekka as if remembering the horrible event. His words came in a whisper. "It was Aetenos. He was jealous of my great accomplishment. When I called for His Light to add a spark of the divine to my spell, he went silent. I was left with insufficient power to complete the spell. It failed.

"Banishment, they said. Banish the Mad One to the North! But I shall have my revenge. The monks of Aetenos die first. Then those fool nobles in the City of Spires."

Sekka smirked at Maugris' tale. If the man only knew the

truth of the matter. "It is a touching tale. Nonetheless, the pace in which you exact your revenge is in your own hands."

"Enough with your stubborn behavior, Hell-born. There is no Ever Hero. If you cannot provide me with what I desire, I will replace you with another who can."

Maugris moved back to a long table piled with ancient parchments. He leaned on its edge for support. He rubbed his chin with his hand. "If I was strong enough to summon you, then there are others whom I could call."

A devious smile creased his weathered face. "I wonder how eager Zizphander would be to carry out my wishes if I offered him his arch-nemesis bound and gagged on a silver platter? Are you prepared to watch the flames of the Red Devil consume your precious Gathos?"

Sekka grew bored with the debate, "Do what you must, or you can. Zizphander would need the same means of establishing a portal great enough for what you ask."

Her devilish desire was to rip him to shreds, but she was still bound. Time, she needed just a bit more time. She approached Maugris delicately. She brushed up against his body with slow and sensual movements.

"Let us not fight. You are mighty, Maugris, and your will shall be done. I can tell you are fatigued. Let me soothe your weary head."

She turned his head to her breasts. His body followed. She held him as a mother would a child. Maugris resisted her embrace at first but finally succumbed to the coolness of her body. The softness of her flesh was too much to endure in his weakened state.

"That's it. Just rest."

Maugris' defenses dropped for a moment. It was just enough of an opening for Sekka to purr an inconspicuous spell of suggestion into his ear.

"I shall open a small portal and bring forth Lord Oziax to

lead your armies; however, remember the Ever Hero is the key to your ultimate vengeance. Find him, and you shall rule whatever realm you wish." She then lifted his head and gently kissed his lips. "Perhaps you would like to start with the one before you?"

Her sheer gown fell to her ankles. Her naked body was a masterpiece of desire. The torchlight caressed her muscular form and lush curves. She stepped out of the pile of rumpled fabric, and slowly pirouetted before the Sorcerer. "Do you like what you see?"

She deftly removed his robes. Maugris mumbled some agreeable words about Lord Oziax. He would put men to the task of finding the one she desired. Her tongue was a shock of ice over his body. The stiffness of his member was a testament that he burned for more. As she had expected, her devious charms would be the first of her powers to break through the shackles of Maugris' binding. Humans were so easy to manipulate.

Their coupling was filled with moans of delight from Maugris. She beckoned her forgotten flock of magicians closer. Their eyes were filled with lust. Craving hands reached out to touch her. She smiled with wicked joy.

Her provocative human form altered its shape. Horns, talons, and teeth grew from her body. Her magicians screamed in horror, but they could not turn away. She compelled them forward and feasted on their flesh. Maugris writhed in ecstasy beneath her terrible form. Soon he was coated in blood.

Sekka mentally whispered the words of a summoning spell into Maugris' mind. He repeated the words aloud, lost as he was in the bliss of her attention. The tear in the Amaranthine Barrier caused by Aetenos' arrival on Gathos had grown wider when she was summoned to the Mortal Realm. Now the path was easy to follow if one knew the way.

A flash of light brightened the chamber, followed by a thunderous boom. The walls shook, and stacks of books tumbled to the floor. The temperature dropped, and frost covered everything in the room. The slaves lined against the far wall shivered in pain as the chords dug deeper into their flesh.

Lord Oziax leaped into the Mortal Realm.

He was a huge demon standing on two muscular legs. One arm ended in five long tentacles cascading from where his elbow would be. Hundreds of small sucking mouths with sharp teeth lined the surface of each tentacle. His broad back was covered in coarse, alabaster hair. His nostrils flared in anticipation of violence.

Lord Oziax had the head of an artic lion. A full mane of thick fur framed his face. Two long canine teeth jutted from his jaws. His skin was the color of bleached bone. He stepped through the broken and mauled bodies as the juice of the dying magicians spread across the floor to Sekka's side and bowed deeply before her.

"What is it you wish of me, my Mistress?"

Sekka was covered in gore. She swiveled her hulking form to face him. "Look at the banquet our little mage has set for us, Lord Oziax." Her wicked grin drooled long strands of swaying bile. Her flesh changed back to her exposed human body. Broad swaths of blood smeared down her neck and covered her breasts and legs.

Lord Oziax's eyes landed on Maugris. "Let me devour the mortal flea at your loins." A purple tongue lolled out of his mouth and curled around his enormous incisors.

Maugris came to his senses. He squirmed out from under Sekka, parting the pool of blood in a long smear. He grabbed his robe and stood indignant before Lord Oziax. Maugris surveyed his study, confused as to what had taken place. He assumed a regal stance.

"Bow down before me, creature. I am your master now."

A deep baritone chuckle resonated from Lord Oziax's throat. He ignored Maugris. "What are your orders, my Queen?"

"Now," Maugris said. He raised his hand to strike Lord Oziax.

Oziax's eyes flashed with anger. "Who is this human worm that stands before Mighty Oziax? I shall peel the skin from your pitiful body for your lack of reverence."

Lord Oziax's body swelled and bristled. He shook where he stood but could do no more. The magic that held Sekka also bound the great demon lord.

"I command you now, Lord Oziax, Demon Warlord of the Frost Legions." Maugris walked closer to Oziax. His confidence grew with each step. "Colorful monikers, but I am unimpressed. A more capable demon lord would have put an end to Zizphander when he was an irrelevant lesser devil. But now, the Red Devil has grown in power, and Oziax has lost his opportunity." Maugris then turned to Sekka. "Perhaps, next time, do not leave a demon to do a devil's work, eh?"

Oziax bellowed out in rage. Black sigils flared to life above his head. The stench of dark magic mixed with the odor of drying blood and entrails. He lunged at Maugris but was held fast by the power of the binding spell. Nonetheless, Maugris took a few steps backward. A nervous expression filled his face.

Sekka draped her arms around Oziax's neck. She whispered in his ear. "Calm yourself, my beautiful beast. Remember why we are here."

She then spoke in a louder voice for Maugris to hear. "Apologize to Maugris and assume a more suitable appearance for your new master."

Lord Oziax followed Sekka's lead. He morphed into his

human form. A tall, muscular man with long, straight hair appeared where the demon once stood.

"There, that's better. Now come, Lord Oziax. There is much to prepare," Sekka said. She walked from the room.

Lord Oziax brushed passed Maugris. "Careful with your words mortal. The Fates are fickle. The path they set is never clear. Your feet may not always tread on such a fortunate ground."

11

KASAI

Giant, finger-shaped spires of granite towered amongst the mountain peaks of the Sarribe Range. Nestled among the natural rock formations was the Monastery of Ordu. It was built to blend with the enduring presence of the mountain without creating distracting blemishes to its rocky surface. Valley forests of pine and oak stubbornly stretched their reach up the sides of the high spires to include the monastery in their wooden embrace. Crest eagles and spire vultures hung lazily in the air on warm thermals that rose from the lower lands.

The monks of Ordu traversed the spire-shaped peaks via a maze of hanging rope bridges. Small bells and colorful ribbons were woven into the hemp strands of the ropes and the acoustics of the mountain range would carry the sounds of the bells for miles, adding a layer of mystery and misdirection, which confused those seeking to infiltrate the ancient haven.

The bells also served a different function. A person unaccustomed to walking the swaying bridges would leave an awkward sound pattern. The sentries could discern who approached based on the melodies of the bridges. Those were precautions from a different time when the monks were hunted and prosecuted by tyrannical kings and bloodthirsty warlords.

The Four Orders of Aetenos were meant to unify all people together under the Laws of Heaven. Unfortunately, this ideal often created a conflicting agenda with less-than-scrupulous rulers outside the religious orders. Spies were sent to infiltrate the sanctuaries of Ordu, Symmetu, Harmonu, and Metho, in order to discover the secrets of the strange monks. In time, assassins were contracted to remove influential members of each Order.

The mountain passes were blocked, and well-known bridges destroyed. Over the years, the locations of the monasteries themselves were lost. Maps were purposely removed from all government archives and only the memories of the highest officials at the High Temple of Illumination and the Master Monks of each Order were entrusted with such valuable information.

The monastery locations were passed from one generation to the next verbally; formal maps were forbidden. The monks took great precaution to thwart unwanted guests from finding their homes. Unfortunately, no fortress could remain hidden forever, nor was it impregnable.

Kasai pulled his outer robe a little closer. Today was blustery day, a cold portent of the winter to come. Brightly colored leaves fell from the trees and swirled like dust devils on the ground. The smell of early winter was in the air. A loose truce had formed between Kasai and Daku during the weeks since the ordeal on the mountain. Thankfully, Daku's anger had lessened with time, as it usually did.

Brothers Jorraih and Morad accompanied them as they walked along a smooth stone path. The two younger acolytes followed a few steps behind. The Brothers collected deadwood for the Monastery fires.

"The Masters are unfair to me, especially Choejor. I am constantly rebuked when the opportunity for advancement is clear. What's worse, I am punished for excelling," Daku said. He kicked a dead branch off the path instead of picking it up. "I have mastered all of the striking positions of the Twenty-One Fire Columns. I am the only one who fully understands the Windu'uni Disciplines. My fire xindu is the most powerful of all the Brothers. It probably rivals the level of the Masters by now."

"I understand Windu'uni," Kasai said.

"Sure you do, Kasai," Daku scoffed.

"You're the one holding on to every slight as if it were your last breath. Let it go. The Masters teach us what we need to learn. Perhaps ask yourself why they treat you as you say. Seek the answer from within," Kasai suggested.

"I already know the answer. They are worried that one day, perhaps soon, I will be their equal. They fear me. They fear the change my fighting methods will bring to the Order. Aetenos left the High Temple of Illumination for the same reasons. That is why they keep me from the more powerful mysteries," Daku snapped back.

"That's not why Aetenos formed the Four Orders," Kasai said.

Daku was churning through more than just that one event in his head. It was his way. He liked to dig up nightmares from the past and make them into present battles.

Jorraih called out, "Hey, are you two going to do some work or just chirp all morning like little birds?" He was small and of similar build to Kasai, with a broad smile and contagious laugh. "Morad and I have already filled up our sacks."

"See Kasai, more taunts. Now it's coming from those of

lesser rank as well. I should teach him the meaning of respect."

"Jorraih means nothing by it. He's just trying to fit in," Kasai said.

The four monks strolled down the winding path until they came across the broken nest of a scarlet swallow. The nest had been blown from its perch and smashed into the dirt. Scattered about the ruined nest were three dead chicks. A fourth had somehow managed to survive the fall. It chirped fearfully for its mother on the unfamiliar ground, while the mother swallow helplessly squawked from a higher branch in the tree.

Morad did his best to repair the nest and then, with careful hands, placed it back into the tree. Jorraih had taken up the helpless chick and gently laid it in the nest.

"There you go, little one," Jorraih said.

"What do you think you two are doing?" Daku said. He snatched the nest and the chick from the safety of the branch.

"What does it look like we are doing? We are going to save the chick. See, the mother is right over there. Now put the nest back in the tree or give it to me," Jorraih said.

Daku hid the nest behind his back. "The mother should not have chosen such a poor spot to build its nest. As Master Choejor says, 'It is the natural way of things.' This chick will die with its siblings."

Kasai realized Daku still felt the pain of humiliation by Master Choejor in the sparring circle. If Daku had to bear the brunt of the Master's example, then all the Brotherhood would feel his pain as well. Daku would not allow himself to become a parody of weakness.

"That's hardly what Master Choejor means. Just give the bird back," Morad said.

"The mother bird needs to learn a lesson. Next time she will take more care when choosing a nesting site," Daku said.

The eyes of the younger monks became anxious. Kasai understood how they felt. Daku was in a raw mood. Kasai saw the telltale spark in Daku's, he wanted a fight, and the slightest provocation would set him off.

"Leave the chick alone. It is not your place to play judge and executioner," Jorraih said. He reached out to try and snatch the nest away from Daku.

Daku was quicker. "Is it not? And who are you to stop me? Come on. I'll let you have the first two strikes without retaliating."

"Daku, just give the bird back to Jorraih. We still have to finish our chores," Kasai said.

"Just listen to Kasai. Besides, you can't hope to best the three of us at once," Morad said.

Daku's face softened as if he had finally come to his senses. Kasai saw through it, though. Daku's expression was always calm before he attacked. Kasai would need to act fast if he was to save Morad from a painful lesson.

Daku snapped the neck of the chick and dropped it back in the nest. "Here."

Morad took the nest. His mouth was wide open.

"No!" Kasai was shocked. "Why?"

"I told you, Kasai, the outside world is cruel. It is the natural way of things." Daku pushed passed them. He continued walking alone on the path, humming a peaceful tune.

The night was calm. A fragrant, sugary aroma drafted up from the turning leaves of the Katsura trees growing in the valley below. The air swept through cracked windows and into the sparse sleeping quarters of the monks. The full moon was bright and bathed the room in soft blue light. Forty-four monks slept on plain cots, all but one rested peacefully. Kasai tossed and turned in a half-sleep. Sweat beaded on his forehead, and the wool blanket tangled around his legs in a knot.

Creatures of fell magic chased him in the dark. He wanted to run, but his legs moved as if they were being sucked into a thick mire. He heard the gnashing teeth of the creatures behind him. They were gaining ground.

The nightmare changed. Kasai watched his mother die by the hands of a foul, eyeless ghoul. Meanwhile, his father ran into the embrace of a fiendish woman draped in a regal, ice-blue gown. She wore a high headdress made of animal horns and human bones. The woman had stark-white hair, white skin, onyx eyes, and indigo lips. She eyed Kasai as she held his father in a lover's embrace. The woman spoke the same word to him every night. "Mine."

Kasai woke with a shiver, and his skin felt clammy. The nightmare appeared more frequently, each iteration revealing more of the story. He looked around the dormitory to see everyone still asleep. Kasai sighed. "Lucky."

Kasai told no one about his dreams; today was no different. He was thankful for his daily routine. It made it easier for him to believe that the unsettling nightmares were nonsense. He reasoned with himself during dawn chores that there was nothing wrong with him. He was calm again by the end of morning meditation. By the end of the day, he had all but forgotten his dreams.

Kasai stretched as he paused for a moment to enjoy the orange glow of the setting sun, the last bit could be seen through the high spires surrounding Ordu. He had yet to finish his dusk chores and would be late for dinner. *Cold stew again*, he thought.

He had drawn outer sweeping duty, again. The stairs and paths outside the monastery walls were cleaned meticulously in the early morning and once more in the early evening. The Masters said the work helped to clear a person's mind of unwanted debris collected from the trials of life. Kasai just saw it as a never-ending cycle of work.

The late autumn sun lit the cliffs and valleys in a luminous glow. The mountains took on a cool, purple hue while the colors of turning leaves held onto the last warmth of the sun. The cold nights came early this time of year, and as the sun descended from sight, the icy blast of chilly winds gusted against the mountainside. Their eerie howls took Kasai out of his reverie.

Kasai thought of his Brothers inside the warm refectory enjoying hot stew in freshly-made bread bowls. His mouth watered with anticipation of food and his stomach let him know it agreed. The faster he finished sweeping, the sooner he would be inside eating his dinner. He arched his back and moved side-to-side.

"Best get on with it," he grumbled.

He had one more section to go before he was finished. *Perhaps tomorrow would bring some warmer weather. Wishful thinking*, he thought and moved to the remaining section of stairs. As Kasai turned to cross the last bridge, he was distracted by small reflections of light coming from the cliff of the East Wall. The top of the cliff housed the Inner Halls and many of the common structures of the monastery.

What was that? He squinted to get a better look and saw that some of his Brothers were dusk climbing. The evening sky bathed their robes, a dark-mustard color. Kasai was unaware of a work detachment assigned to the East Wall this evening. One of the Masters must have scheduled a nighttime scaling exercise. Probably Master Dorje, he was known for forcing Brothers to confront their fear, conquer it, and grow stronger.

Kasai thought back to his experience on the mountain and sympathized with his Brothers on the rock. Kasai watched them scale higher along the sheer wall and silently cheered them on. Night climbing was a challenge, especially for the younger novices. He tried to discern who was leading the climb and who followed. He couldn't recognize the body shapes belonging to any of his Brothers.

"That doesn't seem right." Kasai tilted his head to one side. He noticed the monks moved awkwardly. There was no fluidity to their motion. The monks conserved their strength and used the momentum of their body to flow up and down the wall. Their unique skill of crisscrossing arms, hooking heels, and dropping legs enabled them to grip onto impossible holds. His Brothers moved like elegant spiders along the rock wall.

However, these climbers used brute strength to lunge from one hold to the next. Kasai saw the climbers driving handpicks into the rock. His Brothers didn't need anchor holds to climb a sheer surface. Kasai sharpened his focus for a better look. Were those ropes dangling down from the lead climbers? More climbers followed the lines from below. He broadened his view and saw many groups were scaling the wall. His stomach sank. These weren't monks, and this wasn't a training exercise. The monastery was under attack!

Kasai watched in shock as the invaders crested the cliff and scurried to the monastery walls. They threw grappling hooks that lodged into the crenels of the stone and climbed again. Longswords were strapped to their backs and reflected the last of the sun's glowing light. Within moments the attackers were over the top and in the courtyard.

Black smoke rose in the half-light over the white walls that protected the central buildings. The wind changed. The stench of something greasy and burnt wafted past him. Kasai froze with fear. What was happening? Where were the sentries, and why had no alarm been sounded?

He took a few steps forward. He stopped. What was he doing? If he went directly to the front gate, he would be spotted. The smoke intensified, and now he could see flames lapping up to the sky. Even if he went to the monastery, what could he possibly do? He was only a junior monk. Sparring in a controlled environment was one thing. Fighting real foes was something altogether different. Daku was right. Kasai was not prepared for the real world and the many challenges it held.

The Masters would be able to deal with this threat. But they could not be everywhere at once. His mind froze with hesitation. He had to do something to help. He looked at his hands. His broom was a poor excuse for a proper staff. He would be better off using his hands.

"Don't be stupid, Kasai. You're safe here."

He told himself his reasoning was sound. Daku would organize the older acolytes into fighting groups, and they would mount a defense. He couldn't do anything from here.

Kasai thought of the younglings. They would be led to Zazen Hall for safety. Best to get them out of the way when the fighting started. More smoke appeared over the walls of the monastery. The meditation hall was on fire. The younglings might already be trapped inside.

Intruders crawled over the walls like an infestation of vermin. Kasai heard booming thunderclaps resounded from the courtyard and felt the air shudder. The wind carried the smell of sulfur and spoiled meat. A cold shiver shook his body as Kasai remembered the same horrible odor from his early childhood. It could only mean one thing.

The creatures of evil had returned and were using dark magic against his Brothers. They could already be dead. His family was being stolen from him. *Not again*, he feared.

Now was the time to act. Kasai took a hesitant step forward. The front gate was lost. Was there another access available on the Eastern wall? *Think!* His eyes followed the tracks of a series of bridges. Each path resulted in a dead-end. Time was against him. This portion of the slope was covered in meditation circuits. Each bridge circled back to the same spot.

The wind carried the screams of his Brothers. *Hurry.* His mind raced. *Come on, come on, Kasai. People are counting on you.* His heart pounded in his chest. Sweat beaded on his forehead. He couldn't think. He was useless.

Kasai forced his eyes closed. He inhaled deeply through his nose and let the cool night air fill his chest. He let it out slowly. Again. Breath in, breath out. He tapped into his water xindu to calm the fire in his spirit. He wished he had a better grasp on the xindu mysteries.

Slowly, the level of his water xindu rose. His fear and frustration sank into the memory of a favorite swamp from his childhood. Kasai focused on removing the tangle of false paths before him. He let their patterns dissolve from the maze of possibilities meant to baffle and confuse an enemy.

By doing so, the true way would reveal itself. There! A narrow fissure that collected rainwater and melted snow. The fissure fed it to an interior basin, which the monks used for their water supply. For once, Kasai was thankful for his smaller size. He had to cross two bridges and leave the main path, but then he could easily downclimb to the natural aqueduct.

Kasai raced across the first bridge on sure footing. He

would not abandon his Brothers. He traversed in such a way as to add a new song to the chiming bells, one filled with determination and courage. He reached the fissure without being seen by the invaders. He climbed inside.

The echoes of fighting bounced off the inner walls. Kasai tried his best to keep the sounds of the dying from his mind. Instead, he concentrated on the twists and turns of the natural drainage system.

He gradually descended. The shaft opened to a broader space. Beneath him was the basin that housed the refectory water supply. He scanned the walls for the opening where his Brothers drew water. That was his way into the monastery.

Kasai moved carefully along the slippery surface. The inner walls only offered sharp, tiny nibs for handholds. The tips of his fingers became raw, but he kept moving forward. He thought about what he would do once he reached the top. His best option would be to find one of the Masters. Master Dorje's chamber was closest to the refectory. Kasai would start there.

He emerged from the well shaft and into a small room. He peered into the refectory and saw uneaten food resting on cloth placemats. Water mugs were turned over or had rolled to the floor. In some places, water still dripped from the solid oak table. But otherwise, it was empty.

Kasai ran to Master Dorje's chamber. He was doubtful that he would find him there but decided he needed to start somewhere. Perhaps Master Dorje had left a youngling behind to convey his instructions in case any of the older Brothers had the same idea as Kasai.

The noise of battle was everywhere. Otherworldly screams echoed through the empty stone halls. *What was he doing?* He had no plan and scarcely any real information. Rushing blindly into battle was a poor tactic.

Kasai had traveled these halls for years, but suddenly he

felt disoriented and unsure of which way to go. His mind held too many questions demanding answers. Who had attacked the monastery? What purpose would it serve? The monks of Aetenos had no political affiliation or any real influence in the regal circles of the King's court. They were servants of the land and the people who dwelled there. Nothing more. They were only monks! Who would need to slaughter monks?

The entrance to Master Dorje's chamber was before him. The door was open, and Kasai ran in but stopped short. He gasped in shock when he saw that Master Dorje was dead. The invaders murdered him. But he was not just killed, beheaded.

The Master's body lay in a heap on the floor. His head placed on the windowsill overlooking the courtyard. It was clear the killer had wanted Master Dorje to witness the attack on the monastery, even with dead eyes. There was no evidence of a fight, and nothing was amiss or broken in the room. There was no sign of struggle. It was as if Master Dorje had been taken completely unaware. But that was impossible.

The room twisted and turned as the weight of events pounded into Kasai's mind. His entire body began to tremble. He thought he would fall to the floor. The sounds of battle flooded back to his ears. The mark of Mizzen flared on his forearm, lending him courage.

Kasai could do nothing here and was needed elsewhere. He raced to Master Kunchen's chamber next.

He reached Master Kunchen's chamber panting for breath. The old man was dead as well. His heart had been ripped from his chest. The organ sagged from a dagger driven to the wall. Again, there was no struggle. It made no sense. One does not take a Master of Ordu unaware and end their life so casually.

Kasai was no longer registering the immensity of events unfolding before him. Everything was condensed down to individual moments that could be more easily identified, even if not understood. *What of Master Choejor? Had the same fate befallen the blind Master? Without the Three Masters to lead them, his Brothers were doomed.*

His heart pounded in his chest as he ran in the direction of Master Choejor's chamber. Unconscious tears streamed from the corners of his eyes. He was losing his family again, and just as before, he was helpless to stop it.

He rounded the corner of a hall too fast and tripped over the body of one of his Brothers. The body had been torn to pieces. Terrible gashes were slashed across the larger parts. Kasai couldn't even recognize who had died.

Was this the work of the same killer that had butchered the Masters? There were no bodies of enemies anywhere. Who or what could be powerful enough to kill Masters Dorje and Kunchen without a fight?

The inner hallways filled with smoke, and the air became thin and dark. Kasai changed his route and passed the Hall of Artifacts. It was a sacred area, holding the relics and ancient weapons of the Order of Ordu. The room was filling with smoke. So much would be lost in the fire.

Kasai kept moving. He tried to understand what was happening around him. Taking out the Masters made sense. They were the real threat at the monastery. His Brothers could mount a counterattack, but it seemed unlikely they would be victorious against this foe.

Master Choejor was next or had already been murdered. Kasai's eyes stung. His visibility was dim from heavy smoke. Kasai clenched his fists when he heard the noise of battle getting louder; the enemy was near. He needed something to even the odds. He ran back into the Hall of Artifacts. He'd grab the nearest weapon available and ask forgiveness later.

Thick smoke filled the room. Kasai groped blindly for anything that was not locked behind a thick glass case. Nothing. Where were the keys? Not here. Only the Masters held the keys to these locks. Why hadn't he thought about that earlier? The sounds of fighting grew louder.

He tested the strength of the locks, but they held fast. His eyes watered. Kasai was desperate. He stumbled further into the Hall of Artifacts, searching for anything to help.

A burnt wooden rafter had fallen and smashed through a case in the back of the room. Kasai was half-blind from the smoke and reached for whatever was there. His hand found the familiar shape of a sanjiegun. He grabbed the folded three-sectioned staff and ran to help his Brothers.

The weapon felt oddly warm in his hands and was heating as he approached the fighting. He rubbed the water from his eyes and looked at the weapon more closely.

"Oh no," Kasai groaned.

He held Ninziz-zida, the Fire Serpent. Kasai had no time to put it back and search for another. "Please don't curse me," Kasai pleaded. Reluctantly, he tucked the folded staff into his sash and ran forward. It wasn't long before Kasai came to the entrance of Master Choejor's chamber. Kasai was relieved to hear his old Master's inside. He rushed into the room.

"Master Choejor! I'm here!" Kasai keeled over, trying to catch his breath. He put his hands on his knees for support. Master Choejor's back was to the door, and he was speaking to another monk.

"Ah, Brother Kasai. I'm glad you are here," Master Choejor said with a relaxed yet direct voice. Kasai still huffed. His lungs were on fire. He was amazed at how calm Master Choejor could be in such an intense situation.

"Master Kunchen says he has rallied the senior Brothers to the left wall and brought the younglings to the food storage under the refectory. We must leave with all haste to join the fight."

"But Master Kunchen is dead!" Kasai gasped between gulps of air. Tears streamed down his face. "He's gone."

"Eyes can be deceived in the heat of battle, Brother Kasai. I assure you, I am very much alive," Master Kunchen said. The old Master's head poked around the body of Master Choejor. He eyed Kasai suspiciously, and promptly put some distance between the two monks.

How could this be? He noticed there was something very wrong with Master Kunchen's face. His skin looked false, and his eyes held an expression of wickedness.

Kasai was exhausted. His mind moved faster than his understanding could keep up. He gave up trying to figure things out. Unconsciously, he stripped away what was inconsistent with Master Kunchen and sought the truth.

A black vapor materialized above Master Kunchen's head. Bewildered, Kasai stared in confused fascination. Was it just smoke? The dark mist formed into an unusual symbol. It pulsed outward in an erratic motion. Black tendrils reached out to strike the bright-orange glow that had now appeared above Master Choejor's head. That was new.

"Master Kunchen, I'm sorry. I don't understand. How did you get here? What happened to you?" Kasai said as he tried to gather his thoughts. Had he imagined seeing the murdered body of Master Kunchen? "And what is that black symbol above your head?"

Master Choejor tilted his head to the side. "You see a sigil, Brother Kasai? Tell me what you see immediately. Describe it to me," Master Choejor said his voice held unfamiliar urgency. His body tensed.

"I'm not sure what I am seeing. There is a strange, black rune floating above Master Kunchen. I've never seen the like of it before. Is he sick, Master Choejor?"

Master Choejor's shoulders slumped, and his body deflated for a moment. "You are correct, Brother Kasai. Master Kunchen is dead," Master Choejor said. "This imposter is his assassin."

"Assassin." Kasai couldn't believe what he was hearing. He looked again at the man before him. How could this be? Master Kunchen began to take a few steps towards the open window, giving him a clear view of both monks.

The weight of what had happened to Master Kunchen, Master Dorje and his Brothers, finally came to the forefront of Kasai's awareness like a rushing wave of fire. His fingers curled around Ninziz-zida's segments at his waist. His heart pounded heavily as the fire xindu filled his body with anger, even fury. His mind went from asking too many questions to one focused answer. Hurt the one who hurt you.

The enemy was now before him, smiling like a spoiled child who had gotten his way. Ninziz-zida was already in his hands. He gripped her two end segments and stretched the Fire Serpent in a defensive position, but one that could strike with ease.

His mind filled with new and exotic attack sequences combining the reach of the staff and his own body. A dominant force took control of his actions, just as a puppeteer manipulated a puppet. He did not think to resist the influence, only to act. "Master, what are your orders? I am ready."

The thing that was Master Kunchen sized up Kasai. "You are ready? And what is the little monk ready to do? Stop me when two of the famed Masters of Ordu could not? You are but a boy."

Kasai heard the sounds of battle growing closer as shouts and footsteps advanced towards the chamber. Then Kasai recognized the familiar sound of padded sandals on the stone floor of the hallway.

"Your time is up. My Brothers approach in numbers,"

Kasai said. His entire being wished to strike out at the creature, but his will remained steady. Master Choejor had yet to give his order. He was surprised by the aggression that filled his mind and the desire to engage in battle. His fire xindu had never blazed so fiercely.

The imposter leaped to the windowsill, perched like a gargoyle on a ledge. "Alas, I must bid you farewell. My time grows short, and I must be away on more pressing affairs." The image of Master Kunchen shifted out of focus and revealed something else. Something shimmering and unnatural.

The *thing* on the window ledge deftly tossed a small object to the floor. It exploded and filled the room with billowing smoke. Kasai shielded his eyes and began to cough, but his senses were on alert. He somehow heard the rapid deployment of numerous objects cutting through the air and heading in his direction. He reacted on instinct. Ninziz-zida was a whirlwind of motion.

Time slowed down before his eyes. The confusing nature of the smoke slowed to almost a standstill. Kasai saw the oncoming projectiles appeared as large as bloated apples pushing through the smoke. Ninziz-zida's outer sections deflected the darts with ease, sending broken pieces in all directions. Not one barb managed to penetrate Kasai's defense.

Kasai heard Master Choejor grunt in pain. Events in the room flashed back to real-time. The assassin was gone. Master Choejor laid crumpled on the floor.

"Master Choejor!"

"I shall be fine," Master Choejor said, but not without effort. He tried to stand. "We must help the others. Get me up."

Kasai did as he was asked, but Master Choejor remained unsteady without assistance.

"Master, what was that…thing? What is it? Are you hurt? What happened?"

Master Choejor removed his robe from his left shoulder. He brushed away a small barb that was embedded in his flesh. The skin around the impact point had turned an ugly green with blisters bubbling around the edge.

"It appears I have been poisoned," Master Choejor said in a curious tone. His power tattoos flared as they sought to counter the toxins and repair the wounded flesh. But the skin blistered at a more rapid pace.

"But how? This wound is on your back. How could … oh no. I was not thinking of where the darts were going after I blocked them. Master, I am sorry."

"You defended yourself admirably," Master Choejor said. He looked towards the door with blind eyes. A small group of younger monks barreled into the small chamber. Their eyes were wide with fear. Many had encountered the enemy and had done their best to fight back. Their faces and hands were covered in cuts and bruises. Somehow, they had managed to escape the melee and had fled to the safety of the inner buildings.

"Master Choejor! Brother Kasai! The monastery is overrun. The buildings are burning. Everyone is dying. What should we do?" one of the younglings wailed; his words spilling together. Kasai knew him as Brother Mica.

"Where are the others? Where are the senior Brothers?" Master Choejor asked in a strained voice.

"Whoever is left is fighting in the courtyard. Daku sent me to find all the Masters. He needs help. I found Brothers Tutto, Nindus, and the others in the meditation hall," Mica said.

"Take me to Brother Daku. Have you seen Master Dorje?" Master Choejor said.

"We were hoping he was with you," Mica said.

"Brother Kasai will lead us to the courtyard. We shall lend our help where we can. Hopefully, we will join with Master Dorje along the way," Master Choejor said.

"But…" Kasai decided to hold his tongue. He led the younger monks out of the chamber and towards the courtyard. Destruction was everywhere. The old wood of rafters crackled and popped as the fire ate into their core. Black chunks of wood fell to the floor, followed by filthy streams of charred smoke. The old monastery was crumbling around them. Kasai navigated a path through the burning debris. The monks often had to go back the way they came when collapsed ceilings prevented them from moving forward.

Master Choejor brought up the rear. He spoke reassuring words to the younger Brothers, but they were all moving too slow.

Kasai wanted to tell Master Choejor of the death of Master Dorje but considered the information carefully. He did not want to create more panic in the younger monks. He was barely able to retain his courage himself and could only imagine what was happening in the minds of the young ones. Their vacant eyes told him they were in the grips of the death fear. Kasai would tell Master Choejor about Master Dorje later.

"Let me scout ahead and make sure it is safe," Kasai told the others. He moved quickly down the hall and around a corner, hoping the way to the courtyard was clear.

The corridor shook as if it trembled with the same fear he felt in his heart. The air here was thick and suffocating. A long groan was followed by a deafening crack. He whirled around, retracing his steps to find an entire section of the ceiling had crashed to the stone floor. Dread filled his heart. A tangled pile of burning wood, grey stone, and plaster was heaped in the middle of the corridor. Under the debris were the unmoving arms and legs of the younglings.

"No, no, no!" Kasai cried. He frantically threw fiery pieces of the fallen ceiling to the side. Everything was hot, and his hands soon blistered. His Brothers were gone. Tears of frustration ran down his face.

"Master Choejor! Master Choejor!" Kasai could not find the old monk. Cruel tongues of flame laughed at him as it burned through the wood. Kasai knew there was nothing to be done now. He had lost them all. How could he have missed the compromised ceiling?

Kasai saw movement beyond the rear of the pile. Master Choejor had fallen backward when the ceiling collapsed. He sat up straight and cocked his head to the ceiling. It looked like the Master was meditating or communing with an unseen voice.

"I understand," Master Choejor said into the air. He slowly stood using the wall for support.

"Kasai, you must escape to Gethem. Go to the Temple of Illumination and find Grandmaster Nysulu. He must know what has occurred here. Our sister monasteries must be alerted to this danger, or the same fate will befall them."

"But what of the others? They need our help," Kasai said.

"The Boundless has set you on a different path. I shall gather as many as I can. I am afraid we have lost this day to darkness. There is a foul smell in the air. Somehow the Amaranthine Barrier has been breached. Creatures from the Abyss have returned to the Mortal Realm."

"The Abyss…" Kasai's heart sank as the magnitude of the word registered in his mind. He was reliving his worst fears.

"The monastery is lost. You must warn the others. Their salvation lies with you. Race now to the catacombs as quickly as you can." Master Choejor slumped against the wall. His breathing was shallow.

"Come, Master," Kasai said. "Put your hand on my shoulder. I will not leave without you."

Master Choejor smiled with understanding and nodded slowly. Together, they navigated the torn hallways towards the monastery's catacombs. Kasai grew increasingly worried. Master Choejor was getting weaker instead of stronger, needing frequent rest.

They stopped behind a partially-collapsed ceiling and wall. It provided excellent cover and a clear view out to the courtyard. The fire blazing through the monastery buildings lit the square. Kasai saw a small group of monks fighting off the invaders. Daku led the survivors, but the enemy grossly outnumbered them.

One-by-one the monks were captured in large nets and dragged to the side of the courtyard. Daku was the last to be caught. His wrists were bound, and he was forced to kneel on the ground before the murderous assassin.

The assassin conversed with a group of oversized men in loose clothing resembling monk's robes. Kasai felt a shudder pass through the air. He smelled a pungent mix of sulfur and cinnamon permeate the ash-filled air.

There was a blinding flash, and a lithe, otherworldly creature materialized into the courtyard. She had a feminine form and was both dazzling and deadly to behold. Kasai could not look away. He had read of the different types of demonkind in the monastery library. This creature was a succubus, seductive, and deadly.

The demon shunned modesty and was naked from the waist up. She wore form-fitted leather leggings, which hung low and tight on her slender hips. The demon did very little to cover her seductive curves. Onyx, bone-straight hair shot down her alabaster skin and glistened like black oil running down a sheet of ice.

She marched straight towards the assassin. He bowed cockily in her presence like some flamboyant minstrel in the presence of royalty.

"Is this all that remains?" she growled.

"And an excellent evening to you, too, Sess'thra," the assassin chortled, with a pompous grin. The demon slapped him hard across the face, dropping him to the dirt.

"The monks were meant to be collected and unharmed until tested," Sess'thra growled. "Our Mistress will be furious with what you have done here, Dax."

"My orders were to remove the Masters. Maugris' mindless Vor were to create a distraction and chose carnage." Dax shrugged. "I cannot be held accountable for their bloodlust."

The succubus looked at what remained of the Brotherhood, sneering. "And? Was there success?"

"My dear Sess'thra, you wound me. Success? Of course. All but one Master is no more. The third will be dead soon. He will not be able to resist the unique poison in his veins."

"I was referring to them." Sess'thra looked past Dax. She sauntered over to the bound Brothers, narrow hips swaying, predatory eyes glaring. "Now, let us see if something can be salvaged from this debacle."

Sess'thra moved through the captives. She spun a small amulet over each of their heads. Kasai saw a flash of green every time the stone at its center caught the light of the fires.

"What is she doing?" He whispered but knew Master Choejor would be unable to answer. He feared she was deciding which of his Brothers would be taken as slaves and which would be killed as sacrifices to unholy gods. He forced himself to stay hidden and quiet.

Sess'thra moved between the captives like a snake slithering through the grass, occasionally stopping to grab someone's chin or examine another's arm before shaking her head in disappointment. She glanced back at the assassin. "It will not go well for you if he is already dead," she said, continued her search, passing Daku, and then turning back to inspect him. "That one. Pull him from the rest."

Daku was separated from the group. He looked at her with a mixture of anger, awe, and blatant desire when Sess'thra gave Daku a flirtatious smile as she slithered in his direction. Carnal delight oozed from her movements. She halted a few meters from him and tossed a wicked-looking dagger at his knees.

"You. Pick that up," Sess'thra said in a commanding voice.

Daku picked up the dagger between both hands. He looked questioning at the succubus.

"You're different from the rest. I can smell it. I would wager that no one here sees your true potential as I do. There is a certain glint in your eyes that holds promise for greatness to come.

"I offer you a choice. No longer will you be shackled beneath all this…hypocrisy." Sess'thra waved her hands about the burning monastery. "You shall be transformed into a champion among champions. Yours shall be a life of conquest. You shall have the power which only one such as I can grant. You will come with me and experience all that you desire."

"And in return?" Daku asked.

"Ah, yes, everything must have a price. All I have said shall be yours *when* you slit the throat of every one of these miserable monks. The choice is yours. Shall it be one final stand for Ordu? Will you fight beside your Brothers and friends, or will you choose freedom without consequence?"

The Vor, as Dax had called them, chuckled with deep guttural malice. Daku flipped the dagger backward in his hands and sliced through the leather straps binding his wrists. He then drove the blade into the ground and rubbed the circulation back into his hands.

Daku surveyed the position of the enemy around him. When Daku attacked, Kasai would use the distraction to join his friend. Maybe together they push the creatures back and free the others. That was a long shot, but worth a try. Ninzizzida felt warm in his hands.

Daku flipped the dagger into the air and caught it in a firm grip, then turned and thrust the blade into Brother Hondo's chest. Kasai gasped and quickly covered his mouth.

Daku methodically worked his way through the group of his shocked and helpless Brothers. Ri'sonu fell next, then Brothers Dani, Jonah, and Numan. Daku didn't stop until only two remained.

Kasai clenched his teeth to keep from yelling. He turned away from the grisly sight. "Daku, what have you done?" He whispered with his head low. Kasai then heard the voice of Jarescu yell above the din of burning buildings.

"Have you lost your mind?"

Kasai looked back. Jarescu was kneeling in the dirt. Tears ran down the sides of his face as Daku stalked towards him.

"Times have changed. I finally see real power in front of me. I'm sick of the Masters brainwashing me and telling me there is a Boundless that will grant me power. It's all a hoax. Ordu is a lie," Daku said.

"She's a demon!" Jarescu yelled.

"Demon? Can you not see her? She is a goddess. I see her. I see her so clearly," Daku said. He was speaking to himself as he stared at Sess'thra in a daze.

"It's not too late, Daku. Cut us loose," Cannonball said.

Daku was momentarily broken from his swoon. He looked again at Cannonball and Jarescu. "No, it is only too late for you two. The strong survive, the weak perish. It's the natural way of things."

Daku wore a wicked smile and deftly slit the throat of Brother Jarescu. "Plus, I never liked you."

"Good-bye, Cannonball." Daku stabbed Jia'mu in the chest. A fountain of blood followed the knife's blade when he ripped the dagger out of the chubby monk's body.

Daku walked up to Sess'thra and placed the dagger back in her hands. "I accept."

He glanced back at the carnage he had reaped, satisfied with his work. "They were never my Brothers, and certainly not my friends."

Sess'thra handed the dagger back to him. "No, my lovely pet, keep this as a symbol of our trust. Your ascension shall be glorious." She looked past Daku and straight towards the location where Kasai and Master Choejor had taken refuge. Kasai quickly ducked back behind the debris. He prayed he had not been seen.

"Master, we must go," Kasai said, and Master Choejor nodded.

"We shall gather some traveling supplies and make for the monastery catacombs. If we are lucky, we will reach the wilderness without incident," Master Choejor said.

Kasai supported him as they walked away. Master Choejor's face was white. Kasai knew their chances were slim to none that they would make it outside the monastery walls alive.

"Lucky, lucky, lucky," Kasai said to himself.

12

SHIVERRIG

On a table in his study, Duke Shiverrig unrolled a map of the Sarribe Mountains in southern Baroqia and set a heavy wooden marker at each corner to keep the map stretched open. He studied the Sarribe Pass, marked in red. It wasn't the only entryway into the Kingdom of Sunne, but it was the safest.

Shiverrig would see Baroqia strong again—and he had plans, but he was woefully short of allies, troops, and the wealth needed to purchase mercenaries. He stroked the three-day stubble on his cleft chin as his eyes drifted to the northern kingdom. Dense forests filled the central regions of Baroqia as roads and rivers wound throughout the realm. The land was civilized due to the vision of a long line of House Shiverrig rulers imposing their will upon forest and field.

He reached for another map, this one depicting the northern borderlands of Baroqia and beyond—to the Kingdom of Trosk where Maugris stayed cooped up in his fortress of rock and snow, plotting his revenge. Shiverrig sucked at his teeth. Maugris. What to do about Maugris?

His maps were made of boarhide, a sturdy material that accepted script and design work without ink bleeding through to its backside. The Duke favored these maps. They were a part of his family's history as much as Volkerrum Keep; heirlooms passed down as relics-of-honor from father to son, dating back to the founding of Baroqia. They had traveled with him through blood, mud, and victory.

More charts were rolled out over a long table made from a single slab of thick red oak. Shiverrig was obsessed with the details of any campaign, no matter the size or scope. He assessed his troop deployments, where the land provided natural chokepoints and areas for swifter movement of the infantry and war engines. The more significant frontier settlements were also displayed in graphic detail.

Shiverrig turned to ponder a larger map tacked to the wall behind him. It showed a detailed description of the vast grasslands that spread throughout northern Baroqia. A box was drawn on the map just south of the sloping foothills of the Hoarfrost Mountains. It symbolized the Last Garrison, an old military base used mostly for war games and training. It held hard memories for Shiverrig, memories he intended to erase.

He traced a path with his finger through the Hoarfrost Mountains along Stormwind Pass. The route led to Rachlach Fortress, Maugris' stronghold. Could the sorcerer be trusted? That was a question Shiverrig could not answer with confidence. No matter, he would put together overlapping contingency plans to ensure the outcome of events followed his design. He turned back to the maps on the table, clasping his muscular arms behind his back.

He would tighten his hold on the outer villages throughout Baroqia and secretly draft more conscripts to his cause, not Conrad's. Peasants could choose to live outside of the walls of the kingdom and the politics within, but soon they would need to side with one power or the other. Either way, they would be consumed in the war to come.

"My Duke, I came as soon as I heard the word. Dax has returned," Malachi said as he scurried into the study. "Ordu has fallen. All have been slain."

Duke Shiverrig looked upon his Archvashim. The man's body appeared more bent than straight, and his face had developed blotches of a purplish nature. It was clear he hadn't sleep in days. His lower right arm was wrapped in leather bindings and ended in a mean, iron stump. Malachi was a haggard mess.

"And the demon?" Shiverrig inquired. Words like 'demon' came too easily to his lips in recent weeks. He didn't like it. It was a sour alliance, but a necessary one until he could control the might of the kingdom.

Malachi became crestfallen upon hearing the description of his unrequited love. This was becoming a problem.

"I fear I do not know. Sess'thra travels when and where she will. She leaves without warning and returns the same."

"I'm wary of the time you spend with your dark charges. Our guests are not toys or baubles for your fancy. When they have served their purpose, they will be removed." Shiverrig took a hard look at his advisor in the light. "You look unwell."

Malachi's mood brightened at the mention of the demonkind at Volkerrum Keep. "My Duke, they have so much to offer us. And not just the Vor spawned from Rachlach Fortress. The lesser fiends that have been summoned from Gathos have so many secret things they are willing to tell and do. Fascinating creatures." Malachi absentmindedly brought his left hand to the stump at his right, caressing the edges of iron.

"I see," Shiverrig said. He did nothing to hide his contempt. "Until the disposition of these creatures can be properly assessed, I do not want you to bring them any closer than you must. Sess'thra speaks in honey-coated riddles. Dax is too polite to be trusted, and these Vor are now everywhere. Keep yourself clean of their taint until this is over."

"Of course, my Lord. It shall be as you will."

"Did I hear someone mention my sweet name?" Dax inquired as he glided into the study. Shiverrig took note that a young man dressed in dirty robes trailed the assassin. Not a prisoner, but also not a companion.

"Where did you find this one?" Malachi said. "By the looks of him, I'd say vagabond traveler or monk hopeful for the Temple of Illumination. And one in need of a bath." His face scrunched in disgust from an imagined foul smell.

"Ah, yes, a proper introduction then. I present to you, Daku. No last name, or none that the lad wished to give me. So, let us call him Daku of Ordu. A one-time monk and now an extended agent of the Mistress. We remain hopeful at least," Dax said. He brushed off some dirt from Daku's shoulder and fussed over his robes. "Well as can be, I suppose."

"Come here, boy," Shiverrig ordered. He was impatient to know why a monk from Ordu had survived the culling and been brought to his Keep. Daku moved with fluid ease away from Dax and presented himself to the Duke. He drew back his shoulders and kept a rigid posture.

"From Ordu? How is it that you came to be here?" Shiverrig said.

"I decided it was in my best interests to walk a different path than those at Ordu," Daku said.

"You see! Mor's truth is spoken from one of Aetenos' own. The demigod is truly dead," Malachi said. He jumped forward with keen interest. "The Change of Mor reveals the truth in all things." He stabbed a bony finger into Daku's chest. "Even you!"

Daku raised an indifferent eyebrow. He then fixed his dark eyes on Shiverrig. Daku had the same relaxed reserve that the Grandmaster had during their failed negotiations.

"Malachi, calm yourself. Give the boy some room," Shiverrig said. His Archvashim's fanaticism with Mor was becoming more pronounced since the arrival of the demons. If it clouded his judgment, Shiverrig would need to remove him.

Malachi bowed. "Yes, my Duke." He grumbled something more as he passed Daku but moved to the side.

"I am not interested in Mor or Aetenos. Either will do, or pick another. I care not. I need more able-bodied men under my banner, not the rantings of new worlds to come by another self-inflated prophet," Shiverrig said. "Which are you?"

It was a test. What information had Dax let pass through his lips on the long journey back to Gethem? For now, Shiverrig would consider the boy a spy until proven otherwise.

"A monk's true power comes from mind-over-matter. By using a focused determination of will, one can separate the illusion of mental pain from what is in reality, only physical sensation. A new reality then blossoms within the disciplined mind when this basic principle has been mastered.

"Deities and demigods are inconsequential to my abilities. Stories of Mor or Aetenos are meant to control the masses. They do not grant magical favors to the faithful."

Malachi's eager expression dropped into a menacing glare. "You will become part of the Change of Mor or perish."

Shiverrig frowned.

"Duke Shiverrig, I can be of value. The monks of Ordu were found homeless on the streets of desperate neighborhoods across the lands of Baroqia. They were orphaned or abandoned at an early age. They have nothing.

"Feed them, shelter them, give them an enemy to focus

their anger on, and your ranks will swell. I'll recruit and train them myself."

"An army of street rats pretending to be monks of lost Ordu?" Malachi scoffed.

Daku's eyes narrowed. "Do not push me, old man."

The boy has courage and pride. I can use both, Shiverrig thought.

Dax came to Daku's side and patted him on the back. The assassin was quick to change the subject. "The boy certainly has spirit and a favorable conscience to your cause. He's strong as a bull and not without a quick, fiery fist. Quite the fighter when cornered, mind you. He managed to hold his own against some unpleasant disagreements with my entourage along the way to Volkerrum Keep. Plus, our dear Sess'thra has taken him into her trust."

As a plaything or informant? There was more to this young man than just an afterthought or memento from a raid. He was here for a reason. "Where is that little bird? She is constantly fluttering here and there, yet I am not privy to her movements," Shiverrig said.

Sess'thra appeared like a ghost from the shadows of a forgotten corner of the room. Sulfur and cinnamon followed in her wake. "The monasteries of the Four Orders have fallen. The monks are gone. Hardly the fight I expected. It was all quite disappointing."

Shiverrig heard a slight sigh come from Malachi. The Archvashim rushed to faun over Sess'thra. He reached his good hand out to touch her.

"What did I say about touching me again, worm?" Sess'thra growled.

Malachi immediately pulled back his hand. "I only wished to welcome our wayward dove back to the Keep."

Sess'thra's upper lip curled. She gave Malachi a sidelong

glare when she passed him. "I'm already in a foul enough mood without listening to your weak drivel."

She drew close to Dax. "I was able to test the monks, properly this time. None passed."

Daku pushed forward to stand in front of Sess'thra. "I did what you said. I want what was promised."

"Ah, my young monk. I have not forgotten about you."

Sess'thra raised an amulet with an emerald center above his head. There was a flicker, but then the stone went dark. She sighed. "Still nothing."

Shiverrig sensed the frustration clinging to Sess'thra's typically alluring features. There was another storyline in play. Sekka's real interest in this campaign was taking shape with each piece she moved into place. Maugris seemed content enough to watch those that made him an outcast suffer, but the Arch Devil and her thralls were up to something entirely different.

"I said, I want..." Daku started again.

"I do not care what you want!" Sess'thra barked at Daku. She turned back to Dax.

"Were all the monks within the walls of the Ordu during the raid? Could any have escaped?" The succubus was fire and fury in a moment's notice. She was unbridled passion.

"How would I know? I was busy disposing of the Masters," Dax said.

"Who was missing!" Sess'thra screamed. She rounded on Daku. "You were in the courtyard. You saw them all die. Who wasn't there?"

His eyes went wide with surprise. "I, I don't know. Let me think." Daku looked left and right. "Kasai wasn't there," Daku said at last. "He was absent in the refectory at last bell. I did not see him in the holding area, either. He might have been outside the monastery walls during the attack." Daku softly chuckled. "I knew it. Late for his own funeral."

"Ah, it seems this Kasai may have alluded us," Sess'thra eased back to her provocative demeanor. "Kasai." She gently breathed the name through her teeth. "Such a peaceful name. Like a field of long grass blowing in a gentle breeze."

The succubus stretched out her arm and walked her slender, alabaster fingers up Daku's tattered sleeve. "Could Kasai do anything interesting, any tricks?" Sess'thra purred into Daku's ear.

"He was average. I could best him in the sparring circles with ease. I once engaged four other Brothers simultaneously. I defeated them all. I even fought against a Master. I was next in line to ... "

"Not you!" She cuffed him across the back of his head. "I examined every monk within the monastery walls. Dead or alive, the amulet did not respond, not so much as a glimmer. But I did not think to look to the outer reaches. My advance scouts did not speak of monks being late with their chores."

Sess'thra exchanged a quizzical glance with Dax. Shiverrig let the plot unfold as each piece fell into place. It was valuable information that he could use to his benefit in the future, once he understood its meaning.

"I will ask you again. Did your Kasai do anything special?" Sess'thra said. Her impatience was on the rise.

"Well, he did complete something I couldn't, but I'm sure he cheated," Daku reluctantly said under his breath.

"And what was that?" Sess'thra said.

"He completed the Trial of Pillars."

Sess'thra looked at Dax for some kind of explanation. The assassin shrugged his shoulders.

"It's a maze in the sky. An initiate follows a circuit of columns by jumping from the top of one to the next," Daku said.

"Not much of a test," Sess'thra said. "I presumed you monks were capable of feats of this nature."

Daku rolled his eyes. "Not if you're blind to where the next column stood. It's as more of a mental test than a physical one. Kasai was good, but not that good. Even I could not finish the route. The test is designed to be impossible for any but a Master to complete."

"Could it be he had someone watching over him? A guardian angel, perhaps?" Sess'thra's excitement mounted. "Tell me more. Tell me everything" The purring had returned.

"What do you want to know? Kasai was soft. He had green eyes that changed color according to his mood. I don't know. He loved to protect the weak. I tried to tell him, only the strong survive in this world. But he wouldn't listen."

Dax sided up to Sess'thra and spoke in a conspirator's tone, "Kasai was the name of the monk who interfered before I could finish off the last Master. He saw through my glamour and alerted the blind one to my identity."

Sess'thra wore a devious smile. "He is the one," she said with conviction.

"Kasai? Why does he matter? He's a nobody. You said I was special." Daku looked forlorn.

Shiverrig wondered if the fool was in love with the succubus. That would be a mistake. He feigned boredom with the conversation. "Assassin, please explain why any of this is of interest to me in any way?"

"Because Duke Shiverrig, our lovely Sess'thra speaks of the coming of the next Ever Hero. The Mistress has made it clear that she wants the avatar of Aetenos for her own in the North," Dax said.

"Bad news for her if he was a monk," Shiverrig said. He picked up a map from his desk and studied it to hide his surprise. Could it be true? Had Sekka entered the Mortal Realm?

"Kasai? The Ever Hero? Don't make me laugh. Kasai

wouldn't let his shadow be seen if he didn't have permission first. He's been a milk baby since I met him at Ordu. He's no hero," Daku said. He crossed his arms over his chest. "You have the wrong person."

Shiverrig took a hard look at Dax. Was it true? Had the fool Maugris successfully summoned the devil to the Mortal Realm? Assuming he had, why would she need the Ever Hero alive? It didn't make sense. Maugris wanted the monks of Aetenos dead. Who could blame him? History showed them to be a troublesome lot, and Sekka would be smart to be rid of them as well.

If Aetenos was truly gone, then who would be left to oppose her? Better to have the Ever Hero dead as well. But she had other plans. She needed the Ever Hero alive for something special. But for what? This question lingered in his mind, as did his wondering on who was the real power in the North?

A storm was coming, one that King Conrad would never be able to weather on his own. Unfortunately, Shiverrig was not strong enough to defend the land without absolute control over the Five Armies. If a demonic invasion were imminent, he would need to consider his position in the aftermath.

There were always weak links in any well-planned strategy. Perhaps, a partnership with Sekka, not Maugris, was necessary … until the proper moment to counterattack presented itself. Focus on one enemy at a time, while keeping them all in mind.

"I am not some dullard, keen on prophecies or peasant stories of salvation from the unseen divine. I care not if the monks are gone from the mountains, grasslands, hills, or hovels where they hid. Can we finally move forward as planned?" Shiverrig demanded. He deliberately acted as if he was none-the-wiser of the real motives of his guests.

"What about me and the promises you made me? I want the power you spoke of at the monastery." Daku grabbed Sess'thra by the shoulder to pull her around. He failed to do anything but elicit a sharp hiss from the succubus. Then a sensual smile came to her lips.

"In time, you will have ample opportunity to prove your worth," Sess'thra said. The demon did not try to hide her desire for Daku. It was clear she had other plans for the young man.

"I have real worth right now! I can show you."

Sess'thra ignored Daku. She turned to Dax. "Take Maugris' Vor and score the mountainside, foothills, and forests. Find any remaining monks that could have been outside the walls of Ordu. Bring them here. We want the one named Kasai. I'll wager he did not escape our trap alone. He is your priority. Keep him alive."

"You'll never find him," Daku said. "Not without my help."

"We found our way to your hidden sanctuary easily enough. I'm sure we can manage," Sess'thra said.

"It's obvious the Order was betrayed. However, the paths Kasai now walks are known only by the monks of Ordu. And unless you can raise the dead, you'll need a guide."

"I see, which makes you conveniently indispensable. How timely." Sess'thra eyed Daku with suspicious doubt. "How do I know this is not some trick to protect Kasai?"

"Kasai betrayed me," Daku said. Shiverrig heard the threat in the boy's tone. He was beginning to appreciate the lad.

"The boy was born into the wrong house," Dax said, full of mirth. His laughter circled to Shiverrig, who remained stoic.

"Let me show you my loyalty once more. Let me lead your pack of hunters. I know Kasai. He will come running when he sees a friendly face. Then you will have your prize, and I will have my reward."

The young monk grew bolder now that he had the succubus' attention. He didn't know the game he played with the demon. She was toying with him.

"I have not the patience to wait while you bumble around in the woods, and more so, there is no way a mortal could lead a host of demonkind. You'd be ripped to shreds the moment Dax' back was turned."

"I held my own against them before."

Sess'thra gave Daku a quaint smile. "They were playing with you. You are not ready. There is much in you that would need to change."

She walked away, throwing Daku a teasing pout over her shoulder. "Kasai shall not escape. We have all the information we need."

Dax cleared his throat. "If we are finished here, I shall be on my way."

"Wait!" Daku cried. He looked uncertain. "How? How would I need to change?"

"Be careful of what you ask for, monk," Shiverrig said.

"Oh hush, Duke Shiverrig. You'll scare the boy. I won't need much, just a bit of his soul," Sess'thra said. "Well, to be honest, I'll need all of it."

"My soul? You want my soul?"

Shiverrig saw Daku try to step back, but Sess'thra was quickly within his intimate space. She entwined herself around him before he could create any distance.

"Ordu was a lie. Aetenos is gone and left his monks with nothing. And you have no use for deities and demigods, remember? Why worry about something so intangible as a soul? Hmm? They are overrated at best. Live a life of greatness now. The cold dirt of death offers no salvation, divine or otherwise," Sess'thra whispered lie upon lie in his ear.

Shiverrig watched and waited.

"There may be a way, if you are strong enough," Sess'thra

said. She pushed herself away from Daku. "But I doubt it. Mortals are made of weak stock."

"I am strong! You said I was different."

"In your body, perhaps, but we shall see if your soul also has the strength of your conviction. If you are found worthy, you will prevail. If not, well, your soul was not worth the etheric energy it was given in the first place."

"No, not my soul. Take something else instead." Daku became defensive.

Shiverrig studied the young monk. He was fit and fearless until this point, a supple fighter with a brawler's mentality. He was an easy target to manipulate when his passions rose.

This was an opportunity to gather sorely lacking information about the demon's abilities. The boy had betrayed his Order and was of no use to the Duke, except, maybe, as an experiment.

"You boast of prowess and worth. You demand respect, and yet, when given the solution to attain your goal, you refuse. Strong words fill you, but they are empty. You're just a frightened, young boy.

"Send the assassin about his business. Have him find the monk Kasai, or the Ever Hero or whatever. I tire of this drama. If the boy has no more use to you, then get rid of him."

"But it's my soul."

"What better raw material to use to build the new you? Maybe the Duke is right. You are not ready for such advancement," Sess'thra said.

She dismissed the idea and turned to the assassin. "No more mistakes, Dax. If Kasai is the one the Mistress desires, he must not be harmed."

Shiverrig watched Daku closely. The boy was exhausted and probably hadn't had a solid meal in days. A decision of impatience and ill-consequence was about to be made by the youngster.

"I'll do it. I'll do what you ask," Daku said. He stepped forward and stood proud.

Sess'thra was once again at the boy's side purring in his ear. "A wise decision. You shall be magnificent. The mortals of this world shall bow down in your presence." Before Daku could say another word, she deftly placed a white pearl into his mouth. "Now, swallow."

"Hmmph?"

She gave him a passionate kiss and pushed the pearl deeper into his mouth.

Shiverrig folded one of his arms across his barrel chest and with the other raised his hand to stroke the sides of a rough mustache. I need to shave, he idly thought. Something would happen soon. He was not wrong.

"My body feels warm and filled with energy. Is this what you feel?" Daku said. His eyes were wide with amazement. He stretched his body and curled his hands into fists. "I feel strong."

Fat droplets of sweat formed on his forehead and freely flowed down his face. He looked at his arms and nodded. "Yes. I feel it. Just like you promised."

Blue veins rose to the surface of his exposed skin and pumped hot blood throughout his body. Daku's dark eyes turned pink, and his sandy-brown skin became pale.

"Yes, but not quite like I promised. The demon seed has taken hold," Sess'thra purred. She watched the transformation evolve. "Humans are frail compared to the vigor of demonkind. This is only the beginning."

Daku held an eager expression. "More. I want more."

"Oh, it is coming," Sess'thra said.

The Duke remained skeptical. Nothing with the infernal

born was straightforward or free. A price must always be paid.

"It's wonderful. I feel...wait. I feel cold. Why am I cold? There is...pain."

Shiverrig watched as Daku deliberately slowed his breathing. He chanted foreign words, "Om tare tutarre ture soha, Om tare tutarre ture soha, Om tare tutarre ture soha..." Shiverrig assumed it was a mantra to go beyond the pain. It wasn't working.

Daku's hands trembled. He clamped down on his temples as if to hold his head together. "So much pressure...the pain. The pain...is too much. I've changed my mind. I don't want this!" Daku pleaded. "Make it stop."

"But this is what you wanted," she noted with sweet innocence. Sess'thra stepped back. She watched the young monk's torment with knowing eyes.

Daku's wailing shifted to screams. He dropped to his knees, hunched over from the pain. Malachi's eyes widened, and his head inched forward to take in more of Daku's suffering. The Archvashim licked his dry lips. Shiverrig grabbed him by the collar and pulled him back.

Daku from Ordu was doomed. Shiverrig hoped the mess would be minimal. He stood protectively in front of his table of maps as an eerie silence came over the monk. The room waited.

A deep gurgle resonated from within the monk and turned into a horrible laugh. Daku's pink eyes darted around the room as if looking for an escape. The monk's body expanded. Muscles stretched, ripped, and grew anew. Bones cracked and broke, then reformed to support something ... bigger.

Daku's torso convulsed. Blood vomited from his mouth and sprayed across the floor. He tore off his robes as if they were anathema to his new form. His spine budged along his back, then sharp-edged bone tore through his pale skin as each vertebra swelled and popped back into place.

Daku's body grew into a cruel and vile shape. Where the young monk once knelt was now a beast of ashen muscle and short, white fur. A pale-skinned demon raised itself from the floor. A final, whimpering gasp seeped out of its mouth.

Sess'thra approached the pale demon and laid her hand upon his impressive physique. "Welcome Khalkoroth, Shadow Demon of Gathos."

The demon was massive, standing eight feet tall. It resembled the basic human features of Daku but took on the thick musculature and size of an arctic bear. Khalkoroth's stout muzzle filled with needle-shaped teeth. Instead of paws, the creature had long fingers that flexed in the open air.

The leftover debris of Daku's torn and tattered skin hung from Khalkoroth's hard body. The pale demon grabbed the husk and threw the membrane to the floor. A black vapor trailed from Khalkoroth's body as it moved about in its new form.

The demon's face shifted back to the image of Daku. His pink eyes turned dark. "Help me," a meek and distant voice cried.

Khalkoroth roared, and the pale demon's visage returned. A viscous lather coated its lips. Pink eyes glared in anger.

"This one has a strong will, but he will not escape me." Khalkoroth's voice rumbled through his throat, sounding like boulders grinding beneath the weight of a mountain.

Khalkoroth coughed twice. He vomited a thick mass of bodily fluids and tissues. The mess flowed down its chin and over its smooth chest. He wiped the remains of Daku off his face and smeared it over Sess'thra's mouth. The succubus licked her lips. She provocatively rubbed her body over the pale demon's groin like an animal in heat.

Khalkoroth grabbed Sess'thra and took her in front of

Shiverrig and the Archvashim. It was brutal and savage. Malachi's pallor became ghost white. He looked confused and hurt during their rutting, shaking his head in disbelief. The demon's lust spilled out of his erect member and puddled on the floor.

"Next time, demon, you'll fuck where I tell you to fuck. Malachi, find someone to clean up this mess," Shiverrig ordered.

"Did you enjoy that, Daku?" Sess'thra whispered in Khalkoroth's ear. "I know you can still experience the world around you through Khalkoroth's senses. Such are the gifts I give you."

Khalkoroth momentarily shifted back into the resemblance of Daku, albeit a brutish version of the former monk. There was a visible struggle on the boyish face, mixed with determination. Khalkoroth reasserted control, and the boy vanquished. It appeared the two beings wrestled for control of the shared soul.

The monk had some fight in him. Perhaps, if the boy was strong enough, he could be of use as an informant. How to communicate with him without the beast knowing would be something to consider later.

"Yes, little monk, your thoughts and memories are known to me. It shall be a pleasure tormenting a follower of Aetenos. You will be helpless to watch the destruction I wreak upon his land," Khalkoroth's deep voice filled the room.

Khalkoroth glared at Shiverrig, assessing the level of threat posed by the Duke. He then sniffed Malachi. A feral grin grew on his snout. "What of these mortals? Are they food for Khalkoroth? I have great hunger. I wish to feast on their flesh."

Shiverrig heard a faint gasp escape from Malachi's lips as the Archvashim stepped back.

"These are friends, Khalkoroth. You will treat them as such," Sess'thra said. She playfully winked at Shiverrig.

Khalkoroth stepped close to Shiverrig and took in his scent. The Duke knew battle lust when he saw it. Khalkoroth was eager for violence. This was a challenge.

Shiverrig remained composed. Sess'thra wedged herself between the two, purposefully placing her hands on Shiverrig's chest. She gave the pale demon a stern look.

"Remember Khalkoroth, *friends*."

Khalkoroth gave Shiverrig a smirk. "Yes, friends."

"Now, there is one called Kasai that is of utmost importance to the Mistress," Sess'thra said. "He must be handled with care. You'll find his identity within the soul memories of your host." She twisted around, brushing her hard backside against Shiverrig before handing Khalkoroth an emerald amulet.

"What of this trinket?" Khalkoroth held the amulet in front of his face.

"Keep it for now. The Mistress said it would find its rightful bearer soon."

"And in the meantime?"

"I want you to stay here and watch for our quarry. I suspect if Kasai escapes our net again, he will make his way to the holy temple in the city. If you get bored, look to the priests for entertainment."

Khalkoroth's pink eyes shifted to Malachi, and a wicked smile curled at the edges of his snout. Drool dripped in long strands from his jaws. "That I will."

Shiverrig was unimpressed with the spectacle. He was more concerned about the loyalties and allegiances of the demons and devils entering his lands. "And what of you, Dax? You do not seem to have the mark of frost upon you," Shiverrig said.

"Duke Shiverrig, I am not from the Frost Plane of Gathos,

nor any of the deeper layers of the Abyss. I hail from the Mortal Plane, same as you."

"He is a cambion, a cross-breed mongrel," Khalkoroth snorted with contempt. "The Mistress keeps him only as a curious freak."

"Cambion?"

"Yes, my dear Duke. I am what the pale demon says, a cambion. I was spawned from the union of a changeling demon and a mortal. My childhood was uneventful until my powers matured, and I began to shift from one form to another. I had no control as a youth. What child does?

"My mother and I lived in a small village. The townsfolk did not take kindly to my extraordinary ability. The village preacher labeled my mother a Sunnese witch. He tortured her within a sliver of her life, then put her to the fire. Her screams through the night were enough to turn any kind soul black."

"Yet, you survived."

Dax shrugged his shoulders, "I ran and hid."

"Of course, you hid like a coward. There's too much human in you. A true demon spawn would have destroyed his enemies. I would not have rested until I slaked my thirst for revenge with their blood," Khalkoroth snarled. He let the excited drool fall from the corners of his mouth.

Dax ignored the pale demon's taunts. "My mind was filled with fear. I ran into the forest and transformed from one animal to another. I blended into the woods with ease. The pursuit of the villagers was short-lived.

"I scraped out a meager existence in the forest. I tried to survive by thieving and hunting small game. I was not very successful.

Fortunately, a band of forest brigands took me in, they saw my ability as a gift rather than a curse. They trained me how to steal properly, and of course, how to kill. I excelled at the latter."

"And the villagers who put your mother to the fire?" Shiverrig's curiosity in the cambion's story was piqued.

Dax's eyes gleamed back at Shiverrig. "One-by-one, they turned on each other. I had them utterly convinced their loved ones had committed horrible deeds. 'More firewood!' they said.

"I took a certain satisfaction in hearing the pleas of denial and innocence from the preacher. This was some years later, after I had mastered my shape shifting craft."

"And so, we come to the present. How did you become Sekka's killer?"

"As I developed my talents, I realized I was better off on my own. The small band of thieves I ran with felt I owed them a debt and threatened to kill me. Perhaps I did owe them something."

Dax reflected for a moment. "Nonetheless, I killed them all. Of course, talents of my proclivity attract notice. Eventually, Sess'thra found me. She encouraged me to meet her Mistress. The rest is history."

"He has no loyalty. He moves with the wind. Cambions cannot be trusted," Khalkoroth growled out the words.

"Oh, and you *can*, my foul friend?" Dax laughed. "Why do you think the Mistress keeps you locked up in a little pearl?"

"Do not mock me, changeling." Khalkoroth's voice turned savage. The pale demon's pink eyes looked to the side as if distracted by another's words in his ears. Khalkoroth's face shifted momentarily to the visage of Daku, but then snapped back to that of the demon. The young monk was still fighting for possession of his soul.

"Come Khalkoroth. We have preparations to make. Dax is just teasing you," Sess'thra said. The commanding nature of her voice was at odds with her childlike size. Khalkoroth stomped off behind her with a frustrated gruff.

Good, good, thought Shiverrig. Khalkoroth's lack of control was something he could manipulate once he found the right levers to pull.

"He is the one to watch," Dax said.

"Indeed, he is."

13

SEKKA

Sekka brooded as she walked down barren corridors deep within the bowels of Rachlach Fortress. The binding Maugris had laid upon her was proving to be more difficult to unwind than she initially expected, and her latest attempts had left her in a toxic mood, much to the misery of her unfortunate slaves.

Sekka had cunningly crafted the magic herself, giving the finished summoning spell—and subsequent binding knowledge—to her trusted succubus, Sess'thra. She in turn, who was to deliver it to Maugris, in such a way for him to think he was the original creator. It was a simple thing to accomplish—mere child's play for Sess'thra.

It was a necessary precaution, since Maugris was incapable of weaving the correct path through the Amaranthine Barrier with his limited understanding of deep magic. Left to his own devices, he would have caused her to be torn to shreds, while attempting to pull her through the Barrier.

The spell was laced with loopholes and trapdoors she could exploit later. Maugris had discovered the obvious inconsistencies in the spell and removed them, as she knew he would. But the more obscure ones remained in place. Yet, countering the core magic of the spell was proving more difficult than she initially predicted. Could the Amaranthine Barrier have contributed unique threads that strengthened the binding portion of the spell?

She reminded herself that this had been the only way. If she tampered too much with any part of the spell, it would become unstable and corrupted, and cast her who knows where? In time she would divine the weakest thread within the spell, or within Maugris, and pull it. Still, it was an insult to her majesty that she was his to command.

Sekka entered her scrying chamber. A stand with a basin filled with water was located in the center of the room. The air was stale and heavy as if the basin's enriched waters had recently been used to speak to an ally or spy upon a distant adversary. Was Maugris watching her?

Maugris' obsession with her had become unbearable. The fool thought he was going to *allow* her to be by his side once the conquest of the Three Kingdoms was complete. Such were the hopeful delusions of mortals who overreached their abilities.

Sekka approached the stand and looked down at the basin with contempt. She loathed the need for such aid to communicate with her minions mentally, but until she was completely free of Maugris' binding spell, she had no choice but to use the tools at her disposal.

She spoke dark words in the language of Gathos and parted the water with both hands. The water turned to slush as it folded back over itself. Her fingers traced patterns in the icy film covering the surface. Arcane designs floated lazily in the air and disappeared.

"Show me Oziax." Sekka concentrated on the image of the lord, and soon the demon warlord appeared in the slush.

Lord Oziax walked, in his human form, through a crowd

of her minions from Gathos. He held the regal stature of an aristocrat; finely polished and elegant features, high cheekbones and chiseled jaw. Long alabaster-hued hair flowed from his head and spread luxuriously over an oversized fur coat, unclasped and flowing open. The remains of arctic wolves, snow rabbits, and white-winter elks composed the bulk of his coat. The animals were frozen in place and added a macabre design to his mortal apparel. The antlers, claws, and teeth of the dead beasts jutted out from the fur coat like warped bristles. Under the coat, he had donned form-fitting white-leather armor, covered in strange designs and deeply engraved runes of brilliant-blue.

The massive rune sword, Eishorror, hung on his hip, sheathed in the stretched hide of an abyssal jol'goth. The encased blade radiated an intense cold, which froze the moisture from the air. A white trail of crystal flakes followed him as he moved.

+Lord Oziax, align your senses with mine. I want to enjoy the impending raid. My mood is sour.+ Sekka's thoughts invaded Oziax's mind.

+As you wish, my Queen.+ Oziax sent back.

Sekka felt the connection to Lord Oziax's position become stronger. The walls of the scrying chamber faded away to be replaced by hundreds of straight and tall Asher Pines with greyish, grooved bark and twisted branches sprouting clumps of long needles.

Late afternoon had turned to dusk across the Hoarfrost Mountains. The crisp air and fresh smell of pine sap offended her senses. Her mind was carried forward as the pine trees raced past her in a blur. She descended from the high plateaus and into the lower foothills where Blackwood Cotton trees, Red Chestnuts, and Bur Oaks grew in abundance. The stubborn deciduous trees still held on to their leaves, refusing to relinquish the colorful bounty to winter's grey sleep.

The musky smell of Autumn surrounded her. Crickets could be heard tuning for their nightly chorus. The forest floor was covered in a mulch blanket of red, orange, and brown. Sickening, she thought. Soon this land will feel the wondrous touch of Gathos' chill and be buried under ice and snow.

Lord Oziax now stood at the head of a demonic horde waiting inside the perimeter of trees that surrounded a small hunting village. He uttered a harsh word, and frost gathered on the ground under the feet of the horde. With a wave of his hand, the icy crystals crawled towards the village. A foul spray of mist followed and then swept through the village. The stench of lesser fiends and demons carried the odor of rotten meat and the coming of something worse.

Sekka peered into the village with Lord Oziax's eyes. She spotted an old goatherd leading five goats with a long stick. The man stopped short and staggered for a moment on unsteady legs before dropping to the ground, vomiting whatever sparse contents remained from the day's meal. His goats bleated fearfully and scattered.

Sekka's mouth watered with eagerness for the events to come. If only she could be there for the slaughter. She longed for something wild to chase. She loved equally the intoxication she felt when her victims realized they were doomed and the primal fear on their faces that followed.

Lord Oziax worked his demons into a wild frenzy with the promise of human flesh to rend and devour. Lesser fiends scurried between the legs of hulking abominations or jumped up and down on their backs. The larger beasts barked and snapped their jaws at the bothersome pests. The guttural language of the horde echoed through the trees. A wayward traveler would think the creatures of the forest had suddenly gone mad.

Just as the dire symphony of the horde reached its crescendo, it ceased with a word from its master. Lord Oziax was always one for theatrics. No birds chirped, or insects buzzed. Even the air between trees went still, holding its breath in anticipation.

Lord Oziax had become proficient at raiding the human villages, and the horde followed his orders with precision. If a lesser demon or fiend disobeyed his will, it was destroyed without question. Any challengers to his authority were met with battle, as was the way of demonkind. None were a match for Lord Oziax and his brutal blade. The loser's essence was obliterated and never again able to reform in the rejuvenation pits of Gathos. Such was his promise to the horde.

Lord Oziax barked out another command, and the horde raced forward. The forest trees provided a weak defense against the rampaging monsters. Ancient oaks cried, cracked, and fell to the ground with loud swooshes to the ground. Smaller maple trees exploded under the weight of the massive oaks in a hail of splinters and red leaves. The branches of thick chestnut trees shook and then shattered, tossing their serrated leaves into the air. The forest canopy resembled a thousand colorful birds dashing and darting into flight. Prickly ground bushes were uprooted, thrown into the air, and stampeded under hoof and claw.

Unnatural combinations of man, beast, and otherworldly filth, spawned from the Ice Plane of Gathos, raced out of the forest and into the defenseless village. The living nightmares unleashed horrific mayhem to those within their diabolical reach.

The villagers were overwhelmed with little effort from the horde. Those not killed by the initial onslaught of bloodlust, were herded to the center square by deformed, bearlike demons covered in thorny barbs. The demons held double and thrice-pronged spears, which they used to poke and prod the prisoners into makeshift holding pens.

Other demons with flat faces and birdlike beaks roamed through the holding pens. They placed iron shackles around the necks of the terrified townsfolk. The restraints were attached to long chains which traveled back into the forest mist, where they were held in the massive grip of a pink-skinned giant that rivaled the height of the younger trees.

Sekka knew this Gathos giant well, for he was the only of her lesser juggernauts whom she had summoned. Maugris would have no more until he brought her the Ever Hero. The giant beast was called Morteg the Despoiler in the mortal tongue. His upper torso was that of a man, but he possessed a boar-shaped head with enormous tusks that jutted from his oversized mouth. His lips were slathered in mucus, and ropes of drool dripped down his face to resemble a liquid beard. Morteg stood on four sturdy legs and his long tail was covered in glistening iridescent scales. It swished through the dead leaves and wrapped around the trunk of a tree.

Lord Oziax spoke to Sekka in his thoughts. +Shall we see what we have caught this day, my Queen?+

Even in his mortal form Lord Oziax towered over the villagers. He regarded them knowingly, as a victorious warlord eyed a defeated rival's followers. They would be fodder for darker deeds to come. He stared at the townsfolk with a gleam in his pale-purple eyes, satisfied with himself as he took in the plentiful catch. The villagers huddled in a mass of trembling flesh, holding one another in fear.

+Are you pleased?+

+Carry on, Lord Oziax.+

Withered and desiccated beings, the color of bleached bone, jumped into the pens. Their arms and legs were long and spindly. They wove through the terrified villagers leaving a trail of frosty footprints in the dirt. The demons weeded through the families and grabbed the children from their horrified parents.

The children were hastily corralled into a smaller group to the side, closely watched by grotesque demons resembling bulbous toads. These creatures, with their lidless eyes bulging from their spotted, grey bodies, seemed to see everything simultaneously. As the children screamed in terror, their gazes fixed on the slavering jaws and rounded lips of the ravenous beasts. Desperate cries for their mothers' embrace filled the air, but those who attempted to run were swiftly devoured by the toad-like demons in single, monstrous gulps.

+There's an elusive one.+ Sekka sent to Oziax. They both saw a lone villager slip between cottages. The man raced to a small group of villagers who had been previously undetected by the horde. He wore the short, off-white robe of a healer with a cobalt-blue monk's sash tied around his waist. He quickly reached a family huddled together on the porch of a small cabin.

+Apparently, we have found a true-believer.+ Sekka sent.

+The monk will not survive.+ Lord Oziax replied.

+Check him first, Lord Oziax. Then you may have your fun.+

"Fear not my children. The power of Aetenos shall prevail," the old monk called out so that all could hear. "We shall banish this dreadful host through His blessing."

Lord Oziax motioned to a beast handler and pointed to the monk. The handler unleashed a pack of six quadruped fiends covered in coarse, yellowish quills. The fiends howled in delight as they raced after new prey.

The monk saw the pack and swished his arms together in a broad, rhythmic pattern. The upswept leaves on the porch swirled at his sandaled feet and bounced off his brown leggings. The air shimmered around the family and encased them in a transparent sphere of blueish hue.

Three of the smaller fiendish dogs broke away from the pack and sprinted toward the isolated villagers. Their long jaws snapped together with strands of slobber trailing like ribbons from their gums. Mad hunger drove them senseless, and one after the other, they leaped into the air. The air sparked to life as each fiend struck the barrier protecting the villagers. The sphere flashed with bright-blue light, the fiendish dogs dissolving into black ash.

The remaining pack skidded to a stop; all abyssal creatures knew the toxic smell of divine energy. It was anathema to their flesh and held certain doom for lesser demons. The fiendish dogs backed away in frustration, thwarted from reaching their prize.

The monk held his ground and concentrated on maintaining the barrier. The fiendish dogs scampered along the edge of the aegis. One snapped at another, and the two fought until only one was left alive. The victor gnashed its teeth at its remaining brother.

Lord Oziax looked at the blood and carnage splashed throughout the village. Sekka could feel the satisfaction in his heart. He walked to the monk's barrier as the lesser demons and fiends parted before him in deference.

"The power of Aetenos shall smite you, as it did your cursed minions."

The demon warlord chuckled. "There is strength in your spirit and possibly more in your soul, but how long do you think you can last, old man?" Lord Oziax said.

Lord Oziax gingerly tapped the barrier twice and quickly removed his hand. He blew on his burnt finger and contemplated the wall of light preventing the fiends from their savory morsels.

"Such a distant song Aetenos now sings, if any at all," Lord Oziax said, absentmindedly. He inhaled a deep draught of air and placed his entire out-stretched palm on the barrier. He lowered his head and murmured throaty words with complex syllables as he exhaled. The runes on his garments came to life. The barrier protecting the villagers faded.

Lord Oziax raised his pale-purple eyes at the monk. "What now, old man?"

"Thou shall burn in the Holy Fire of Righteousness!" the monk denounced. He jumped off the porch and into action. He conjured a pillar of fire that engulfed Lord Oziax. The fiendish dogs scurrying at the warlord's feet burst into flames and then cindered to ash.

The rest of the horde moved aside as they saw what the holy fire could do. The column of flame rose into the air and bathed the small village in divine light. The old monk dropped to his knees, exhausted from the release of so much fire xindu energy.

"The power of Aetenos saves us!" one of the villagers proclaimed.

"The Heavenly Mother and her Son of Light have protected us!" another said.

"Father Dante is a monk of the Four Orders?" a third villager said. "He never said a word."

A cheer of sorts came about from the villagers in the holding pen. Most were still in shock and awe of what they had witnessed. They stared wide-eyed at the column of flame. Then Lord Oziax stepped unharmed through the conflagration.

"Not today, I'm afraid," Lord Oziax said. He brushed at the smoldering furs to tap away any adolescent flame that threatened to rekindle. "Anything else?"

The old man's energy was spent. He looked up at the

smoking figure of Oziax. Sekka saw defiance in the man's eyes.

+He will need to be broken, Lord Oziax. But see the youngling entering the square?+

Oziax saw a child walking towards the chaos instead of fleeing from it. The little girl rubbed her eyes and called for her mother between sobs. One of the prisoners in the holding pen saw her too. He pushed past a demon bear thing and sprang over the wall of overturned carts to rescue the young child.

Her sleepy eyes recognized him immediately, then grew wide as a pack of lithe demons with curved beaks leaped on his back and ripped him to shreds. Blood and viscera burst in the air as the villager struggled in vain against the demons. The child went down with less of a fight.

"Well, that was unfortunate," Oziax said, "but not unexpected." His voice was a rich baritone, and each word echoed in his throat with an animalistic growl. He paused to think of what a human noble might say in this situation.

"I'm dreadfully sorry for this bit of inconvenience, but your dear neighbor to the North, Maugris the Infinite, demands the pleasure of your company." The sound of malice in his voice mocked the pleasantries of his words. Lord Oziax could not keep the grin from his mouth. He savored the pungent smell of fear now reeking from the peasants.

"I am the Great Demon Lord, Oziax, High General of her majesty Sekka's Frost Legions, and Baron of the Frozen Wastelands of Thresh. I am at your service," he bowed deeply.

"What do you want with us?" Father Dante said.

"I mean to escort you safely through the high peaks of the Hoarfrost Mountains and beyond to Rachlach Fortress.

There you will work to till the frozen soil and harvest the food for the army of the North."

"Maugris the Mad! You send our souls to oblivion. In the name of Aetenos, the Light Bringer and the Smiter of Darkness, I command you, begone!" Father Dante said. He did his best to stand. His commanding voice helped to stabilize the growing fear and moans of the villagers.

"I shall smite you, demon, as Aetenos once did long ago. We shall not be fuel for dark sorceries!" he said. Father Dante glared at the creatures surrounding him. The howls and screeches of the abominations grew louder.

+ They shall be a grand batch for the ice pyre. Such fear. However, the child was not enough. The defiant one brings them hope. Take the monk.+ Sekka commanded.

Oziax motioned to two tall demons with bloated midsections. Puss wept from their eyes. He then pointed at the old man. "Bring him."

The tall demons grabbed Father Dante with their long limbs. Rough, white hands secured the old man and dragged him to their master. They dropped the monk in a frosted puddle of mud at Lord Oziax's feet. The frozen dirt cracked and bit sharply into the monk's hands and knees.

"Why, oh why, must you mortals always make this more difficult than it need be? Aetenos is no longer with you. He rots in the deepest hole in the Mistress' Keep." Nearby demons laughed and nodded their cursed heads in agreement.

Father Dante glared up from the puddle of reddish muck and raised himself to his knees. "Begone! In the name of the Light Bringer and the return of his Ever Hero! Foul creature, begone!"

"Ah, now we are getting somewhere. You speak of the avatar of Aetenos. Yes? Could he be you, old man?" Lord Oziax took a small amulet from a pouch at his belt and held it over the monk's head. An emerald sparkled and twirled at its end, but that was all.

+He is useless.+ Sekka voiced in Lord Oziax's mind.

"Sadly, you are not the one. Well then, would you know where I might find this human hero with the soul of a demigod? Hmm?"

"He shall be with us when our need is greatest!"

"I would think that time is now, don't you?"

"Go back to the Deep Dark," Father Dante said. He slumped defeated in the cold mud. "He shall come."

Lord Oziax looked around the ruined village and waited a moment. He even held his hand to his ear as if listening. "It appears he will not come this day. More's the pity. For if you are not the Ever Hero, nor able to provide the information concerning his whereabouts, then you are little use to me."

A wolfish smile broadened on Lord Oziax's face. He unsheathed his terrible blade and held it even with Father Dante's eyes. An icy chill filled the air as frost fell from the vile weapon, and the nervous sweat dripping from the monk's forehead froze in place.

"This is Eishorror, and she is a most frigid wench." Lord Oziax swung the sword in a low arc and sliced clear through Father Dante's neck. The cut was so quick and precise that there was no blood. The old man's body turned blue and crystalized instantly. Lord Oziax deftly kicked the decapitated head into the air. A winged creature grabbed it midflight. The airborne demon glided to a nearby rooftop and consumed its prize.

A hush came over the villagers as they stared in disbelief as the body of Father Dante collapsed in the mud.

+A nice touch.+ Sekka thought. She was enjoying the show.

"Now, where were we? Ah yes, travel arrangements," Lord Oziax said. He turned to the villagers in the holding pen.

"Please, take us and leave the children behind. What could Maugris need with small children? They are but infants," lamented one young mother. Her tears ran through the grim on her face. Her dirty hands came together in prayer above her head.

"They will not survive the harsh passage north," sobbed another. She bowed and cowered in the mud of the pen.

Lord Oziax tapped his finger to his lip three times. "Indeed. The journey north would be a bit extreme for the youngsters. You make a fair request. And to show you I am a just host, I decree, the children shall remain!" Lord Oziax said. He dramatically swept his arms through the air in a grandiose manner. "Your prayers have been answered."

A glimmer of encouragement came to the faces of many of the villagers. Although their doom was sealed, at least their children would be saved. "Besides, they have a more immediate use," Lord Oziax said as he turned to the demonic horde behind him. "Enjoy."

The villager's eyes grew wide in disbelief. They watched in horror as the wretched demons pounced on their helpless children. A bloody mist floated like a crimson cloud through the square. The monsters left nothing but slashed and tattered clothing and red-stained dirt once they had their fill.

Oziax signaled Morteg the Despoiler to begin. The chains drew taut. The villagers were pulled to their feet and forced to march to their doom. The old and grief-stricken who could no longer walk were dragged.

A gangly and sinewy demon approached Lord Oziax as the horde left the pillaged village. His face bore the scarring indicative of advanced rank. "Till the soil, Lord? There is no soil in the North. It is frozen rock as far as the eye can see. The ground is barren."

"I thought it best to have something to entertain us along the way. We shall flay them one-by-one and mount them on posts marking our progress north. If the Ever Hero has risen, this should create a trail of carnage easy enough for that miserable soul to follow."

"And what of the quota set by Maugris? The sorcerer's demands were very clear."

"That petty magician shall have his share of soul-slaves to sacrifice in the name of the Mistress. We will have plenty to spare from the next village." Both demons laughed and followed the horde into the cold mist of the dark forest.

+Can you taste the sweetness of their dashed hopes, my Queen?+

+You have done well, Lord Oziax. You have entertained me well and lifted my mood. Your rewards shall be great upon delivery of the Ever Hero. I have something special planned for you once my prize is in my grasp.+

+Thank you, my Queen. I shall have reward enough when Eishorror takes the head of that miserable wrench, Maugris.+

Sekka severed the connection to Lord Oziax. Her vision returned to the stone walls of the scrying chamber. She smoothed the thin layer of icy film on the water's surface and traced new designs in the slush. It was time to see what progress her nemesis Zizphander had made, if any, towards reaching the Ice Plane of Gathos.

Sekka reached out to the minds of her border scouts. Only one remained. Fresh frost formed on the walls as Sekka cast her spell and established a connection to her minion, who answered her summons with dire news.

+What story of the borders? Where are the other scouts?+

+The Red Devil has taken his first steps into Gathos. The outer limits of Falseshore are ablaze. The others did not survive Zizphander's fury.+

Sekka looked upon the desolation through her servant's eyes. Great rivers of magma flowed where thick ice had once laid dormant for thousands of years. The land boiled and bubbled like a sea of fire. Geysers of red magma erupted into the air, then fell back into the lava flow. Scalding hot steam whistled out the pending death song of her land. Zizphander had reached the outer borders of her realm and was circumventing the plane, creating a wall of fire around its edge.

Sekka took it all in with a calm reserve. *He is taunting me. He means to lure me out into the open and engage him in direct battle.* Time was growing short. She pondered his location for a moment. Why was she not notified about his exact movements? How had he reached Gathos so quickly without her knowledge?

She should have been warned. This was precisely the type of information lesser devils used to win favor or at least her attention. There should have been more buffers to slow him down, smaller skirmishes with allied devils as he passed through their realms. But there was nothing.

Betrayal within her dominion came to mind. *But if Zizphander knew my present location, he would have already pounced on Furia Keep. There was a grander scheme being played, but by whom?*

"Lord Oziax, you must be quick. Time works against Gathos." She spoke aloud, lost in her musings when Maugris interrupted her thoughts.

"Are you talking to my errand boy, Oziax? Has he the slaves I demanded?"

"Leave me," Sekka said. But she had no control over the sorcerer.

"Where is my army? And not this piecemeal rabble you insist is all you can bring me. I demand the great beasts of Gathos to lay waste to Baroqia. Where are the famed behemoths?" Maugris' impatience had reached its limits.

Sekka's hand deftly brushed through the slushy water and any remnants of the conversation with her scout. "You fail to bring me the raw material needed to fulfill your request," Sekka said with ease. "A Chaos Gate must be opened, and to do this, you must give me the soul of the Ever Hero. Only in this manner can I bring forth the greater beasts."

"There is no Ever Hero to be found!" Maugris screamed. "I have indulged your foolish whims long enough. My resources are taxed. The spies have found nothing. The Ever Hero is a myth! I have had enough of your excuses. I shall have my revenge on those who saw fit to banish me to this frozen desolation." He waved his arms and hands frantically as if to encompass the entire realm on the North.

"You are drained. It is clear from your complexion and disposition." The unconscious strain of fighting back Sekka's constant mental probing was exacting a high toll on the sorcerer. His skin was pale and drawn tight across the bones of his face. His bloodshot eyes were set back in dark hollows. Sekka reached out her hand to soothe Maugris' gaunt cheek.

His face twitched as if her touch burned his skin. His eyes flashed with madness. "Do not insult me with your false compassion!"

Sekka withdrew her hand. The hint of a smile peeked at the corners of her mouth. Not long now, she thought. The relentless riptide of magical currents she sent into Maugris' mind was wearing him down. Her mental barrage was slowly eroding his willpower and resolve.

The power struggle between the two foes was formidable. Maugris was forced to draw deeply from the well of eldritch energy to increase his magical resistance to her probe. However, pure magic was not inherent in humans, and it claimed too much of their life force as payment. Maugris' fate would be no different.

"What have you been up to?" Sekka said. Her words dripped with a mother's suspicion towards a naughty child. Could he be secretly communing with Zizphander?

"My actions and whereabouts are my own," Maugris said defiantly. He wore the guilty countenance of a conspirator. "Do not forget who is master, devil."

"I only ask in that I may assist you in summoning more demonkind. Your new wizard cabal does not possess enough strength to bring forth anything of merit from the Abyss. If you want to summon another who is equal to Morteg, then you will be forced to devour the life force of all your remaining wizards.

"What will you do when you have no more wizards? The greater juggernauts of Gathos demand a high tax, and you will have nothing of value to sacrifice. The powerful behemoths such as Cymeryes will ignore you." She watched him calculate possibilities, frowning as he realized she was right.

"The juggernauts will do. I must have all of them! And I want them now!" He smashed his fist into an open palm. "No more tricks. Do as I command, devil, or you will know my wrath."

"You cannot command me to do something that is not within my power to provide. I will tell you again. Only a Chaos Gate has the means to bypass the Amaranthine Barrier and transport the true power of Gathos into the Mortal Realm. This is the only way you will achieve your goal."

Her mind raced through possible scenarios. The combined energy of soul-slaves from any one of the great cities found in the Three Kingdoms would be more than enough to topple Zizphander. The remaining cities would provide her with a surplus of infernal currency. She would have power enough to bargain her way into the highest echelons of power in the Abyss, perhaps even a position among the Great Three.

Her imagination traveled beyond the Three Kingdoms of Hanna and into the broader world of mortals. If she could open a Chaos Gate, the potential for soul energy would be limitless. Nay, she would not demand a mere position among the Great Three. She would topple them!

As her lust for power grew, so did her excitement to inflict pain. She was tempted to rip the heart from Maugris' chest and feast upon it before his very eyes. Her arm was held in check by the power of the binding spell.

She returned to matters at hand. The invasion of Hanna must be quick. All would be lost if Zizphander attacked while her physical presence was still trapped in the Mortal Realm. She must have the soul of the Ever Hero. She must!

Maugris marched over to the scrying bowl and looked to the frosted water. The slush had settled, and nothing remained of the previous spell Sekka had cast.

"Do not pander to me. I grow weary of your excuses. Summon my army, or I will replace you in the most humiliating way. And you will never see Furia Keep or your precious Gathos again." Maugris stormed out of the chamber.

"Your time is short, magician. Very short," Sekka said through clenched teeth.

14

KASAI

"Master, why are we not being followed?" Kasai said. He took most of Master Choejor's weight on his shoulder.

"I suspect the enemy is busy checking the bodies of our dead. They are looking for something, or someone," Master Choejor replied. He spoke with more of a wheeze than a voice. "Now is our best opportunity to reach the lower levels."

"Let me grab a travel pack first. We'll need supplies."

Kasai returned promptly and the two monks fled through the smoky passages that led to the catacombs. They blended with the shadows like thieves in the night. There was no alarm that their passing had been discovered. "Lucky, lucky, lucky," Kasai whispered.

Eventually, Kasai heard the whistle of night air rustling through the catacombs like lonely ghosts. They hobbled into the moldy, subterranean chambers and disturbed a nest of mice. The small shadows scampered in a hundred directions underfoot. Kasai held his breath as the squeals of the red-eyed rodents echoed off the walls of the old passages. They turned a corner and the silhouette of the outer gate was in sight, their last door to freedom.

Upon opening, the small iron portcullis practically caterwauled from disuse. Kasai's heart beat faster. He gave the gate a quick shove to end its rebellious wail. He cautiously stepped out and did a quick survey of the area. The harvest moon was high in the night sky, bathing the entire grounds in soft blue light. Their way was clearly illuminated, leaving them naked to anyone who happened to look in their direction.

Kasai felt just like one of the frightened mice that had scurried for a proper hiding place. His senses were alert for sign of danger as they raced down a rarely trodden footpath and into a copse of trees. Like fugitives, they scampered low to the ground, wary of being spotted by hostile eyes.

Surprisingly, Master Choejor took the lead, albeit stumbling as he went, somehow managing to flawlessly navigate his way along the trail with unseeing eyes and unsteady legs. Soon they came to their first bridge.

"Master, the bells."

"Those who attacked the monastery will not know the song of the bells. They will assume it is nothing but the wind," Master Choejor said.

Kasai looked up to the monastery walls and then across the open gap. This was a very long bridge. He looked far below where the cliff wall vanished from sight.

"If anyone happened to look our way while we crossed…"

"The Boundless will hide our passage," Master Choejor said. Then muffled a cough as best he could.

"Just the same, we should traverse the underside," Kasai said. He looked closely at Master Choejor. He looked bad. The poison continued to leech away the Master's strength. The old monk coughed again; this time in the sleeve of his robe.

Kasai took some rope from the small travel pack he had appropriated from the monastery supply chamber. Luckily the storeroom had been enroute to the lower vaults that led to the catacombs.

"Master Choejor, I ask with great respect, will you allow me to assist you across the bridge?"

Master Choejor nodded once in agreement and offered no resistance. Kasai strapped his Master on his back and secured the ropes around his own chest. Kasai knelt down carefully to the lower side of the bridge and grabbed a handful of weathered rope.

"So this is why Master Dorje made us climb with rocks in our packs," Kasai said, hoping to add a little levity and calm his own frayed nerves.

They moved together like two awkward spiders buffeted by the wind. Fear of losing his grip threatened to break his concentration. Kasai grunted with each reach and grab. Somehow, he remained focused. Safety drew closer with each lunge and successful grab.

Midway across the span, Kasai came to a halt.

"I need to rest," Kasai said. "Are you ok, Master?"

Kasai hooked his legs between connecting pieces of rope and let his arms rest one at a time. Master Choejor's arms and legs were wrapped around Kasai's torso like a jungle sloth.

"I will be fine. Do not worry for me," Master Choejor said. "You have much of your father's strength. A bright spirit to move the body forward."

"With all respect, Master, I take after my mother. My father was a liar and a coward. A disgrace to those who looked upon him as their protector."

"Those are harsh words coming from the son of Jarei Ch'ou. I knew of a different man. One that gave of himself more than he thought of his own needs. Did you know your father was a great healer? He was able to blend his xindu energies together and use the unique energy to mend broken bones and cure the infirmed. It is a rare gift, though I suspect with the right training you would be able to do the same."

Training? What good was training when the entire monastery had been overrun so quickly? Kasai thought.

"Master, please do not refer to my father as if he were a saint. He abandoned us, my mother, and me when we needed him most. He ran away to save himself from those…creatures, instead of protecting us."

"Yes, Master Kunchen has told me the unfortunate story of how you came to us at Ordu. He was sorry he could not save your mother when he found you both, lost in the wilderness as you were. Her wounds were too great for even his skill."

"I know," Kasai said. He remained silent and thoughtful.

"Let us be on our way, Brother Kasai. The assassin may return with greater numbers when they discover our absence. They may already have our scent."

"I don't suppose you have any safety nets below us here, do you?"

"Not this time, my son. If we fall, we will fall for a very long time. Trust in the Boundless to guide your hands."

Luckily, the autumn winds held their breath, and the air remained still. Kasai and Master Choejor reached the far side and climbed back to solid ground undetected. A few steps later, they were under cover of trees. Kasai untied Master Choejor and lowered him to the ground. He placed the small travel pack behind the old monk's head.

"Rest, Master."

Kasai's shoulders and forearms burned from fatigue. He looked back to the monastery walls and saw tiny torch lights bobbing across the many bridges and moving along the edges of the cliffs. The monastery had been overrun and they needed to keep moving. Kasai knew they had been lucky so far but doubted it would last.

"They shouldn't be able to see us from here," Kasai said. He rubbed his arms to increase circulation. "Who would do such a thing to peaceful monks?"

The forest was alive with activity. Kasai noticed gashes in the trunks of nearby trees and traced his fingers along the grooves.

"What's this?" Kasai said then looked nervously into the wooded shadows.

"Vargru," Master Choejor said. He sat quietly. His head was tilted to the sky.

"Master Choejor?"

"The vargru mark their territory. This pack has given us fair warning. We are outside the protective boundaries of Ordu. We now trespass on their domain."

Kasai had been wary of enemy pursuit all night and worried that the poison from the assassin's dart would continue to hinder his Master's movement. He had hoped the shadows from the forest canopy would provide enough cover to conceal their location while he figured out what to do next. And now this. The vargru would not need sight to guide them.

"Master, we should move on. The enemy has made progress down the Eastern Slope. They will find the lower bridges soon."

Master Choejor rose slowly and nodded in agreement. Kasai inspected the festering wound and realized the Master would need medical attention very soon.

Kasai spotted a patch of peppermint and removed a handful of the bumpy, spade-shaped leaves from the plants. He offered a few of the bitter, yet flavorful leaves to Master Choejor. He took a few for himself.

"Come, Master. Let us put some distance between us and

our pursuers." They moved at Master Choejor's pace through the trees and half-submerged boulders. Kasai offered his support whenever Master Choejor grunted in discomfort. Kasai suggested short rests whenever possible, although he felt the enemy's presence behind every shadow or unfamiliar noise.

Their garments were ill-equipped to handle Autumn's cold night air. Kasai chastised himself for not thinking to grab two heavier robes or a travel shelter to keep them warm and dry while they slept. As if on cue, the wind changed direction and blew cold air down from the mountains. It would only get colder along their journey to the Temple of Illumination in Gethem.

There was nothing for it now. He decided to risk a small fire to give them a bit of warmth. Kasai grabbed the travel pack and rummaged through its contents. The bag contained items meant for a few day's excursion away from the monastery, nothing more. There was a small clay bowl for eating and drinking, a small pot for boiling water, some waybread and dried jerky, a canteen, some flint and tinder, a fishing line with a lure, and a compass. He sighed. It would have to be enough.

He found a large, slanted rock, jutting out from the ground. It would provide enough cover to shield the firelight from distant pursuers.

"We are in luck," Master Choejor said with a half-smile. He pulled his knees to his chest and wrapped his arms closer around his legs, waiting for the fire to warm his body. "The night wind blows our scent downwind, away from pursuit."

Kasai looked into the direction they were headed. But what if something worse waits for us along this path? Upwards, through the loose canopy of swaying trees he saw a thousand shining stars in the dark sky. At least it wasn't raining, he chuckled ironically to himself.

"Just rest a bit, Master Choejor. I'll make you some tea."

Kasai gathered leafy herbs not far from where they camped. He was fortunate to also find wild ginger and wolfberry growing nearby. He put the roots and berries into a small pouch and returned to their makeshift camp.

Kasai placed the ingredients into the small bowl then ground them into a fine meal with a rock. Next came boiling water from the pot he had placed next to the fire. The elixir wouldn't cure Master Choejor, but it might ease his discomfort.

"Master, drink this. It will lessen the inflammation of your wound," Kasai said. He could smell the wound in Master Choejor's back. That was worrisome.

Kasai shook his head in disbelief as if things couldn't get any worse. Now he had to contend with vargru. He knew something of the creature's lore from his studies. The sorcerer, Maugris, or his witches or warlocks had mutated the animals of the forest and turned them into horrors to help lay waste to the frontier villages. The vargru were abominations driven to madness ... and they hunted in packs.

Kasai was roused from his musings by a distant screech. He looked at Master Choejor to see if he heard it too. Master Choejor sat quietly, enjoying his tea. Kasai strained to listen for another, but there was none.

"They won't bother us," Kasai said, mostly to calm his nerves.

He heard strange and exotic sounds, some deep and guttural, some high-pitched, clicking and clucking. The forest was saturated with noise. He tried to distinguish which if any of the sounds were threatening. His imagination played cruel tricks on his hearing. Nerves, it was just his nerves getting the better of him. He took a deep breath.

Then he heard the screech again. And then another, like the first but closer.

Master Choejor handed the clay bowl back to Kasai and leaned against a small boulder to rest. "I've always enjoyed this time of year the most. Such wonderful colors all around."

Kasai looked at Master Choejor with incredulous wonder. Colors?

"Master, we cannot rest now. I fear we are being hunted by more than just the attackers of the monastery."

Kasai began breaking down the small camp and gathering up their meager supplies.

"Yes, Brother Kasai, I too have heard the song of the vargru. They shall be along soon enough. But first, sit a moment more with me. Let us speak together of the Boundless."

"Now, Master?"

"There is always time for now, Brother Kasai. There is more you must learn before the end." Master Choejor paused for a moment. "Your mind is strong, but already too full of answers for one so young. This is what keeps you separated from truly understanding the Boundless. Perhaps even more so now."

"I am open to the Boundless, Master. I just wish I could see it."

"The Boundless if formless, yet you see it everywhere with your open eyes and your listening ears. You feel it in the temperature in the air, and the wetness of water, or the thickness of the earth. All these things are alive, and they speak through a universal language of vibrations. You need only learn to decipher their message as you did atop the pillars.

"When you do this, you will see, feel, and hear a different world. Silence your mind, and the melodies change."

"I understand, Master."

"Do you? I wonder. I sense little harmony with the alignment of your xindu energies."

"Forgive me, Master. I'm more comfortable trusting the strength in my body rather than something intangible or magical." Kasai said. He hoped that would end the conversation.

"Magical? Now you sound like Brother Daku. You both mistrust what you cannot control. The known is no more your friend than the unknown."

"Daku...How could he do those things?" Kasai shuddered.

"Brother Daku's journey was set in motion long before that dreadful event."

"But Master, the Way of Ordu should have prevented him from…"

"From what? Do you think the Way of Ordu has the power to sway a soul from its predestined journey?"

"Yes! If not, then what good are the lessons and the training?" Kasai looked at his Master in bewilderment. He sat back against the side of another boulder and rubbed his temples. "None of this makes any sense."

"Kasai's vision blurred, and he suddenly felt very weak. Disturbing images overloaded his mind. Daku was Kasai's spiritual Brother and his friend. He was a difficult person to deal with, but that was because most people didn't understand his code of friendship. You were either with Daku or against him, there was no middle ground. He demanded unconditional loyalty and respect. But to murder his Brothers? What could have possessed him to that extreme?

He saw his dead Brothers in his mind, and then the assassin…and…the alluring demon. He quickly shut her from his thoughts. His thoughts became a confusing jumble of images without meaning. The world he knew had been turned inside out.

Master Choejor was speaking. The tone of his words was soothing. Kasai became calm.

"We all have a seed within us that matures to fruition

over our days. During the time we are given, the sapling matures and grows into the highest and strongest tree possible.

"The amount of water, sun, and care that is given to the seed will not change the type of tree that grows. Perhaps it will stunt or accelerate the growth, but it cannot change the nature of the tree."

"I understand, Master." Kasai lied. He didn't understand. Seeds and trees did not help him comprehend how Daku could have strayed so far from the path of the Light. There was a whirlwind of conflicting thoughts and emotions crashing against the walls of his sense of reason.

"Come, Master, let's be on our way."

Kasai did his best to push thoughts of Daku the Killer out of his mind. He had more pressing concerns to solve. Kasai needed to get Master Choejor to a healer that could counteract the poison in his blood. The City of Gethem seemed to be an eternity away. The weary monks pushed on for a few more hours before stopping for the night.

The deep forest never slept. Kasai could understand why. It was the noisiest place he had ever experienced. Night birds chirped and hooted, and an occasional wolf howled into the dark sky. The clicking sound of insects was relentless. Kasai felt as if they crawled mercilessly over his body. The horrible screeches persisted. Their wails sounding like mocking laughter.

Kasai's body ached. The grueling flight from the monastery had not been kind to his sore muscles. Kasai searched for sleep that his mind could not find. He drifted in and out of a nightmarish haze.

The events of the last twelve hours replayed over and over in his head. He saw the image of Master Kunchen flicker in and out of focus. He saw smoke and darts sailing towards him in slow motion. Ninziz-zida reacted in a blur of movement as the three sections that made up the staff flashed out to shatter or block each projectile.

Kasai saw in sharp magnification the one dart he had inadvertently deflected into his Master. He could see the poisoned tip in great detail as it ripped through loose robes and impaled itself into his Master's flesh.

He felt the suffocating weight of massive rocks heavy on his chest. The shifting image of Master Kunchen finally settled to the face of the assassin. It changed again to a mask resembling the face of Daku. His friend leered down at him while he was trapped under the rocks.

"I told you. But you wouldn't listen," Daku said. "Now look at me."

A rough hand took away the mask to reveal something else, something unnatural. Pink eyes filled with malice and hate stared back at him. Then the *thing* faded from sight.

15

DESDEMONIA

Desdemonia sat at the stoop of her small cottage. It wasn't much, but it was home, of a sort. The morning sun hadn't yet chased away the chill in the air. The skin on her exposed arms was like gooseflesh, but she didn't mind. She appreciated the sensation. She stretched out her legs and drew arcs in the dirt with her heels.

Blackbirds and robins chirped in the nearby trees. The leaves were well through the color shift, and every day more fell to the ground. She blew a rogue strand of hair from her face. She watched if fall back into the same place, then tucked it behind her ear.

"Another day in paradise," she sighed.

She was lonely. It was always worse this time of year. Autumn brought memories of brighter days learning her craft from her parents and playing hide-and-seek with the village idiot. He wasn't really an idiot. He just didn't have any magic in him. Not one bit. It was a rare condition amongst the Sunnese. But she didn't care. She liked him for who he was, not what he could do.

She could have found another village to take her in as a stray, but that would mean staying in Sunne, and more bad memories. She needed to move on and find a new life, somewhere away from the jungle. She would go someplace where there wouldn't be so many reminders of what she lost.

The fragrant blooms from the late Autumn flowers wouldn't let her forget. They came on the winds from the south and through the Sarribe Pass into Baroqia. The jungle found her and wouldn't let her go. Desdemonia couldn't escape her past.

She glanced to her right and saw three chickens pecking at stones at her feet. She rolled her eyes. "Rocks are rocks, you dumb birds."

She cast a simple spell, and seeds tumbled to the ground. The chickens clucked happily and enjoyed their breakfast. "Now, a little something for me."

She walked to the fruit trees growing in the clearing that made up her yard. She climbed the fig tree first and gathered a handful of the small fruit. "Maybe an apple as well." She hummed a tune as she gathered her breakfast.

She heard a telltale screech in the distance. It was far enough away not to be a problem. The vargru were only dangerous when then hunted in numbers. Maybe this one was just lonely too. She heard a rustle in the brush beyond the tree line. Something was out there, something big.

She put her hands on her hips. "Not now. I don't want to play. I'm hungry."

The rustling stopped. A heavy grumble came from the bush.

"If you're going to sulk, then I'm going inside." She waited a minute. "Fine. But you're staying outside this time."

Desdemonia walked back to the cottage to enjoy her figs. She forgot about the apple. Her little home was cozy, and she liked it that way.

"There was no room in here for that big oaf anyway," she said. She washed the figs in a bucket of water, cut them in half and drizzled just a bit of honey over them. She sat on a small bench under a small table. Her fingers knocked the figs back and forth.

"What do you think, Gauldi. Maybe we should move again." She spoke loud enough, so her voice projected outside. "I don't know. Where would we go? A city? Ha! Never." She popped a fig half in her mouth. "What is that tree-bark-for-brains up to now? Gualdumor! What are you doing?"

She went outside and noticed immediately that the birds had stopped chirping. She heard a second screech and a third. The vargru were on the hunt.

"When will they learn?" she said. "C'mon, Gauldi. It seems the old alpha wants to test my boundaries again."

Desdemonia ran into the forest. The trees across the clearing swayed aside as something large followed in her direction. Then whatever it was pushing through the trees vanished as if swallowed by the earth.

16

KASAI

Kasai awoke from a restless sleep, covered in morning dew. He was shivering, his body was sore, and ached with fatigue. Kasai wrapped his arms around his body to keep from shaking. He lied to himself, saying it was from the chill in the morning air, not the dream. He looked over at Master Choejor and saw his skin was pale blue. *This shouldn't be happening*, he fretted.

"I'll get some more fuel for the fire," Kasai said to himself as he quickly gathered some loose twigs and leaves for kindling. When he returned, Master Choejor was awake. "Master, does your injury still bother you? I shall heat more tea. It will soothe your pain and help you regain your strength."

"Thank you, my son," Choejor muttered. His voice was soft and distant. "We must continue to the Temple of Illumination in Gethem. I must speak with Grandmaster Nysulu. Something terrible is upon us. Something bigger than the destruction of Ordu."

"Yes, Master. We will be on our way after some breakfast.

Please forgive me for saying so, but your skin lacks the warmth of your heart. Something is not right."

"Fear not for me," Master Choejor said. He propped himself up to a sitting position. "I shall persevere." The old man grinned briefly as some of his old humor returned.

A breeze blew through the tree canopy above them. The thick branches swayed back and forth, releasing brilliant red, yellow, and orange leaves. The sunlight intensified their color as they spiraled down to the ground.

"They look like mid-summer lanterns," Kasai said.

"As with all things, their beauty shines true in the light," Master Choejor said. He wiped a trickle of blood from the edge of his mouth.

"All things, Master? You cannot also mean to include the evil that attacked the monastery, or what Daku did?"

"All things have their natural place in the Great Balance. When something is pure to itself and follows its natural way, you will see its truth. When you understand the truth of a thing, you can then appreciate its beauty.

"All too often, we are seduced by the Great Manipulator or evil, as you call it. Our emotions turn against us. Our bodies no longer listen to our will. Our minds play tricks on us, and soon we have become pawns to a darker power. We give in to the ease of its disordered desires. Thus, we surrender our light and become an instrument of darkness."

"I don't understand, Master. How can evil control the pure at heart?"

"Be mindful of the kinks in your armor, Brother Kasai, for we all have many. Evil searches for weaknesses to exploit and does so in subtle ways. We are most vulnerable when we are unaware of the manipulation. Beware the doppelganger disguised as truth."

"How will I be able to see evil for what it truly is, Master?"

"You saw the truth of the assassin beneath his glamour. That was a fine feat. Sadly, Masters Dorje and Kunchen could not see the truth before it was too late. Nor did I sense the changeling's presence."

"Changeling," Kasai whispered, scarcely believing the truth of what that word meant. All of this seemed unreal. However, the scattered memories of his earliest childhood told him a different story. The monsters were real. He looked hesitantly at Master Choejor.

"I don't know how that happened. I was scared at first and wanted to flee. But then I remembered the younglings. I knew they would need help during the battle. So, I went back.

"When I reached the inner sanctum, I saw the fires and broken bodies. I was closest to Master Dorje's chamber and sought his guidance. His Light had been extinguished when I found him. I am sorry I did not say so earlier, Master."

"I understand. I assumed as much from the assassin's bold words. Please continue."

"I saw death in every hall and room. I ran to find Master Kunchen. I saw him dead, as you now know. I knew you would be next, if not already dead, so I ran to find you.

"I realized I was weaponless as I ran past the Hall of Artifacts. I ran back to look for anything that would help, but all the weapons were locked in their cabinets. I noticed the ceiling had fallen over one case. My eyes watered from so much smoke, and I could not see clearly. Though I did not know it at the time, my hand grabbed Ninziz-zida. I tucked the collapsed staff into my sash and ran out of the room."

"Did you now?" Master Choejor said with surprising interest.

"Please forgive me, Master. Let me return the Fire Serpent to you now. I am unworthy of such a weapon."

"The Fire Serpent indeed. She is an unwilling ally if she is mismatched. The mere fact that you hold her freely speaks of a partnership between weapon and wielder that is rare. Keep her for now. You will find she is both a fierce weapon and a motherly protector to those she respects. Now, please continue."

"I barely remember it all. I ran into your chamber. Master Kunchen was there when he should not have been. I could not think clearly. But then, a warm calmness took me." Kasai paused to reflect on the clarity of that moment. "It was then that I saw the blackness come alive above Master Kunchen's head. You were bathed in amber light. I saw a sigil of the same hue floating above your head. I felt relief.

"The movement in the room slowed to a standstill. Everything shimmered with vibrant color. The darts fired at us became inflated, and the smoke seemed frozen in the air. Ninziz-zida acted of her own will and directed my movements."

"Interesting. Can you see my sigil now?"

"Yes, when I concentrate, but the impression is faint. It's more of a whisper now. I fear it has something to do with the sickness inside you."

Master Choejor sat back in contemplation.

"Brother Kasai, each of us possesses an inner sight that helps guide our steps and shows us the truth. Most of us are unwilling to use it, and we remain blind. I am quite baffled how you saw behind the veil so effortlessly. This ability is gained only from advanced training, which you would not have been exposed to at Ordu. Also, I have never witnessed an initiate having the depth of mental control to time-shift.

"Had I not heard your words of warning in my chamber and the subsequent outcome, I would not believe them to be true."

"Am I sick, Master?"

"Sick? Oh no, my boy. You are not sick. These are accomplishments few Reverend Grandmasters have attained over decades of study and meditation." Master Choejor chuckled. "And you speak of them as if they were commonplace. What it means and how it has come to pass, I do not yet know."

Fear crossed Kasai's face. He looked at the ancient weapon anxiously. "Am I being manipulated by Ninziz-zida's dark magic? Is that why this has happened to me? I have no love for sorcery or the ill-effects it causes those who wield it. It's unnatural. Please, take the Fire Serpent back. I don't want it."

Master Choejor thought for a moment. "I have never known the Ninziz-zida to grant any special abilities to its wielder outside of boosting the wielder's martial prowess. But she never accepted me as an equal partner. I shall meditate upon this and open myself to the Boundless for answers. You shall do the same."

And the matter was decided. The two monks sat in silence for a time, lost in their thoughts. Kasai stared at the compressed sanjiegun, wondering how any of this could get any worse. He needed something else to do, anything other than meditation.

"You should eat something to help keep your strength up. Please rest. I'll fix us up something before we continue."

After a small meal of way-bread and jerk, Kasai broke camp and the two monks trekked deeper into the wilderness. The sounds and smells of the forest amazed Kasai. Life was abundant here, but there was also death in the air.

Kasai and Master Choejor came across the carcass of a massive wild boar near the edge of a shallow stream. It had been dead for a time, but oddly enough, no other animals had come to feed on the remains. Kasai suspected he knew what had taken down the great brute.

The claw marks on the boar's flesh were the same as those gouged into the trees when they first entered the forest. The safe confines of the monastery seemed so very far away. There was savage danger here. Not far away, a howl shattered the daytime din and liveliness of the forest. A profound, unnatural silence dropped over the trees. Kasai and Master Choejor stopped along the path and listened.

In barely an audible whisper, Kasai asked, "What was that?" He tried to gauge the proximity of the clamor. *How close? Maybe a mile.* He figured the predators must be following along the same path they had traveled.

Kasai moved Master Choejor off the path and into the denser woods. Perhaps they could find suitable shelter or a more defensible position like a high rock, or a cave, or anything besides being caught on the open trail. A deep gurgle sounded ahead of them. Kasai pushed Master Choejor off to the right. They didn't take ten steps before they heard another menacing growl coming from behind a dead tree that had been felled in a storm.

A series of squeals forced Kasai to put his hands to his ears. He turned Master Choejor to go in a different direction, but again the hunters were already there, waiting. Kasai realized they were being surrounded. The vargru had found them and were closing in for the kill.

"Master, there is but one way we have open to us, but I fear this is by design," Kasai said through huffing breaths.

"Your instincts are right; however, we must continue to move forward. The numbers surrounding us are too many to overcome," Master Choejor said. "Perhaps there is salvation ahead where there is none behind."

"We'll need to run." Kasai knew the confrontation was inevitable. They would not escape the vargru. Kasai hoisted Master Choejor onto his back. He wasn't sure how fast he would be able to run, or how far, but he would run until he could run no more.

The wild chase began. Kasai used his peripheral vision to

keep track of the vargru on either side of him. He caught fleeting glimpses of fangs and claws, ripping up trees and throwing storms of leafy mulch into the air.

Kasai's childhood nightmares came back to him in a wave of fear. He recalled his vow to protect those he loved, and this gave him renewed strength to run. He was determined not to lose another family member to creatures of darkness. But what hope did he have?

The vargru glided fast through the forest. Nothing seems to hamper the monsters' strides. Kasai had managed to avoid punches and kicks from his Brothers during sparring because of his agility and speed, but against these mutated killers, he was too slow.

Master Choejor's body jostled on his back. Every screech and wail brought the monstrosities closer. *Just keep running*, he thought. *Don't stop.*

Kasai's lungs were a fiery furnace filled with hot coals. His legs burned with fatigue. How much longer could he last? The vargru charged forward. Their pounding feet shook the ground. He narrowly missed stumps, rocks, and fallen branches as he ran. *When would one finally snag him and send them both to the forest floor? Just keep running.* He hoped an opportunity for escape presented itself before he was spent. But he doubted it.

The dense forest opened to a small meadow surrounded by sheer cliffs on three sides. The environment would be considered idyllic under different circumstances. Kasai knew they were trapped.

Two vargru erupted out of the woods a moment later. Each sprinted to either side of Kasai and forced him to run straight. They were as large as the bears of the deep forest. Their fur was patterned like camouflaged cats, and stunted antlers grew down their backs. Their heads tapered into the canine snouts of wolves.

Steep rock walls loomed ominously over Kasai, draining him of hope. Escape was impossible. He slowed down since there was no sense wasting any more of his strength. The vargru mirrored his steps. Each had five pink eyes that rolled in enlarged milky clouds. Yet, they did not attack.

Kasai's legs trembled from exhaustion and threatened to buckle beneath him. Master Choejor set himself on the ground. Kasai knew their only option was to climb the rock wall. Maybe alone he could scale the rock face fast enough to escape, but that was a big 'maybe.'

I won't leave Master Choejor, he thought. Somewhere in the back of his mind, he heard Daku laughing.

"Master, our path ends here. There is nowhere to go but up the rock wall," Kasai said. He frantically looked for an alternative escape route, but he saw none.

"We will need to fight."

"Clever beasts," Master Choejor said. He extended his hands and rotated his body as if to discern the locations of the vargru. "I will deal with these abominations. Get to the Temple of Illumination in Gethem. Find Grandmaster Nysulu. Tell him what has happened at Ordu."

Master Choejor stepped forward to draw the attention of the two vargru. "Why are you waiting? Climb the wall now!"

Three more vargru bounded out of the forest. And lastly, one great beast entered the meadow. Its body was covered in twigs and loose debris. The alpha vargru bellowed out a high-pitched chortle to its pack mates, and they responded with submissive chirps.

The three vargru slowed to a leisurely pace and spread out. Their prey had nowhere to go. Kasai looked up the rock wall and then back to his Master. Master Choejor breathed in deeply and readied himself in a defensive position. But in truth, the assassin's poison had sapped too much of the

Master's strength. He was sacrificing himself to give Kasai time to escape.

Kasai grabbed Ninziz-zida from his sash.

"No Master, we shall face this trial together, as one with the Boundless at our side." He thought he caught a satisfied smile from Master Choejor's mouth before more coughing brought blood instead.

Kasai would fight for as long as he could. He hoped his Master would be proud of him, but he held none for victory. There were too many of the enormous creatures.

All of Kasai's training was predicated on stopping the fight once his opponent offered submission. But this was different. Kasai could almost feel the primordial hunger from the vargru was over him like a wave of aggression. Fear traveled through his body and knotted in his muscles. His heart pounded in his chest, and his limbs grew weak.

As if sensing weakness, the two side vargru charged directly at him and lunged with splayed claws and gnashing teeth. One of Ninziz-zida's end segments flashed out with astonishing speed. It cracked against the skull of the first vargru, and then without hesitation, Kasai's body twisted so he could stab the butt-end of its other end segment into the eye of the second. The vargru drew back, reassessing their prey.

Kasai was amazed at the quickness of his attacks. Ninziz-zida hummed in his hands. It was as if the *sanjiegun* moved of its own volition and made his body follow. It created a protective barrier around him, then whipped out fast as a viper whenever a vargru came within range. Kasai felt a flash of hope but then realized the vargru had succeeded in widening the distance between him and Master Choejor.

Master Choejor had engaged the other three vargru. Somehow, he had regained some strength and was keeping the pack of unnatural horrors at bay. The Master's movements were fluid and effortless. He redirected the force of each attack away from himself, sometimes sending the frustrated beast headlong into the ground. Kasai stared in awe.

Ninziz-zida burned hot in his hands. Kasai stupidly looked at the weapon in surprise. He realized too late the sensation was a warning. White light filled his sight. The shock of the blow was like no other he had ever felt. Kasai was bent in half as his feet left the ground. A sharp pressure built in his side. Broken ribs. How many he did not know.

The air left his lungs as he hit the ground. The pain was excruciating. He knew that was it when a tall shape blocked out the light of the sun. He shut his eyes and waited for the sharp bite of the vargru to finish him.

"Kasai! Kasai!" Master Choejor said. "Stand if you can." Master Choejor stood over him. His hands glowed white-hot.

Kasai clenched his teeth through the pain. He held Ninziz-zida loosely in his hands and stood. Breathing was difficult. The vargru did not wait to pounce. The one closest to Kasai lunged into the air like a cannonball shot.

Kasai's arms thrust forward with the staff to intercept. The sections of Ninziz-zida miraculously aligned together into a rigid rod. The impact of the strike shook Kasai's arms and left them tingling up to his shoulders. The vargru fell, but slowly regained its feet. It shook its head like a dog in the rain.

Kasai struck again but missed his mark. He was no match for these unnatural predators. Fear was clouding his thinking and slowing his responses. Daku was right. He had never learned to do what was necessary to win. He always held back against his Brothers at Ordu. He never struck the killing blow.

Ninziz-zida changed back into three sections. Kasai spun the staff in such a way so that the outer parts created a broader, figure-eight patterned pinwheel. Master Choejor was not faring any better as the vargru attacked from multiple directions at once.

Master Choejor cried out in pain. Kasai spared a glance and saw that the old monk had fallen to his knees. Master Choejor tried to stand, but a second vargru shouldered into him, bowling him over. In a heartbeat, the third vargru had him pinned to the ground. The other two circled to enjoy the kill.

Kasai tried desperately to get back to his Master's side. He struck out widely at the nearest vargru. It dodged his blows and snapped at his legs. The other vargru jumped to the rock wall and climbed.

The beast leaped into the air, intent on attacking Kasai from above. Kasai saw the threat but was in no position to defend himself. He braced himself for the impact.

Three bolts of blue energy slammed into the vargru's side. Kasai almost stumbled in surprise. The shots were not enough to kill the creature but knocked it to the ground near his feet. Kasai wasted no time. He compressed Ninziz-zida into one hand and used the sections as a bludgeon. He hit the back of the vargru's head as hard as he could. The vargru's skull cracked.

Kasai looked to see who or what had saved him. A lone figure entered the meadow from the far right. She walked with the gait of a young woman. She was dressed in the colors of the forest and wore tight-fitted leathers with a hooded frock. She fired more blue bolts into the back of one of the vargru closest to Master Choejor.

Kasai took advantage of the distraction. He struck the vargru pinning Master Choejor. Ninziz-zida flared with heat as the two outer sections repeatedly bashed and battered the monster's side. The vargru lunged at Kasai and swiped his leg with one of its massive paws. Kasai fell back to the ground. The vargru pressed the attack.

Kasai back-peddled like a crab. Then he kicked his legs up and over his body. He pushed off the ground with his hands, holding tight to Ninziz-zida's middle segment. He arched backward and landing in a standing position. The acrobatic movement momentarily transfixed the vargru.

Kasai drove the end segment of the staff down the vargru's throat. Ninziz-zida blazed with bright light. The vargru's eyes bulged as the end of the staff punctured through its neck. A warm sensation rushed up Kasai's arms, and he felt an odd sensation of gratitude. Kasai looked at the three-sectioned staff with amazement and no small amount of trepidation. Kasai wondered if the cursed staff was relishing the kill.

The vargru's mutated body collapsed to the ground with only its head remaining upright. Kasai pulled Ninziz-zida out of the monster's mouth. He dared for a moment to check on Master Choejor. Unbelievably, the old monk was slowly raising himself off the ground.

The alpha vargru barked out a series of high-pitched screeches. The vargru hovering around Master Choejor scattered and regrouped. The three younger vargru raced towards the woman. Two ran straight at her while the third circled to attack from the side. The alpha held back, waiting like an experienced general surveying the battlefield.

The woman went straight for the vargru. Her movement was more of a spiraling dance rather than a sprint. She moved her arms in rhythmic gestures while she twirled through the air. Kasai saw strange, autumn-colored runes trailing from her hands. The magic rose higher and twisted in the air behind her head. She acted if she didn't care about the danger closing in on her. She spread her arms wide, keeping her palms down over the grassy field.

The grass between her and speeding vargru trembled and convulsed. Both vargru leaped into the air. In the same moment, the living earth erupted between them, morphing into the shape of a giant humanoid. Dirt, grass, and flowers covered its outer skin. Thick roots spiraled together, then overlapped to make up its arms and legs. Branches and leaves sprouted from all directions across its vast bulk.

The earth golem snatched one of the vargru from the air with an enormous hand. It snapped its neck with a quick flex. The golem then twisted its body with incredible speed and caught the second vargru by its hind legs and hurled it across the field. The vargru somersaulted awkwardly through the air and landed hard with a loud crack. The golem turned to the alpha, while still holding the first vargru tightly by its neck.

The alpha moved forward slowly, sniffing the air and assessing the golem's strength. The golem let the dead vargru fall from his hand. The alpha snorted in some form of animalistic disgust. The arrival of the newcomers had stolen his advantage, and it called to its remaining packmate. The runt scurried to its leader, and both bolted into the forest.

Kasai breathed out a long sigh of relief. He saw the woman communicating with the earth golem. They both looked in Kasai's direction. It seemed they were deciding his fate.

The woman approached. Kasai's mind screamed out in warning, Wood Witch! She was coming for them, probably to take as slaves or boil in a stew. He raised Ninziz-zida in defense.

"That's close enough. What do you want?" Kasai said. His ribs felt like they were moving on their own. He slumped to one side.

The golem roared. The rumble of its earthly voice

vibrated through Kasai. The woman put her hand on the golem.

"That's enough, Gauldumor. Don't mind him. He can be a bit of a bully sometimes," she said. "Are you hurt?"

Kasai was surprised by the softness of her voice. "We are fine. We do not need your help."

"Kasai, it will be all right," Master Choejor said. He was finally up. He put a reassuring hand on Kasai's shoulder. "I do not believe the Forest Dweller means us any harm."

"Listen to him, Gauldi, not even a thank you," the woman said over her shoulder to her giant creation. "Of course, we don't mean you any harm, old monk. You're lucky I happened along as I did."

Kasai refused to lower Ninziz-zida. The Fire Serpent's section glowed a dull mauve. He had no trust of Forest Dwellers and their mysterious ways. Kasai felt Master's Choejor's hand slide off his shoulder. The old monk had dropped to the ground.

"Come now, boy. I can see your father is not well. Let me have a look at him." The woman took a few steps toward Master Choejor.

"Stay back! Do not touch him."

Gauldumor growled menacingly.

"Gauldi, hush. It's Kasai, right? I'm Desdemonia, and that big mud pie is Gauldumor. Kasai, listen, your father is hurt. I can help him. If I do anything unnatural, then you are free to strike me with your pretty sticks. Ok?" The woman took away the hood and revealed her young face. Black locks of thick hair cascaded down her back. "Do we have a deal?"

Kasai didn't say anything but didn't prevent her from moving closer to Master Choejor, either. Desdemonia waved her hands over the prone monk's body. Kasai smelled lavender and blueberries as a soft blueish glow lapped against her palms. She gently touched Choejor, and the flames caressed his body as well.

"Gauldi, help me roll him over," Desdemonia said. She examined him thoroughly and found the source of his sickness. "Oh, that's a nasty sting."

She uttered strange words and brought her hand down over Master Choejor's wound. The soft, blueish flamed turned dark.

"What are you doing?" Kasai said anxiously.

"Shh," Desdemonia whispered sternly.

White puss oozed from the wound, and then it closed shut. Desdemonia selected some reddish herbs from a small pouch on her thigh and crushed them on a nearby rock. She collected the pulped pieces into her hand, spit on them, then squeezed her palm tight. Again, the soft, blue flame engulfed her hand, and the sweet smell of berries wafted through the air.

She put the paste on the closed wound and bound it to his body with sticky leaves from a different pouch. Desdemonia looked up at Kasai with kind eyes as dark as coal.

"See, that wasn't so terrible," she said. "The wound is closed for now. He will feel some strength return. But he needs rest. Whatever is infecting him is beyond my cure craft. Now, let's have a look at you." The seriousness had left her face, and a pleasant smile took its place.

Kasai looked at Desdemona in both awe and suspicion. "You're a…that was Elemenati magic," he said. He took a step backward with a frowned.

"I can see by that unfavorable expression you do not approve," Desdemonia said. She had the apathetic tone of one who had endured this conversation too many times before. Her hands rested on her hips. "I told you, Gauldi, another day in paradise."

"You made…that," Kasai said. He took another step backward. His ribs screamed in agony. He scrunched to one side to lessen the pain. It didn't work.

"Yes, I called upon the ancient pacts between the Earth Goddess and First Dwellers to raise Gauldumor. Right now, the only thing saving your father is the healing power of the forest."

She spoke in a melodic, richly accentuated voice. Kasai couldn't place it. Perhaps she was from a jungle tribe in Sunne. How she had come to pass the Sarribe Mountains was a riddle. He looked upon his rescuer with new eyes, and his pulse quickened. She was beautiful.

Based on the books he studied in the monastery library; her clothes were form-fitting as befitted the traditional attire of a Forest Dweller. They were made of a flexible material that allowed her to move silently past trees and bush with nothing loose to snap a branch and give away her position. Bands of deer hide crisscrossed her legs and wound up her torso, keeping the material snug to her body. Charms and thin pouches were woven into the straps for ease of access. Her outer garment was sleeveless and revealed arms with the muscular definition of one who was trained to defend herself.

Desdemonia's eyes briefly caught the light of the rising sun. The color shifted from dark charcoal to smoldering amber. Kasai had never seen eyes so bright before. He was mesmerized by their inner fire. He stared at her, dumbfounded, the pain in his side forgotten.

Her slender feminine shape stirred a queer feeling in his gut. He was unsure why his heart thumped against the walls of his chest. He tried to say something to break the silence, but his mouth was bone dry.

It wasn't as if he had never seen a woman before. While at the monastery, he had studied numerous anatomical diagrams of both men and women. The images showed meridian lines and primary energy zones, as well as pressure points and vulnerable nerve clusters.

All of that was forgotten as he looked upon the supple and sinuous figure of Desdemonia. He saw strength in her body as well as a feminine allure. Kasai noted the marks of old scars that traveled up her forearms. She was a fighter and a healer, just like the monks of Ordu.

Desdemonia was no village damsel lost in the woods. She was a daughter of the forest who was one with the wilderness. Somehow, that made him nervous.

Kasai stared at Desdemonia's comely, yet bewitching face. Her golden gaze drew him in for a second time, and he was spellbound by her smart, bright eyes. Eyes that demanded his attention and made him uncomfortable. She smiled at him, and his insides leaped.

"Something to say?" Desdemonia said with a raised eyebrow.

The wind shifted and pulled at her long raven locks. Thick strands of hair swam before her amber eyes and cast them back into shadow. The pain in his side returned and snapped him out of his reverie.

"You are a witch then?" Kasai said, not knowing what else to say. He quickly added, "And he is not my *father*. My father is dead and gone."

17

SHIVERRIG

Duke Shiverrig leaned back against the wooden chair at his desk and read from an oversized book. The worn leather cover felt good in his hands. It was old and familiar. The book was filled with the historical events of the Shiverrig Clan, dating back to when the first Aj-Kahun, Baroq Shiverrig, led his burly, pale-skinned warriors across the Eastern Ocean. They arrived on sleek wooded ships trimmed with sail and oar; intent on conquest.

It was Baroq Shiverrig's vision to tame the wilds of new land and bring its native people to heel under his reign. The Aj-Kahun ruled with absolute power and imposed his will with sword and spear. He conquered all that dwelled in the hills and forests, between the cold and jagged Hoarfrost Mountains to the north, and tall peaks of the Sarribe Mountains to the south.

Duke Shiverrig turned another page. A crude diagram extended over two pages of what was now known as the Kingdom of Baroqia. The able-bodied men of the middle lands were conscripted into his warband, and soon the warband became an army. The women and children were used as slave labor to service his war machine or tend to the farmlands, ensuring the harvest came in to feed his warriors.

Shiverrig traced the borders of Baroqia then extended his path into the Kingdoms of Sunne and Trosk. He exhaled in frustration.

"The pages of my life will not be meaningless. Baroqia must grow," he said. He turned another page.

Gangs of ogre were discovered in the deep forests and initially thought to be perfect fighters due to their size and strength. This notion fell out of favor when the great brutes were assimilated into the army. The body of an ogre was ripe for war, but their bloodlust and lack of discipline made them a liability in battle. The results were catastrophic, and most were slaughtered or used in the slave pits for sport.

The Aj-Kahun's rule remained uncontested for decades. His armies swelled to vast numbers and were filled with colossal soldiers that defied understanding. Rumors spread that the great conqueror and his scions had intermingled their bloodline with that of the ogre slaves. It was pure speculation, and any who spoke out against the newly appointed King Shiverrig were rarely heard from again.

New bloodlines were introduced into the population, and over time the size and stature of the army normalized. Yet, the Shiverrig scions remained as giants amongst men.

"Better times," Shiverrig said.

He closed the book and placed it on the desk. He stood feeling quietly agitated as if he wanted to be in several places at once. He abruptly left his study. Things were taking too long.

He reached the sparring chamber. Twenty of his elite soldiers were already in the room. Shiverrig was taller than most men with a perfectly proportioned physique. His broad shoulders and thick legs supported the massive slabs of packed muscle across his frame. He moved with the grace and skill of a mountain cat.

Practice swords and shields clashed together. The clatter of a disarmed weapon hit the stone floor and skidded to his feet. Shiverrig picked it up and walked to the central mat. He stood barefoot, wearing loose pants and a thin shirt. His men, however, wore padded armor consisting of quilted layers of cloth and batting. He drew in a breath to center himself.

"Begin," he said.

His opponents came at him one-by-one or many at a time. It didn't matter. Gerun Shiverrig was a brute. He never held back, always being the aggressor. He reigned vicious blows down on his opponents with the sword or his bare hands.

His soldiers were systematically dispatched and sent sprawling to the floor. He had already laid low a dozen men when Sess'thra sauntered into the room. She wore soft leather boots and leggings. The vest she wore, loosely tied in the front, barely contained her alabaster flesh. She propped herself up against the weapons rack.

"I see the steward has finally found you something appropriate to wear," Shiverrig said. He was not thrilled to see her here. He knew his men would quickly fall under her seductive spell. They were useless to him if they were distracted. Their efficiency in training would diminish, and he had barely worked up a sweat.

"Clothing is such a bother, yet Sess'thra still obeys her master," the succubus said with a crooked smile. "Seems the mighty Duke Shiverrig does not have much of a challenge this day."

She picked up a blunt dagger and twirled it in the middle

of her palm. "Perhaps I should call Khalkoroth for playtime. He would be happy to oblige you."

"Call your pet abomination, then. I could use a good brawl," Shiverrig said.

In truth, he wanted to know more about how demons fought. Their outer strength was apparent enough, but was that magically enhanced? And how did they fare without the use of deadly poison? He would need to consult with his mages, and possibly have them create a charm for him for both scenarios.

Sess'thra pouted. She threw the blunt dagger fast into a dummy target. The blade struck what would have been the heart of a real man. It managed to stay embedded in the practice doll. The succubus sashayed up to Shiverrig. She reached out and wiped a bead of sweat from the side of his rough face.

"And here I thought you would ask me to dance." Sess'thra gave him another pout while her tail twitched seductively in the air. She backed away with outstretched arms. "As you can see, I am now unarmed."

The Duke's men collected in a ring around the two. Most were rubbing bruises or sore muscles, while some stared helplessly at the succubus. The challenge had been declared, that much was clear. They waited eagerly for their Duke to respond.

Shiverrig decided a tussle with the succubus could work to his advantage, and it would be a good lesson for his men. They all needed to understand their uncommon allies' strengths and weaknesses. He walked away from Sess'thra and placed his practice sword on the weapons rack.

"I am unarmed as well, but how do I know you do not come here bearing your Mistress' gifts?"

"You don't. But be at ease, the Mistress has not informed

me of any recent slights from Gethem or its Duke. This bout is purely for my pleasure."

"Grappling only," Shiverrig said.

"Until submission," Sess'thra purred.

"Then, let us dance." Shiverrig took a fighter's stance and waved Sess'thra forward. He remained in the center of the sparring mat while she rounded his position.

Her lithe figure was like a child compared to his massive build. She looked at him in admiration and awe, but that was just a feint. He had observed her in the battle against Grandmaster Nysulu. She was a handful, but how deadly was she without the aid of poison or magic? That was what he intended to discover.

Sess'thra launched herself at Shiverrig with a kick to his midsection. The Duke caught the blow in both hands with ease. He knew something more was coming and was ready when she twisted out of his grip and swept her tail across his calves. His sturdy legs withstood the impact of the blow. His men cheered.

"I like a man with strong legs." She gave him a playful wink.

Shiverrig moved fast to counterstrike. He grabbed Sess'thra's right arm and twisted it around her back. She arched backward and laid her head against the Duke's chest.

"An enticing position," she remarked. Her free hand playfully traveled up his left leg. The Duke pivoted and shot his knee out and down to the backside of Sess'thra's right leg. The move forced her to the mat. Shiverrig followed her down.

Sess'thra folded with the momentum and twisted the two into a roll before hitting the floor. The Duke found himself on his back with Sess'thra's backside lying over him. He involuntarily became aroused with the weight of her body draped over his.

"My, my, my, you are full of surprises," Sess'thra purred.

Don't give in to her tricks. She is just trying to confuse you into making a mistake, he thought. She twisted out of his arm lock and twirled to mount his chest. Her crooked smile returned. Shiverrig grabbed the loose fabric of Sess'thra's vest from behind her back and pulled. The succubus somersaulted acrobatically through the air and landed in a standing position. Shiverrig drew his legs back and leaped to his feet.

Shiverrig rushed Sess'thra. She jumped into the air to avoid his tackle. He caught her by one leg and slammed her back to the floor. He pounced upon her, grabbed her wrists above her head, and held her arms down with his knees. His men cheered again, but he knew the succubus was toying with him. She was making this too easy and enjoying the sexual provocation of her actions.

"Shall I submit here, or would you like to continue this in private? Trust me, I don't mind being watched," Sess'thra spoke loud enough for all to hear. Her tail twitched in the air behind him. A page cleared its young voice.

"My apologies, my lord Shiverrig. I have news from the City of Spires."

Shiverrig swiveled his head to see a page standing in the doorway. His spies had returned. The outcome of this bout could wait. He released Sess'thra and hurried from the sparring chamber.

"Summon Malachi. I'll want his input," Shiverrig said to the page.

"Who's next?" Shiverrig heard the succubus say as he left the room.

Shiverrig went directly to his strategy room. It was perched at the top of a high tower within the main castle walls. A sturdy table sat central to the chamber, with a sheaf of paper, an inkwell with a pen for written decrees, but no chairs. The Duke preferred to stand while deciding the fates of those who fell under his rule.

Ten arched windows, positioned to spiral around the inner wall, added the cleanliness of natural light instead of candles or torches to the room. Somehow it made Shiverrig feel pure when bathed in the outside light.

The city stretched out beneath him. Gethem was the first walled encampment that grew into a town and then into a thriving city. It was the hub of commerce for Baroqia. Ports filled the coastline of Gethem; ships from the Three Kingdoms came with their unique wares, leaving with goods bound for markets beyond.

Gethem bore the gritty marks of its history on every street corner. The city's narrow alleys and bustling markets were often thronged with characters of dubious repute, yet there was an unyielding honesty about them rooted deeply in their proud heritage. Every citizen of Gethem could recount their ancestors back to the original bands of conquerors who had claimed these lands. Such a legacy fostered a fierce loyalty to their own, making them wary of outsiders.

Amidst these imperfections, Shiverrig found a resilient spirit in his city. The populace adhered strictly to the edicts of their Duke, a testament to their enduring allegiance. In Shiverrig's eyes, Gethem deserved to remain the capital of Baroqia, a bastion of tradition and strength. However, the political tides shifted when House Conrad ascended to power, relocating the capital to the more picturesque and affluent city of Qaqal.

The new capital, with its lavish apartments and tranquil views of undulating hills and dense forests, appealed to the sensibilities of the nobility. The elite preferred the sanitized beauty of Qaqal over the industrial soot and labor of Gethem. From their lofty perches, why should the nobles spare a thought for the toil and troubles of those below, as long as their wealth—measured in overflowing coffers of gold and silver—remained untouched by the struggles of the common folk?

"They're all soft," Shiverrig scoffed.

The image of overflowing coffers reminded him of House Conrad's treachery. The nobles had so easily been manipulated with the promise of gold. Damn Maugris and his wayward spell! A storm of passion swirled in Shiverrig's heart.

He turned from the window of the strategy room as Malachi entered with a stocky man named Pathias. Shiverrig had been waiting for weeks for a reliable report from Qaqal. He was concerned about the lack of information flowing to him. "What news, Pathias? Be direct," Shiverrig said without pleasantries.

"King Conrad has decreed Baroqia will take up arms against the North. He will soon call upon the four Great Houses to bring their respective portions of the Five Armies together in Qaqal. The individual armies will be dismantled and consolidate into the newly named King's Army. The king will bestow a temporary title of Second General to you, Lord Fritta, and Duke Manda.

"He will then divide up the armed forces into new legions and grant leadership as he sees fit. Rumors fly that Baron Rokig will be named First General of the King's Army. He will be assigned ten thousand men, mostly coming from the Standing Army of Gethem. I have heard he will order them north and east to secure the outer territories. It is uncertain what roles you and the remaining lords will play."

"Of course, Baron Rokig, the king's lackey. I would expect no less from that spineless sycophant. Continue," Shiverrig said in a calm tone, yet internally the storm in his heart raged with new fury.

"Each Lord will retain a token host at their keep,

enforcing the king's law, although King Conrad will soon demand the presence of the Knights of Gethem in the Capital City to bolster his personal security." Pathias bowed. His report had ended.

"Why now? What has happened to change the king's stance on Maugris in the North?" Shiverrig's mind raced to potential betrayals, and those that might benefit as House Shiverrig grew weaker.

"That is all I presently know, my Duke," Pathias said, bowing once more.

The Duke paced the hard floor of the circular chamber. "He would dismantle my standing army and spread my troops across Baroqia. It is a bold move and one I would not expect Conrad to make on his own." Shiverrig pondered for a moment. "Who is advising the king? He knows I will not surrender my troops as willingly as Baron Rokig."

Malachi walked to a window with his hands clasped behind his back. "This is precisely why he does it. The king will force you to play your hand for power but on his terms. He gathers the kingdom's armies to him in case you strike," Malachi said. "If you agree to his demands, he will bleed your strength slowly. House of Shiverrig will become a frail husk of its former glory. A memory to be scattered in the wind."

"Spare me your poetry, Malachi. It's exactly what I would have done to him if I had the favor of the other Great Houses. But why now?"

"My Duke, you have been rather verbose with your ill-will towards the rule of House Conrad of late," Malachi said. He raised his eyebrows as if this was an obvious statement.

"He's scared," Shiverrig said. "He needs something to solidify his rule. A war would ... "

Sess'thra walked into the strategy room, uninvited, cozying up to Shiverrig. "Your men bore me," she cooed, walking her fingers up the duke's arm. "They break too easily." She winked seductively at Malachi as her hands massaged Shiverrig's bare, muscular arms.

The Duke ignored the remark. He peeled her body off his as if he were removing the slick membrane of a sticky fruit. He was not in the mood for her games. "The timing is not quite right to crush Conrad. I have enough men in key positions within the noble houses, but not enough to sway the balance of power. I cannot strike without the alliance of either Duke Manda or Lord Fritta. I need their men if I wish to hold the throne."

Shiverrig paced across the small chamber.

"I could promise Duke Manda the Baron's lands and its holdings in return for his assistance. It might be enough to sway him. There is no love lost between the two, and he would become the second richest House in Baroqia.

"Lord Fritta has always been a wildcard. I'm not sure where his alliance lies. House Fritta will watch and wait. Of the two, I trust and respect Fritta more. He honors tradition."

The Duke turned to Pathias. "I need to know when Conrad will move his troops against Maugris. Get me the routes of supply lines he intends to run. Have the heavy war engines been mobilized outside the city gates yet? What numbers will he keep in reserve behind the city walls?

"Speak to your brethren inside the walls of Lords Fritta's and Duke Manda's Keeps. See if either will acquiesce to the king's demands or resist. I suspect Duke Manda will go along willingly with the king. His ambitions go no further than the easiest way to fill his coffers with more gold. He will surely finance the war effort, and therefore will follow whatever the king wishes. Also, have your shadow men keep their eyes and ears open for dissenters against our House in Gethem. I want names and family connections."

"Yes, my Duke. It shall be done." Pathias bowed one last time before departing the chamber.

Sess'thra moved in front of the Duke. "Tread lightly, Duke Shiverrig. Now is not the time for heroics and hurt pride. The flow of Maugris' plans must not be interrupted. It would not end well for you to change the outcome of his war."

"I care not for the Mad One's desires," Shiverrig said. He took a step to the side of Sess'thra. "I cannot allow Conrad to continue on this course."

"Then let me say it a different way. My Mistress would be most displeased if you altered the events now set in motion. There are other moving pieces whose success or failure depends on the completion of your tasks." Sess'thra moved back in front of Shiverrig to make sure he fully understood her message.

"Are you threatening me?" Shiverrig's outward calm demeanor evaporated. She stood her ground against his fury, which caused his desire for her to increase. He wanted to break her.

"I am merely stating the obvious consequential events." Sess'thra's alluring stare had him captivated. Shiverrig could not look away.

"My Lord, perhaps we have overlooked an interesting partnership. The influence of the Demigod of Change has brought about a new radial faction called the Cult of Shokuei. They follow the teachings of Mor and are rising in prominence in the outer cities and villages," Malachi said.

"The time of war grows near. It is time to bring your pieces of power to their proper places on the board," Malachi said. "The Cult of Shokuei would be a valuable tool to create unrest from within Qaqal and the outer townships. Their influence could have a profound effect on the nobles backing the king."

Shiverrig turned his head towards Malachi as if hearing him for the first time. Sess'thra grabbed his chin and forced him to look back into her purple eyes.

"You must commit now to the higher ideals of the Ice Queen or choose to be fodder for Lord Oziax's demon horde. And I wouldn't want the latter for my dear Duke." She pressed close to Shiverrig. "The Frost Legion shall soon arrive, and the frigid tide will flow."

"The Shiverrig Clan tamed these lands, and I shall not dishonor my ancestors any longer. The rule of this false king must end. I am the strength and might of the land, not House Conrad." He pressed his finger down on Sess'thra's forehead. "How could you understand such a thing as honor, demon?"

"The concept is not so different, though *honor* has little meaning in the Abyss; power suits the Infernal and Ice Planes better. But do not mistake this idea for mere physical strength. Indeed, cunning and deception are equally vital, serving as the true measures of gaining what one desires."

Shiverrig felt the pliable form of Sess'thra body press forcefully against his. Her figure melted around his body as her arms and hands wandered up his spine. His desire for her rose, and his body responded. Shiverrig saw Sess'thra in a new way. The succubus was wise, and she wanted only to serve her master. He could almost taste her desire on his lips.

"Sess'thra, you have a valid point." Shiverrig turned his head to Malachi. "Send a squad of loyal knights to Qaqal as an honor guard for the king. Make sure they keep me informed. That will be all." Shiverrig looked back to Sess'thra, not bothering to watch Malachi leave the room or caring if he did. He returned her embrace, much to his surprise.

His eyes devoured the succubus, while his mind played through different ways to possess her. She looked up at him, longing for the attention his body promised. "Are you done playing the disparaged son of a twice-dead king? We have unfinished business together."

Sess'thra climbed up Shiverrig's chest and kissed him hard. She bit down on his bottom lip and drew blood.

"You do enjoy tormenting my Archvashim," Shiverrig said when he pulled away from her kiss. He wiped a few drops of fresh blood from his mouth. He lifted Sess'thra's vest over her head and dropped it to the floor. The afternoon sunlight lit her alabaster flesh in warm hues.

Shiverrig devoured her breasts. He barely noticed when she removed his pants or when she removed her own. The Duke swept the contents of the table to the floor. Her legs dangled over the edge when he mounted her.

Sess'thra's nails dug into his back and bit deeply into his shoulder. She bucked under his weight and drove him deeper between her legs as he climaxed. Ecstasy filled his body as he filled her with his seed.

It was soon over. Shiverrig fumbled to collect his clothing. His thoughts were jumbled and hazy as he dressed. Sess'thra slid off the table with a cunning smile on her lips. "I see before me a lordly Duke among the immortals of Gathos. There is strength in you, Gerun Shiverrig. But first, you must bow to the rule of Maugris and the Mistress. Do this, and great power awaits you. The Three Kingdoms of Hanna is only the beginning."

Shiverrig's vision spun. He heard himself talking but wasn't sure of what he was saying. "There is wisdom in your words, Sess'thra. I will honor my arrangement with the North. I will not alter Maugris' timetable." He sounded like a drunken cur. The room seemed to shift with each step he took.

"I'm glad you have come to your senses, my Duke. Now, if you'll excuse me, I have an orange-robed fly to catch." Sess'thra blew Malachi a kiss and strolled lightly out of the room. She didn't bother to dress.

The effects of rutting with Sess'thra wore off soon after

she departed. His mind cleared. "I'll play your game, for now, succubus." Shiverrig knew wars left armies weak and depleted, no matter the victor. He would hold back his elite forces and use the rest sparingly until he was assured of one side's victory over the other. Threats and false promises did not concern him. In the end, ultimate rule would once more belong to House Shiverrig.

18

SEKKA

The strength of a summoning spell—and its subsequent bond of holding over the summoned—adhered to a straightforward tenet; the summoner must always maintain control of the magic. The spell creates a contest of wills between the two opposing forces; one to maintain dominance, the other seeking to escape. No creature, whether infernal, divine, or otherwise desired to be controlled by another. It's the natural way of things.

Maugris was a capable sorcerer, but his strength was finite. He was only mortal, after all. The depth of his spellcraft was shallow when compared with the abilities of an infernal-born devil. Maugris lacked the patience to properly construct spells that were impervious to improvisation or suggestion. His obsessions created mental distractions, which left his spells open to attack from a more advanced spellcaster, such as herself.

She waited until Maugris had depleted both his magical and mental endurance and then stealthily wove thin threads of corrosive magic into the invisible bonds of his binding spell. She patiently exploited minuscule weaknesses in his spell-craft that were unseen by mortal means. Freedom was only a matter of time.

Maugris had ranted and raved that she was twisting the meaning of his commands, and of course, that was precisely what she was doing.

"Let me make this crystal clear. I want the entire Frost Legion, here, in Rachlach Fortress, now! I want my war!" he screamed. He paced the floor of his study with agitation. Her answer was always the same. "Bring me the Ever Hero, and all of Hanna will fall. Until that time, all I can give you are lesser demons. The effort taxes me to my limits."

Sekka feigned exhaustion. She could summon an army of lesser demons if she wanted to, but until the binding spell was broken, they would be under Maugris' control, not hers.

"The Amaranthine Barrier is too strong. I will need the raw energy of ten thousand soul-slaves to bring forth anything bigger."

"Ten thousand? All of the frontier villages combined do not amount to that number!" Maugris screamed.

"Cull your remaining wizards. The magical sacrifice may be enough for another lesser juggernaut such as Morteg." She lied. "Now, I must rest." She lied again.

Whenever Maugris' frustration reached its apex, she slyly tempted him with a bit more knowledge to summon her minions without her assistance. He took it without question, as she knew he would. His lust for power was insatiable.

"I feel no such fatigue," he boasted. "I will summon another demon lord such as Lord Oziax to lead my armies." His attempts failed, as she knew they would. He glared at the Arch Devil. "I want the juggernauts! Bring them!"

"Be patient. The foot soldiers of Gathos will suffice to wage your war," she said with detached interest. "In time you will have enough."

"I will need more than just foot soldiers. Can't you understand I will need the behemoths to bring down the walls of the great cities? Do you know nothing of siege-craft? If you are incapable of doing what I ask on your own, then give me the knowledge I need to do it myself. If you cannot, I will find another who can." His face twisted in a sinister grimace.

Sekka looked deeply into his eyes. He was bluffing. There was no one else ready to take her place as his bondslave. Nonetheless, she was forced to teach him the lore of summoning one of the truly magnificent beasts of Gathos, for it was in her power to do so, and she was still under his yoke.

"There are rules to this game you play, rules which cannot be broken. A portal must remain open long enough to admit a juggernaut, and your wizards to not possess the etheric energy needed for such a duration of time. They will all die in the attempt, as will the summoned giant. A behemoth requires so much more." She shook her head. "It cannot be done."

"Give me what I need!" He screamed.

"I have told you what I need to accomplish what you ask. I warn you, to attempt such a summoning on your own will go badly."

She knew he would still try. She was counting on it. Maugris eventually learned to summon lesser demons and fiends on his own. But the well of eldritch magic he drank from took more than it gave, and his ability to resist her corrosive charm was continually being taxed.

She continued to add buffers and parasitic channels to divert Maugris' magical energy away from the strength of the binding spell. Maugris would not know his plight until it was too late. With any luck, the transition would be so subtle that he would be none the wiser when the shackles of binding finally dissolved—and that was a delicious thought.

. . .

At long last, the day Sekka stole back her freedom had arrived. Maugris and his cabal of wizards would attempt to summon a greater demon from the Gathos. She would ensure that he succeeded this time, but the cost would be high.

Sitting alone in her chambers in deep concentration, Sekka worked through the multiple stages of the incantation one more time. Her counter-spell should work.

If she timed the spell correctly, it would take hold when Maugris was at his weakest. She was taking a big chance. If her spell failed, it could alert Maugris to the true precarious nature of his sorcery. He would naturally reestablish the binding enchantments of his spell and his own magical wards. That would set her back months in her work. She did not have the time to begin again. The counter-spell could also cause her to be self-banished from the Mortal Realm, for she would no longer have a host connection. Returning to Gathos in such a manner would be a painful process that would leave her debilitated. She would be vulnerable to the likes of Zizphander, or worse. But her options were limited —and time was running out.

+Is everything in order, Lord Oziax?+

+Yes, My Queen. I have done as you commanded. I primed the chamber myself.+

+Excellent.+

+I have long anticipated this day. Maugris will learn the folly of his actions. His pain will bleed off him as his blood seeps through his pores.+

+Don't be rash. Maugris still has a role to play. Your time with the mortal will come, but not before I possess the Ever Hero of Aetenos. Am I clear?+

+Yes, my Queen.+

+Very well. Ahh, I feel the beckoning. My time has arrived.+

Sekka's physical form was pulled from her room and materialized in the same spherical chamber that had summoned her from Gathos. The air tasted stale and worn. She hovered in mid-air opposite Maugris. His wizard cabal was already in position in the spaces between the points of the three-dimensional, silver-chain star. The slaves no longer struggled as the drugs took hold of their movements, but still left them entirely coherent for the inevitable pain.

"Does this not bring fond memories, my slave?" Maugris said haughtily. "We have accomplished much together, Sekka, but you have taught me too well."

"You remain the master, Lord Maugris. Your summoning shall be a great accomplishment. Even Lord Oziax will be impressed," Sekka said, playing into his ego as much as she dared.

"I care not for the adoration of that beast. I intend to replace him with a true General. One that will obey my commands without question."

"You cannot mean Lord Narthoth?" She raised her eyebrows in mock surprise.

"The same," Maugris said with a faint smile. "This day shall mark a turning point in my ascendency with the Dark Arts. Nothing shall stand in my way now."

Maugris prepared to cast the taxing spell to summon Lord Narthoth, a Valgothi Warlord whose influence and command in the Frost Legion were rivaled only by Lord Oziax. The timing of her counter-spell would need to be flawless.

Maugris wove his summoning spell, and his strength ebbed away. At the same time, Sekka carefully added the final touches of counter-magic to disrupt his binding spell on her. She laid down one subtle layer after another. Too much, too soon, and Maugris would feel the currents of magic tug against him.

The torches in the chamber grew dim as the arrival of Lord Narthoth sucked the oxygen from the room. The silver chains crisscrossing the chamber shook violently and became blurred in space. The temperature in the room dropped, and the pungent smell of dark magic filled the chamber.

Maugris moved through the final phases of his spell. Sapphire blue runes rose from the silver chains as they should but were then quickly extinguished by indigo sigils of power. The dark sigils drifted down to fuse with the chain. Sekka glanced from the corner of her eye at Maugris. He was none the wiser to her subterfuge. His eyes were closed tight in concentration as he uttered his intricate spell.

A pinprick of light formed in the center of the three-dimensional star. Ice crystals formed a layer of thin frost over the silver chains. The light grew brighter, followed by a wave of force that pinned the wizards against the walls of the chamber.

Lord Narthoth materialized in the center of the star. His roar echoed throughout the chamber. The crisscrossing chains wrapped around his material form and ensnared him in place. The greater demon howled in pain as the silver chains burned his skin. A thick mane of white hair bristled along his back. The knots and braids tied into his hair thrashed back and forth, following the movements of his bat-shaped head. His face contorted with rage. Black, beady eyes glared menacingly at Maugris and his wizard cabal.

Lord Narthoth's dark-blue wings remained furled behind his back, locked in place by the constricting chains. His hind legs, resembling those of a predatory cat, were built for speed. They jerked and stretched, trying to find some invisible purchase in the air. He had powerful shoulders and arms, with multiple protrusions of jagged, ice shards growing from his elbows.

His arms ended in oversized hands tipped with claws meant for rending and tearing. Circling his torso were five smaller arms with crablike pinchers instead of hands, which clacked and snapped in the air. A long tail, ending in tufts of white fur, angrily swished and whipped through the air.

"Lord Narthoth, I am Maugris the Infinite. You will call me Master. I command you to obey me!"

Lord Narthoth flexed his arms and legs against his bindings, but they held tight. He strained to look to the right. His black eyes found Sekka. "You have betrayed your oath!"

Sekka ignored Lord Narthoth's theatrical performance. She cast the final stanza of her spell. Lord Narthoth roared again. He pulled aggressively on the silver chains, but they would not break.

"It is pointless to resist," Maugris boasted. "What hope do you have to break the bonds that have held your queen to my will?"

"She is no longer my queen! I shall destroy her once I have devoured your soul!"

"Your threats are feathers in the wind," Maugris said over the din of clanging chains.

Maugris chanted the final spell that would dissolve the silver into the demon's body, thus binding the demon to his will. But the long chain links did not infuse with the beast.

Lord Narthoth chuckled. He jerked fast on one of the chains that held him in place. It snapped easily. His eyes narrowed, finding Maugris and holding him in check. "Your words do not match your skill, little mage." Lord Narthoth broke the link to another chain, and the long strand fell away from him. "I'm going to enjoy this."

"No, no, no!" Maugris' face distorted in confusion. His cabal of wizards was frozen in fear. Lord Narthoth unwrapped the last of the chains and tossed it away.

The demon's wings unfurled, and with blinding speed, he

pounced on the nearest wizard. A head flew in the air. Lord Narthoth moved quickly to the next. The wizard's wards were no match for the strength and fury of the greater demon.

Maugris screamed out words of power, but he lacked the required energy to give them strength.

"Narthoth the Bleeder comes for you, foolish mortal."

"Sekka! I command you to stop Narthoth!" Maugris wailed in desperation.

The familiar compulsion to obey was absent. She felt nothing. Her counter-spell had worked! She was now as free as Lord Narthoth. She acted quickly, knowing that any hesitation on her part would alert Maugris to what she had achieved. She cast a simple spell at the demon. Sticky web spun from her fingers. Lord Narthoth dissolved the strands with contempt.

"You reek of weakness. Narthoth will devour your essence and rule Gathos!"

"Banish him! He will destroy us all!" Sekka said with as much worry as she could muster. She had to play her part, even at the expense of her pride.

"She cannot help you now." Lord Narthoth shook his head at Maugris. "Your fear is ripe. I can taste it in the air."

Maugris was frantic. He looked left and right with eyes wide from fear. He pushed away from Lord Narthoth. He reached inside his sleeve and hastily threw something small at the demon. Lord Narthoth caught the small object in one hand with amusement.

"A pebble to stop Narthoth?"

"Obliterate!" Maugris cried out.

Lord Narthoth tried to drop the obliteration pearl, but it expanded past his hand and engulfed his entire body. The milky white substance then collapsed upon itself and shrunk to its original size. Lord Narthoth was gone. The pearl fell to the bottom of the chamber with a deafening thud.

Maugris' chest heaved, searching for breath. His wild eyes shifted in every direction before throwing his head back, laughing like a mad man.

"I live!" he exclaimed.

Sekka stared at him in wonder. Maugris' eyes eventually found hers.

"Surprised?"

"Quite so," Sekka admitted.

"I know the deep desires of those who follow me. The temptation to steal my power will always be too great for some, so I remain prepared. I've expected betrayal since your arrival."

"It is no small feat to construct a Pearl of Oblivion," Sekka said.

"Child's play," he sneered. "Let this be a lesson to you, I cannot be defeated." Maugris searched for a reaction. She gave him none. He scowled and reached inside his sleeve again. This time he held a small vial. He popped the stopper and drank the fill of its contents.

He looked about the chamber. "So much wasted." A few moments later, he teleported out of the chamber.

He was a liar. The Pearl of Oblivion must have taken years to create. "Enjoy your small victory." A devious smile crept across her face. The counter-spell had worked, but there was still much to do.

+Lord Oziax. Our time has come.+

19

KASAI

Kasai followed Desdemonia along a deer path that wound its way through the ancient oak trees and sprawling clusters of ferns. The colors of the forest blazed deep purple, bright yellow and vermillion all around him. He tried to recall the events of the previous days. Everything had become murky impressions, rather than distinct images.

A thin branch snapped back and stung him in the face. He looked up and saw the witch standing in front of him, giggling. She then twirled away and ran ahead down the path.

Master Choejor's hand rested upon his shoulder. Kasai was happy he could lend his Master some support. Desdemonia was lost from sight, although Kasai could hear her plain enough as she sang a tune into the heady forest air. The lyrics were unusual and in a foreign tongue unknown to Kasai.

"Why must she be so loud?" he questioned.

Kasai's shoulders slumped. He felt heavy and slow. The intensity of fighting with the vargru had worn off, and his body felt rigid and stiff. He was sore everywhere. His mind drifted to thoughts of his Brothers at Ordu. The family he had left behind, again. All gone. All dead.

"Kasai, I sense you walk with heavy steps," Master Choejor voice was sluggish as he shuffled behind Kasai. Desdemonia's healing magic had given Master Choejor a respite from the pain, but she had said it was only temporary. They needed to get to Gethem before the poison entirely took him.

"I was just thinking about Ordu," Kasai replied. He spotted Desdemonia reappearing on the trail and pranced about like a minstrel entertaining the peasant folk. His head tilted to the side, and after a few moments, he realized he was staring at her. The sun poked through the high branches of the forest in beams of apricot light. She glowed like honey each time she danced through one.

"She should stop singing, or at least lower her voice," Kasai whispered under his breath. "I fear for our safety. What if more of those creatures are lurking in this forest?"

"No, don't ask her to stop. I'm enjoying the song. It reminds me of my homeland. She sings of the jungle during the monsoon."

Kasai shook his head. Was he the only sensible one? He looked ahead and watched Desdemonia curtsy to a stump with two small saplings growing from its roots. She locked her elbow around the shaft of one and circled to the second. She saw him and laughed joyfully.

"Come and join me for a dance!"

He was sure he would do no such thing, turning his attention to Master Choejor. "Is the witch's magic the same as xindu energy?"

"You will find many different powers in the world. Xindu energy is but one. Desdemonia's magic is not the Song of Aetenos, nor the Change of Mor, which draws from darker sources, but the overlap between the two. It comes from the same vast ocean of energy that binds the worlds together.

"It is known by many names. We call it Elemenati magic. The Forest Dwellers refer to it as the Gift of Nayche. Many from the jungle kingdom of the Sunne are high practitioners of this art. Her companion Gauldumor is a fine example of the manifestation of this magic. He was derived from the physical elements of the world we inhabit."

"How can you tell, Master Choejor? Forgive me, but you cannot see the earth golem, can you?" Kasai looked behind him. He saw the lumbering giant keeping pace with the group. It glared back at him and snorted a *humph* of steamy air. The golem's rock eyes bore into Kasai and made him turn away.

"I can smell the old bark that encases his strength, hear the pondering steps that shake the ground. I can taste the decaying leaves and earthy roots that make up his great bulk. The magic within his construct changes the flow of air as he gets close. I can see him well enough. Can you?"

"I don't think he likes me much," Kasai muttered under his breath.

Master Choejor continued, "Those who follow the Way of Nayche believe the essence of their loved ones returns to the goddess when they die. One day they will be born again, or reawakened as they say, such as the life cycle of the golem."

"Is reincarnation real, Master?"

"Who can say? When you are one with the Boundless, all things become possible, in one shape or another. A tree falls in the forest. It decomposes to feed the nearby saplings with nutrients. The vacant space in the canopy lets in the sunshine to warm the leaves of the younger trees below, and so life continues, taking with it a part of the old, fallen tree."

Kasai remained silent. He believed magic of any kind was evil. Now he had been saved by magic and healed by magic—

the embodiment of that power was a dancing gypsy who wouldn't stop winking at him.

"But can *she* be trusted? She is still a witch, after all."

"Trusted? Who knows? Our options are limited now, wouldn't you say?" Master Choejor chuckled. "However, I sense no ill-intent from the young woman. There is no room for evil in a body filled with joy. You must be mindful of deciding the merit of a person based on tired labels or monikers. Each of us has our own story to tell."

"Yes, Master. I will try." Kasai saw Desdemonia walking his way again. The woman could not walk in a straight line.

"Ah, listen to them, Gauldumor. The monks keep so many secrets from us." Desdemonia's voice was filled with laugher. She brushed passed Kasai and marched up to the earth golem like a soldier in the King's army. "We will keep secrets too! And then we can trade them all away by the fire later tonight."

The late afternoon sun was fading. Soon it would be night. Desdemonia skipped and danced along the trail without worry. There was gaiety in each word she spoke, no matter how nonsensical. Kasai wondered at her sanity.

"And perhaps share a few secrets together in private, eh love?" Desdemonia gave Kasai another exaggerated wink and a mock elbow to his side as she danced back ahead of him to lead the party.

"What? No. I mean, who? Why do you keep calling me that?" Kasai stammered through words that made no sense. He couldn't think. If matters weren't troublesome enough, now this forest pixie was teasing him. "Do you have to be so loud? Aren't you fearful of another attack?"

"Here? Now? With Gauldumor raised by our side?" She looked back at Kasai with puzzlement written across her face.

"Doesn't seem like you have much to be afraid of then." Kasai secretly wished he could say the same for himself.

"Oh, to lose my soul to the Deep Dark would be a horror beyond words," Desdemonia replied, "or to die bound and helpless under the cruel whims of another. Demons. Don't like demons either. What else?" She rolled her eyes, looking up to the right. "Hmm ... a bird shitting on your head would be bad. Ya, I know it's supposed to be good luck and all, but when it happens it's a mess to clean."

"But ... isn't Gauldumor ... a ...?"

"What? Is he a creature of darkness? Of course not. Gauldi, he thinks you're a demon!" Kasai flushed in embarrassment. Her hysterical laugher didn't help much either. He looked to Master Choejor for support, but his Master was chuckling along with the witch.

"Gauldumor is a Guardian of the Forest. He has a soul just as much as you or me. His is the essence of the living trees and the flowing rivers, the soft grass underfoot and the fragrant pollens that move through the branches," Desdemonia explained. "He is all of this and more."

"He truly has a soul?" Kasai was still confused.

"Yes, a soul. Don't they teach you anything in monk school? All living creatures have a soul. Now, those prickly demons are different. They don't have one, and that's why they are constantly trying to get ours. But if you know their name, their true and secret name, then you can control them to do your bidding."

"Really?"

Desdemonia's eyes grew wide, and she stared deeply at Kasai. Her hands waved in the air. "Yesssss!" She jumped away and stomped out a different dance and a much louder song, laughing joyfully between verses.

He was sure another pack of vargru would hear her and follow the sound of her voice to their next campsite. They would attack en masse, and not even the earth golem would be enough to hold the creatures back. But in his nineteen years of life, he had never seen hair so thick or black or long. It flowed like an onyx river down her back. He just wanted to touch it.

Desdemonia danced back to Kasai. Her eyes sparkled in the orange half-light, and again he was dazzled and amazed. "You have a riddle in your mind that doesn't know its way out. Am I right, love?"

How did she know? Had she cast a spell? So many unanswered questions and his mind raced to every possible outcome no matter how farfetched.

"Do not call me that. My name is Kasai Ch'ou, all right?" Kasai blurted out. He didn't mean for his words to sound ungrateful or overly blunt, but they did. He took a breath and relaxed. His mind was spinning in circles. "I apologize. You spoke of a safe place. Master Choejor needs rest. Will we be there soon?"

"Soon? We are here now, silly." Desdemonia danced through a well-camouflaged opening in the densely-packed trees. In the clearing stood a small cottage, entirely hidden from sight, meshing naturally with the trees and boulders surrounding it.

20

DESDEMONIA

Desdemonia stood at ease in front of Gauldumor, hands clasping her elbows behind her back. She leaned back and craned her head to meet the creature's eyes.

"The boy has been touched; his destiny no longer his own. The paths of time are in flux with that one," Gauldumor's deep voice rumbled.

"I know, I know. I sensed it too. The monk is on the precipice. His decisions will affect many," Desdemonia added while absentmindedly tracing a pattern in the dirt with her foot.

"Light and Darkness are at war over his soul. He is a prize for each." Gauldumor bent forward and edged in closer to Desdemonia. "He shall face a difficult decision, one that will affect many by its outcome. Return them to the glade where you found them."

"Maybe we can help them?"

"He is not for you. If you value your soul, you will be done with him." He spoke as a parent would do to a carefree child.

"I can't just leave them alone in the forest."

"Then I will end them both while I remain above the soil."

"You'll do no such thing." She pointed her finger at the earth golem and gave him a playful slap under the chin. "You may be right, Gauldi. Time will tell. But for now, we must do what we can to help them. I will lead them out of the forest and away from here."

"You have the stubbornness of your father and the loving heart of your mother. Choose your path carefully, or your fate may follow theirs."

"Thank you, my dear protector and faithful friend." She patted the earth golem lovingly on the chest. "I will be careful. There is something important about this one, even if he doesn't know it yet."

"I tell you again, let them go."

"Without a guide? The old alpha would have them within a day."

"If that is their fate, let it be so." The earth golem raised itself up straight and folded its great arms across its thick chest. "Do not be tempted, child. I have seen that look in your eyes before."

"Stop worrying. I'll be fine."

"Very well. The deep earth beckons me to return. Call, and I shall come. But if you leave this forest, know I can no longer help you."

"I know, I know. Off with ya then, you big oaf."

Desdemonia watched Gauldumor melt back into the fertile forest soil. The earth golem left behind a heap of loam that soon congealed with the mossy brown ground and was gone.

She tied her hair back in a knot behind her head. "It's not the same for you."

"Ouch!"

"Who's there?" Desdemonia spun quickly. It was Kasai.

He stood with a stack of firewood in his arms. One had apparently fallen on his foot. He attempted to pick it up but only succeeded in dropping the rest. He stood dumbfounded, holding a small twig with an awkward, sheepish grin.

"I didn't mean to listen, but well, I was collecting and wood and turned the corner of the cottage," Kasai stammered, looking back the way he came.

He must have heard everything. She walked towards him, and his expression changed from embarrassment to apprehension. He thinks I'm going to turn him into a toad, the poor dear. She couldn't help but laugh.

"Well, Gauldi sure doesn't like you. Don't worry, love, I'll protect you. I'll get you and your father out of the forest. In the meantime, it will be nice to have some company. I've always wanted a kid brother." She patted him on the top of his smooth forehead.

"Kid brother? I am not a child. This is my nineteenth summer, or there about. And I told you, Master Choejor is not my father. He is my mentor and a Master of Ordu." Kasai tossed the twig. He picked up the fallen wood. "I'll have you know the monks of Ordu are renowned and well respected."

"A monk of Ordu, are we? That's nice. Are you coming? I'm starving." She walked inside.

Master Choejor rested quietly on a small cot near the fire. A medium-sized pot rested in a stand above the flame, filled with a stew she started hours ago. The savory smell of the vegetables and herbs from her garden made her mouth water and her stomach growl. Dinner was almost ready. It seemed like a lifetime since the morning's fig halves.

"Have a seat, and I'll serve you a bowl," Desdemonia pointed to a small bench that sat next to a wooden table. Kasai sat down as instructed. Desdemonia returned with two steaming bowls of stew.

"Well, slide over, I'm not eating on the floor," she said as she put both bowls down. She then brought over two wooden spoons and cups filled with water. Kasai slid over and watched her sit down next to him. There was barely enough room for two, and their sides touched.

She felt him stiffen. "Relax. I won't bite," she said. She had to admit she was a bit drawn to the monk. Her pulse quickened as she felt the warmth of his body next to hers. Something was endearing about his awkwardness.

"What were you doing in the middle of the deep forest?" she asked casually between each spoonful of stew. She was almost halfway through her bowl when he decided to answer.

"I ... cannot say," Kasai stared into the steam that rose from his bowl.

"That's right, you monks like your secrets. Don't worry, we all have them. Start eating. It looks like you need a good meal."

Kasai took a tentative sip of the stew. She saw him glance sideways at her.

"Just eat," she said without looking at him.

Kasai did as he was told. He ate quickly and finished before she did.

"Do your parents live nearby?" Kasai said. "How did you learn to make an earth golem. Are there more of you nearby?"

He clearly did not want to talk about himself or why they were running for their lives in the forest.

"My parents are dead." Desdemonia finished her stew and got up from the bench.

"Oh. I'm sorry."

"It happened when I was young ... when we lived together in the forest village of Shryse." At his confused look, she added, "Just outside the jungle basin south of the Sarribe." When he nodded, she continued. "A traveling band of merchants came to our village eager to trade furs and metals for magical items. They had heard of a family in the region that could enchant items and imbue them with special powers." She paused. *Why I am I telling him so much?* "My family was known for such deeds." She busied herself with cleaning her bowl and spoon.

"What happened?" Kasai shifted on the bench to face her.

"When they brought forth their swords and spears, my father told them we were healers, not killers. We honored the land and all living things that were a part of it. He told the merchants he would not enchant their weapons of war.

"We were all relieved when they left. Unfortunately, they returned a week later, at night. They abducted my mother and me and forced my father to enchant their blades. A fight broke out, and other villagers got entangled.

"The merchants were not men of commerce at all. They were a savage band of thieves. When the killing began, it did not stop. My father died protecting my mother and me. We fled together until an arrow found my mother's heart. I alone escaped into the jungle."

Desdemonia stopped talking and went to the pot. She stared into the fire, and absentmindedly used the ladle to stir the stew. "I await now for their awakening. Perhaps if I am lucky, I will find them again in this lifetime."

"When they wake? I don't understand."

Desdemonia turned around with a smile on her face. "I shall tell you more of the jungles of Sunne and the ways of my people in exchange for a kiss!"

Kasai went white as a ghost. "What? No. I'm a monk. I don't kiss."

"You're not a dead monk, are you?" Desdemonia approached him with a sly smile. He was so easy to tease. "You have pretty eyes. Did you know they turn sage green when you are happy?"

"What, what are you doing? Stop. I'm not happy," Kasai said. He was so nervous. That made her want to tease him even more. She pinched his arm hard.

"Ouch! What was that for?" Kasai rubbed his arm.

"Not dead yet," Desdemonia said. She twirled away to wake Master Choejor for some dinner. Her laughter filled the room.

21

KASAI

Strong southern winds blew across the dense forest canopy for the next three days. Old trees creaked as bough and branch swayed in the warm air. Waves of leaves rustled over the heads of the three unlikely companions as columns of sunlight poured into the forest. The bodies of tiny insects flickered in and out of the beams as they drifted aimlessly across the swatches of light.

Kasai and Desdemonia walked side-by-side along a leave covered path with Master Choejor trailing a few steps behind. Kasai was relieved the Master had regained some of his strength. It was the first bit of good news in what seemed like an age of running, fighting, and hiding from danger.

"Why does your earth golem not walk with us? Or is he traveling under our feet?" Kasai minded his steps. He hoped he wasn't offending the golem in any way.

"Gauldi? He's not mine to command," Desdemonia said. She turned to Master Choejor. "Seriously, what do you teach them in that monastery? Doesn't he know anything about anything?"

Kasai wore a broad grin. Now she would hear some tales. She would think twice before calling him a 'kid' again. But Master Choejor only chuckled lightly and said no more. A devilish smile lit Desdemonia's lips while she waited for an answer.

"It's not like that. Master Choejor, tell her. I learned plenty at Ordu."

"Anyways, there's a lagoon fed by an underground hot spring, not a half day's trek from here. The warm water is said to have rejuvenating qualities and will help ease the pain your Master is experiencing. He hides his discomfort well."

"I'll have you know, the monks of Ordu are taught to elevate our minds above physical trauma. Pain is nothing more than a mental illusion; a sensation to experience, observe, and then let pass. A tickle or a slap can be perceived in the same way, depending on the strength of one's mind." Kasai said in somewhat of a haughty voice. "Master Choejor is a Master Monk of Ordu. He is hiding nothing. He has gone beyond the pain."

"If you say so, Mister Special," Desdemonia rolled her eyes.

Kasai didn't care what the witch thought about Ordu, or about him. He was above pain, too, just like his Master.

"Plus, the warm water is ideal for kissing," Desdemonia said with a crooked smile. She proceeded to skip in a circle around Kasai. Kasai's tower of superiority crumbled to the ground. She never once missed an opportunity to provoke him.

"Kissing? With you? Didn't I just say that I am a monk of Ordu?"

How could she be so daft? She frustrated him to no end with all her dancing and laughing and teasing. Couldn't she see he was serious? His world radiated at a higher, more cerebral level. He would not taint his purity of mind and body by succumbing to such a base desire as physical interaction. Even in his head, he sounded like an idiot.

He watched Desdemonia spin in a pirouette. He figured they were roughly the same age, although maybe the witch had seen a few more summers than he, but not many. One moment she was a frolicking gypsy, singing, and prancing without care; the next, she became a warrior druidess of the forest. Kasai didn't know if she was fearless or just crazy, or both.

He concentrated on her image. The glow of her aura surged around her in a wild frenzy of yellows and greens. The streaking colors reminded Kasai of two cats playing together in the grass. One chased the other until it was caught. They tumbled together for a bit, then leaped to their feet and renewed the chase. She was as wild as the forest.

He focused on her more intently to test his newly discovered inner sight. A mandala of complex organic shapes and colors spiraled above Desdemonia's head. He saw the purity of nature in symbolic form. Master Choejor was right about her. She was not an enemy.

Desdemonia also possessed high levels of fire xindu. Kasai didn't need any special skills to see that aspect of the witch. But as he looked deeper, he saw something else.

"Water xindu?" He tilted his head to the side. The two energies clashed together like the rapids of a fiery river. But there was an odd sense of harmony to how they flowed.

Desdemonia was passionate, but unlike Daku, her heart was filled with tenderness rather than cruelty. At least Kasai hoped so. He couldn't figure her out. Daku, Desdemonia, who's next? *Why do I always attract crazy people?*

Kasai thought of Daku. *What happened?* It still seemed impossible to imagine. *How could he?* Kasai pushed the horrible thoughts from his mind. He would sift through them all later, once Master Choejor was safe in Gethem.

Eventually, Desdemonia's lagoon came into view. The path curved, and now they walked parallel to the steaming water. Kasai heard small waves lapping up against a hidden shore. There was a distinct smell of salt in the air.

"This spot will do. We will make camp here," Desdemonia said. "Master Choejor, I have something for you that I took from my home. Perhaps it will ease some of your pain." She handed him a small vial filled with dark liquid.

"I told you he is a Master Monk of Ordu," Kasai interjected. "Hey, stop that. What are you doing? He doesn't need that."

"Thank you, sweet child. I appreciate your kindness," Master Choejor said. He took a sniff of the contents and scrunched his nose. "Mm...valerian root. It will certainly let me rest."

"Why won't you listen to me? I know what is best for Master Choejor."

Desdemonia gave Kasai a triumphant smirk. He just dismissed her with a shake of his head. She annoyed him to no end but would not engage in another one of her games.

"Fine. I'll get the camp set up." He removed the bowl and some herbs from his travel bag. Once he made a small fire, he would fix Master Choejor a proper tea.

"I'll scout ahead and make sure we are alone," Desdemonia said.

Ninziz-zida whispered to Kasai in strange tongues. It sounded more like the buzz of a horsefly. And like the pest, its message was incessant, shapeless, and had no meaning. Its only purpose was to ensure one knew it was there. Kasai massaged his temples. His head had not stopped hurting since taking Ninziz-zida from the Hall of Artifacts. He took the staff from his sash and held it before him.

"What do you want from me?" he said. He didn't expect the ancient weapon to answer. But maybe the buzzing could stop. He laid Ninziz-zida down upon a smooth boulder across the campsite. A little separation couldn't hurt.

Desdemonia called to him from further down the path. She didn't sound like she was in any danger, but she was undoubtedly a troublemaker. Kasai got up and obediently followed the direction of her voice. He marveled at the different colors and sounds he encountered along the forest path. There were incredible amounts of life here. Soon enough, he saw her close to the water's edge.

"It's about time. Come on, let's go for a swim," Desdemonia said. She shed her clothing down to her undergarments. She ran into the water and within moments was waist-deep in the hot pool.

"What are you waiting for? The water's perfect."

Kasai immediately looked away. "I don't think that's a good idea, Desdemonia. I need to watch over Master Choejor." He tried to quell the rapid thumping in his chest.

"You said yourself he's a Master Monk of Orduuuuuu. I'm sure he can take care of himself. And it's Des."

"What?"

"Call me Des. Desdemonia is so formal, especially if you are planning on saying sweet things to me in the water." Her laughter filled the air. The playful gypsy had returned.

Kasai watched her wade further into the dark water as the rising steam swirled in the wake of her body. He stood there like a statue, bewildered and fascinated.

He should say something witty in reply. A clever gibe to show her he was already two steps ahead of her. If she wanted to play games, he would show her some real skills.

"Now you're all wet and … I like being umm, dry. I think I hear Master Choejor calling me." He sulked disheartened back to the campsite. Why couldn't he just keep his mouth shut?

Kasai plopped down on his haunches. What a fool. He looked at the lagoon through the trees. There was something in the rock wall across the steaming water. It was some kind of dark grotto, as best as he could reckon. A thunderous waterfall dumped a steady supply of mountain water to its right.

Kasai turned to hand his Master Choejor some hot tea and found him already asleep. He was propped against a weathered stump, napping peacefully. The vial of valerian root was empty. That was good. Master Choejor needed as much rest as he could get.

Perhaps he should trust her more. Master Choejor seemed to be at ease with the witch. Kasai looked back at the water. Desdemonia had turned right and walked across his line of sight. She stopped and arched backward. Her chest and breasts rose into the air as she submerged the back of her head into the warm water.

Kasai's insides lurched. He quickly averted his eyes, but peeked again, nonetheless. She squeezed the water from her hair. She looked back at the shoreline, shrugged her shoulders, and dove into the steaming water.

He scolded himself for being unfriendly and disrespectful, if he was honest, for his cowardice as well. Who wouldn't jump at this opportunity? He glanced back and saw Desdemonia wading deeper into the lagoon. "What's wrong with me. I like swimming," Kasai grumbled as his heart thumped like a caged beast inside his chest. She was unlike anyone he had ever met before. He allowed himself a small chuckle. "As if you are some sort of expert on women."

The noon sun towered overhead. Kasai wondered why no birds flew in the sky. "Come to think of it. I don't hear any chirping, either." He feared the vargru had found them again. He caught a glimpse of a sharp sparkle at the edge of the ridge where the waterfall started its plunge. Kasai looked more closely, but whatever was there was now gone.

His senses remained alert. Something was not right with this lagoon, and he looked to the water. The pool was empty. An uneasy feeling crept up Kasai's spine. Where was Desdemonia?

He heard a chorus of unearthly howls. He stood up to get a better vantage of the cliff wall. Three dark blurs dropped from the cliff's edge and splashed into the water. Desdemonia finally resurfaced, but she was unaware of what had entered the lagoon.

She bobbed up and down for a moment and scanned the shoreline. Kasai knew she was searching for him. Three giants broke through the mist behind her. Two of them waded towards her while the third dove under the water. Kasai realized the sound of the waterfall masked their approach.

She continued to play in the water, blind to the approaching danger. He needed to warn her. Kasai raced to the clearing where she had entered the lagoon. He reached for Ninziz-zida. Gone! He had left the Fire Serpent at the camp.

"Stupid!" He panicked and began waving and pointing frantically behind her. Desdemonia waved back. She was still trying to coerce him to join her.

Kasai finally saw the recognition of danger in her face. She spun around as the giants closed in on her. Kasai took a few steps into the water. An image of a snarling vargru came to mind. He needed the staff.

"Stupid, stupid, stupid!" He raced back to the camp to retrieve Ninziz-zida.

Kasai heard Desdemonia chanting. It sounded like water

splashing against the walls of a box. Through the trees, he saw her point at the lead giant, and a watery column enveloped its maligned body. The giant frantically pushed the water away from its face, but he couldn't escape. Its movement slowed, and it sunk beneath the surface.

"One down," he said when he reached the camp. Master Choejor was snoring peacefully. Kasai didn't know how long the effects of the potion would last, and he doubted he could wake the Master if he tried. He quickly decided Master Choejor was safe for now.

Where was Gauldumor? Kasai wondered. They would need the earth golem's strength.

Kasai snatched up Ninziz-zida, and the three-sectioned staff felt warm and reassuring in his grip. The buzzing sound he usually heard coming from the staff shifted in his mind. Kasai pieced together its message.

'You need only me.'

A piercing yowl came from the direction of the water, and Kasai sprinted back to the entrance of the lagoon. He heard Desdemonia begin the chant a second time. When he reached the clearing, he stabbed Ninziz-zida in the soft soil. Kasai tore off his outer robe and kicked away his sandals. The loose clothing would only slow him down in the water.

He picked up the Fire Serpent, and the staff ached for battle. Kasai waded into the steaming water with Ninziz-zida held above his head.

The second giant came fast. It howled and snarled and beat its chest, but Desdemonia remained calm and sized up her next target. Bright blue sigils of power fanned out behind her back. The swirling patterns pushed the steam away as they spun.

Desdemonia raised her arm to cast her next spell. The water erupted behind her. The third giant finally surfaced.

His massive hands grabbed her, pinning her arms to her sides. The blue sigils of power vanished along with her spell.

"That was my brother, witch!" said the giant as it drove forward in the water. He finally reached her and grabbed her by the throat. "No more magic from you!"

He was a brutish thing with scar tissue crisscrossing his face and arms. He lifted her in the air as if she were a child. The giant brought her head close to his own. His swollen tongue lolled out of a black-toothed mouth, and he slathered her in grey mucus from cheek to mouth. "Not that we care, right, Ruffo?"

"The more for the two of us, eh?" Ruffo said. He continued to hold Desdemonia's arms tight. He had filthy red hair that was packed together in long ropey coils.

Desdemonia's body was full of storm and defiance. She kicked the giant facing her in the stomach. He doubled over. Ruffo twisted her in the air and dunked her under the water.

Kasai was moving too slow. The water deepened, and he could no longer walk on the soft bottom. He tucked Ninzizzida under one arm and swam on his side. The red-headed man-beast dragged Desdemonia back towards the cave as she struggled to the surface for air. The giants roared with laughter as Ruffo dunked her again. Kasai fretted he would not reach her in time.

Ruffo pulled her up again. "I like the feisty ones. Better for sport."

The second giant with the scarred body struck Desdemonia with a powerful backhand across the face. Water sprayed across the lagoon from the impact of the blow. Desdemonia's body sagged lifelessly in the giant's mighty hands. "She be easy now."

"We fuck, and then we eat," Ruffo said. "You finally taste forest witch."

"I'm first this time!" The scarred giant pleaded.

Kasai's heart filled with equal measures of despair and fury as the giants carried her towards the cave. Luckily, they had not seen him through the mist. He followed as best he could, but he could not keep up with their long strides. They quickly outpaced him and disappeared into the entrance of the cave.

Kasai hated himself for being unprepared. Ninziz-zida whispered something that felt like a reprimand for being left behind. He tried to tune out the staff's clamor in his mind. Finally, his feet hit the soft bottom again. He tucked Ninziz-zida into his sash and rushed out of the water.

The low bank on the far side of the lagoon was easy enough to climb. His eyes stung from the saltwater, but the smell outside the cave was worse. It almost made him faint. Bones and offal littered the ground. Rats gnawed on the scraps of what must have been the leftovers of a recent kill. Kasai put his hand over his mouth and nose and ran into the cave.

Mold, mildew, and some other kind of shiny matter was splashed against the inner walls of the entrance. Blood? Urine? It was difficult to discern. The light became scarce as he ran deeper into the cave. Then he noticed a glow coming from the staff. He looked more closely and saw tiny red flames rippled along Ninziz-zida's surface. The fire moved over his hand as if he was part of the staff. He was alarmed at first, but he didn't feel any pain.

"Please don't possess me," Kasai said with apprehension, but he kept moving.

He heard bestial howls echoing from the darkness. When he rounded a corner, he saw flickering light slapping against a far rock wall. He approached the next bend and cautiously peered around the corner.

The two giants leaped across a blazing fire while hollering and shoving each other in a jubilant and primitive dance. They were naked and sullied, one slightly larger than the other. The lagoon water did little to wash the filth from their malformed bodies. They had coarse hair of red and black that resembled a horse's mane, filled with dirt, twigs, and Aetenos knows what else.

They grappled together. Ruffo howled in delight when one knocked the other down. He waved his hard member at the scarred giant on the cavern floor, but then swiveled in the direction of Desdemonia. She laid on the ground with her wrists bound behind her back. A filthy rag was stuffed in her mouth.

Was she unconscious? Dead? There were soiled knives strewn all about the cavern floor. He couldn't tell if she had been cut or not. It was too difficult to see from this vantage point.

"I'm going to have to kill them," Kasai realized. He knew offensive strikes, of course, but had spent his time mastering more the defensive forms which focused on protecting the people around him.

But now he was alone, and his defensive skills would not be enough to save Desdemonia. He cycled through the few hit to kill strikes he knew. They didn't seem to be enough against such large foes.

Ninziz-zida twitched in his hand as if insulted by his thoughts. Kasai looked down at the Fire Serpent in wonder. A warm glow washed up his arms, and the mysterious voice in his head became singular and focused. Images of fighting positions and angles of attack rolled through his mind.

He felt Ninziz-zida request access to his fire xindu as one friend might ask another for a favor. It purred to him with a promise of partnership, not possession. Kasai acquiesced to the Fire Serpent's desire. What choice did he have? Desdemonia was doomed if he didn't act quickly.

Summoning his fire xindu, Kasai channeled it into the

staff. The slow ripples of flame on Ninziz-zida segments began to grow. Miraculously, the fire still did not burn him.

'Together,' Ninziz-zida sent into Kasai's mind.

Kasai nodded. "I understand. You shall strike, I shall defend. Together we will be whole." Kasai gripped Ninziz-zida's segments tightly and slipped into the giant's lair. He spun one of Ninziz-zida's outer sections in a glowing figure-eight pattern while the other part whipped back and forth across his waist. The giants were startled for a moment, then jumped to attack.

Ruffo, with the mangy red mane, came first. The giant unwisely grabbed Ninziz-zida's outer segment, and flames blazed across his hand and forearm. Ruffo's high-pitched scream filled the small cavern. He desperately tried to douse the fire.

Ninziz-zida connected itself into a straight staff. Kasai thrust forward and impaled the end into Ruffo's chest. Kasai pulled the staff back, and Ninziz-zida split back into three sections. The motion was fluid and exact as if Kasai and Ninziz-zida shared the same thought. Ruffo sank to the cavern floor, burning.

The black-haired giant with a scarred face grabbed a spear with a barbed head. He cautiously circled to the left, pushing Kasai in the opposite direction and away from the lair's entrance. Kasai carefully stepped over Ruffo's smoldering body. Ninziz-zida blazed in his hands. Too late, Kasai realized the giant was not dead.

Ruffo grabbed at Kasai's ankle. He missed but succeeded in tangling Kasai's legs with his arm. Kasai fell to the floor. Dust and dirt blinded him. He rolled quickly onto his back and tried desperately to push away from Ruffo.

The scarred giant howled in glee. He raced forward and tried to jab Kasai with his spear. Kasai rolled to one side and avoided the blow. The spear point scrapped against the ground and sent chips of stone into the air.

The giant stepped over Kasai's body. This time he aimed carefully. He raised the spear in two hands over his head. Kasai's luck had run out. In this position, Ninziz-zida could not hope to stop such a mighty blow.

The giant stopped mid-thrust. Something had locked up his muscles and shoved him forward a step. His torso vibrated unnaturally. Large, white bumps boiled up from his skin until they burst.

The giant screamed in agony when his midsection burst. The two halves of his body fell to the cavern floor. Kasai was amazed to see Master Choejor's standing where the giant once stood. His outstretched hand vibrated with shimmering, white energy. Ruffo tried to rise, but fell back to the floor, dead.

"Master Choejor! I thought you were asleep. How did you…"

"One does not become a Master of Ordu by sleeping with both eyes closed." The smile on his lips was short-lived as Master Choejor sank to his hands and knees. Blood vomited from his mouth.

"We must be on our way to Gethem," Master Choejor gasped between fits of coughing and spitting up phlegm. "I will be fine. Tend to Desdemonia."

"Desdemonia, Desdemonia, wake up. Are you hurt?" Kasai unbound her wrists and removed the dirty cloth from her mouth. He gently rocked her awake until she opened her eyes, sleepily taking in the new environment. She rested her eyes on Kasai.

"Hello, Handsome." Her smile returned, and she propped herself up on an elbow. For once, Kasai was relieved to hear her playful banter.

A faint voice came from the back of the lair. "Help me."

Kasai grabbed a torch from the wall and followed the sound of the voice. The cavern sloped into a curving tunnel that opened to a second, smaller area, where Kasai found a little person chained to a rock. At first, Kasai mistakenly thought she was just a young girl. She was huddled next to a group of dead pilgrims. The stench of the decomposing bodies was unbearable. The pilgrims wore the clothes of priestesses of the Immortal Mother.

"Please, please, help me," she cried, her dirty face streaked with tears. Magenta-hued eyes the shape of thin almonds slanted upwards at the corners, like the tips of thorns.

Kasai nodded. He looked around to find something to unlock the chains. Off to the side, he saw a weathered chest. Inside were odd blades, bones, some coin and luckily, a set of rusted keys.

"I've found someone. She needs help."

Kasai unlocked the heavy shackles and helped the young priestess to her feet. Her unnaturally pale skin and was in sharp contrast to her jet-black hair, which she wore in a style he'd not seen before. Her bone straight hair was cut sharply across her forehead, falling like a curtain to just above her shoulders where it ended like a solid wall.

"Oh, thank you. Thank you," she whimpered. "They were horrors. I had given up all hope. They … they were going to … going to …" She broke down, shuddering as more tears streaked her face. She swooned, and Kasai caught her. She clung to him while heavy sobs racked her small body.

"Shh, shh, you're safe now. You have nothing more to fear from them. My name is Kasai."

"Thank you, Kasai." She looked at him with thoughtful eyes. "I like your name, Kasai. I am Reese."

Kasai gently pushed her away though she was reluctant to let go.

"What happened to you?" he asked.

"We were on pilgrimage ... to the Temple of Illumination and ... Shrine of the Immortal Mother... Pray for the coming ... of the Ever Hero ... peace in the land."

Reese could barely speak. She was still in shock. Superficial scratches and cuts covered her body; fortunately, nothing was broken.

Reese looked to the bodies of the other pilgrims and wept again. Kasai wasn't sure how to act. When he patted her on the shoulder, she wrapped unnaturally strong arms around his torso. She was unnaturally strong for such a young woman.

"Kasai, what's happening? Who's there with you? You need to come back," Desdemonia called out. She limped to the back of the cave. "Master Choejor is not well."

Kasai set Reese aside and ran to Master Choejor. He was on his back with blood coating his mouth, and his breath came in shallow gasps.

"Can you help him?" Kasai looked imploringly at Desdemonia.

"Not here. I have no components to use. We need to get him back to my home."

"He won't make it," Kasai said. Reese had followed them and knelt next to the old monk.

"Let me try," Reese said. The light of the central fire revealed more of her features. Kasai thought he saw something familiar about the young priestess. He couldn't quite put his finger on it, though. She had the vague appearance of someone he remembered from a dream.

Reese whispered strange words over Master Choejor's body as she reached out and grabbed Kasai's hand. An oddly shaped ring was wrapped around her index finger that was black as night. She placed her other hand over Master Choejor's head, and Kasai momentarily lost his balance, but his vertigo left him as quickly as it had arrived.

Kasai looked at Desdemonia for an answer to his curious instability. Maybe it was some form of magic she recognized. Desdemonia shrugged her shoulders. She watched Reese with suspicious eyes. Master Choejor coughed once more, and then his face softened. His breathing became less erratic and calm.

Reese brought the side of her head over Master Choejor's mouth and nose to listen to his breathing. She whispered strange words close to his mouth. Desdemonia wedged herself between the priestess and Master Choejor and wiped the blood from his mouth. "I can take it from here."

"He will be all right, but needs rest," Reese explained. She rocked back on her heels. "The Immortal Mother provides and has granted him her favor."

Kasai was filled with relief. "We travel to the Temple of Illumination as well. The Monastery of Ordu has been attacked, and we must alert Grandmaster Nysulu before the other monasteries fall to the same fate. Master Choejor has been poisoned. Only the High Healers can save him now." The words tumbled out of Kasai's mouth.

"Kasai, you say too much! We don't know anything about her," Desdemonia said. She took an aggressive step towards Reese. "Who are you? You say you're a priestess? What denomination of the Immortal Mother do you follow? Your clothing doesn't look like it fits you well. Why were you saved and not the others?"

Reese fled behind Kasai's back. She held tight to the fabric of his vest with her small, shaking hands.

"Desdemonia, she saved Master Choejor. That is enough to know for now. Leave her be. We can help her reach Gethem." Kasai turned around to face Reese. Her magenta eyes glistened with fear.

"You may join us to Gethem if you like," he said. Reese nodded, seeming happy with the pronouncement happily.

She glanced at Desdemonia for her reaction, not quite meeting her eyes. Kasai attributed it to shyness. "We'll stay here the night and then be on our way in the morning," Kasai said.

"I'll take first watch," Desdemonia said. She turned in a huff to the tunnel exit.

22

SHIVERRIG

"Pathias, what have you learned? Be quick," Shiverrig inquired of his man. They spoke in hushed tones while walking through the King's Palace in Qaqal.

"My shadow men within the Great Houses have been activated."

"Good, good. And the scouting reports of enemy strength and movement?"

"All altered before reaching Baron Rokig. The majority of the scouts used by the Crown were trained in Gethem. Tradition has its rewards, lord," Pathias said.

"Excellent work, Pathias. The king is desperate for a victory. He will blindly blunder along until he trips into his own coffin. All we have to do is keep the lid open."

They reached a door with two guards on either side of the entrance. "It won't be long now. Have Malachi send word to the North."

"Yes, my lord." Pathias bowed and walked away.

Shiverrig eyed the guards. Each bowed in deference as he pushed passed them and entered the King's War Council.

"Is he insane? He does this on the eve of declaring war?"

Shiverrig's voice bellowed into the room. Lord Fritta, Duke Manda, and the king's lackey, Baron Rokig, were already present. King Conrad had yet to arrive.

Shiverrig took the last remaining seat on the side of a magnificent marble table in the center of the room. A grand map of the Three Kingdoms of Hanna was laid over its smooth surface. Figurines had been neatly placed, showing dispositions of armies. Rokig was busy adjusting the placement of auxiliary troops while pontificating to the others of his vast military knowledge and experience. The man had never taken up a sword and shield against a real enemy in his life.

What did any of these fools know about warfare? All he saw were children playing war games with toys on a map. Out of the bunch, maybe Fritta had a decent mind for battle. But the others, especially the king, were products of pretend military tours at the Last Garrison.

Shiverrig took in the contents of the room. Ceiling-to-floor banners lined the walls. Each depicted an act of bravery and courage from a historic event in the development of the realm. He expected to see scions of House Shiverrig commanding troops or vanquishing foes. But instead, the dominant persona had been changed to an insignificant family member of House Conrad. All lies! The actual history of the realm had been rewritten in one generation.

"The function of the Five Armies has always been to keep power spread out amongst the Lords of the Realm," Shiverrig said. "No Great House should have absolute control over the others. It has been this way from the very beginning. The Crown must have a counterweight to keep it balanced."

Fritta and Manda sat at opposite sides of the long table. Fritta's arms were crossed against his chest. He nodded his head in agreement with Shiverrig's pronouncement but said nothing more. The king's proclamation would become a death sentence to anyone opposing the Crown.

Manda sat back in his chair with a leather-bound ledger tucked under his arm. Sorting through the contents of a fruit plate to his left, he plucked a handful of plump, purple grapes, and tossed them past garishly colored lips, one after another. He seemed unconcerned who controlled the Five Armies or if a new King's Army was formed. Shiverrig had expected as much from Manda. His family's influence in the court had been established through their extensive mercantile holdings. He wasn't a military leader, nor had ambitions to be one. He let others run campaigns, preferring to finance them. He was only concerned about the interest he was able to charge on his way to a tidy profit, and of course, debt repayment. War was good for business .ii his business.

King Conrad finally arrived. His crown still sloped on his narrow forehead. He was flanked by his son, Prince Dane, a boy in his sixteenth year, and Baron Rokig to the right. Rokig had eschewed his family's coat-of-arms and wore in the livery of House Conrad. He pinned unearned medals of honor to the oversized lapel of his jacket. He was a grand image of a heroic general of old. None of it was true.

"Desperate times call for desperate measures, Duke Shiverrig," Conrad said. "The realm requires a stable and merciful king to lead during times of fire and sorrow."

"One king, one rule, sire," Rokig affirmed, his sycophant's voice unable to be syrupier.

"You are all here as my Generals, yet only one can lead the realm's forces to victory," Conrad said.

"And who might that lord be? Rokig?" Shiverrig pointed first to the opportunistic man who married into wealth, and then across the king to his son. "Or, perhaps Prince Dane? A boy with no practical experience in warfare, whose family now holds the throne due to the criminal trickery of a disingenuous grandfather?"

"Hold your tongue, Shiverrig. You are here at my sufferance and out of the respect that is due to your family's contribution to the kingdom—not because of you. You became obsolete the day your father died."

"You dare!"

"I am the king. I will dare as much as I like. You will do as you are told. Know your place and be grateful you still have a position at this table."

"Gerun, hold your tongue. Let us hear the king's strategy. Perhaps it is sound," Fritta soothed, his tone fatherly. He was the eddy that calmed the storm waters before they reached the harbor. His deep-set eyes pointed out the additional guards behind Shiverrig.

Shiverrig stood defiantly. "Speak then."

He knew he was risking much the more he baited Conrad. He would show the other lords present he would not be dismissed so easily. Conrad waved Rokig to begin.

Rokig glowered at Shiverrig at the insult to his honor. He pointed to the map. "As you can see, our forces greatly outnumber anything the North can muster."

Rokig then placed a large figurine across the northern mountain range on the map. "Maugris will descend the Hoarfrost Mountains via Storm Wind Pass. The King's Army will be waiting for him at the Grassland Plains just outside the Last Garrison. The might of our full military on display will convince Maugris of the futility of an invasion into Baroqia."

"You feel superior numbers alone will destroy the enemy's morale," Shiverrig said. His brows lowered and knit together in consternation.

"I do," Rokig said. "If they do not break immediately, we shall rush Maugris' army of ragtag barbarians, overwhelm them and break their will to fight. The barbarians will drop their weapons and flee the field. They have no spirit for war. They came only for easy plunder, not to die. Maugris will see his forces scattered and will withdraw back to Rachlach Fortress. I'd wager he sues for peace within a fortnight.

"The king shall allow Maugris and what is left of his meager army passage back to the north. A war reparations tax will be levied, and Maugris will be forever bled of resources."

Rokig made a point to look squarely into Shiverrig's eyes. "In this way, the king wins a decisive victory without the spill of Baroqian blood. This is warfare at a more intellectual and humane level."

Rokig took his place once more to the side of the king. He raised his brows in an expression of superiority and challenge like the arrogant peacock he was.

Shiverrig approached the table. He snatched up a figurine representing a block of enemy troops and rattled it in his palm. "The king's strategy is weak. It affords the enemy multiple avenues of escape. They will not retreat, but to regroup in numbers and attack our forces from unprotected sides."

Shiverrig placed the piece in his hand down and moved other figurines into new positions across the map. "You underestimate the resolve of what lurks in the North."

Manda was bored. Fritta, however, gave a slight nod of understanding. However, Conrad was a simpleton and could not see three steps ahead of himself. Rokig scoffed at the new placement of the figurines.

"The Crown has gathered enough information to validate our strategy. We will be more than prepared for whatever the North sends into battle," Rokig said.

"This will not be a ragtag group of barbarian tribesmen looking to fill their pockets with some Southland trinkets. It will be an army created by a maligned sorcerer intent on destroying all of Baroqia," Shiverrig declared.

"Shiverrig," Rokig rolled his eyes.

"My king, there are vast poppy fields ready for harvest along the lower hills of the Hoarfrost. The cotton fields that extend into the plains are also ripe. Storm Wind Pass lies but a day's journey north," Manda said.

"I see. It will be unfavorable to lose those crops due to the ravages of an invading army," Conrad said. A tinge of worry coated his words.

"Quite so. Last year's harvest came in three percent below the year before. Many nobles have tied their debt payment to this year's harvest," Manda said. He took the ledger from under his arm. He turned a few pages to confirm his analysis. "The pageantry of war will benefit your current acceptance rate with the Lesser Houses, but the destruction of the land and its valuable crop yields will cause irreparable harm to your reputation as a qualified leader during times of strife."

He shrugged his shoulders. "The scions of House Shiverrig have always been known as the War Kings. If it's a war you want to win, give the command to Shiverrig. The percentages of victory, and a safe harvest, more than triple in his favor."

"Finally, Manda, you have contributed something of value," Shiverrig said. Manda pursed his lips in a childish expression.

Rokig was quick to interject. "My king, the royal mages have assured me there is nothing to fear from the Mad Magician. They have the means of canceling his corrupt magic. He will be contained. The harvest will be safe."

Fritta cleared his throat. "Sire, with all due respect to the Crown, your strategy promotes participation in a war but not one that will lead to ultimate victory. Even if you win here, the conflict will persist, and your enemy will return. Our aim here is to end the threat from the North, is it not?"

Fritta's statement was true to form. He was a rock, never moved by emotion. Like Shiverrig, he was a man of the realm. Baroqia came first, its ruler's ego second. Fritta saw through the frill and concentrated on the real objective.

"Lord Fritta is correct!" Shiverrig jumped to confirm the typically taciturn lord's assessment. "This time, Maugris must be destroyed. Banishment gave him time to lick his wounds and recover. Now he is back with a greater force.

"And if the Knights of Gethem are to be used in battle, they will be used to ensure victory. The king's strategy is flawed. I will not sacrifice my men in a battle that will never be won. Such an ill-conceived plan must have come from you, Rokig. You will race forward-thinking victory is assured just as Maugris' trap snaps shut." Shiverrig gave Fritta a warrior's nod. Perhaps he had found the partnership he needed to topple Conrad.

"They are not *your* men, Duke Shiverrig. They are men of the realm, and therefore, my men," King Conrad said. "And neither Baron Rokig nor Prince Dane will be at the head of the King's Army. It will be me."

"You?" Shiverrig said. "That is interesting."

Shiverrig looked back to the map and the figurines. "Very interesting, indeed. I suggest we place regiments of infantry and spearmen here, here, and here. Fritta's ballista will be moved to the hills to the right and left. Their range will hold the enemy war machines back. Our archers will stall the enemy's ground advancement. Depending on how Maugris brings his troops to battle, we can remain flexible with our own infantry's position."

He placed the figurines that represented the fighting forces of Baroqia on the map. The combined infantry of House Fritta, House Manda, and House Rokig will engage the enemy with sword and spear. I will lead a division of cavalry behind Maugris' forces and cut off his retreat, here.

"Send the conscripts forward as fodder to draw the enemy into the range of the archers and ballista. Hope that Maugris' inexperience in large terrain warfare compels him to commit his cavalry too early. He will run them into the waiting tips of our spear men's lances."

Fritta nodded favorably. "The regiments attack from three sides, merge as one and connect with the cavalry division. We do not allow for an enemy retreat."

"That's right. We cut them down to the last man. Then, we regroup to reassess our strength. In short order, we march on his lair. This time, we uproot the vile weed once and for all."

"All very impressive, if not a bit of overkill. Baroqian soldiers will die in this type of exchange, which is not to my liking," King Conrad said. "I have a hunch there will be no need to fight, and I like my hunch."

Baron Rokig chuckled at the king's remark, but Fritta held a concerned expression. Shiverrig caught him shake his head disapprovingly. It was just a small gesture, but it was there.

"Sire, maybe we should at least consider Shiverrig's ideas. If on the odd chance Maugris does something unexpected, it would be well to have our forces properly positioned."

The king studied the players and their positions on the map. "Yes, yes, of course. Shiverrig's plan has some merit, but there are obvious holes and details to be worked out. If his strategy is accepted, then it will be me leading the cavalry. The king shall cut the head from the beast."

Rokig pondered the placement of Shiverrig's figurines with a critical eye. "What great force do you believe Maugris to possess? You plan for war beyond the means of an outcast magician. He has been holed up in his mountain fortress for years. He is a recluse. What army could he possibly muster? The Northern Tribes present no threat. They are wanderers with hardly a scrap of military training or discipline."

Shiverrig shook his head. "Declaring war on Maugris is not the same as inviting him to a county fair where the jousting matches are fixed with collapsible lances. The duels will not be fought with blunt, wooden weapons. We must prepare for every possible scenario."

Rokig continued to press Shiverrig. "You are forcing a fight that could easily be avoided. If the battle is over too quickly, you will be denied glory through bloodshed. Is that what you fear, or is it something else? If you know something more, I suggest you share it."

Shiverrig held his tongue. He was busy calculating potential numbers of wounded and dead on either side. He considered areas of terrain for positional advantage or disadvantage. He was keen to predict where the killing fields of battle would form. He would direct their position as much as possible.

King Conrad would lead them all to ultimate ruin, and Shiverrig couldn't have been happier. Battle was an unpredictable thing. When the killing began, even the most experienced fighter could lose their ability to think and reason. Accidents were plentiful.

When the smoke cleared, who could know the reason a rogue arrow, a spooked horse, or misguided round from friendly ballista fire found Conrad instead of the enemy? The battlefield offered so many beautiful ways for a king to die.

23

KASAI

"You didn't tell me one bit of your troubles when I first asked. I had to coax and coddle every single word out of you. But oh, this cute little thing crosses your path, and you just spout like a fountain," Desdemonia whispered angrily to Kasai. She grabbed his arm and turned him to face her. "She is too helpless, too convenient, and I don't like her."

"Des, you imagine snakes in the grass where there are none."

Desdemonia's amber eyes blazed back at him. He hoped she wasn't about to cast a spell on him.

"Listen to me. Reese is no good. The forest knows nothing of her. It's as if she just appeared out of thin air."

Kasai ignored the warning look from Desdemonia. He just stared straight ahead.

"Send her away, Kasai. No good can come of this."

"Just like you wanted to send me away?"

"That was Gauldumor, not me. Please, don't think such things about me."

"What are you two whispering about up there?" Reese

inquired. She had eagerly volunteered to support Master Choejor as they walked along a well-traveled path. The forest had thinned, and a more settled land took shape.

Desdemonia turned her head towards Reese. "I'm educating Kasai on some of the unique fauna found in the wild. Not everything here is as helpless as it looks."

Desdemonia turned her head back and faced forward. "Her wounds are many, but superficial scratches at best. Where are the deep bruises from being held against her will? Where are the rope burns from struggle? Not a single broken bone, not a one."

"I don't know, Des. Maybe she healed herself. Listen, she's been through a lot. Those giants killed all the other pilgrims, and she was to be next. Can you imagine how scary that must've been for her? She's just a kid. We can't just abandon her now. Where's your heart?"

"That's right. Reese is a perfect, precious little thing, isn't she? You're not thinking straight. Can you not see that she is *too* beautiful, *too* vulnerable? She's just the kind of helpless waif that would inspire warmth and care from an overprotective monk who just lost everything. And don't think I'm jealous because I'm not."

"You're not making any sense. Why would you be jealous?"

"Ugh. Now you're truly under a witch's spell." She shook her head in frustration and stormed off ahead of the group.

"What's with her?" Kasai shrugged his shoulders. She wasn't wrong, Reese was beautiful. If she needed protection, then that is what he would give her. His training at Ordu had prepared him to be a shield to those in need. It was one of the Pillars of Aetenos, after all. And Reese had healed Master Choejor at a desperate hour, and Kasai felt he owed her a debt for that kindness.

Eventually, the forest opened to a small grass field.

Kasai saw the outskirts of a hamlet, and beyond the city walls of Gethem. The outer edge of the town seemed peaceful, the homey smell of burning wood wafting through the air. Kasai envisioned sitting in front of a warm fire, enjoying a hot meal, trading stories with his Brothers. How long had it been since fleeing the monastery? A few weeks? Maybe a month? So much had changed since those days.

There was an oddly familiar tang to the taste in the air. Kasai remembered a similar smell from his early youth but couldn't place it in his memories. The afternoon meat was being prepared for the afternoon meal. It wasn't cooking—it was burning.

Soon this nightmare would be over. Master Choejor would finally get the aid he needed and just in time. The Master would know what to do next. Kasai breathed a sigh of relief. He was uncomfortable making decisions that affected others.

"Des!" he called out.

She stopped and turned. Her mood was sour. "What do *you* want?"

"Look! We've reached Gethem." Kasai pointed to the distant walls of the city.

"And?" Desdemonia stood impatiently with her hands on her hips until Kasai reached her.

"You've led us safely out of the forest."

"Of course I did."

"Well, you can return home now. Master Choejor and I are grateful to you. We couldn't have made it this far without you." Kasai bowed humbly. When he raised his head, he saw a hint of sadness in Desdemonia's eyes.

"I think it's best if we stay together a little longer. There is a foul scent in the air. Something is not right here. I'll wait until you and Master Choejor are safely inside the Temple before I leave." She looked suspiciously to the hamlet, and then to Reese. Her eyes narrowed just a bit.

"Don't worry, Reese will be fine too. The priestesses of her order will look after her," Kasai said.

"Then you won't need to worry about her, either," Desdemonia said. Her eyes had become dark and heavy.

Kasai was about to reply when Reese came forward, filled with excitement.

"Look! It's Gethem. We are saved! The Immortal Mother has guided us true." She handed Master Choejor to Desdemonia and hugged Kasai in a heartfelt embrace. "You did it!"

"Immortal Mother?" Des looked incredulously at Reese. "Let's just get this over with."

The four companions entered the outskirts of the hamlet. Modest huts were built sporadically on the edge of the small town, growing denser as the party walked towards its center. The smell of something burning became more pronounced. *Wood*, Kasai thought, *but something else as well*. Then he noticed that the thin columns of black smoke became thicker as they rose into the sky.

His first thought was the night of the raid at Ordu. The sights and smells were so similar. *Stop it. Not all the world is so horrible*, he thought. *Maybe, there's a festival in the main square*. By his reckoning, Aetenos' Day of Ascendance was still a few weeks away. *Perhaps these townspeople are celebrating something else*.

He smelled roasted pig on the fire, or was it some other kind of animal? He wasn't quite sure. Either way, his mouth watered at the thought of slabs of bacon and fresh ale. His stomach growled with every step.

"I bet you didn't know we could make ale at Ordu," Kasai said to Des.

"Fascinating," Des replied, but she wasn't paying much attention. "Maybe we should turn back."

"Turn back? Now?" Kasai said.

"Or get to Gethem a different way. Something doesn't feel right."

"You've been saying since the cave. It will be fine. Come on."

The townspeople stopped what they were doing, watching silently as Kasai, and the others made their way into town. Soon a small following trailed behind them, speaking in hushed tones. Kasai figured they were just curious people. They did make up an odd lot. Two mysterious monks of Ordu, a Forest Dweller, and a priestess of the Immortal Mother were an unlikely fellowship.

These townspeople appeared to be simple folk of meager means. They dressed in clothes designed for working the fields and some carried farm tools in hand. The group behind Kasai and the others grew larger.

"I don't like this," Desdemonia said.

As if on cue, the voice of the crowd rose above a murmur. Kasai heard discouraging words like "witch," and "dark magic, and "evil."

Some of the townsfolk covered their mouths and pointed their fingers at Desdemonia. They traced symbols in the air to ward off evil spirits. Kasai spied other individuals standing in place, twitching erratically—black drool leaked from their mouths as they cast vapid stares from dead eyes.

The street leading to the center of the hamlet was walled off by a haphazard arrangement of boards, broken doors, and overturned carts. People milled about the entrance searching for something forgotten or lost. The townspeople, as one, turned and watched them approach. Their faces glared menacingly at Desdemonia. The murmurs from the group behind them grew to shouts.

"Kasai, we need to get out of here, now," Desdemonia said.

"I think you're right."

Kasai pivoted the group around only to see that the crowd behind had swollen. They seemed to be only mildly interested in Kasai, Master Choejor, and Reese. Their focus was centered on Desdemonia. They reached for her, cautiously at first but then with more determination. Desdemonia pushed away from their groping hands, but there were too many of them.

The crowd turned into a mob.

In a quick surge, the townspeople flowed in a massive current of flesh that swarmed around Desdemonia. She was cut off from Kasai and the others. The mob carried her through the makeshift barrier and into the town's square. Kasai tried in vain to reach her, but too many bodies filled the gap between them.

He saw Reese was frozen with fear. He could not leave Master Choejor with her like this. The crowd would trample them both.

"We must get Master Choejor to safety," Kasai shouted over the noise of the crowd. He grabbed Master Choejor's arm and worked his way out of the mob. He was hard-pressed to find an opening through the sea of people.

Reese snapped to attention. She moved in front of him and drove the manic townspeople out of their way. Kasai was amazed at her strength, and it wasn't long before she pushed through the crowd. Kasai spotted a narrow alley between two small buildings.

"We'll be safe here," he said. The pupils of her magenta-hued eyes had dialed to swollen black disks. She had the look of a preternatural hunter.

"Stay here with Master Choejor. I'm going back for Des," Kasai said.

"Stay with me, Kasai! The Wood Witch can take care of herself. Don't leave me alone. I can't be alone, not again,"

Reese said. The hard edge vanished, and tears welled up in her eyes. She was visibly trembling.

Kasai was unsure what to do. He couldn't just leave Reese and Master Choejor alone. She looked so frail. If the mob discovered them, he could lose them too. But Desdemonia was in danger right now.

"I'll be right back. Just don't move from this spot."

He raced to save Desdemonia. He followed the crowd through the wooded barrier. Kasai gasped in horror at what he saw on the other side. Crucifixes in the shape of an X lined the ground, creating a semi-circle around a central platform. Bodies were spread against the roughly cut wood in various stages of decomposition.

Massive scaffoldings draped limp bodies from thick ropes. Black ravens lined the top beams over the dead bodies. Two jumped from their perch, squawking angrily at each other. Loose feathers sputtered from their wings as they competed for a piece of loose flesh from a dead man's face. The choice eyeballs were already taken. Eventually, the victor ripped it free and flew into the grey sky. The other trailed close behind, refusing to give up.

Charred bodies slumped from blackened stakes over smoldering wood. He followed the movement of the mob to a high stake surrounded by fresh timber. Three men held Desdemonia, while a fourth was busy tying her to the stake. The mob's wild hysteria grew. They demanded another victim to satiate their bloodlust.

The center of the town was a sea of madness. How was this possible? What would cause decent people to act in such cruel and horrific ways? Kasai was shocked as he raced passed latecomers to the next spectacle.

He drove into the heart of the crowd, pushing and pulling his way towards Desdemonia. She thrashed against her bonds to escape, but the ropes held. Naked bodies caked with muddy filth gyrated against Kasai in a macabre dance. Their hands pressed against him and tried to encourage him to join their madness.

Kasai pushed the naked zealots back. He climbed awkwardly atop the loose wood and sticks. Desdemonia's eyes were bright amber, alive with fright.

"Call Gauldumor!" Kasai shouted over the deafening crowd. He looked frantically for a way to free Desdemonia.

"I can't! The forest binds Gauldi. He cannot travel beyond its deep roots. Free my arms, and my spells will flow!"

Kasai tried to untie the ropes, but the knots were too tight. Fear sweat poured from his forehead, and panic clouded his thoughts. Ninziz-zida grew hot in his sash. Kasai looked out at the angry mob, but he could never stop them all.

It was happening again. All he wanted to do was protect those he cared for and loved. He failed to save his parents, his Masters, his Brothers, and now Desdemona. He had lost so many. He felt powerless.

"Let the light of your heart spread as my Light once did." The fatherly voice returned.

Kasai barely heard the message. He was focused on four flaming torches bobbing their way through the crowd. Each was thrown towards the kindling wood at their feet.

The fire caught fast. The mark of Oh-hur on his forearm responded involuntarily. The temperature of the flame dissipated as the power tattoo protected him. But Des didn't have a unique tattoo to ward off the flames.

The fire spread. Kasai was desperate. He needed a knife to cut the rope. He stomped at the flames with his feet. But he only succeeded in spreading the fire. He searched the crowd for a sympathetic face. A sea of insanity stared back at him.

"Burn! Burn! Burn!" The townspeople shouted. "Burn the

witch!" Some thrust pitchforks or short swords in the air, while others raised their fists in anger.

"Kasai, the fire, it burns! Help me!" Desdemonia wailed.

Kasai felt helpless. His power tattoo would not protect him infinitely, and the fire would burn them both if he didn't do something soon. Kasai searched through his memories of Ordu. He couldn't concentrate on anything but the flames.

"Focus. Calm. Light." Kasai heard the voice in his mind again.

"Aetenos?" It was the first name that came to mind.

"Let me in. I will light your way."

Desdemonia's shrill screams pierced Kasai's heart.

"Help me!" Kasai shouted. He lowered his guard and allowed the voice's mystic presence to guide him. Then a wave of cooling sensation coursed through his body. Kasai felt his intense need to protect grow stronger. It was his shield and weapon at once.

Where before his panic had unraveled his thoughts, now the soothing energy helped focus his concentration. The cooling sensation within him swelled to an overwhelming force. It pushed against the barriers of his awareness. It wanted to grow, to live.

Kasai was barely aware of the white light seeping from his body like a soft mist. It flowed down below his feet and smothered the flames of the pyre. The light expanded upwards and encased Kasai and Desdemonia in a loving embrace.

Desdemonia was no longer screaming. She was calm and serene. Kasai saw a look of wonder in her eyes.

The enraged mob raged and yelled as they rushed the stake with more lit torches. Pitchforks and swords raised in the air. They would not allow the witch to survive this day. Kasai felt the angry surge of the crowd. The mob was blind to the light flowing from him.

Kasai tried to control the energy, but it was bigger than him, bigger than the fire, bigger than the mob and the entire hamlet. When he could no longer contain it, he let the massive force go. Blinding, white light exploded out of his pores in a violent release of energy.

The mob, blown off their feet, had fallen like freshly-scythed wheat, laying in a circular pattern around the wooden stake. Some of the townspeople smoldered and burst into flame.

Kasai's body glowed and flared with righteous light before fading, as if it were never there. He jumped to the ground and picked up a fallen blade to cut Desdemonia's bounds. She hugged him tightly, their embrace as pure as the white light. The two leaped from the smoking pyre and ran out of the square. Soon they came to where Kasai had left Reese and Master Choejor. Kasai was aware of two men following them from the square.

"We do not want any more trouble," Kasai warned. He took Ninziz-zida from his sash. The men slowed their approach and showed their hands, free of weapons. In unison, they and dropped to a knee and bowed their heads.

"We offer our service to the Argent Hammer of the Divine Fist," one of the men proclaimed. He wore dark leather breeches and a dark, form-fitted shirt. He was lean and muscular. Two long daggers were tied to either side of his waist. The collar of his shirt had an embroidered shape of a three-pronged wheel. The arms of the emblem spun counterclockwise. Kasai recognized it as a symbol of Aetenos.

Rugged in appearance, the man had straight black hair slowly giving way to grey. Kasai guessed he'd seen more than thirty winters.

"Aetenos' blessing is upon you, young one," the man said. "We are Followers of the Light. We have waited long years for the rise of the next Ever Hero. I am Pallo Katan."

His bright blue eyes held a father's authority. "This is my brother, Veers, but most know him as Run-Run." The other nodded his head enthusiastically but remained silent.

Veer's face was expressive, especially his green eyes. They reminded Kasai of Spring's first tender shoots stretching up through the last remaining snows of winter. He had a stubble beard and auburn shoulder-length hair, the cinnamon color of a turning leaf.

Veers was dressed in similar clothing as his brother, wearing the same blue, three-pronged symbol on his collar, but overall his appearance was shaggy and unkempt. Kasai saw that Veers, or Run-Run as he was called, wore bits and pieces of bush and grass tangled in his hair.

Run-Run was slender and wiry. When he stood, he moved with fluid grace. He looked younger than Pallo, perhaps in his late twenties. Run-Run did not say a word but stared at Kasai in adulation. Kasai shifted uneasily. He didn't like so much attention.

"Come, we must leave this place. The townspeople are under the influence of the Change of Mor. They will gather their senses soon enough and be back to finish what they started."

Kasai was about to respond when Desdemonia stepped forward. She pointed to Gethem. "Can you get us to the Temple of Illumination?"

Pallo and Run-Run looked to each other with unease. Run-Run's brow furrowed, and Pallo signed with his hands in response. Kasai wondered what was exchanged between the two brothers.

"If that is the wish of the Ever Hero, it shall be done. But we must be quick," Pallo said. Run-Run nodded his agreement but kept a worried face.

"I don't trust them. We should find a different way. Just

us," Reese said. She looked from behind Kasai as if to shield herself from their view.

Kasai turned around and placed his palms on Reese's narrow shoulders. "Reese, I think they are friends. And by the looks of things, we'll need all the help we can get," Kasai said. He tried his best to be reassuring.

Reese looked up at Kasai with saucer-shaped eyes. "I followed you as far as the barrier. I saw what happened. How... I've never seen anything like it. The holy books promised of the coming of a savior. You are the promised one. We have been searching for you."

"Not you too," Kasai sighed.

"The Song of Aetenos sings brightly in you," Pallo said.

Master Choejor began to vomit blood where he sat on the ground. Kasai pushed thoughts of demigods and Ever Heroes from his mind. Master Choejor had to get to the High Healers.

Pallo and Run-Run gathered Master Choejor in their arms. They walked deeper into the alley. "Come, there are other ways to get into Gethem besides through the main gates."

They moved quickly to an inconspicuous door, which opened into the rear portion of a tavern. Kasai and the others entered a dark room. The floor was sticky, the air smelling of old smoke and stale mead. Chairs were flipped upside-down, arranged haphazardly upon long oak tables.

Pallo and Run-Run lead the way to a blank section of the wall. Pallo gently transferred Master Choejor's weight to Run-Run and produced a silver key from an inner pocket. He used it to unlock a small door that was invisible to Kasai until it was opened. Inside was a small landing and a descending staircase.

"Who are you people?" Reese inquired suspiciously.

"I have said, I am Pallo. He is my brother, Run-Run. We

are..." but before he could say more, Run-Run interrupted him with a grunt. "We are Followers of the Light."

Kasai quickly scanned their auras. Faint blue, dagger-like shards shimmered in circling spirals that traveled in a circuit from their feet to their heads and back again. The shards seemed to point in the direction of Reese no matter the position they occupied over the men's bodies. Kasai wondered why the auras of followers of Aetenos would be at odds with the aura of a priestess of the Immortal Mother.

Kasai looked to see if Reese's aura did the same in return, but surprisingly, he could not make out any discernable shapes or symbols surrounding the young priestess. Her aura remained unfocused as if constantly in motion.

The staircase descended into another small landing. The walls and floor were covered with wooden boards. A tight corridor traveled into shadow to the right and left. Pallo reached into a belt pouch and took out a palm-sized stone, while Run-Run did the same. The brothers hit the stones against the wall a few times until they glowed with an inner light. Pallo handed his stone to Kasai, and Run-Run gave his to Desdemonia.

"We will travel under the chaos," Pallo said. He pointed down the right corridor. "Lead the way, Ever Hero."

"You are mistaken. I am just a monk," Kasai said as he moved to the front of the group.

"I want to be right next to Kasai," Reese said fast. She locked her arm inside of his.

"Des, maybe we should spread the light out so everyone can see," Kasai said.

Kasai thought he caught Reese give Desdemonia a nasty look. Des just shook her head and walked to the rear.

"Everyone ready? Ok, let's go," Kasai said. It wasn't long before the wooden panels were gone, and the corridor turned into an excavated tunnel of packed earth.

"How far does the tunnel go?" Kasai asked.

"We will walk for three hours. The end will bring us up into the center of Gethem. But you must know, the city has changed, and not for the better," Pallo opined.

They walked along in silence, boots slapping the cool, moist surface below, arms sometimes brushing clammy walls. The tunnel was cold and damp. Eventually, they reached another staircase that ascended to an upper platform. Pallo unlocked another hidden door with the same silver key, and they entered a vacant tunic and cloak shop where the window curtains were drawn.

"Where is the shop owner?" Desdemonia asked. "Why isn't anyone here?"

"He is a friend of Aetenos," Pallo said and explained no more.

Kasai and Des handed the rocks back to the brothers.

"How far now?" Kasai said.

"Not far," Pallo responded. He opened the front door; the noise immediately assaulted their ears. Kasai had read that Gethem was considered the King's Jewel for centuries. House Shiverrig imposed strict orders over the populace. Anyone disobeying the law was dealt with swiftly. But as Pallo had said, things had changed.

The streets of Gethem had been transformed into a sprawling, savage arena of mayhem and misery. The stench of death hung heavy in the air. How could such suffering be allowed to happen? Where were the duke's men to enforce law and order?

Kasai heard the click-clack of animal hooves on cobblestone. A column of armed knights in polished armor rode atop massive horses clad in long chainmail, leading an extensive train of wagons filled with supplies. The heraldry of House Shiverrig was draped over their backs and the coverings of the wagon loads.

"They're leaving the city on their way to war," Pallo pointed out.

The harsh noises and oppressive smells were overwhelming; Kasai longed for the silence of the monastery and the sounds of the mountains. The ambient clamor of suffering and screams was deafening. Even the forest seemed tranquil by comparison.

Long lines of impaled bodies and rotted heads littered the street. The ground was wet and muddy and dotted with deep burgundy puddles.

"What fresh hell is this?" Desdemonia said.

"Gethem bleeds for reasons known only to the Duke," Pallo said.

The clouds hung low, filling the atmosphere with oppressive gloom as no sunlight could pierce the thick veil. Men and women dance naked through the chilly streets, gyrating beneath the slow deaths of neighbors that had been nailed to rough, wooden beams.

A disheveled and dirty man stood facing a stone wall, screaming obscenities inches away from its surface. His arms flailed in chaotic exclamation as if addressing an enthusiastic audience and stirring them to revolt. He then cocked his head back and rammed it into the wall. A wicked gash opened on his forehead. The insane man ran to another section of the wall with blood streaming down his face. Once there, he started his tirade again.

"Gethem has turned from the Light of Aetenos. These people have lost themselves to the Change of Mor," Pallo said. "The hamlet was but a taste of the depravity that has befallen sweet Gethem."

"What do they hope to achieve?" Desdemonia said.

"They seek salvation by freeing themselves from the constraints of the flesh," Pallo said. Run-Run rolled his eyes and drew a revolving circle in the air beside his temple.

"Let's keep moving," Pallo said.

The city spread out, folding back upon itself with hundreds of switchback streets. Pollution poured mercilessly from rusty spouts into already dirty waterways. There were bridges and canals around every street corner where filth was swept freely into the water and mixed with the slow-moving, thick current.

Judicators in tall conical headgear prowled through the masses of hysterical worshippers. They grabbed people, seemingly at random, for trial. The crowd would cheer every time a recruit was selected for the Change of Mor. The judicators were followed by packs of filthy sycophants, wearing hooded frocks. They scurried about with muddy feet, stopping only to lash themselves with hand-held whips.

Feral dogs ran amok, holding human body parts in their mouths. The weaker animals gave up their bounty to the strong and, in turn, stole from lesser beasts.

The thick smoke hung low in the sky and kept the stench of charred flesh in the air. Black ash drifted about as if an abyssal snowstorm fell on Gethem. Kasai thought he might vomit. He kept walking, trying only to focus on reaching the Temple.

Pallo successfully navigated the group through a back alley, which opened to another street surprisingly clear of mayhem. Ahead of them stood the Temple of Illumination.

The Temple began with three short steps that led to a modest one-story gateway. Orange-stained columns rose on either side of rust-colored double doors. The columns supported rows of arches with curled ends that pointed to the heavens.

The entrance had been vandalized. The iconographic images and artifacts usually found on the main doors of any monastery had been torn off.

The Temple's sacred structures wound around a central

tower, presumably where the Grandmaster took office. The corners of the tiled roofs also curled upwards to symbolize the enlightened souls that transcended the mundane world. However, the windows had been boarded up or bricked over. The Temple no longer radiated the glory of Aetenos or the power of the Immortal Mother.

"Is this it? I expected something more," Desdemonia said.

Pallo and Run-Run walked Master Choejor up the stairs to the doors. "The loss of Aetenos has brought much suffering to the lands of Hanna. This is the work of Mor, or worse," Pallo said sadly. He looked upon the once immaculate temple and then back to the city of Gethem. "A great evil has risen. It blows its foul breath through the lands, infecting all who taste its foul air."

Kasai agreed with Desdemonia. He had expected something more from the Temple of Illumination since Ordu was kept spotless. Kasai would know. He was always cleaning.

One who followed the Way of Aetenos did not lavish himself in decadent ornamentation or precious things. His role was to serve others and to be a shield to those in need. What he saw upon the outer façade was complete disdain for the spirit of the demigod and his followers.

His eyes wandered to Reese. Was she a precious thing or someone in need of a shield? Either way, it would not matter. Soon she would be back with the other priestesses of her order, and Des would be gone, too.

He had traveled many miles and endured much hardship to reach the Temple. Now that he had finally arrived, he wasn't sure he wanted the journey to end. Another fit of coughing wracked Master Choejor, and fresh blood wet his lips. He sagged in the arms of Pallo and Run-Run.

"We must go inside and find the High Healers," Kasai said. He took the first step towards the Temple doors. Saving

Master Choejor was the priority, not his mixed feelings towards his new friends.

Desdemonia remained standing in the street. Her hands locked in fists firmly on her hips. "Kasai, haven't you wondered why Gethem allows such atrocities to continue? Or what your Temple is doing to protect these people? Are you sure there are healers in there?"

She looked to another square further down the street. "These people aren't evil, but they are most definitely under some dark spell."

"And you would know," Reese said. Her voice was noticeably hostile. "Isn't it time for the Wood Witch to be running along? Go back to your forest, Desdemonia. Kasai doesn't need you anymore. He is among his kind now."

Reese took Kasai by the arm and led him the rest of the way up the stairs.

"In that case, I'm coming too," Desdemonia said. She marched up the steps and joined Kasai and Reese at the doors.

24

SEKKA

Sekka stood at the center of her inner chamber, watching with interest in her mirror the patterns of blood dripping from her naked mortal body in the matted sable of a tattered rug. Outside the circle of the mat, butchered slaves were tossed about the furniture or piled on the stone floor in messy heaps of torn flesh.

She had chosen a group of slaves to take as lovers, albeit for a brief time, and enjoyed their company. She reveled in the feel of human skin upon skin. It was so delicate. It was electric. Eventually, her dagger found their hearts at the precise moment of climax. The mixture of death and release was an intoxicating splash of bliss and misery. She savored every drop.

Others had felt the wrath of her bestial form. That usually came after the session of so-called lovemaking. She tended to need something more to satiate her demonic passion. Those unfortunate slaves were ripped to pieces by her talons and teeth. Their shredded remains still dripped down the walls and puddled on the floor. But no matter how often she tried to distract herself, she could not find peace.

Now that Maugris' spell of binding was broken, she could communicate with her thralls on the Gathos with ease. Sekka licked wet blood from her lips. She spoke a final syllable and completed the ritual of sending.

+Chedipe.+

The connection was instantaneous. Chedipe was startled from her work. She looked up as if Sekka stood before her.

+Open your senses to me.+ Sekka commanded.

+My Queen. The hour is desperate. You must return!+

+Show me the monk.+

Chedipe's eyes, now her eyes, looked down on the bloodied and bruised body of Aetenos. He had been removed from the stone wall of his prison cell and moved to a bigger room. Presently, he was stretched on a flat table. His wrists were bound above his head and chained to the edge of the table. His legs were spread and shackled at the ankles. Carving instruments laid jumbled and bloodied on the table between his flayed legs.

+What news do you have for me?+

+Zizphander comes. His armies have begun the march to Furia Keep. Gathos burns!+ Chedipe's mind was saturated with anxiety. Sekka pushed the demon witch's fear aside. She needed answers.

+What has Aetenos revealed?+

+He refuses Chedipe. The monk speaks in riddles of madness.+

+I told you not to break his mind.+

+No, my Queen, he is not broken. His mind is crafty. He has hidden it where Chedipe cannot find it. Chedipe will dig deeper. She will find the information you seek.+

Sekka had used subterfuge and coaxing to discover the whereabouts of the next Ever Hero. She failed. She entered his mind and tried to take the information by force. She was rebuffed. She hoped by now Chedipe would have had more success, but still, Aetenos had revealed nothing. Again, failure.

Aetenos' eyes cracked open. He looked up at Chedipe, but Sekka knew, somehow, he saw her instead. One of his disgusting, lighthearted smiles, broadened his lips. Was he mocking her?

Sekka forced Chedipe's face closer to his. "Why do you endure so much for the mortals? Their faith in you has faltered. You are a forgotten thing to them."

Aetenos said nothing. He simply continued to smile.

Chedipe paced the floor of the torture chamber. Sekka's mental influence betrayed the control she had over the demon witch's body. When she spoke next, her voice inadvertently came out of Chedipe's mouth.

"I must have his secret before Zizphander learns of my absence. What was overlooked?"

"Reached too far…again. Enemies…at doorstep. Take advantage…your folly. Late to flee…Gathos." Aetenos chuckle through bruised lips.

"You know nothing!" Sekka glared at him through Chedipe's eyes.

"A hero has risen … grows stronger. Defeat you … above and below. Same fate as before. Unless Zizzzphan … der." Aetenos' eyes closed, and he went silent. However, the smile remained on his face.

+Heal his wounds and secure him outside. Make sure he is protected from the cold. He is useless to me dead.+ Sekka commanded Chedipe.

Sekka severed the connection to Chedipe. This was wonderful news! The Ever Hero had finally risen. If Aetenos would not reveal his location, then she would bring his avatar to her.

+Lord Oziax.+
+Yes, my Queen.+

+Meet me in Maugris' throne room. It is time to force the war with the South.+ She looked at her body in the mirror again. +I will be along shortly. Say nothing until I arrive.+

Magical, floating globes were interspersed along the corridor leading to Maugris' throne room. They generated a sorcerous, emerald light that played against the uneven rock of the walls.

The corridor was carved from dark grey hematite, which made up much of Rachlach Fortress' inner chambers. The natural iron in the stone gave the walls the appearance of shining, green metal.

When Sekka arrived, Maugris sat uncomfortably in his black throne. Dark runes of power were etched into the surface of the broad chair. Oziax stood beneath him at the foot of the dais. The tension was thick between the two.

Maugris stood as he spotted her, pointing his finger in accusation. "I will not commit to a war with the South until I possess the greater demons of Gathos. I have demanded this from the start!"

"You will do as the Queen commands," Lord Oziax said.

"What did you say? You and your Queen are nothing."

"You are a brave mortal behind your shield of binding. If I were free of your bond, I would tear your heart from your body and devour it before your eyes," Oziax snarled up at Maugris.

"But you are not free, are you? It is a wonder I still allow you to exist."

Sekka arrived at the dais. She faced Lord Oziax and eyed the demon warlord knowingly.

+I told you to hold your tongue.+

She turned to Maugris. "Lord Maugris, an army gathers in the South. The time for war has come."

"I am well aware of what is happening in Baroqia. Let them come. Conrad's host will freeze in the mountains before they find me."

"This is a fortuitous opportunity. One that should not be squandered."

"Have you brought me the behemoths and juggernauts of Gathos? No? Then this conversation is pointless."

"My lord, we are so very close to achieving all that you desire. I have been alerted the Ever Hero has risen. He must be lured to Rachlach Fortress."

"Ever Hero, Ever Hero," he mocked, sneering at her. His face twisted, turning purple as he screamed, "Ever Hero!" He threw his hands in the air. "This obsession of yours has pushed my patience to its limit."

"My obsession is driven by your desire, my lord. A world of demonkind awaits your command, but I need the means to bring them to you. The war with the South will compel Aetenos' avatar to come forward. Once he is in our grasps, I will have the means to open the Chaos Gate."

"The answer is still no. I will decide when the appropriate hour is to invade the South." Maugris gathered himself into his robes on the throne chair.

"Perhaps it would be best to speak of other, more favorable developments. Duke Shiverrig has pledged his loyalty to your cause," Sekka said.

"Gerun Shiverrig, the son of Gareth Shiverrig?"

"The very same. The combined strength of House Shiverrig's armies and the current demon horde shall be enough to assure victory over those who wronged you long ago."

"A Shiverrig will only embrace a cause as long as it fits his agenda. They are a family of vipers. But no matter. When this is over, all of the Great Houses will fall," Maugris said.

"Then let us begin the reign of Maugris the Infinite."

"Give me what I command."

"I cannot."

"Bah. It is clear I sucked the wrong devil from the Abyss. There will be no war until I am ready. I am quite content to remain here and bide my time."

"Maugris, do not be cruel. Lord Oziax will lead the horde into Baroqia and take the fight to the Southerners."

"He will do nothing of the sort. Did you know the fiends haunting these cold halls are fond of whispering secrets? They speak of foul-play and betrayal. The demon Narthoth should not have been able to break the wards of my binding spell. I wonder if it was not Lord Oziax that sabotaged the summoning chamber."

Lord Oziax bristled at Maugris' words. A challenge had been issued.

"I have heard enough. It is time for this insufferable mortal to learn his place." Lord Oziax took a step towards the dais.

"You will not take another step." Maugris cast a contemptuous glare at Lord Oziax, which faded as the demon warlord put his foot on the first step of the dais. Maugris' bold attitude was replaced by questioning doubt.

"Oziax! I command you to stop!" Maugris shouted.

Lord Oziax's eyes narrowed at Maugris. A sinister grin of canine teeth filled his mouth. The demon lord took another step.

+STOP!+ Sekka bellowed into Oziax's mind. She sent a burst of mental force that brought him to his knees.

Maugris released a clenched breath. His superior countenance returned quickly.

"You see? Look how he cowers," Maugris stepped down to where Lord Oziax knelt. He jabbed a bony finger into the demon warlord's forehead. "You are nothing."

Lord Oziax pushed against Maugris' finger and slowly rose. His eyes sunk into his head. Razor-thin lines appeared over the demon's exposed skin. A white mane of hair grew long past his shoulders.

The temperature in the room dropped, and the air smelled of a coming storm. Maugris hesitated, then backed away. "What's this?"

+Obey him, or I will destroy you myself.+ Sekka said with calm determination.

Lord Oziax's head twitched to the side. He lowered his head in submission. +Why do we need him, my Queen? Give him to me. His death will be slow and sweet.+

+No. You will do nothing until the Ever Hero is mine. Is that understood?+

Lord Oziax did not respond. He raised his head towards Maugris. His body seethed with hatred.

+OZIAX!+

+Understood, my Queen.+

"One wonders what value your Queen sees in you."

"If not Lord Oziax, then who? I have said countless times that the demons of Gathos will not follow a mortal, even one of your abilities. Lord Oziax is well respected and feared among the horde. There is no other they will follow at Rachlach Fortress."

"Then bring me one they will! Am I not being clear?" The emotional angst radiating from Maugris was raw and palpable. "You consistently find ways to twist my demands into suggestions and then afterthoughts."

"My lord Maugris, we are at an impasse. As I have said, if you wish to bring forth anything of merit from Gathos, you will need to open a Chaos Gate. I cannot do the impossible, no matter how often or insistently you ask. The Ever Hero is the key to your triumph."

Maugris was no longer listening. He tapped his fingers together in front of his mouth. His eyes were filled with suspicion. "Leave me now. I wish to hear the sound of my own thoughts and no others."

Lord Oziax begrudgingly backed away from the throne dais. He gave a short, obligatory bow to Maugris and left the room. Damn that impatient beast. Maugris would soon realize the truth. Perhaps Lord Oziax was right. What did it matter now? She could take control of the horde, but the longer she siphoned Maugris' resources, the more she could conserve her own. She would need all of her strength when she encountered Aetenos' Ever Hero. Aetenos was wrong. She would not suffer the same fate as before. This time she would win.

Where was Sess'thra? She had not given her a report of any kind for days. Her silence was unnerving. "I'll throttle that little minx if she's neglecting her duties again and fucking for her own pleasure."

25

KASAI

Kasai pushed open the Temple's red double doors. He was not surprised they were unlocked. All were welcome inside the hallowed halls of the Temple of Illumination. The street clamor poured into the entry chamber. Kasai closed the doors quickly once everyone was inside. The entryway was deserted, and he was puzzled when there was no one to greet them.

"Shouldn't someone be here?" Desdemonia asked.

"Yes," he confirmed, looking past the entryway. There should have been a novice monk stationed at the door to offer weary travelers a cup of freshwater. Where was the sound of monks chanting verses of the sutra? All he could hear was the muffled chaos of the street. Kasai exchanged a nervous glance with Desdemonia.

His expectations of the Temple of Illumination had always been grand, but this was a dreary and untended place. The halls lacked the serenity that was familiar to him at Ordu. There was an oppressive heaviness in the air that Kasai couldn't quite place. The misery of Gethem had seeped into the Temple's foundation and corrupted the peaceful harmony of the building. He suddenly longed for the chiming bells of Ordu.

"Let's try to find someone that can direct us to the healers," Kasai said.

He spotted an older temple monk down the hall. Kasai was surprised his robes were dyed bright red. Typically, monks wore rusty-orange or bright, yellow-colored robes, never bright red. The Master Monks dressed in light blues, like Master Choejor. Kasai guessed this was the attire of a city-temple monk versus one studying at Ordu, or any of the other three Orders of Aetenos.

"Wait!" Kasai called out.

The temple monk stopped abruptly. His look of surprise turned to uncertainty and then concern. Kasai did not see any distinguishing marks of Aetenos upon the monk's robes. Nothing about this Temple made any sense.

"What's going on here?" the temple monk asked. He examined Master Choejor's soiled and tattered robes. He looked at the others with a troubled expression, then focused his attention on Kasai. "You two are from…?"

"We come from the mountain monastery of Ordu," Kasai answered.

"Ordu," the temple monk repeated. "Is that so?"

"Yes, we have traveled far to see the High Healers. He is Master Choejor. He has been poisoned by something that cannot be purged. A terrible fate has befallen the Order. I must speak with Grandmaster Nysulu," Kasai said.

"A Master from Ordu." The temple monk's eyes darted to each member of the party. "Yes, yes, you must come quickly. My name is Jai. I will bring you directly to the Grandmaster."

Jai led Kasai and the others down a dimly lit hall where only a few candles sputtered in sconces along the walls. The stained-glass windows depicting Aetenos' journeys through the lands of Hanna had been painted black. A deep worry took hold in Kasai's gut. He felt Desdemonia's nearness as they walked.

"This is bad," she whispered.

"I know. I know," Kasia said. He caught up to the temple monk. "Jai, what is going on here?"

Jai picked up his pace. "Hurry now. It's not far."

"Are we going to the High Healers? Will Grandmaster Nysulu be there?"

"The Grandmaster of the Seventh Heaven has passed from this realm of suffering," Jai said over his shoulder. There was no remorse in his voice.

"Dead? Grandmaster Nysulu is dead? But how? When?" Kasai was stunned.

The uneasy feeling of worry in his gut became a tight knot. His intuition warned him not to trust this temple monk and to leave this place immediately. There would be no salvation here for him or his companions. But Master Choejor needed deep healing. Where else could he go? There was no time. If the healers were here, then they would help.

He had been thrust into events beyond his understanding since the attack on Ordu. Kasai felt like the ground had opened up beneath him. No matter how quickly he backpedaled, he could not escape the crumbling edge.

"Come. Come. Eto Vyliche, the new Grandmaster of Eternity, will answer your questions," Jai said.

Kasai looked at Des, and her eyes were filled with doubt. Reese seemed perfectly content. When their eyes met, she gave Kasai a reassuring yet, somewhat misplaced wink. "We're almost there; the Shrine of the Immortal Mother is located close to the receiving room of the Grandmaster." Reese's smile seemed benign.

They entered a large room where the newly appointed

Grandmaster stood speaking to another monk. Grandmaster Vyliche exaggerated an air of self-importance. His delicate hair fell in long thin strands down to the middle of his back, and he wore a magnificent red robe with embroidered gold symbols circling the sleeve cuffs and collar. Five temple monks, in less ornate bright-red robes, stood along the far wall of the room.

"Please, only those from the Monastery of Ordu may approach his Holiness. The others must remain back with me," Jai said.

Kasai took Master Choejor from Pallo and Run-Run, shouldering his weakened Master's weight on his shoulders as he slowly approached the Grandmaster. Kasai hoped the smaller monk standing next to him was a High Healer. The monk didn't look like a Healer, and Kasai did not sense any compassion in him. He looked crafty. And the monk shimmered strangely in the light when he moved. Kasai remembered seeing that shimmer before, but he couldn't recall where. It made the hair on the back of his neck rise.

Kasai briefly looked back at Desdemonia with trepidation. She mirrored his unease. She shook her head side-to-side in short, quick moves. Reese, however, looked enthusiastic, as if waiting eagerly for something to happen.

Kasai looked more deeply into the auras of the temple monks in the room. Although they were too far away for an accurate reading, he clearly saw ashen vapors surrounding the monks. Even the Grandmaster's aura was no more than a few flecks of bright blue struggling to avoid muddy-black tendrils that wrapped and unwrapped around his body like constrictors.

Kasai's heart sank. The Temple of Illumination had turned from the light of Aetenos and into a house of darkness.

Kasai reached the Grandmaster, and quickly told him of

the trouble at Ordu, the poison infecting Master Choejor and their flight from the monastery. Master Choejor hung so heavily from Kasai's shoulder; he appeared nearly dead. The crafty-looking monk moved closer as he examined the frail Master.

"Yet, you two somehow survived the massacre of Ordu," Grandmaster Vyliche stated. He slowly evaluated Kasai with a scrutinizing eye. "Good, good. It is a wonder you managed to reach us at all. Were there any others who survived that dreadful day?"

"I do not know, Grandmaster. There could be others. I fear the other monasteries shall suffer the same fate if they are not warned." Kasai looked nervously around the room. The five temple monks fidgeted aggressively along the back wall.

"The other three monasteries of Aetenos have already fallen. The Four Orders are no more," the Grandmaster said matter-of-factly.

A cold sweat edged down Kasai's back. He was too late. His heart thumped heavily in his chest. All of the monasteries had been destroyed. Gone. His eyes searched for some kind of answer.

"I see this is news to you, young friend. Come, I shall tell you the entire tale, but not here. This information is sacred to the Temple and not for the ears of the uninitiated." Grandmaster Vyliche looked to where Desdemonia and the others stood. "Let us adjourn to my private chambers. Master Lanak will accompany us. I believe he can shed more light on these terrible events." The crafty-looking monk bowed deeply.

"Grandmaster Vyliche, I humbly request that Master Choejor be brought to the High Healers first. He needs immediate attention. He is very sick."

"Indeed. I'll send for a healer to join us. Come, I wish to hear more of your story. Your friends may take their respite in the garden. Brother Jai, see that they are comfortable." The Grandmaster's tone made it clear this was not a suggestion but a command. He turned and walked across the room to a far door.

Kasai followed the Grandmaster, though his instinct screamed, RUN! Everything about Gethem, the Temple of Illumination, and the temple monks within were wrong. Kasai concentrated intensely on seeing the aura of Master Lanak. The ashen vapor above his head shifted into the black sigil he had seen at Ordu, the day the assassin's dart pierced Master Choejor's flesh.

Kasai's heart raced faster. Master Lanak was the changeling! The five temple monks along the back wall approached slowly. He observed similar black sigils fade into reality above their heads. He turned and looked at the temple monk, Jai. Darkness surrounded his soul, as well.

Why hadn't he listened to Desdemonia's warning? Now he had walked his companions into a trap. The Temple of Illumination was filled with vipers, and Kasai had stumbled blindly into their pit.

The despair of Gethem was permitted to thrive because the spiritual leaders had embraced a darker evil. They had turned their backs on the people they were meant to heal and protect. Kasai stopped walking.

"Will the changeling be accompanying us, Grandmaster?" Kasai asked as he pointed to Master Lanak. He was surprised at his own words. But the *things* in the room were imposters or worse. He reached for Ninziz-zida. The Fire Serpent's sentient connection to Kasai responded with her approval. His instincts were correct.

The Grandmaster turned and tilted his head at Kasai. "What did you say, young man?"

Master Lanak looked at Grandmaster Vyliche in mock surprise, and then a knowing smile crossed his face. "I believe the lost monk from Ordu owes me an apology, Grandmaster Vyliche," Master Lanak said. He drew a short dagger concealed in his robe and pointed it at Master Choejor. "And a life. I see the last Master has not yet found the deep sleep from my dart's kiss. She is quite an aggressive leech. Once she has developed a taste for something, she eats her fill ... from the inside out."

"Assassin," Kasai cried out with disgust. Ninziz-zida's segments flamed in his hands.

"Yes, that is quite a clever talent you possess," Dax said beneath the outer disguise of Master Lanak. He nodded something of approval towards Kasai.

Master Choejor coughed up more blood. With great effort, the frail monk rose out of his stupor. Master Choejor moved protectively in front of Kasai and took up a shaky defense.

"Leave now, my son, while there is time. Flee this unholy place," he muttered.

Kasai moved beside Master Choejor. He uncoiled Ninziz-zida and readied her in a striking grip. He cried out to his companions, "Assassins!"

"Where? Who?" Desdemona responded as she dropped down in a defensive posture. Her hands glowed bright azure. Short swords flashed in the hands of Pallo and Run-Run as they moved forward to help Kasai. Reese backed against the wall, distancing herself from the others.

Grandmaster Vyliche sighed with impatience and held up his hands. He turned back towards Master Choejor. Quick as a snake, he struck Master Choejor in the temple with the first two fingers of his right hand. Master Choejor crumbled to the floor.

"Deal with this mess, Dax. Ordu should no longer exist. Kill them all," Grandmaster Vyliche said and turned to leave the room once more.

"It will be my pleasure," Dax said, swinging his attention to Kasai.

"Aetenos, help me," Kasai said absentmindedly. He had never actually prayed to the demigod before, and he honestly didn't know how. However, the thought of Aetenos at his side gave Kasai a righteous fury. His fire xindu ignited throughout his body.

"Aetenos, if your Song is truly with me, let me hear it now. Give me the strength to save Master Choejor."

Ninziz-zida welcomed the sensation of holy righteousness to fuel her flame. She blazed brighter as she tapped into the flow of Kasai's xindu energy.

Dax dropped the disguise of Master Lanak.

"Thank you for saving me the trouble of hunting you down. Sess'thra will be jealous that I found you first."

"You talk too much," Kasai said. He whipped the outer sections of Ninziz-zida in circular arcs probing the assassin's defenses. Ninziz-zida's red fire lit up the center of the room.

Dax stabbed forward, hoping to catch Kasai off guard. Kasai pivoted, striking a blow across the assassin's exposed wrist—bones cracked. Twisting his body, Kasai flicked his other wrist, batting the dagger away with Ninziz-zida's opposite end-section. The staff sent sensations of triumph into Kasai's mind.

Dax sneered, cradling his shattered wrist. Kasai whirled, expanding Ninziz-zida's segments; blazing bright red as he funneled more of his fire xindu into the ancient weapon. Dax's expression turned to defeat as Kasai swung Ninziz-zida down to finish the assassin. His strike was stopped by two temple monks who tackled him from behind. Kasai was astonished at their strength, but he soon knew the reason why. Their faces changed from human to monstrous fiends as their malformed mouths snapped inches from his own. Their breath stunk of rotten eggs.

They fell hard on the floor. Ninziz-zida collapsed into a tight three-sectioned baton as Dax raced to the back of the room, holding his injured wrist. He twisted a sconce on the wall, and a hidden door panel slid open.

Kasai used Ninziz-zida to bludgeon the head of one of the assailants. The strike of the Fire Serpent's wrath burned the fiendish monk with an otherworldly flame. He rolled to the side, flames festering, consuming his robes. A chilling scream left the monster's lips as Ninziz-zida's holy fire burned him to ashes.

Kasai hit the second fiend with a knee to its gut and jumped to his feet.

"Des! There!" Kasai yelled.

Blue energy swirled around Desdemonia; glyphs of power radiated from her body. Numerous deadly darts shot from her magic hands into the back of the second attacker. The fiendish monk arched in pain, whirling to face Desdemonia.

"Fire, Des! Use fire!" Kasai yelled.

Des nodded that she understood. She spoke ancient words of power and formed a small ball of fire in her hands. She threw it at the fiendish monk; he burst into flames and dropped to the floor to roll and snuff out the fire. Des' magical fire flared again, consumed him, turning him to black ash. It smelled horrid.

Three more temple monks in the ruby red colors of the Grandmaster of Eternity poured into the room, carrying short, curved blades. Holy pretense dropped as they warped into creatures spawned from madness.

A lumbering monstrosity covered entirely in short, white hair appeared from the passage. It looked pale and unwholesome, the size of an upright bear, it pushed aside the smaller killers, the temperature plummeted as it advanced. From his nose and snout, thick ropes of snot and drool splashed freely, the ends clinging to his naked chest as they cooled. The pale demon licked his lips, exposing rows of razor-sharp teeth.

Spying Kasai, the demon halted. Their eyes met and both widened as the creature's face softened and shifted slightly to resemble Daku. Just as quickly, the likeness disappeared and the image of Daku was lost.

"Kasai!" It bellowed out with a repulsive laugh. "We have been waiting for you. Daku has told me all about you."

A temple monk ran at Kasai in the center of the room. Desdemona shot a focused funnel of wind into his chest, sending him windmilling into the air. His red robes billowed around him as he smashed into the stone wall across the room. When Desdemonia cut the air, the monk dropped to the floor, a dark smear trailing after his slide down the wall.

"That's enough!" Jai held Reese tight with a dagger at her neck. Pallo and Run-Run sprang to her aid. Pallo's short sword somehow peeled Jai's weapon away from her neck and Run-Run stripped her away from the older temple monk. Jai ran from the room, and Reese was safe.

"Kassssssai..." the aberration taunted him. "Shall we spar once more?"

Kasai saw the demon was close to the body of Master Choejor.

"Where is Daku? What have you done with him?" Kasai shouted.

"He's right here. Inside me. I sometimes hear him weeping in the corner of my mind. I laugh at his misery. His soul is mine."

The demon moved to stand over the prone body of Master Choejor.

"Ah, dear Choejor. Daku bids your greetings, but it will be Khalkoroth who takes you to the darkness." Khalkoroth began to hum a tune, and then words came to his song.

"Off we go, off we go.

The Halls of Madness awaits all who go.
Off we go, off we go.
To those who follow, let them know.
In blood, you'll be, from head to toe.
Off we go, off we go."

Ninziz-zida was eager to attack, but Kasai held her back. Kasai could see the mannerism and movement of his lost Brother when the demon moved. Daku was in there, somewhere. If he destroyed this monster, would he not kill his best friend in the process? And how could he fight with Master Choejor at risk?

"Kasai! Move!" Desdemonia cried out. She'd conjured more fire in her hands and hurled it at the demon. Kasai ducked as the small fireball soared over his head.

Vermillion flames splashed over the demon's body, causing a green rock around his neck to flare with emerald light. The demon snickered as the flames were sucked into its core.

"Anything else?" he taunted before leaping hard and fast.

Ninziz-zida flashed out to strike but couldn't get through the demon's defense. Her fire did not burn the pale demon as it did the other fiends. The demon caught Kasai with a sweeping blow, sending him sprawling to the ground. Leaping forward, he straddled Kasai, glaring at him. He brought his claws down , the segments of Ninziz-zida in his hands deflecting the blow.

"You never did know how to win," Khalkoroth mocked, using Daku's voice.

Kasai thrust Ninziz-zida into its face, but the pale demon swatted the segments aside with an enraged growl. Its strength was overwhelming. Kasai knew he wouldn't be able to withstand such punishment.

"I can hear Daku wailing inside. Perhaps he longed for those special sticks in a past life. Another thing he will never have," the Thing said as it slashed his claws across Kasai's hands. The pain was excruciating. A second blow swatted Ninziz-zida across the floor. The flames of the Fire Serpent sputtered out.

"You've lost your precious Ninziz-zida. Now you are doomed!"

Kasai brought his hands up to block the next blow. He was desperate. "Aetenos! Help me!"

"Believe in me and be shielded from the darkness."

"I believe! I believe!" Kasai yelled out with desperation.

Khalkoroth picked Kasai up and raised him to his face. Kasai struggled, but the creature held him tight, lips peeled back revealing needle-sharp teeth. "This will be over soon."

Kasai brought his feet up against the pale demon's chest and pushed with all his might. His robe tore where the claws held them, and Kasai flew backward, crashing into a table. He had nothing left. He was totally spent. Beaten. This abomination would kill him now.

Kasai saw the prone body of Master Choejor lying on the floor. He willed himself to get up. Master Choejor still needed him. Kasai managed a kneeling position but felt panic rising to drown him in its murky darkness—he forced it down. *I will not fail Master Choejor.*

Khalkoroth stomped closer. Kasai took a deep breath and bowed his head to his chest, steadying his resolve. "Aetenos, hear me. I believe. Hear me." The words were calm and meaningful. He lifted his head, watching the demon approach.

"Praying will not save you now," Khalkoroth spat, his massive arms high over his head, ready to smash Kasai into oblivion.

"I am here, my son. I have always been here with you."

"I know," Kasai whispered, raising his hands as the demon's fists swept down.

A shield of energy rippled in the air. The demon pounded again and again on the invisible aegis, furious at being denied his killing blow, howling like a crazed wolf. Kasai rolled to the side and kicked as hard as he could into the demon's knee. It stumbled back a few paces but quickly regained his footing.

"Ah...Brother Kasai. Look at how many things have changed. But your clever tricks will not save you." The demon came at him again.

Desdemonia ran up while firing blue bolts at the demon's back. Once again, the amulet that hung from his neck absorbed the magic. Khalkoroth swiveled his head in her direction.

"What is this pest? Something wild and dirty you found in the woods?"

Desdemonia pushed her hands into pouches on her thighs. When she pulled them out, there were long bear claws attached to gloves on her hands. She leaped on the demon's back and repeatedly raked her razor-sharp claws across its face while shouting strange, unfamiliar names.

Ninziz-zida lay on the floor, and Kasai scrambled to retrieve her. Khalkoroth grabbed Desdemonia by the hair, ripped her off his back. As it lifted its massive arm back to thrust claw-hands through her chest, Kasai leaped into the air and snapped Ninziz-zida into the demon's face. Khalkoroth snarled something ancient and evil and dropped Desdemonia to the ground. With its hair on fire and raw, burned skin, its pink eyes burned with hatred. The burning smelled putrid and poisonous.

Kasai backed away to draw the demon after him, but Reese suddenly jumped in front of the hulking killer.

"Halt!" she demanded in her childlike voice. She thrust up her hand in Khalkoroth's face. The demon eyed the onyx ring on Reese's finger with uncertainty, then narrowed his demonic eyes at her. Reese thrust her hand up into his face. "Stop!"

"Where did you get that ring?" Khalkoroth sounded confused.

"In the name of the Immortal Mother, I command you to stop!" Reese shouted again, with newly found authority.

"Who are you to command Khalkoroth?" The pale demon took a step back, uncertain of the power of the priestess.

"Reese, no! He is too strong!" Kasai cried out.

Reese began chanting something in an exotic language. She raised her other hand, and the monster stepped back in pain. Reese seemed to hold sway over its behavior as it retreated. But it saw Master Choejor still on the floor and jumped at the monk.

"You stupid monk. You never could see the truth." Khalkoroth's booming laughter filled the room. He threw Master Choejor over his shoulder.

"To Rachlach, I go. To Rachlach, I go!
Poor Choejor's hollow head is broken and low.
To Rachlach, I go. To Rachlach, all will go!"

The room suddenly grew dim as the Thing that called itself Khalkoroth gathered the shadows into a haze of darkness around itself. Kasai rushed forward, but the darkness was quickly gone, taking with it the demon and Master Choejor. Only faint maniacal laughter lingered in the air.

Kasai looked anxiously around the room, searching for what he knew was already gone. Pieces of ash swirled on the floor. Pallo and Run-Run were alive; battered and bruised, but alive. They had dispatched the other temple monks while Kasai and Desdemonia battled with the demon. Reese seemed unharmed. Desdemonia was on the floor and not moving. Kasai ran to her, thinking the worse.

"Des, Des!" He rolled her over.

Her eyes flared open in alarm, then softened as she saw

his face. "Give us a kiss, Handsome," she said with a wide grin. The jovial gypsy was back.

"Really?" Kasai rolled his eyes. "Come on, Des, get up. We need to find Master Choejor." Kasai scanned the room. Where could they have gone? He heard more temple monks coming through the hidden passage.

"Ever Hero, we must flee while we can. We will find your Master, but not here," Pallo pressed.

Kasai knew Pallo was right, more danger approached.

"The demon said something about taking Master Choejor to Rachlach. Did he mean Rachlach Fortress in Trosk?" Reese wondered aloud to the group. She was already leaving the room, beckoning the others to follow.

"Yes, I heard Rachlach as well, but how do we get there?" Kasai said.

Pallo and Run-Run looked at each other. "We know the way," Pallo said. "Run-Run can guide us once from the wilderness."

The Temple of Illumination was suspiciously empty as Kasai and the others ran outside into the streets. Run-Run took the lead, followed Kasai, Des, and Reese. Pallo was the rearguard. They skirted in and out of alleyways, passing unused storefronts. Kasai noticed many repeating symbols of long triangles arranged around a central point to mark the general location of secret handles for concealed doorways or trapdoors.

"How do you know of these secret ways?" Kasai asked as they ducked under a shallow ceiling and crawled along a narrow passage that opened into a tunnel.

"There's a scourge upon the lands of Hanna. It has infested the Northern Kingdom and is now infecting Baroqia. The jungles of Sunne will soon be overcome as well," Pallo said. "We are Spire Runners by trade, and part of a swelling resistance called the Kibo Gensai. We are devoted followers of Gen Mol, the First of Aetenos, and these are our secret passageways."

"The first? Do you mean his first follower?" Kasai said.

"Gen Mol was the first Ever Hero," Pallo said. Run-Run nudged his brother.

"We remain in secret due to the oppressive subjugation of Aetenos' followers. The factions of Mor have become warped by an unholy alliance with a diabolical evil. They are too numerous and too powerful to stand against in the open."

Run-Run nudged Pallo, again, in the direction they needed to go. "We must keep going," Pallo said. As they reached the end of the tunnel, Pallo pressed a smooth rock in the wall. The wall slid to the right, the afternoon light filling the exit. They now faced north, the forest only a short distance away.

"We are the daggers that pierce the darkness," Pallo declared just before they ran for the trees. "The Kibo Gensai have long searched for signs of the return of Aetenos and the rise of his next Ever Hero."

When everyone was concealed within the tree line, the two brothers dropped to one knee in front of Kasai. "We are the servants of the Divine Fist and his Argent Hammer, the Ever Hero. We are your sworn protectors during the time of transformation."

Kasai looked at them as if they were mad. "Get up, get up! What are you doing? There's not going to be any transformation. Not for me..., I'm no Ever Hero. I'm nobody. Nothing. Only a simple monk from Ordu." He shook his head in disbelief.

Pallo reached up and took Kasai's hands in his own. "You are much more. You bear the mark. You are the one who shall grant salvation to the worthy." Pallo then turned Kasai's hands upright to reveal cobalt-blue symbols on his palms, shinning like two freshly-inked tattoos. The design on each hand was in the shape of an open spiral.

"What's this? Kasai exclaimed.

"The Prophecy is revealed. The Ever Hero has risen," Pallo said.

Run-Run nodded eagerly. His grin was missing two teeth.

26

DESDEMONIA

Desdemonia huffed dismissively, "I don't care. Kasai can do what he wants." She lingered at the back of the group, lost in her thoughts, as they trekked through the forest. Ahead, Kasai was constantly engaged in conversation with the annoyingly clingy Reese. It was clear that Reese had developed a deep attachment to him; she was always by his side, close as a second skin. Desdemonia noticed how Reese flirted unabashedly with Kasai, though she doubted it would lead to anything substantial, after all, Kasai was a monk from Ordu. *Whatever that meant*, she fumed.

The morning air was crisp, and the smells of the forest were a cleansing relief from the filth of Gethem. Small birds flitted from branch to branch, chirping incessantly as the travelers walked beneath them. Desdemonia missed her little cottage in the woods and the squirrels that came to eat nuts out of her hand.

They had been traveling for ten full days without incident due to the clever trailblazing of the brothers. Run-Run typically scouted ahead, as he did this morning to see that the way was clear. Pallo followed his brother's markers and lead the group through the undisturbed forest. They were keen to stay off well-traveled paths.

Pallo also kept a watchful eye on Reese. Desdemonia was glad she wasn't the only one that suspected something not quite right with the priestess. Kasai, of course, was an idiot. He only saw the good in everyone.

She could only imagine what Kasai must be feeling right now. No one could explain the strange markings on his palms. The brothers were convinced he was the next Ever Hero. Wow. *What an incredible burden.*

She had heard of a strange phenomenon that altered the bodies of raving zealots, but in her heart, she knew Kasai wasn't mad.

"Maybe a poor judge of character, but he's not crazy," she commented to herself. She watched him trace the blue spiral on one of his palms. *Could he really hear the Song of Aetenos?* Her eyes drifted to Reese. The tension she felt with the priestess had been mounting since arriving at the Temple. There was something about that one that made her skin crawl. The confrontation with the demon, Khalkoroth, was still heavy on her mind.

Kasai struck up a conversation with Pallo, leaving left Reese by herself. Seizing the opportunity, Desdemonia quickly caught up to her. "Reese, I've been meaning to ask you something," she said, hoping to sound as friendly as possible.

"What do you want?" Reese's mouth creased into a frown.

Even when Reese was unpleasant, she was still beautiful. No law said a priestess of the Immortal Mother had to be ugly, Desdemonia reminded herself. But Reese had an uncanny, flawless beauty. And somehow, that made Desdemonia uncomfortable.

Staring at her with sharp, magenta eyes, Reese stated impatiently, "Yes?"

"You were very brave to stand up to the demon the way you did," Desdemonia began.

"How would you know? You were lying on the floor being useless."

Desdemonia bit back a sharp retort, determined to be civil towards the young priestess. She needed answers. "Yes, well, Pallo told me what happened afterward. What did you say to the demon that made him back away? Pallo said you commanded him to leave, and he did."

Reese became pensive, fingering the black ring she wore. An impish smile came to her mouth. "I don't know. Kasai was in danger. I couldn't lose him. Not after all he's done for me. I jumped in the path of the demon and said the first thing that came to my mind. It was a verse my mother sang to me as a child to ward off evil spirits."

Desdemonia eyed Reese with skepticism. "You expect me to believe you recited a nursery rhyme and pushed back a greater demon?"

"I know. Who would believe it?" Reese put her hand to her mouth, then giggled like a young child. She abruptly stopped laughing and became serious.

"I want to make something perfectly clear to you. Don't get in my way."

"In your way of what?" Desdemonia asked, genuinely confused.

"Oh, don't play that game with me. I see how you look at him when you think no one is watching. He's mine."

"Who, Kasai? You're crazy."

"You have no idea." Reese glared. "This is your only warning."

Desdemonia looked away, perplexed at the instant hostility. Collecting her thoughts, she turned back to Reese, another question on her tongue when Kasai rejoined the pair. Reese practically leaped into his arms.

"Hi, Kasai. Desdemonia and I were just commenting on what a nice morning it is. Don't you agree?"

"Sure," Kasai said, appearing uncomfortable by Reese's enthusiastic embrace.

"When you're finished," Desdemonia comments, "I want to show you something. I took this from Khalkoroth." She held a delicate chain that was attached to a small amulet. There were intricate runes inscribed over the central piece. The emerald jewel in its center sparkled bright-green when it caught the light.

"Des, you shouldn't have that. It's evil. Destroy it now!" Kasai reached out to take the amulet away from her.

Desdemonia pulled the amulet back to her chest. "Not so fast. It might not be evil. Didn't you see how the amulet absorbed magic?"

"Yes, and it was around the neck of a demon that wanted to kill us, Des. Maybe it only absorbs good magic."

"I don't know. I want to study it more. Plus, we will need more than my simple spells and your flashy sticks where we are going."

Reese cast a suspicious eye towards Desdemonia and pulled Kasai's attention back to her. "Never trust the words of sorcerers or *witches*. I think she wants to make slaves of us all. Desdemonia makes me nervous."

"Don't be ridiculous. Des is a friend," Kasai said.

Reese leaned closer to Kasai and whispered, "Let her keep the trinket and send her away. We don't need her anymore. The Immortal Mother watches over us." Her magenta eyes gleamed with eagerness.

"Ugh, I'm standing right here. I can hear you," Desdemonia snapped. "And I'm not going anywhere."

"We'll see about that," Reese said.

Run-Run returned to the group to interrupt the standoff. He hurriedly spoke to Pallo using grunts and quick hand gestures. Pallo nodded in understanding.

"A war column approaches from Gethem. The Knights of Gethem lead a long trail of armed townsfolk and wagons swollen with supplies. We could merge with the local conscripts and see about retaining some additional supplies. We are ill-equipped to cross the Hoarfrost. Winter will catch us soon, and we will need warmer clothing.

"Run-Run suspects the column travels to the Last Garrison. It's large enough to serve as a command center for the coming battle. We can walk with them until we reach that point, then take Stormwind Pass to get to Rachlach Fortress."

"And the Sorcerer," Reese said, glumly.

"Run-Run is right. We are not prepared for the cold," Kasai said. "What do you think, Des, should we join the war column?"

Reese quickly interjected, "I don't like it. Let's keep away from those mean soldiers. We can wait until they pass and continue alone," She took Kasai's hand and tried to pull him in a new direction, away from the group. "The Immortal Mother provides."

Desdemonia held out her arm to prevent Reese from going any farther. "The closer we get to the mountains, the more likely we are to run into the enemy. There is safety in numbers until we have a better idea of what lies ahead."

"What is the wish of the Ever Hero?" Pallo said. "He shall decide our path."

"Blending in with the regular folks seems like a smart idea. Plus, we are heading in the right direction. We can make our move to rescue Master Choejor when the opportunity presents itself."

"It shall be done as the Ever Hero commands," Pallo said.

Run-Run bowed and vanished among the forest trees.

"Where's he going?" Desdemonia asked.

"He goes to secure our ingress within the column. Hopefully, there will be others of the Kibo Gensai that will help us gather supplies," Pallo said.

"Why do you call him Run-Run?" Kasai asked.

Pallo chuckled a bit to himself. "We were trained to be Spire Runners at a very young age. My brother was the fastest of us all. Quick as a rabbit, that one. He could run at pace for hours without losing the scent of a trail. I swear, my brother has the nose of a hound. No one could match his speed or stamina."

"Spire Runners? I am unfamiliar with this title," Kasai said.

Pallo hesitated. "Interesting. I would think a monk of Ordu would be well versed in the history of the realm."

"They don't teach them much in the mountains," Desdemonia said.

"Pallo, pay no attention to her," Kasai deflected. "Please, go on."

"When first the stones of Volkerrum Keep were laid in Gethem, runners were used to race across the land to bring messages from one small village to the next. This was how Baroq Shiverrig, the great Aj-Kahun of his time, kept his subjects informed of his will.

"Eventually, other cities grew and prospered throughout the realm, most notably, Qaqal."

"The City of Spires," Kasai added, proving he knew something of the outside world.

"Yes, exactly, the City of Spires. Over time the idea of runners caught on with the noble class in Qaqal. The Spire Runners, as they became called, knew the fastest routes to convey not only the King's Law but also the secrets of their rivals for power."

"Secrets," Desdemonia interjected.

"Yes, secrets," Pallo continued. "Valuable secrets of such importance that the Spire Runners were in danger for their lives. In the same way messenger birds could be shot from the sky, Spire Runners could be caught and made to reveal what they knew. Hence, we trained ourselves in many martial forms, becoming proficient with blade and fist alike."

"City life." Desdemonia shook her head. "At least one knows where they stand in the forest. What about Run-Run? He never talks."

"His is a sad tale. Years ago, my brother was caught by a pack of zealots. They were maniacal worshippers of Mor. They forced him to renounce his faith in Aetenos. Run-Run would not, so they cut out his tongue as a reward for his devotion."

"Oh no," Desdemonia said. "I'm so sorry."

Pallo nodded sadly. "But let us not dwell in the past. We must be ready to move upon Run-Run's return."

It wasn't long before the party meshed with the slow-moving column of supply wagons and war engines destined for the coming battle with the North. Warhorses plodded along with heavy steps through worn and muddy roads, and their tails swished away fat flies that trailed their muscular flanks.

The last breath of Autumn was giving way to the cold slumber of winter. Instead of crisp air bringing the smell and flavor of snow to the lands, there was a bitter reek drifting on the winds.

Desdemonia couldn't shake the feeling they were being watched, or worse, hunted. The presence of a predator was close. She could feel it lurking in shadows and following their every move.

She watched Kasai move through the different groups of soldiers and conscripts. No matter how much he declined the moniker, the title of Ever Hero followed him. Rumors of the return of the Ever Hero had spread fast from the townsfolk outside of Gethem.

Pallo and Run-Run didn't help matters, either. They refused to see him as anything but a holy savior. The two brothers rarely left his side and acted as bodyguards and servants.

Somehow, Kasai remained humble through all the adulation. He was a unique soul with a pure heart. They were a good team together, unless Reese showed up to act like a wedge between them. Strangely, since they joined with the war column, Reese had been absent for long periods.

"Good riddance," Desdemonia snorted. "Lord knows what type of mischief that so-called priestess is causing." She didn't believe for an instant that Reese was spreading the good word of the Immortal Mother to the troops. She caught the sight of orange robes bookended by two black shadows as Kasai and the brothers made their way closer. His face looked worn and drawn.

"Their eyes are on me everywhere I go," Kasai said.

"Whose eyes?"

"Everyone's." Kasai's hands went out to encompass the war column.

"Well, you know … you should be honored," Desdemonia quipped, poking him in the arm. "Not everyone gets to be the savior of Hanna." She shouldn't jest, he was having a hard enough time already.

"Funny," Kasai responded, though he wasn't laughing. He looked down at her finger where it was pressing against his arm and moved to take it in his hand. He shifted his gaze to meet hers. "Des, they have it all wrong. I'm just a monk. Nothing more, nothing less. I don't know why all this is happening, but to think it's because I somehow possess the spirit of Aetenos is just fantasy." Kasai sighed, dropping her hand. "The weight of their expectations is great."

Run-Run gave a grunt, nudging Pallo before pointing in the direction of a small group of townsfolk approaching, dressed in makeshift war gear of padded armor and mismatched helms. They held old, dull swords that should be used for something other than killing. Pallo and Run-Run were quick to occupy the space between Kasai and the oncoming townsfolk. Desdemonia thought they looked harmless enough.

A man of roughly forty summers with a short, thick beard, salted with age, and a balding head, spoke for the group. He had heavy eyes, filled with caring and stature that expressed years of hardship.

He looked with cautious interest at Pallo and Run-Run, then addressed Kasai politely. Desdemonia felt slightly insulted at being left out. "Here we go again."

"I am Lorne from East Valor. The land yields less each year, and the people suffer. I am fearful for my family's safety. Watch over me, Ever Hero, so that I may return to them when this is over." He bowed low to Kasai. The rest of the group did the same.

Kasai glanced at Desdemonia, his expression seeming to ask if now she understood. He did his best to straighten each member of the group. "Please, please, stop bowing."

"The prophecy reveals itself. Your arrival has been foretold," Pallo said with zealous conviction. "Behold, the Mark of Aetenos! Have courage, my friends. The Ever Hero walks with you." Pallo raised one of Kasai's arms to the crowd and showed the symbol of power on his palm.

"Pallo, enough," Kasai implored. He pulled his arm down, but the damage had been done.

"The Open Palm," one of the townsfolk remarked in awe. "The prophecy reveals itself."

"The Divine Fist and his Ever Hero are among us. Aetenos has returned," another exclaimed aloud. Other conscripts and now soldiers heard the townsfolk's exclamations. They drew near.

"He bears the Mark!" Lorne said. "Show them, show them all!"

Kasai reluctantly did as he was asked. The men before him gasped. They bowed their head in reverence or knelt before Kasai. More soldiers came. It wasn't long before Kasai was surrounded by at least fifty kneeling worshippers. Each had their head bowed, and one hand raised, palm facing towards their savior.

"Well, we can forget about blending in with the militia now," Desdemonia snarked. She hoped the sorcerer didn't already have spies wading through the army ranks. But that would be wishful thinking.

27

KASAI

Alone, Kasai walked through a frigid wasteland with nothing more than his burnt orange robe. The cold air burned his exposed skin. The encampment had changed to open tundra. Kasai saw his breath cloud in front of his eyes. When it cleared, the barren landscape had transformed into a cold and dark interior. Where was Des?

Ice stalactites hung from the ceiling. He looked about the room, seeing sharp and dangerous looking tools on a small, waist-high bench. Underneath, spatters of blood stood out against the frozen white floor. The outline of a woman took shape in the shadows.

"Des, is that you?"

"Ah, there you are, my elusive monk. I wonder as you do, are you the One?"

"Reese?"

"Now, step a bit closer and let me see your handsome face. That's it, just a bit closer."

Kasai could not stop himself from obeying. His feet slid forward on the slick floor of their own volition. "Reese?

Show yourself. Who's there?" Kasai said to the shifting image.

"I can be many things. Whatever your heart desires," the woman whispered.

"Why are you hiding?" Kasai's voice wavered. A warning of danger crept up his spine.

"Let me show you."

The form of the woman changed, darkness wrapping around her in a shifting haze of shadow. Kasai saw the shape of her body become flesh. She was magnificent. Perfect. He took a step closer.

The darkness gave way to a flurry of brightness. Now she was shrouded in a swirling cloud of snow. A headdress of bones grew from her head. Kasai recoiled in shock. He knew this woman. The apparition from Ordu had found him again. The nightmare continued.

She grew in stature to tower over him. She pulled a limp body from behind her back. She held it up for Kasai to see. Kasai's eyes widened in horror. He recognized the face of his father. The apparition then showed him the body of Master Choejor. The old monk's body was ashen and broken.

"The frail hopes of forgotten fathers are calling you. Come to me. Save them if you can."

Kasai gasped. His body felt unnaturally hot. Pinpricks covered his skin. He felt a profound sadness as his stomach heaved into his throat. He couldn't move, no matter how hard he tried to twist or turn his body.

The apparition slammed the two bodies together until they shattered like glass. The pieces fell out of sight. She took a step closer to Kasai.

Fear washed over him. He tried to reach for Ninziz-zida, but his arm was anchored to his side. He searched for anything that could help him escape.

"Who are you? What do you want from me?" Kasai said.

The woman's body grew until only a colossal face remained in Kasai's field of view. He saw the woman's long neck, slender chin, and full mouth. The rest was lost in swirling white snow that spread throughout the entire room.

A seductive smile formed. Kasai was drawn against his will to the enticing lips. The mouth opened wide, and he saw rows and rows of sharp, arrowhead-like teeth. Her smooth jaw lurched forward and snapped at him, inches from his face. He stared, frozen in fear.

Kasai snapped awake, heart pounding, lying on his back in a puddle of clammy sweat. The early morning moon cast its pale light over the encampment of Shiverrig's army in the fields surrounding the Last Garrison. Dawn was still a few hours away.

At some point during the night, Reese had returned and lain down next to him. She was lying across his outstretched arm. Her arm laid across his body. Her small hand had somehow snaked beneath his robes and rested just below his navel.

Kasai looked around. Desdemonia was curled up at the edge of their small camp with her back to Kasai. He carefully removed Reese's hand and pushed her gently aside.

He stood up. The feeling of helplessness still clung to his body. He rubbed his hands over his smooth scalp and down his long, black braid of hair. He stretched in the cold, pre-dawn air. He looked around the camp for a quiet place to meditate.

"You see with the eyes of the Ever Hero," Pallo said. He was tending a small campfire nearby.

"What?"

"The visions are real."

Kasai had no answer. He moved to sit closer to Pallo. The warmth of the fire put him at ease. Kasai soon heard the familiar sound of steel plates clanking together from heavy footsteps. Soon, three armed knights wearing the house colors of Duke Shiverrig came into view. A snarling mastiff emblazoned the purple and rose light shirts they wore over their armor.

"You shall come with us, now," the lead knight said. There was no introduction or explanation.

Pallo jumped in front of Kasai with his daggers drawn. The knights did not bother to remove their swords.

"Now," said a second knight.

"Pallo, it will be all right. I do not sense ill-will from these men. It is probably best to go while everyone still sleeps. I do not want to cause a disturbance."

"As you wish. I will be close if the need arises," Pallo whispered to Kasai.

Kasai was brought to a large tent where guards dressed in plate armor stood two apiece to each side of the entrance, their steel bodies reflecting the yellow light of campfires and torches. They parted the mastiff icons embroidered into the canvas panels between them, admitting Kasai to stand in the busy command center.

Like bees surrounding their matriarch, busy advisors and lieutenants circled the towering duke and they discussed contingency plans and assignments, pointing at maps unrolled on the table in the center of the room. Shiverrig looked up and noticed Kasai, frowning in disapproval, which was replaced by a look of annoyance. "You. Come closer." He raised his voice and spoke to the room, commanding its attention. "This is the one creating the disturbance among my men?" Shiverrig asked.

Kasai took three steps closer. Shiverrig gave him a thorough scrutiny. "You don't look like much."

"No, sir," Kasai responded.

"Well, let's have it boy, should I address you as Sir Ever Hero?"

"No, sir. Maybe. I don't know," Kasai vacillated. He wasn't sure what he should reveal to this man. The Duke of Gethem couldn't be trusted. He had turned a blind eye to the suffering of his subjects within the once-great port city.

"Trust me, boy. You are not the Ever Hero; there is no such thing. The idea of a mighty avatar walking the lands with the powers of a god is absurd. Even the so-called mages Great Houses employ are little more than petty carnival acts. It's all lies and myths used to quell the hearts of the weak-minded. There are no saviors."

Kasai studied the duke's aura. A volcanic blossom of blood-red anger continuously erupted around the man. Shiverrig possessed violent anger and immeasurable fury. He walked to another table that held the figurines of troop placement atop a map of the immediate area.

"Life and death," Shiverrig contemplated his words and then continued, "all revolve around blood and steel. True heroes are forged from battle and conquest. True heroes are men that fight and die to protect the realm their family forged with their own hands. Yes, a true hero must protect the lands and its people from would-be usurpers and duplicitous diplomats."

Shiverrig studied the map for a moment. He moved some of the king's pieces to a new location and added more, bearing his family's colors. He gently pushed them all over on the map. Shiverrig brought his hand to his chin and rubbed the rough stubble.

Kasai noticed the Duke make a slight, silent nod to himself, then picked up the pieces and returned them to their original location on the map. He turned his gaze back to Kasai.

"You know something of what I speak. The Monks of Aetenos are renowned for coming to the aid of the people in times of need, are they not?"

"Yes, Duke Shiverrig. We are taught to protect and serve, to be a shield from darkness and a healer when the land falls ill."

"Exactly! There is a sickness in the land that must be purged. The people need a symbol to rally behind. Although you are not the blood of kings, you can still be of great use to me. If the people are convinced you are their Ever Hero, and it gives them courage in the coming battle, then so be it. You shall be their hero."

"Duke Shiverrig, I am just a simple monk from Ordu."

"Ordu, you say? I was told the hidden monastery was no more. Yet you survived."

"Yes. I was more fortunate than most."

"Indeed." Shiverrig studied Kasai more closely. "Yes, yes, well, you need not worry about evading death a second time. You will remain behind in the medical tents. I can't have a rogue arrow find your heart, or an enemy sword sever you in half."

"I beg your pardon, Duke Shiverrig, that was not my meaning."

"I don't care, it's mine." He looked around the room for a page that wasn't there. "Blast, where is Morgan? Tell that useless page to provide the monk with a medical supply horse. Perhaps he can use some of the famed monk healing on my troops during the coming battle."

Shiverrig called to his guards. "Get him to the armory. I want him covered head-to-toe. Nothing too fancy." Shiverrig turned to Kasai. "The armor will protect you when I cannot. Under no circumstances are you to engage the enemy. Are we clear?"

"Yes, Duke Shiverrig," Kasai bowed.

"Then, that is all." He waved Kasai away, returning his attention to the table and is commanders.

Kasai was taken to the tent housing the knight's armory

and given armor, shield, and sword. Although using a sword and shield were not wholly foreign to him, he walked awkwardly in the plate mail.

He felt off-balanced and claustrophobic. The armor was loose in some areas and too tight in others. He could not feel the energy vibrations of the outside world. Perhaps he was one step closer to understanding the Boundless now that he was cut off from it.

A page was waiting for Kasai when he left the armory. The boy held the reigns to a small, spotted pony, that was burdened with packs of healing supplies, water, and little vials of dark liquid. Kasai wondered if it was the same valerian root Desdemonia had given Master Choejor to let him sleep.

"Sir, Ever Hero, sir, I am Morgan. I am to be your page. I am to go where you go."

"You mean to keep an eye on me and make sure I don't do something stupid, right?" Kasai said, trying to bring some brevity to the conversation.

"Yes, well, something like that, Sir Ever Hero."

"Please, just Kasai."

Kasai smiled at the young boy. He was dressed in the livery of House Shiverrig and had oily, black hair, cropped at the shoulders. Morgan did his best to carry himself in a noble and knightly way, but Kasai could see there was great fear behind his soft eyes. War was no place for children, no matter their upbringing or family heritage.

Kasai returned to camp, but his companions were not present. He assumed they had gone to secure supplies or help where they could. Kasai picked up Ninziz-zida and tucked the Fire Serpent under one of the saddlebags with the rest of the supplies.

Although he had agreed not to march into battle with the

regular soldiers, he knew from experience to keep the ancient Fire Serpent close at hand when danger was near.

Kasai walked through the ranks of the reserves. Morgan was always just a step behind, leading the pony. The youngster followed Kasai as if his life depended on it. Perhaps it did.

The plate mail chafed and confined his movement to a slow crawl. How could anyone fight in such a cumbersome shell? He wondered if he could wield Ninziz-zida effectively if the need arose.

Kasai and Morgan walked through the masses of reserves and met other monks along the way. Somehow, they had survived the monastery massacres. He spoke briefly with them, trying to answer questions, but he felt increasingly uneasy in the presence. Most were adolescent lads that had somehow managed to survive the wilds, only to be conscripted into Shiverrig's army.

The tale of his miraculous feat in the hamlet had spread like wildfire during a dry summer. The ragtag groups of monks looked at him in awe. Some asked to see the Mark of Aetenos on his palms, while others asked if Kasai could speak directly to Aetenos. It was the same everywhere throughout the encampment. The people assumed he was something that he wasn't. They desperately needed a savior. He just wasn't it. "Blessings to you, Ever Hero, and bless of the return of Aetenos," the monks would say repeatedly.

"Thank you, Brothers, and blessings to you as well," Kasai responded politely, but he felt no different inside. He didn't feel heroic or invincible. The truth was Kasai felt helpless and afraid. If it weren't for Desdemonia, Master Choejor, and then Reese saving him, he would have been dead three times already. How was he supposed to be a hero when he couldn't even take care of himself?

His thoughts drifted to Master Choejor. His Master was

somewhere beyond the Hoarfrost Mountains, trapped and suffering at the hands of Khalkoroth. Kasai was haunted by the image of Daku's face appearing and disappearing on the surface of the demon's head. Daku was trapped as well, but could he be saved?

A majestic horn sounded, and the call-to-arms rang out among the early morning campfires. Kasai and Morgan found a high outcropping of boulders that jutted out from a sloping hill. They managed to climb to the top to get a better vantage of the battlefield.

Morgan pointed to a group of large tents with long, colorful banners. The flags flapped and snapped in the wind. "Look, there is Lord Fritta's tent. You can tell by the eagle with its spread wings. And that one there is Duke Manda's. See the diving hawk? The great boar of Baron Rokig's is to the far left. He was made General of the King's Army. A command that should have gone to my Lord Shiverrig."

Morgan was quite a knowledgeable youngster. He explained to Kasai how the Duke's forefathers had come to Baroqia so many years ago to tame the land. The Shiverrig clan laid the foundations of what had become the Kingdom of Baroqia, ruling as kings for countless generations.

Things were different now, however. The power to rule the kingdom had changed. During a time of crisis, it was the gold of House Conrad, not the military power of the House Shiverrig, had paved the way for salvation. Kasai didn't have the heart to tell him he knew at least that much of the history of Baroqia.

"And do you see that great tent with the pouncing griffon? That is King Conrad's tent. My Lord Shiverrig said the king came to watch the victory over the North while he took his tea. He said the king would not personally fight. He said the king was a coward."

Kasai remembered the anger that radiated from Duke

Shiverrig. He wasn't surprised to hear such words had been spoken from the duke. Kasai followed Morgan's litany of family histories as he pointed to the icons and emblems on different tents. Troops began to pour out of the traveling barracks, running to muster points to stand by their lords.

"Do you know anything about warcraft, Ever Hero?"

"Please, Morgan, it's just Kasai. My training at Ordu encompassed all forms of military strategies from significant battles to small skirmishes."

"Have you been in many wars?" Morgan said.

"None. I lived in a place where war was something only read in books."

The horn pealed a different cadence. The armored ranks of the King's Army assembled. Row after row of locked shields and spears tips formed behind the mass of conscripts and peasants relegated to the front.

Kasai peered into the fields just to the front of the lines where the King's Army were still shuffling and jostling into place. He saw the enemy with little difficulty. Barbarian tribesmen from the Far North wielded great broadswords and wore heavy furs on their backs. Their long hair whipped in the early morning wind. There was a small assortment of horsemen, but they were scattered haphazardly throughout the foot soldiers.

"Why would they bring so few to war? The King's Army will make short work of them," Kasai speculated.

The small band of northern barbarians smashed their axes to their shields and shouted curses at the top of their lungs. Without cause or cue, the Northerners charged the men of the King's Army. Burly riders on saddleless horses trotted behind men running full speed, hoping to be the first to engage the enemy.

A trumpet blared from the ranks of men. Mounted knights bearing the flag of General Rokig bolted down a corridor between the fidgeting conscripts into the open field.

"This may be over very quickly," Kasai said with no lack of relief.

A war horn's bone-chilling wail shrieked out over the grasslands; the ground split, tearing open to reveal a colossal beast crawling up from the black dirt. It had the upper torso of a man and the malformed head of a lion. Enormous tusks rolled out of its mouth. Four monstrous legs powered it onto the grassy field. The beast bellowed a preternatural challenge to the men of the King's Army. A warrior in dull, white armor climbed up upon the beast's back. When the beast was fully above ground, The warrior blew from his horn a second time, and the ground trembled.

"Look!" Morgan squealed, his quaking young betraying his youth.

Kasai saw it too. A vast horde of child-sized, unworldly beings spewed from hundreds of previously-hidden holes in the surrounding fields. Misshapen forms and hulking monsters followed in their wake. Kasai saw glimpses of feathered wings and barbed tails, long hooked beaks, and broad snouts rolling through the mass of creatures of chaos.

"Aetenos, help us," Kasai said. "This enemy is beyond men."

A great stench preceded the horde. The air became filled with the stale odor of old death. A frigid wind washed over the King's Army like the precursor of a terrible blizzard. Kasai looked to the reserve troops and saw fear mounting in their hearts.

Nightmares given form stomped and screeched. Their numbers grew as more escaped from the underground tunnels. A raw coldness crept up Kasai's spine. It was an absolute horror. It was death. His mind failed to comprehend what his eyes were seeing.

Rokig's cavalry raced across the open field to engage the barbarians.

"They are too far away," Kasai said. "Stop. Stop!"

The cavalry continued their long charge, eventually crashing into the pack of barbarians, scattering them into smaller groups. Those on foot were brought down quickly under the trampling hooves and the sharp lances of Rokig's knights. The Northern horsemen peeled off quickly to return to the demon horde. Kasai wondered why General Rokig had committed such an ill-advised charge.

"General Rokig has drawn first blood!" Morgan's excitement was short-lived when a flock of bat-winged creatures dove down from the dense grey clouds.

"He's overextended and has lost the support of the archers. The spears and swords cannot cover his retreat," Kasai enlightened his young page. He squeezed his eyes shut, wincing when he heard the ear-piercing screams of the warhorses.

28

SHIVERRIG

Duke Shiverrig sat restlessly on a magnificent black destrier; the early morning's chill lingered on the open fields. The horse shimmied from side-to-side, snorting warm clouds of air through its enlarged nostrils, perhaps sensing his irritation. It

His troops regulated to the southern flank; the king didn't want any competition when he rode the enemy army down. The barbarians had shown their numbers, and as expected, they were few.

The thunder of hooves caught Shiverrig's attention. He opened his spyglass and watched with keen interest as Rokig launched a premature cavalry charge. An experienced general would have seen it for the apparent feint it was. Rokig took the bait. He led half of his mounted knights into battle. The peal of General Rokig's war horn rang out over the clamor of moving troops and nervous draft horses.

"The fly races to the spoiled meat," Shiverrig said. "Ready men. We move on my signal."

The duke rested his spyglass on his thigh, calculating the likelihood of survival for Rokig's cavalry charge. The fool had driven his contingent too far, outside the range of the archers. If the subsequent calvary-infantry melee was not exhaustive, Rokig's group might survive, but Shiverrig was certain the enemy was hoping for just this sort of blind-headed blunder and suspected what was coming next.

A fantastic wail curdled through the air. The ground opened, and a creature from nightmare pulled itself onto the grassy plain. A rider stood on its back with a sword that looked like a long, shard of ice. A second peal of the rider's horn signaled the beginning of the end for Rokig. Hidden tunnel doors opened, and Hell vomited its minions onto the battlefield.

A dark cloud descended on Rokig's far-flung knights. Shiverrig raised his spyglass again and saw queer, bat-like creatures swarm into focus, darting down from low cloud cover to harry the knights. When the winged demons could not pierce the steel of the knight's armor, they gave their full attention to the exposed flanks of the warhorses.

The Duke heard another horn blow. The conscripts and foot soldiers charged the field. Only a token host of reserve troops remained behind. There was no semblance of order to the advancing footmen and no cohesion of lines drawn up to support an orderly retreat.

"And the flow of folly begins," Shiverrig said. He swiveled his spyglass to the enemy warlord, who stood on the back of his war beast.

The warlord raised his sword and blew one last screeching note from his horn. Abyssal creatures rushed across the open field as the demonic horde was unleashed. The poorly equipped conscripts and half-armored, but undisciplined, foot soldiers of the King's Army slowed to a stop.

The enemy slammed into the king's infantry with wild fury. Ill-prepared to deal with such a brutal foe, their will to fight faltered. Many stood frozen in fear as demons pounced on them and rendered them to pieces.

The demon horde drove the soldiers back, killing everyone in their path. The infantry fell back on each other, bodies piling up under the onslaught. Monstrous shrieks were drowned out by human screams. This battle was over before it began. Without a protected front or compact battle groups, Conrad's scattered and poorly disciplined troops quickly fell to the horde. The rest of the morning would be messy blood work.

"Oh, I warned you. Yes, I did," Shiverrig said. He trained his spyglass to Conrad's camp. Knights bearing the colors of House Conrad surrounded the king's tent. A lone rider emerged. The knights formed a protective barrier around him, and as a whole, they galloped hard in the opposite direction of the battle.

"Had your fill of playing war hero, have you?" Shiverrig said.

He signaled his knights. "We go to the king!"

Shiverrig and his knights left the encampment in a cloud of dust and debris. He had accounted for this contingency. The rats always abandon the sinking ship before the cold waters take it. Mortimer Conrad was no different. He had no taste for actual battle.

Hearing the cries of men dying was very different from moving clay figurines on a map. No one ever talked about the smell of death, but it was awful, repulsive to the living. Conrad had always been a coward. He should have ended Gerun long ago, just as Mortimer's father had deposed Gerun's father in these very same fields. "Oh, no, no. Don't think I have forgotten." Shiverrig raced to catch the king. If his allies in the North had done their part, Conrad would be heavily engaged by the enemy when they arrived. That was a big 'if.'

Up ahead, Shiverrig saw a beautiful sight.

"Dax, you perfectly wicked creature," Shiverrig chortled. The North had not betrayed him. The king and his accompaniment of knights were surrounded by a thirty, maybe forty barbarians. The scene was set for Shiverrig to ride in and make a heroic statement. Which he would. Today was the day he saved Baroqia.

"Shiverrig! The enemy besets us!" King Conrad shouted. "To your king! To your king!"

Shiverrig halted his advance. The barbarians leveled heavy crossbows at the king's knights. A guttural command was shouted, and the bolts were let loose. More than half of the knights died slumped in their saddles or fell to the ground to be broken by their horse's hooves.

The barbarians saw Shiverrig's company and scattered across the field or escaped into nearby holes.

"Get them! Get them all!" King Conrad cried.

The king's knights gave chase. Ten of them curled back to form a loose circle around the king.

"The battle did not go as you planned, eh Mortimer?" Duke Shiverrig said as he calmly rode up to the king. His destrier snorted and pranced closely to the king's horse. King Conrad's mare shied away from the intimidating warhorse.

"You will address me as your king!"

"You should have followed my strategy at the war council, Mortimer. Soldier's lives would have been saved. Lives I would have put to better use in the coming war. But no matter, we would have eventually come to this moment, you and I."

King Conrad was puzzled. "This moment?"

"Yes, this moment, Mortimer." Shiverrig's eyes followed the trails of the king's knights as they darted after the fleeing enemy. "No accounting for an untrained guard." He unsheathed his great bastard sword.

Conrad's eyes widened in shock. "Are you mad? I am your king! My men here will witness your treasonous betrayal and cut you down where you stand."

Shivering laughed. "These men?" Shiverrig pointed to the mounted knights closing the circle about the king. "These are MY men. The ones you insisted taking from Gethem's Elite Guard, or had you forgotten?"

Conrad drew a sword that had never been bloodied in battle or otherwise. It was too heavy for his hands, and the point drooped low. Shiverrig shook his head with disappointment.

"You could have been a wealthy noble and lived a long life, had you simply acknowledged my rightful claim to the throne when I came of age. The history of the land shall now be honored."

Shiverrig blocked the King's pathetic thrust with ease and jabbed his sword into Conrad's shoulder. The sword fell from his hand and clattered uselessly on some small stones.

"I yield! I yield! The kingdom is yours!" King Conrad cried.

"It's far too late for that."

Duke Shiverrig deftly sliced his sword back across Conrad's exposed neck. The cut was deep enough to cut the carotid artery. Conrad's lifeblood spurted out over his unblemished armor. Shiverrig tore off Conrad's loose-fitting helm and tossed it to the ground. He then grabbed a handful of Conrad's hair and gave a swift jerk, pulling the dead king from his horse.

Shiverrig spat on the pitiful form of his nemesis.

"Round up the remains of this rabble. Kill the Northerners and any of Conrad's remaining knights."

A squad of Shiverrig's knights galloped away.

"Throw the dead together. Make it appear we arrived too late to protect the king from the ambush."

Shiverrig took in the carnage. Justice was served.

The Knights of Gethem quickly dispatched the remaining guardsmen of the king. Most of Conrad's men were elevated to knighthood by excessive financial contribution to House Conrad's coffers. Some of the Northerners managed to escape, but that was little matter. Shiverrig's objective had been achieved.

It was now time to collect his men. Lord Fritta had agreed to terms of Shiverrig's ascension to the throne if the King should fall, and with luck, Lord Manda would comply as well. What would that princess of a man care as long as the coin flowed?

Duke Shiverrig turned his horse to lead his knights from the killing field. He spotted a lone figure approaching on a twisted beast. The figure shimmered in the late morning light and wore a broad grin as he clapped his hands together in applause.

"Sekka, the Frost Queen of Gathos, congratulates you on a job well done, Duke Shiverrig. The battle was easily won, as expected. The Mistress wishes to meet with you and express her gratitude to you in person," Dax said.

"Curious, that it's Sekka, not Maugris, who brings congratulations."

"Maugris, yes. I'm sure he would like to express his pleasure as well," Dax said. The twinkle in his eye spoke volumes to Shiverrig of who indeed held power in the North.

"Her desire for celebration is untimely. I have other pressing business in Qaqal."

Shiverrig signaled his knights to gather close. He pointed at a nearby squire. "You there, get word to my man, Pathias. Have him alert Lord Fritta that the king has fallen to an enemy ambush. This battle is lost. All soldiers are to regroup at the Broken Boulder Crossroads. Have Pathias send another man to Lord Manda with the same message."

Shiverrig rounded his horseback to Dax. "Tell your Queen that her precious Ever Hero was in my possession before the fighting began. I instructed our mutual friend to walk with him like a second shadow. I know not what has become of him, but I have done my part."

"All is as it should be, Duke Shiverrig." Dax bowed again in his saddle. "I bid you good fortune until we meet again."

The Duke addressed his men. "Knights of Gethem, we march to the City of Spires and the throne of Baroqia!" The knights cheered and raised their swords. They fell into rank and proceeded to follow their beloved Duke.

29

KASAI

Sharp horns sounded as the King's Army raced to engage the enemy with a rush of infantry. General Rokig and his men frantically fought the flying creatures as the bat-like things swarmed around the knights.

Eventually, the winged demons turned their attention to the warhorses. Kasai heard the animals scream. Soon each horse was covered in flapping wings. The horses ran, kicking and bucking, but could not dislodge the demons. Riders fell to the ground as they were shucked off their terrified mounts.

The infantry finally joined the desperate knights in the middle of the battlefield. Before the soldiers could take up proper defensive lines, the demon horde attacked with fury. They slammed into the king's disoriented army in a giant wave of claws, hooked beaks, and gnashing teeth. Wings beat, and barbed tails pierced men until they died.

Fear overwhelmed the troops. They stood motionless as creatures from their nightmares became real before their eyes. Soldiers were slaughtered where they stood. The demon warlord slid off his mount and effortlessly carved a gruesome path towards General Rokig and his horseless knights.

"If the general falls, it will be the end of the infantry," Kasai warned.

The demon warlord ruthlessly slew everything in his path. No one could stand against him or his horrible sword and survive. Bodies were cloven in half or shattered into spraying shards of ice. As their ranks were destroyed, the men turned and ran. The King's Army had failed miserably.

The soldiers held back in reserve began to panic. They saw the frontline troops fleeing the field, and knew their turn was coming. Kasai could smell the reek of their desperation. In some cases, it puddled at their feet. A captain rode forward on a bloodied horse and yelled out, "Wedge formation, now! Push forward hard and drive the enemy forces back. Keep ramming ahead until you reach General Rokig. Do not stop! If you fail, we die!"

Kasai could see the faces of the men below him. None of them were listening to the captain. They looked out to the battlefield to where the slaughter was the greatest. They were being sent to their deaths to support the retreat of the Rokig cavalry and the first wave of infantry.

Suddenly, a collective roar spread across the battlefield. Kasai looked back to the battle and saw the demon warlord had struck down General Rokig. The general lay headless on the ground with a circle of dead knights piled around the demon.

The soldier's morale was broken; men fled for their lives. Monsters pounced on their backs and dragged them to the ground. It was a day of ruin for the King's Army and, possibly, the Kingdom of Baroqia. The horde shrieked its unnatural symphony of animalistic victory. Who could stop such a force?

The reserve troops were barely able to shuffle into a

defensible position. Fear glued their feet to the ground. If the reserves didn't stop the horde, the monsters would run free across Baroqia. The army needed someone to rally them together and keep courage and bravery in their hearts. General Rokig was gone. The army was disintegrating. A new hero must emerge, or all would be lost.

Kasai looked to the tent of King Conrad. His leadership and presence on the battlefield were needed now more than ever. A group of knights was in a defensive circle around the entrance. A mounted rider trotted out of the large tent and took his position inside the semi-circle of armor and steel.

"Look, Morgan, King Conrad is coming out of the griffon tent. He will lead the army."

The king emerged clad in shining armor as if on parade. But the king and his knights galloped away, fleeing the battlefield.

"I don't understand," Kasai professed as he watched in disbelief.

"Coward," Morgan responded matter-of-factly, his face also turned to witness the betrayal of the king.

Kasai observed the young page, for the first time noticing that Morgan's eyes were a unique pale-magenta.

"Come, Ever Hero. We do not want to be trapped up here when the demons come," Morgan said.

Kasai simply nodded, carefully climbing down the boulders as he followed Morgan, his armor making every move a chore. Morgan reached the bottom first and untied the supply pony he had left at a small tree. Kasai thought of his friends and hoped they were all right. Had Pallo and Run-Run joined the fight? Were Des and Reese tending to the incoming wounded? What would happen when the demon horde reached the encampment? None of them would be safe.

"Morgan, there is something I must do. Help me remove this shell."

"But my duke clearly instructed me to keep you out of harm's way. Those plates are important. They will keep you safe. You are too valuable."

"I can't move properly. Please, help me."

"What do you intend to do?" Morgan said. He slowly shook his head from left to right as he reached for a buckle.

"Something stupid. Now please, unbuckle what I cannot reach in the back."

The armor dropped to the ground. Nearby, soldiers heard it clang. They looked at Kasai, wondering what he was doing. Nobody removed their armor during battle. Morgan gave him a quick nod of approval. The young page almost seemed eager to see what would happen next.

"Where are you going, monk?" one of the soldiers demanded. The young man pointed his sword at Kasai. His old, chipped blade shook nervously in the air.

Kasai's eyes went to the battlefield. The slaughter was getting worse. There was only one way to stop it. "I must go."

The reserve soldiers stared at Kasai with anger in their eyes.

"Deserter!"

"Coward!"

"You're no Ever Hero! We are all doomed!"

"You were supposed to protect us from harm!"

They accused him with desperate voices. Kasai knew they were terrified. "I'm sorry. My place is not here with you."

The soldiers saw the sword and shield gifted to him by Duke Shiverrig lying on the ground. Hatred filled their faces.

"Go and hide, you traitorous monk. Your time will come soon enough. None of us will survive this day."

Kasai gathered his burnt-orange robe tighter. He did his

best to smooth out the wrinkles caused by the heavy armor. He turned to the supply pony and reached under the saddlebag. Ninziz-zida felt good in his hand.

The ancient weapon glowed amber, eager to be wielded once more. Kasai sighed. I must do this thing, though it surely will cost me everything. Ninziz-zida heard his thought and passed on feelings of partnership, trust, and power. The ancient weapon coaxed him to share his fire xindu energy with her. He drew in a deep, slow breath. So be it.

Ninziz-zida came alive. She pressed into his mind whirling striking movements and intricate patterns of defense. Would it be enough? He recalled the words of Master Dorje when he received the power tattoo for courage. It seemed like ages ago. 'You shall fill the hearts of those around you with the bravery in your soul and the courage in your heart. As you are strong of will, so shall you inspire the will of others.'

Kasai found his courage, and the Mark of Mizzen glowed on his forearm. He thought about Desdemonia. A slight smile crossed his lips when he thought of the frolicking gypsy, dancing through the forest when they first met. He wished he could have said goodbye.

In the distance, the allied army was trying desperately to regroup. Small, isolated pockets of resistance began to form. The demon horde was a swirling tide of death around them, preventing them from connecting. The demon warlord directed them from where he stood.

'The Great Balance must remain.' Kasai heard the prophetic words of Master Dorje in his head. "And as General Rokig fell, so must the enemy's leader," he said to himself.

The ground vibrated with the pounding of warfare.

Kasai's exposed feet felt the energy of the cold soil as his toes dug into the earth. The sensation of war was foreign and harsh to him. It overwhelmed his senses.

He closed his eyes and calmed his breathing once more. It must be this way. He knew the soldiers' anger was understandable, if not warranted. He turned away from their mistaken expressions of betrayal and began the long walk towards the battlefield.

Kasai held the three segments of Ninziz-zida in one hand as he approached the front line of the reserve ranks. He surveyed the field and the quickest route to his goal. Kasai felt a firm grip take his arm and turned to see who had grabbed him from behind.

"Brother Kasai?" It was Brother Maru from Ordu. Kasai was just as surprised as Maru to see the other alive.

"Maru? I'm happy to see you are still among us, Brother, although I wish it were under better circumstances."

"You're heading into the madness? You can't make any difference. You're wasting your life."

"I must try, Maru."

"You'll be ripped apart!"

"I have Ninziz-zida to guide me." Kasai held out the ancient weapon for Maru to see.

"You hold the Fire Serpent," Maru said and looked at Ninziz-zida with reverence, but he backed away in confusion. "How?" Then focus returned to the young monk's eyes. "Kasai, look at me. This battle is over. We must regroup with the remaining monks and do what we can to heal the wounded. We will lead them to safety away from this place. There will be another time."

"Maru, you are very wise for such a youngling. That is a sound plan and one aligned with the Boundless. The Masters would be proud to hear you say those words in a time like this. You and the others will be greatly needed in the days that follow."

Kasai looked back to the battlefield. Retreating soldiers pushed past them and into the ranks of the waiting reserves. "The Boundless has set a different path for me. Be well, my friend."

Kasai left Maru's side and jogged onto the field. While others fled, he alone moved towards the chaos. Wounded men stumbled back to what they thought was the safety of the reserve troops. Messenger horses with empty saddles galloped back to the encampment. Their fear struck eyes were wide as saucers.

Kasai focused his concentration on the ink-black auras of the creatures from the Abyss. They were everywhere he looked. They fought on the ground or flew in the air over the battle. How could mere men withstand such a foe when fear tore away their resolve to fight?

Without a focal point to keep their hearts and minds aligned as one, the men of the army lost hope. The death of Rokig had broken them. Kasai picked up his pace and ran towards the scattering pockets of men still fighting for their lives. The trampled grass was no longer golden brown, but red with blood.

Ninziz-zida pulsed in his hand and kept time with the pounding of his heart. The fighting swelled around him. The smell of fresh blood and metal shavings filled his nose.

The screaming was everywhere. Demons ripped the entrails from living men and gorged themselves on the warm meat of their victims. Kasai's mind began to fray. There were too many possibilities, too many targets, too many lives to save. His hands squeezed Ninziz-zida tightly.

The ancient artifact sensed Kasai's fear and confusion. Warmth radiated up his arm and filled his body with strength and purpose. Kasai's vision cleared, and his mind became lucid. The movement of fighting slowed down around him, yet he knew his own body was moving faster.

Kasai ran towards a warrior who had fallen under the savage blows of a demon with silver scales and white fur. The demon knocked away the soldier's sword, chortling through a mouth filled with dangling cilia. It grabbed the soldier's shield and tossed it to the ground. The white-furred demon raised its jagged spear to deliver the killing blow.

Kasai launched into the air, sailing over the prone soldier. Ninziz-zida's end segment flashed out in a blaze of yellow fire. The demon's head was vaporized into red mist. Its body crumbled to the ground and settled into a pile of ash.

Ninziz-zida sent sensations of conviction and strength into Kasai. Somehow, like before, he knew what the ancient weapon said. *'I am the Great Fire Serpent! I am Ninziz-zida! I will blaze brightly into the soulless Darkness!'*

The ancient weapon was challenging the entire enemy horde.

Kasai thought he now understood Ninziz-zida. The Fire Serpent did not want to possess his soul and make him into a slave. The weapon was crafted to destroy evil, and the greater the evil it encountered, the more powerful it became.

Ninziz-zida was alive in his hands. The mental connection the two shared was acute, and he realized they needed each other; they were meant to be together. Ninziz-zida had been dormant for many, long years waiting in the monastery's Hall of Artifacts. Now she had awakened and had somehow chosen Kasai as her champion.

Kasai held Ninziz-zida with both hands. Her sections pulsed with eagerness to continue the attack. Kasai closed his eyes and concentrated on opening all channels of his xindu energies to the artifact. Perhaps Ninziz-zida could transmute his energy into her fighting spirit. He breathed in deeply and let out a long, slow, cleansing breath.

"Ninziz-zida, we are of singular purpose. As I give myself to the Boundless, I now open myself to you. Show me your righteous flame. Let us confront this horror together, as one."

Ninziz-zida's three sections burst forth with bright-orange flames in his hands.

'As one.'

Kasai and Ninziz-zida became an unbroken force of attack and defense as they struck down the enemy demons and barbarians. He was a whirling dervish, moving like a blur from one killing strike to another.

His lightning-fast strikes left his enemies defenseless and ruined. Hundreds of barbarian bones shattered, and the creatures of the Abyss were vaporized into ash. A cyclone of Ninziz-zida's fire whipped around Kasai as he rushed toward the demon warlord.

Kasai climbed over the ring of dead knights and soldiers, while the warlord stood preoccupied in the middle, white armor was dented and smeared with human blood. Smeared handprints showed the slain warriors' last attempts to hold the demon back.

Kasai approached slowly, while the warlord admired the armored head of General Rokig. The general's headless body laid at the warlord's feet. The demon lifted Rokig's head high over his own, drinking the fluids leaking from the severed neck. Finally, he spotted Kasai from the corner of his eye.

"The Great Warlord Oziax welcomes you to your death, mortal," he stated with mocking bow. He casually pointed his demonic sword at Kasai and uttered a sharp sounding word. A blast of ice shot from the blade. Kasai spun Ninziz-zida's end sections into a shield of fire, melting the ice fragments in the flame.

"Clever trick, monk," Oziax said. He dropped Rokig's head and leaped at Kasai.

Kasai held the middle section of Ninziz-zida and spun

the end segments in a curved figure-eight pattern. The staff wiped from one side of his body to the other. Kasai sent one of the staff sections out to attack Oziax, but the demon's sword parry was faster, and Kasai's strike missed its mark.

A terrible hiss and groan resounded as the two weapons clashed together again and again. Kasai felt Ninziz-zida's frustration and focused more of his fire xindu into the enchanted weapon.

Kasai grabbed the tail of the Fire Serpent and whipped the rest at Oziax. Kasai snapped the staff back just as it connected to Oziax's shoulder guard on his sword arm. The armor cracked and sizzled. Oziax ripped the useless armor away, exposing his alabaster arm and shoulder.

Oziax bellowed in rage and drove harder into Kasai. The power of the demon was almost overwhelming. Kasai shuffled back in defense, but Oziax slashed his sword forward and struck Kasai on the knuckles of his right hand. Kasai pulled his hand back but lost his grip on the section he was holding.

The demon pivoted sharply and grabbed Ninziz-zida. Oziax gritted in pain as Ninziz-zida's flames burned hot in his hand. But Oziax held on tight and ripped the Fire Serpent out of Kasai's hand, tossing her wide to the side and out of reach.

Oziax swung his ice sword at Kasai's head and then at his gut. Kasai jumped back in a series of somersaults to avoid the terrible blade.

"Stay still, little butterfly."

Kasai spun back again but tumbled over the circle of dead men that made up their mini arena, scrambling to his knees as quickly as he could. Oziax was already there, striking down with a mighty blow Kasai could not dodge. He reacted the only way he could, reaching up to clamp the sword between his hands. Blue light erupted from the cobalt marks on his palms.

"Impossible! No one can stop the might of Eishorror," Oziax shouted as he threw Kasai off the sword. Kasai tumbled away. He stood up fast and was rewarded by a terrible backhand across his face.

Kasai was battered, bruised, cut, and now bloodied. Even with Ninziz-zida in hand, he had only managed to annoy the demon warlord. He was running out of tricks.

Oziax charged forward. Kasai shifted his weight and collapsed at his knees. As Oziax's sword arm passed overhead, Kasai sprung back up. He shaped his hand like a knife and delivered a sharp strike to the nerve cluster in the demon's exposed shoulder. It paralyzed Oziax's arm, and his ice sword dropped to the ground. Kasai breathed a quick sigh of relief.

Oziax howled in pain and frustration as he tried to raise his dead arm. Glaring at Kasai, he said, "You cannot win. Let me show you."

Oziax took two steps back and began to change into something grotesque and horrible. His armor fell off his body, his form swelling and distorting itself. His legs transformed into something akin to the back legs of a horse or satyr with cloven hooves.

The hand that could still move, grew long tentacles where fingers were before. Each tentacle had hundreds of suction cups with sharp barbs protruding from the center.

Oziax's facial features drew back into a brutish animal skull. The old flesh stretched across its surface and tore in places. Long black horns sprouted, curling upward from his forehead.

His back became covered in coarse, white hair, the rest of his skin the color of bleached bones suffering too long in the sun. Kasai watched the transformation with fascination and dread. He couldn't breathe. His lungs felt like a burning furnace consuming all the air around him, suffocating him in the process.

The demon stomped forward, deadly and invincible. Without Ninziz-zida, all he had were his feeble skills.

"I am nothing without Ninziz-zida. Nothing. I can't fight this thing. It's finished," Kasai thought.

"This is not the end. You must have faith. You must believe."

"I do believe," Kasai said, and he did. He believed he heard the Song of Aetenos in his head. But it wasn't enough.

"In yourself."

The voice in his head was right. Kasai pushed the doubt from his mind. He would have faith in himself. It didn't matter if he was the Ever Hero or not. At this moment, he would choose to believe that he was.

Kasai drew deeply from the reservoirs of his xindu energy. The life forces connected to the Boundless demanded a heavy toll, and he surrendered himself as payment. His xindu energies expanded to claim the spirit of his offering. Fire, water, air, and earth energy overlapped for the first time. The sensation was powerful and exhilarating.

"I must end this now. There is no more to give."

Kasai's body vibrated. A transparent membrane of silvery-blue light shimmered around him. He heard the distant echo of Aetenos' voice in his mind.

"I am the Divine Fist, and you shall be my argent hammer to smite the darkness."

Now, there would be no more confusion, no hesitation, just clarity of purpose. Kasai's eyes lifted to the heavens.

"I will."

Oziax lunged head-first like a charging bull. Kasai flashed to the right. He shot his arms out and struck the side of Oziax's head with his open palms. The noise of battle was sucked into a sliver of silence before a dynamic BOOM resounded across the battlefield. A dome of energy expanded outward, ripping open the debris-filled air. The slain bodies of General Rokig's elite guard rolled and tossed like broken ragdolls.

Oziax reeled sideways, dazed and unbalanced. He shook his head like a wild beast shaking water from its dense mane. Glaring at Kasai, a wicked smile came to his face when he regained his balance.

Panting, Kasai could hardly stand. He had never known such exhaustion and could barely keep his head up. But it didn't matter anymore. He had done his best, though it wasn't enough. Death came for him in the form of a wicked beast. But for some reason, an image of Desdemonia laughing and dancing came to mind. It would be, perhaps his last pleasant thought in this world of horror he could not escape.

Oziax's steps became more erratic and exaggerated. He overcompensated to prevent himself from falling but only became more unbalanced. The murderous smile faded as black ichor oozed from his fleshless nostrils before leaking from his eyes and bubbling out of his ears.

The demon fell to his knees. The tentacles of his left hand wrapped around his bestial head. Oziax threw his head back and unleashed a primordial roar just before his head exploded. Tiny pieces of brain and skull jettisoned over the bodies of the dead and then withered to ash. Oziax's headless body sank to the trampled ground and slowly dissolved to a pile of black ash.

Kasai barely registered what had happened. He rested his head on his chest. It was over. He just wanted to sleep. No more fighting. No more suffering. No more anything. He felt his body go light and hoped the afterlife would be kind. His eyes closed, and his ears went deaf to the sounds of battle around him.

. . .

When Kasai finally opened his eyes, smoke and ash were billowing in the air. He was lying flat on his back in the open encampment of the King's Army. The sharp sounds of mayhem amplified as his hearing returned. A small group of people surrounded him, including Pallo, who all but hovered. Behind him, two knights unfamiliar knights approached. "Your page found us after you took to the field. You are either mad, or there is a courage in your heart unknown to men. We fought to reach your side and arrived to witness some kind of miracle," the knight said in a voice filled with awe. "We carried you here but held little hope you would survive long enough to receive proper healing." He stared at Kasai with wonder in his eyes.

"Morgan ... is he safe?" Kasai asked.

The second knight spoke. "The remaining knights rallied behind the incredible turn in the battle you caused ... with your bare hands." He looked at his own hands, shaking his head in bewilderment. "With their leader destroyed, the horde broke ranks and scattered. They lost themselves in a sea of carnage. They killed anything in their immediate vicinity, including their own. The weak fell prey to the strong, none could escape the hunger of the horde. I spied a fell, white fiend picking through the ash corpse of their headless warlord. Vile creatures. No respect for the dead."

"Duke Shiverrig will want to hear more of your bravery and the story behind your magic," the first knight said eagerly.

Kasai massaged his throbbing head. "It's not magic." He raised himself on one elbow to search the room. "Where is Des?"

"I am here," she said, shouldering her way between the

two knights. "Seems you have a knack for finding trouble no matter where you go."

"And Reese?"

"I am here, Kasai," Reese said, kneeling at the end of his cot. "I saw what you did to that ... monster. Only a True-born of the Immortal Mother has such strength. How ... did you do that?" Reese asked.

Pallo kneeled by the side of the cot. "The prophecy is unwoven. The Ever Hero of the Divine Fist now walks the land."

"Reese," Kasai said with genuine affection. "I'm glad you are safe." He looked for Run-Run, then turned his head towards Pallo. "Where is your brother? He didn't—"

"Run-Run secures supplies. We assumed you would want to continue the search for your Master. He has found loyal friends that would be honored to join the Ever Hero in his quest.

"The road will not be easy. We must move with stealth and precision. The enemy is scattered but hungry for mortal souls."

Kasai lifted himself from the cot but fell back again.

"Ninziz-zida. I lost the Fire Serpent during the battle. I must retrieve her."

"Rest easy, Ever Hero. I found her when we found you." Pallo presented Kasai with a long, wrapped length of cloth. "She was hot to the touch. I could not hold the staff with my bare hands for any amount of time."

Kasai breathed a sigh of relief. He clutched Ninziz-zida tightly. The familiar shape and weight of the weapon gave him comfort.

Reese edged in closer to Kasai. She reached out a tentative hand to touch the cobalt mark on his left palm. "You ... really are the Ever Hero. The prophecy is true. The reincarnation of Aetenos is here." Reese knelt before the cot in supplication. "Our savior has returned."

"Reese, please. Stop. I am still just Kasai." He sat at the edge of the cot. He was a bit shaky but well enough to move. "We have done all we can here. I am well enough to travel. Master Choejor needs us," Kasai said, determination renewed.

30

DESDEMONIA

The King's Army had scattered. Extensive amounts of supplies, tents, armor, equipment, and war machines were left unattended. Riderless horses formed herds and bolted away from the carnage into the open fields. The demon horde divided into smaller groups; some chased down the fleeing soldiers while others fought amongst themselves. The victor sat in the middle of the slain and ate its fill.

Earlier, Run-Run had gathered enough horses for everyone, and the small party carefully navigated away from the overrun encampment. They outran anything that was too lazy to give chase. There were plenty of slow-moving foot soldiers to occupy the attention of the horde. Soon, the battlefield was well out of view.

The open fields provided no shelter, but at least they could see enemies coming from afar. While the rest of the party kept a watchful eye for pursuit, Desdemonia scanned the ground ahead. She had no desire to be on the surprise end of a sneak attack.

The party rode throughout the rest of the day until the

glowing orange sun silently slipped below the jagged mountain peaks of the Hoarfrost Mountains. Pallo, at the lead, put his hand up to signal a stop. In the distance, Desdemonia spotted three riders approaching from the south.

"Men of the King's Army?" Kasai asked.

"Not soldiers," Pallo answered.

The three riders rode their mounts hard until they reached the others and brought their lathered horses to a stop. Desdemonia noted they wore the mark of Aetenos on their jacket collars; she wasn't keen on new faces, but knew they'd need help where they were headed. She overheard Pallo discussing the route to Storm Wind Pass with one of the riders.

"We will camp here for the night," Pallo said when they were finished.

Desdemonia dismounted. Her body was sore and tired. She looked to see how Kasai fared; he looked exhausted—face was drawn with his eyes that looked apologetic, like everything that had happened was somehow his fault.

Run-Run tended to the horses, he was a natural with animals. Desdemonia could tell he was a friend of the forest. She wondered if Kasai was…or could be.

Desdemonia heard a sharp whistle; Pallo waved his brother and the three newcomers over to him. The three men quit their tasks and jogged over to Pallo. They chatted for a moment before walking purposefully to Kasai. Desdemonia followed.

"Time for introductions," she sighed. She just wanted to sleep.

The five men stopped as one in front of Kasai. Pallo pointed at each newcomer in turn.

"Ever Hero, may I introduce Airis, Rafar, and Orin. They are all experienced spire runners and trusted members of the Kibo Gensai. Orin is most familiar with the terrain of the

Hoarfrost. He will act as our guide once we reach the foothills."

Rafar stepped forward and put two fingers to his forehead and bowed deeply. He was a tall man, the tallest of the group. He wore his hair tied back behind his head, allowing only a few thick strands to fall in front of his face. His intense, dark eyes never left Kasai. "I am honored and humbled to walk with the Ever Hero of our time. Please accept my swords as your own."

Airis was next. He wore a broad grin when he took a step forward. He was a young man, filled with enthusiasm and determination. He had a boyish face and eyes that had seen too much sorrow. He had wavy, dirty-blonde hair that he wore tied up above his head in a topknot.

"Run-Run, the Miko Nuna sends her greetings and eagerly awaits your safe return," Airis said. There was laughter in his voice.

Rafar just shook his head.

"Run-Run, what did I tell you about that one? Don't get mixed up with the crazy ones."

Run-Run looked at his brother and then somehow found Desdemonia's eyes. His bashful expression was endearing. She had liked him immediately. He maintained a level of happiness that most people dreamed of, and yet, he had suffered great hardship. He had a pure soul.

Desdemonia watched Reese move about the basic camp. She wore the clothes of a priestess and said the words of one devoted to the Immortal Mother, but everything about her was off by just a little. She made too many tiny mistakes. Any of them could go unnoticed, but when added up, they told a different story. Kasai once said Desdemonia saw snakes in the grass when there were none.

I know a snake when I see one; Desdemonia narrowed her eyes, keeping a keen watch on Reese as she listened to Pallo introduce the third newcomer as Orin. The man had closely cropped jet-black hair. He had a clean-shaven face that proudly displayed thin scars that covered his cheek and jaw.

"Greetings, Orin," Kasai said. He pointed casually at the scar tissue on Orin's face. "Have you seen many battles?"

"No more or less than any of us, Ever Hero. Orin is a good fighter with quick steel," Pallo responded, in place of Orin, who bowed, but remained silent. His eyes shifted to Desdemonia and then to Pallo.

"And the scars? Now that I see them more clearly, they seem to be intentional," Kasai said.

This time, Orin spoke for himself, "We of the Kibo Gensai have devoted ourselves, mind, body, and soul, to fight the enemies of the Light. I am a man of singularity in my faith. The marks are not limited to my face. I notch my flesh with a count of every foul creature I have slain in the name of Aetenos. The unmarked portions of my body are a grim reminder that there is more holy work to be done."

"There are more?" Kasai said in astonishment.

Pallo nodded. He circled his finger over all of Orin's body. Orin stepped back, but not before eying Desdemonia with a baleful look.

She gave him a friendly wink in return. *Here's another one that's going to be a problem*, she thought. Orin's eyes were dark and sharp. He looked the type that liked to brood. She felt his scrutinizing gaze like a dagger thrust. Somehow, Orin's hawk-like stare made her feel unwanted or tainted in some way. *Bah. I'm just tired. He's the newcomer, not me.*

Kasai cleared his throat. "I'm not very good at this sort of thing," he started then took a breath to collect his thoughts. "I will honestly tell you I do not know what it means to be an Ever Hero of Aetenos. Who could? And since there were no lessons on the subject at Ordu, I am making this up as I go." He grinned at Desdemonia, knowing he beat her to the joke. She smiled warmly back at him. *He's learning.*

"I do know what is right and what is wrong. I know the importance of protecting the vulnerable spots of the Brother fighting by your side and being protected in kind. Together, we are stronger.

"I go to keep a promise to rescue my Master from an evil that is beyond my comprehension, and quite possibly my skill. I cannot ask you to follow me, for I do not know what horror awaits us in the mountains. If you do, I will be honored by your companionship."

The Kibo Gensai bowed in unison. They returned to their horses and unpacked their bedrolls.

"Nice speech. Uplifting and filled with the promise of a great victory," Desdemonia commented with a grin of her own.

"Funny," Kasai said. "Have you seen Reese?" He looked about the camp.

"Maybe she fell in a ditch," Desdemonia chuckled, sounding hopeful.

"Very nice." Kasai's horse became agitated. "What's spooked you, girl?"

Reese seemingly appeared from around the other side of Kasai's horse. "Oh, I'm still here. I'll be with you until the end." Reese gave Desdemonia a crooked smile.

"Lovely," Desdemonia gibed under her breath.

"I hope we can eat soon. I'm famished," Kasai said. He walked over to where Run-Run was unpacking a sack of food.

"Remember what I said, witch. Do not get in my way." Reese shouldered past Desdemonia to join Kasai and Run-Run.

"This just keeps getting better," Desdemonia deadpanned.

She unstrapped her saddle and slapped her horse on the rear, sending it to graze.

The next morning the party awoke at first light. Everyone was sore from yesterday's long ride. They ate a quick breakfast before breaking camp. Desdemonia climbed atop her horse. Kasai fumbled along as he usually did. He tripped over more things than she could count. The members of the Kibo Gensai looked at him as if he were a sacred thing. *So much bowing*, she thought, shaking her head amused, allowing herself a little chuckle.

"It's a day's ride to the beginning of Storm Wind Pass. Orin will take us through the mountain trails once we leave the Pass. We will find Rachlach Fortress on the morrow of the third," Pallo said as the small party made their way East.

"If we're lucky," Orin said.

"Isn't it curious that we have not encountered any enemy patrols?" Desdemonia commented.

"The Immortal Mother protects her children in their time of greatest need," Reese countered. "Everything is as it should be."

Desdemonia looked skeptically at the priestess. "Or we are heading straight into a well-placed ambush."

"Let's be happy luck is on our side for once," Kasai suggested as he trotted past the two women. "And stop your bickering."

The party traveled on without incident to the entrance Storm Wind Pass. "We must leave the horses here and travel light on foot. Airis will take the horses into the forest foothills a few miles to the south. He will await our return there," Pallo said to the group.

"This makes no sense. Ten thousand footsteps must have passed this way to battle, yet they leave no one behind?"

Desdemonia pointed out. "Where's the broken gear, or shit, or something?"

Pallo looked all about and nodded in agreement. "Orin, surely there should be sentries of some kind along the mountain pass."

Orin unsheathed one of his short swords. He narrowed his eyes. "Best to be ready."

"Ever Hero, what can you sense?" Pallo asked.

"Can you sense danger, too?" Desdemonia said. She'd be impressed if he could. "That would be handy."

He shrugged his shoulders. "It doesn't really work like that."

Reese sighed. "You all worry too much. There are no sentries because the battle was a slaughter. There's no need to guard what the dead cannot steal."

"What do you think, Des?" Kasai asked.

Reese interjected before Desdemonia could respond. "There is nothing more to say. A higher-power watches over us and has cleared the way for the Ever Hero."

Desdemonia gave Reese a cross look, "Doubtful," she said before catching up to Kasai. He was walking with heavy steps again. She could tell he had something on his mind, beyond the present. *It's the amulet.* Every time she brought it up, he shut her down. He refused to listen to any form of reason. "Kasai?" Des began softly when they walked side-by-side.

"Des, if it's about the amulet again, I will listen, but you know how I feel about it. Dark magic is dark magic, no matter the point of view," he said. He was short, almost angry. Something was definitely on his mind.

"I don't want to talk about the amulet," she said, protectively grasping the rock hanging from her neck. "Forget it, Kasai. I can see you are in a mood."

"I apologize, Des. Please continue."

Desdemonia could not help but look askance at him. She

was unsure if she wanted to discuss the amulet or not. She decided it was best to change the subject.

"We have been traveling together for quite some time now. And well, as you know, I've been on my own since my early years. Just me and Gauldi. But he really isn't much of a talker if you know what I mean. And well, I thought ... after all this is over, maybe you and Master Choejor would like to stay with me in the forest." She was surprised that tumbled out of her mouth so easily. "There, I said it."

"The forest? With you and that creature who would like nothing more than to split me in two?"

"That's just Gauldi's way. Okay, not the forest. We can go anywhere. Maybe back to Sunne."

"You must know I need to return to Ordu. It will need to be rebuilt. That's Master Choejor's and my home."

"You don't have to say no straight off like it's a stupid idea. Is it because of Reese?" Desdemonia fumed yet felt crestfallen on the inside. She should have kept her idea to herself.

"Reese? What does she have to do with anything? She's not coming to Ordu."

"Why must you be so dense? I see the way she's always whispering in your ear, telling you things in private. She's poisoned your heart against me. Don't deny it."

"Reese? What? Poisoning my heart?"

Desdemonia looked directly into his eyes. "Yes, Kasai, your heart. Have you no feelings for me after all that we have shared?"

Kasai's eyes grew wide. He fidgeted as he walked. He kicked a stone on the road, and then another.

"Well?" Desdemonia said.

"Of course, I have feelings for you. We're friends."

"Nothing more?" She cozied up to him, her grin broadening.

"I don't know. Sometimes you make me feel dizzy."

"Dizzy? That's hardly romantic," Desdemonia cuffed him upside his head. But inside, she was smiling. "You apparently have no idea what I am talking about. I'm such a fool." She threw her hands up in the air.

"Des, that's not it."

"Well, what is it then? Spill it."

Kasai was about to answer when the dark shape of a cargo net spun over their heads, falling around them before being cinched tight. The rest of the party were ensnared in the same way. Howls erupted from the sides of the pass. Fiendish creatures sprang from their hiding places, brandishing serrated blades.

"Trespassers are always welcome," one fiend garbled in a coarse version of the common tongue. The fiend had a long, white snout and sharp horns cascading down its back.

"Need more slaves," a second fiend said. It prodded Rafar with its sword. "He tall one. Maybe fight well."

A brutish thug pushed through the group, tossing aside the lesser fiend with the pitched fork. He glared menacingly at the other hellions. Each cowered under his commanding presence. "Bind hands and collect weapons. Sekka sees them alive."

"Looks like we've found the sentries," Desdemonia said. "Just lovely."

31

KASAI

The fiends surrounded the prisoners. They prodded them along with their serrated blades and jagged daggers. Kasai's group was herded into the fortress of the enemy.

Kasai had imagined an eerie, black keep with sweeping buttresses and snow-covered towers, but he saw no such things. A sudden squall carried a mini storm of snow; rough terrain blurred in a haze of dirty white. The party was led through a slot carved into the side of the rocky pass. The opening led into a cavern, which slowly reduced to an excavated tunnel ending in an iron door.

The lone demon who commanded the group took out a set of rusted keys to unlock the worn door. He shoved the party inside and commanded all but one of the fiends to remain outside.

"Martuk alone get reward for bring souls to Queen of Ice," the demon said. He pointed proudly to his hairy chest. He grabbed the smaller fiend. "You take bag filled with Martuk new weapons. Follow Martuk now!"

Martuk then pushed Kasai and the others along the corridor. The tunnel was cold and dimly lit. Kasai trudged along beside Pallo; his mood was grim.

"I suppose you think your Ever Hero has some mystical power to get us out of this jam," Kasai whispered to Pallo.

"Fear not. We have everything in hand. Run-Run and Rafar are cutting their bonds now. Orin and I have already freed ourselves."

Run-Run walked behind Desdemonia and Reese. Kasai caught a glimpse of the Kibo Gensai removing a small shiv from the cuff of his sleeve. He deftly positioned the blade in his fingers and sliced through the coarse ropes.

"We of the Kibo Gensai have our special talents, too, Ever Hero," Pallo winked knowingly at Kasai.

Orin and Run-Run fell upon Martuk. One used his shiv to slit the demon's throat, while the other thrust the hard metal through the demon's yellow eye. Pallo and Rafar did likewise to the fiend carrying the weapons, the latter caught the sack of weapons before it fell to the floor with a clatter. It happened fast and silently.

Run-Run freed Kasai, Des, and Reese while Orin took the sack from Rafar and handed out the weapons, except Kasai's. He hesitated, an expression of worry crossing his face.

"I'll take her out," Kasai reassured Orin, taking the sack from the Kibo Gensai warrior. Ninziz-zida's smooth segments slid into his hands. The ancient artifact responded in kind.

"It smells of old, dead magic here. It clings to the walls," Desdemonia commented.

"Come, this way," Reese called out, taking the lead. Her lithe body swayed with newfound confidence.

"Reese? Wait, Reese, where are you going?" Kasai caught up to her and pulled her by the arm to stop. She looked at Kasai with pure innocence.

"The Immortal Mother guides me. This way is clear."

Kasai looked to the others for their opinion. It was clear the Kibo Gensai would follow him wherever he went. Desdemonia's expression remained skeptical and suspicious when it concerned Reese.

"I don't know. This feels awfully like the Temple," Desdemonia said.

The ease of dispatching the guards did seem rather convenient. Kasai looked down the corridor Reese intended to follow. It was empty.

"One way is as good as the next until we can discover the location of Master Choejor. Ok, Reese, you have the lead."

Reese tossed Desdemonia a smug look. She took Kasai's hand and swaggered ahead of the group. She led them down numerous corridors, always deliberate in the direction she chose.

"Something is amiss. Our way has been made remarkably clear since leaving the encampment," Orin said in a low voice. "We are being led by an invisible leash."

"Agreed. Run-Run and I feel the same," Pallo replied.

Kasai knew they were right. No amount of luck lasted this long. Each corridor Reese led them down was as vacant as the last.

"Can we stop for a moment and devise some sort of plan?" Desdemonia commented.

"Not much longer now," Reese said. "The pull on the Immortal Mother is strongest in this direction." She turned a corner that stretched down another long corridor, which opened to a large room. It was awash with pale hues from overhead lights.

"Kasssaaai. I have been waiting for you. Why did you dally? You made Master Choejor endured so much more pain by your tardiness," Khalkoroth taunted as the party entered the room. A deep gurgle chuckled from his throat. The demon squatted over a small altar holding a thick chain that wrapped around a man's waist. Kasai recognized the broken figure of Master Choejor under a pile of shredded blue robes.

Khalkoroth pointed a gloomy finger at Desdemonia. "I see you still have my favorite trinket, Wood Witch. I'll have it back."

The pale demon leaped off the altar and pulled hard on the chain, dragging Master Choejor to the floor. The stone surface was unforgiving. Master Choejor let out a painful moan.

"But first some unfinished business. I wanted you to be witnesses to my little ceremony of transference. Your best friend Daku willingly provided me with a satisfactory vessel to enjoy this world." Khalkoroth drooled viscous sludge from his mouth. The creature's pink eyes blazed with malice and cruelty. "Therefore, I owe him a debt."

Kasai saw the frightened face of Daku appear over the demon's features. His eyes were wide with fear and desperation. "Daku, fight! Don't give up!"

Khalkoroth chuckled. He wiped his brutish hand over his face and smeared the visage of Daku away. "I have all the memories of Daku here with me. Each one is such a tasty titbit of his mortality. It seems Master Choejor was quite a problem for my young monk. So many painful and embarrassing lessons."

Khalkoroth lifted the chain into the air, raising Master Choejor so they were face-to-face. "Daku never liked you, Choejor. Your death will serve as payment of my debt."

The pale demon pulled his free arm back and extended the long-fingered claws of his hand, then thrust his hand through Choejor's chest, ripping out his heart. A slight sigh escaped Choejor's lips before all life left him. "Thus, I seal the soul pact of transference between us."

"Daku! NO!" Kasai yelled.

Blood dripped from Khalkoroth's hand. He casually dropped the wet heart on the floor and squished it under his foot.

"Reese stay behind us. Your rhyme may not work to confuse the beast a second time," Pallo directed. The Kibo Gensai fanned out, approaching the pale demon in a broad semi-circle.

"Kasssaaai, look what I found sifting through the messy remains of your handiwork." Khalkoroth reached behind his back and pulled Eishorror from its sheath. He waved it casually in the air. "It is an arrogant weapon, with no love for you, Kasai."

Khalkoroth eyed the warriors surrounding him. He scrutinized the ice sword. "Such an exquisite blade yearns to freeze the warmth of your blood. Maybe it feeds on the living? I really don't know. Oziax was never one to share his toys. But sadly, Eishorror is not for today. I have been instructed otherwise."

Khalkoroth placed the sword on the ground. He lunged at Pallo with surprising speed. The older warrior barely dodged the sweeping blow that followed. The Kibo Gensai struck as a pack of wolves. Run-Run flashed in to strike Khalkoroth's exposed flank, while the others harassed Khalkoroth with feints and thrusts. Although skilled fighters, their mundane weapons could not penetrate the infernal flesh of the demon.

Desdemonia held back. The Kibo Gensai moved around the demon too fast, and her magic would not know friend from foe. Reese backed away to corridor entrance.

"Kasai! Snap out of it! We need you!" Desdemonia shouted.

"Master Choejor is gone. I couldn't save him. He was counting on me. I failed him." Kasai gritted his teeth, wiping away tears.

"Only you have the power to stop this creature," Desdemonia pleaded.

Kasai saw his companions fighting the demon but were losing. He focused his sadness on Khalkoroth. It all came back to Daku. Daku the hothead. Daku the bully. Daku the Slayer of Ordu!

Kasai's fire xindu flared red hot. It burned through his despair to ignite his anger. "Dakuuuuuu!" Kasai shouted, pointing Ninziz-zida at Khalkoroth. Ninziz-zida blazed bright red. Kasai leaped to his feet with tears streamed down his cheeks.

Khalkoroth spoke through a hateful grin, "The weakling Daku is gone. Only Khalkoroth remains."

Kasai felt the intense wrath of Ninziz-zida as if it were his own. The ancient weapon revered all who followed the Light of Aetenos. She would have her revenge.

Kasai spun Ninziz-zida in a flaming circle. Red flames lapped against his hands. The fire burning along the sticks changed to orange, then to yellow, and eventually blazed forth in righteous blue. Daku was gone. It was time to end this creature.

The Kibo Gensai continued to badger Khalkoroth, attacking with overlapping short swords and daggers. Khalkoroth lunged at Rafar. The warrior was too slow and lost his face to the demon's long claws.

Kasai raced forward. He struck Khalkoroth's open side. The strike penetrated Khalkoroth's magical protection and pushed the demon back. Blue fire erupted over the demon's pale skin and hair. Khalkoroth shrieked. He stumbled backward and frantically snuffed out the flames.

"Pallo, move your men back," Kasai said with absolute determination.

As Khalkoroth hobbled away, his foot brushed up against

Eishorror's hilt. He snatched up the blade from the floor. His white fur left a trail of smoke from Ninziz-zida's touch.

Kasai closed the gap with three long strides and jabbed Ninziz-zida forward, once, twice, three times. Ninziz-zida was too fast. Each thrust found unprotected flesh. Khalkoroth howled in pain, while Ninziz-zida hissed her elation in Kasai's mind.

Kasai whipped around as fast as a spinning tornado and kicked Khalkoroth in the mid-section. The demon doubled over. He held Ninziz-zida collapsed and in two hands. Kasai raised the Fire Serpent high to strike down on the demon's head.

Kasai paused. He knew this strike would end Khalkoroth, and Daku would go with him.

"Do it, Kasai. Do it. Kill me!" It was Daku's voice. His sad face looked up at Kasai through the bestial features of the demon.

"Daku?"

Khalkoroth laughed. "Just a voice, little monk. I have others." He spoke in the voice of Master Choejor, "Help me, my son. Save me!"

Kasai knew then that nothing of his friend remained. He raised Ninziz-zida higher. Khalkoroth raised his gnarled hand and uttered a strange, black word, the sound of which made Kasai shudder. The shadows in the room expanded until all was thrust into darkness.

"Not again, demon," Kasai said. He held his open palm above his head. "Aetenos! Light!"

Silvery-blue light flooded from Kasai's hand, and the darkness was banished. But Khalkoroth was gone.

Desdemonia ran to Kasai's side. "Did you do it? Did you kill him?"

"I assumed the blessing would merely illuminate the

area." Kasai searched about the room for ash or hidden doors.

"Look! The beast runs!" Orin shouted. He pointed across the room. Khalkoroth bounded down a second corridor on all four limbs.

"We must catch him!" Kasai said.

"Kasai, wait!" Desdemonia grabbed his arm tight. "This is work for the King's Army now. Let someone else bear the responsibility of rooting out the evil in this dark place. Let someone else lead. There is nothing more for you to do here."

"I must avenge my Master!" Kasai's eyes were wide, frenzied. "Don't you understand? I must do something."

"Then just walk away, Kasai. Master Choejor is gone. Come with me. Back to the forest and be at peace."

"Walk away? No. I have lost too much. Master Choejor must be avenged!"

"What about me? Will you risk losing me too?" Des spoke quietly.

"This responsibility has fallen to me. It's my destiny."

"Who says so? Anyone could have been chosen. Forsake the Song. Let another rise up in your place."

"Perhaps another could, but it was me that was chosen. I must do what was asked of me."

"What about what I am asking of you?" Desdemona pleaded. "This world has too much pain and suffering. I want to return to my forest, where there is peace. Come with me. Let's leave this horrible place together."

"Des, you don't understand," Kasai said. He slowly shook his head.

"I do understand. This is too big for us. Come, my love, while there is still time. Your duty to Master Choejor has ended. Please, I do not want to lose you, too. I need you."

"Des, I need…" He beheld Desdemonia's sad, amber eyes.

Feelings of warmth and love quelled Kasai's fire xindu energy and calmed his anger.

Desdemonia nodded forward with affirmation. Her eyes watched him, anticipating his answer. "Tell me. Tell me what you need."

"Kasssaaai," Khalkoroth taunted from the end of the corridor.

Kasai stared down the corridor at the demon. The weight of his failure to save Master Choejor rekindled his hatred for the pale demon. His fire xindu blazed forth with volcanic might within his soul. All the suppressed pain and sadness of losing the loved ones in his life erupted within him at once.

Kasai took his arm away from Desdemonia's grasp. "There shall be no peace in the land while this corruption exists. I will destroy these demons before they can take more innocent lives. I will stop Khalkoroth. And Maugris if he's here. No matter what comes against me, I will fight."

Desdemonia bowed her head in resignation. "Then it's settled. I will walk this path with you. I will fight by your side until the end. Regardless of the cost."

"Kassaaai... Kassaaai... I'm waiting," Khalkoroth's deep voice echoed through the corridor. "Still holding back, little brother?"

Kasai led his group into a great hall supported by rough-cut buttresses. The walls cast a metallic-green sheen from sorcerous globes floating across the ceiling. Kasai saw Khalkoroth limping to a dark dais at the far side of the room. He bowed to the two figures upon the dais, then moved off to the side and blended into the shadows.

The figures were shrouded in darkness. One sat upon a back-lit throne, and to his side stood the silhouette of a tall woman with shapely curves. She wore a tall headdress that trailed down her back.

A sultry voice called from the dais. "Rachlach Fortress

welcomes the Ever Hero of Aetenos." The woman stepped into the full light. Her headdress was strewn with bleached bones that rattled when she turned her head to the man seated on the throne.

"You see, Maugris. I told you he will come."

Kasai gasped. The apparition from his nightmares was here now, perfectly depicted and very much alive. The woman nodded in recognition at the ancient weapon in Kasai's hands.

"And he shall bear the fabled Fire Serpent into battle against the Darkness, as his progenitor once did."

Maugris rose from his throne. He wore an elegant attire of purple satin robes, embroidered with beautiful, golden runes.

"This is who you have been searching for all this time? This boy is the Ever Hero of Aetenos?" Maugris said with contempt.

The woman's eyes bore into Kasai. Her gaze was mesmerizing, and Kasai felt helpless and weak under her scrutiny. Then Desdemonia was in front of him. Her hands took hold of his arms and shook him out of his stupor. Des was always there for him. She gave him renewed strength.

"Kasai! We must run! We cannot win. She is not of this land," Desdemonia implored Kasai. She shook him again to make sure he was listening to her.

"I know, Des. I know."

"No, Kasai, you do not know! That is Sekka. She is a greater devil from the Lower Planes! Listen to me, please! For once, listen to me!"

Kasai looked squarely into Desdemonia's amber eyes. "Des, it must be this way. The path ends here."

Desperation swelled in Desdemonia's eyes. "Then take the amulet. The charm will protect you against their magic."

Kasai shook his head. "No, I have a different faith to protect me now."

"Ugh, you're as stubborn as Gauldumor. Fine, we do it your way." Desdemonia's hands glowed with swirling blue light. Azure sigils of power glittered, penetrating the green light of the room. The Kibo Gensai formed a line in front of Kasai. Reese took up a stance behind Desdemonia.

Kasai stepped through the line of Kibo Gensai. He rapidly twirled Ninziz-zida's end section into a spinning shield. Blue fire burst from the ancient weapon as it too recognized its old foe upon the dais.

Maugris was furious at such a challenge.

"I shall not be mocked by a boy! You all will die!" Lightning burst from Maugris' hands. It bounced off the floor to break into separate chains, striking the Kibo Gensai warriors, tossing them like rag dolls into the static-replete air. Their twisted bodies smacked into the stone of the floor, where they lay smoking. An acrid, pungent odor filled the room.

Ninziz-zida's magical components deflected much of the lightning, but not all of it. Kasai's body was wracked by spasms of shocking pain. Des raced to his side, ready to attack. The amulet around her neck had absorbed the brunt of the dark magic. The green emerald at its center throbbed like a beacon.

Kasai recovered enough to see Reese standing nearby. She was unharmed. He turned back to the dais. Sekka's cruel eyes were studying his movements with keen interest. Desdemonia reached out and gathered a portion of Ninziz-zida's blue flame into her hand.

"Your fancy sticks like me, too," Des said with a grin. She gave him a playful wink as she added her Elemenati magic to the flame and crafted a swirling column of blue fire at her side. She grabbed a handful of flame and molded it into a ball. Then threw it at Maugris. The sorcerer dismissed it with a contemptuous wave of his hand.

"You will all pay for your trespass," Maugris said. He threw a fireball of his own. The fiery magic washed the room in vermillion light as it sped towards Desdemonia. It exploded in an array of shimmering cinders when it reached her. The amulet at her neck briefly flared bright green as it absorbed the last of the fiery ball's heat.

Maugris hurled a curse and a second fireball at Desdemonia. Again, the amulet protected her from his spell. "Impossible!" he cried.

Desdemonia peppered him with smaller blue, fireballs but Maugris canceled her magic with barely a word.

"The witch possesses an interesting item." His shifty eyes glared at Sekka. "But let's see how much your Ever Hero can take." Maugris pointed at the floor beneath Kasai's feet. He turned his other palm upright with his fingers pointing to the ceiling.

Kasai felt a quick warning from Ninziz-zida. He instinctively directed the weapon downward in time to smash the stones spikes that shot upwards beneath his feet. Nonetheless, one jagged stone got through his defense and gave him a horrible gash on the outer side of his leg. Kasai fell to one knee in pain.

"This feeble boy is the key?" Maugris questioned Sekka in disbelief.

Sekka observed everything like a spectator at a grand duel. "Kill him then, if you think you can."

Desdemonia raced to Kasai's aid. She reached into one of her shirt pockets and took out a small vial. "Drink!" she said. Kasai took a draught of the thick liquid and immediately felt the pain in his leg subside.

"It's got a bit of a kick," Kasai said.

Desdemonia helped him to stand. Maugris descended the dais.

"I cannot get close enough," Kasai said through his teeth.

"I know, leave that to me. I have a plan. You attack. I'll defend." She looked deeply into his eyes. "Trust me."

Kasai nodded his agreement to the familiar style of fighting. Desdemonia's amber eyes sparkled back at him. She tapped her finger to the side of her head. "Smart."

Her gypsy smile returned for just a moment. Then a stern look of determination crossed her face. "Stay behind me until we are close enough."

"Right."

Kasai and Desdemonia ran towards the dais just as Maugris cast a black cloud of gas. The amulet sucked the foul vapor into its center. Kasai darted past Desdemonia, unleashing Ninziz-zida in a swirling barrage of strikes. Cobalt flames whipped from Ninziz-zida's segments, but her attacks were rebuffed.

Maugris' protective aegis flared against Ninziz-zida's wrath and kept the sticks at bay. Maugris laughed. "How long do you think you can keep this up?"

Kasai heard Master Choejor's words in his head. 'You maintain boundaries where there are none and, therefore, are easily defeated. Give yourself fully to the Boundless and receive its gift in return.' Kasai knew he must fully embrace the Boundless if he had any hope of surviving this fight.

Kasai dropped into a flash meditative state. He let go of his fears of magic, of loss, of failure, of the need to control. He let his xindu energies rise on their own accord. A powerful force called to him. It demanded more, and Kasai gave it willingly.

The Boundless gave its energy back to him in return.

Kasai felt a new connection to a vast power. His xindu energies rose to levels he had never experienced before. He felt as if he was drawing from the raw elements that flowed through the land; fire from volcanoes, water from the sea, earth from mountains, and air from the sky.

Kasai felt the might of the Ever Hero within him. He funneled his xindu energy into Ninziz-zida. The azure glow of her flame burst from the segments in a blinding, blue light.

"Des, step back."

Kasai spun the Ninziz-zida to each side, raising her above his head; the momentum increasing the power building within the staff. Desdemonia backed away from the broad swings of the ancient weapon.

Kasai whipped the end section down on Maugris' shoulder. The magical barrier protecting the sorcerer failed. Maugris' left shoulder shattered. His arm hung useless at his side.

Kasai swung Ninziz-zida around again and connected with Maugris' ribs. The sorcerer backed away, gasping for breath. It finally came to him in screams as Ninziz-zida's fire ate through his robe and dug deep into his flesh.

Kasai shot the heel of his foot into Maugris' knee, and the sorcerer collapsed to the stone floor. Blue fire blazed over his crumpled body. Kasai took a step back. Des moved back to where Reese stood. Kasai looked to Sekka.

She raised a curious eyebrow. "Impressive. Let's see how far you've come," Sekka said with a wicked grin. She looked passed Kasai to Reese. "Sess'thra, now."

Kasai spun around and saw Reese transform into the demon succubus from that last, dreadful day at Ordu. The succubus' almond-shaped eyes grew round with anticipation as she slid behind Desdemonia.

"I told you to stay out of my way, witch," Sess'thra said as she stabbed Desdemonia in the back with a small dagger. Kasai saw pain and sadness fill Desdemonia's face. She melted to the floor.

"NO!" Kasai yelled as he ran to Desdemonia. Ninziz-zida fire trailed behind him.

Sess'thra took to the air and landed at the foot of the dais just as Sekka descended the steps.

"Well done," Sekka applauded.

Sess'thra bowed her head as Sekka walked past her and over to the smoldering ruin of Maugris' body. She looked down at him with uncaring eyes.

"Heal me, devil," Maugris pleaded in a frail voice. Sekka sneered down at the broken sorcerer.

"My dear Maugris. You have played your part well. However, your immediate use is at an end."

"I command you to destroy my enemies," Maugris said through gritted teeth. He slowly raised one charred hand to point at Kasai.

Sekka laughed with sinister amusement. "You command me to do nothing." She crouched down and took Maugris' chin in her hand. "You are a tiny, insignificant thing."

Maugris was shocked. "I ... I command you." His words lacked strength, and his head dropped to the floor.

"Do not fear, Maugris. I may still have use for you in time." Sekka stood, turning her attention to Kasai.

Kasai had barely listened to the exchange between Maugris and Sekka. He was at Desdemonia's side with Ninziz-zida resting on the floor nearby, its fire rippled along the lengths of its segments.

"Love, please don't let her take my soul…" Desdemonia's eyes searched Kasai's for understanding.

"Never, Des, never." Kasai wept. His tears fueled his anger, and Ninziz-zida blazed blue once more. "I should have listened. I should have turned away when you asked. I'm so sorry."

Desdemonia lifted the amulet from her neck and held the

chain out to Kasai. "Take it. Keep you safe." Her body went limp in his arms, and the amulet fell to the floor.

Kasai looked at the marks on his palms. "Aetenos, please heal her." Nothing happened. Kasai feared it was too late. Sadness and anger swelled in his heart.

He reached into his soul and called upon the newly discovered power of the Ever Hero. He took up Ninziz-zida and gathered strength from the ancient weapon. She was eager to confront her age-old foe. But something in his heart knew it would not be enough.

He contemplated using the amulet.

"What is wrong, Ever Hero? Surely the Chosen of Aetenos does not fear me," Sekka taunted. "Perhaps you would like to take Maugris' place and join me in the conquest of this realm? I can be anything you desire."

"You are nothing that I desire." Kasai brushed away his tears. He made himself ready for this final confrontation.

"No? Well then, as I have said before to another of your ilk, I have other, more aggressive forms, if that is more to your liking." Sekka ripped off the clothing she wore. The headdress of bones clattered to the floor as her naked body shimmered with dark magic. Kasai's breath frosted before his face as the temperature in the room dropped.

Sekka arched her back forwards, and four great horns sprouted from her head. The horns curled around themselves, and massive teeth grew from her extended jaw. As she stood upright, her human legs changed to a more avian form, equipped with talons that dug into the stone floor.

Sekka towered over Kasai. Coarse, albino fur covered her back and shoulders. She flexed her powerful arms. A crown of bones materialized and floated above her head with glowing sigils, pulsing with power.

Sekka shrieked menacingly. Ninziz-zida's blue flame gave Kasai courage, and he held his ground. Sekka uttered a strange word, and swirling black tendrils lashed out at Kasai. Ninziz-zida reacted with blazing speed. Her segments shattered all but one of the tendrils, which wrapped around Kasai's leg.

Kasai's body froze like a block of ice. Ninziz-zida immediately sent Kasai's fire xindu back to him. The heat thawed the frigid paralysis, but his movements were incredibly slow.

Sekka attacked again. Lightning flashed from the floor, ceiling, and walls and struck Kasai from all sides. He was raised off the ground and tossed close to Desdemonia's prone body. The pain was greater than any he had ever felt.

"Aetenos…" Kasai whispered the name. Yet, no inner voice responded to his call.

+The Great Monk cannot hear you, Ever Hero. This room is your doom.+ Sekka's voice pounded in Kasai's mind.

His life and the lives of his companions would be over if he didn't stop Sekka now. Maugris was nothing compared to her raw power. He needed something more.

Kasai coughed up blood, then spotted the amulet on the floor.

His fingers slowly walked across the cold floor and tangled around the amulet's chain. He grimaced as he got to his feet. Kasai held the amulet up against Sekka. The center of the charm dangled before him.

+It will not help you against me+ Sekka sent into his mind.

She chanted in a dark and dangerous language, which Kasai could not understand. With a flick of her wrist, she sent a magical dart at Kasai. The amulet took in the magic. It worked for him as well!

With renewed confidence, Kasai put the amulet around his neck and took Ninziz-zida in both hands. Sekka's bestial eyes opened wide, and long strands of drool looped from between her inner teeth. Her mouth gaped open with a guttural sound of triumph.

She raised her bestial hand and pointed at Kasai. One last dark word echoed into the frigid air. Kasai readied himself and trusted the amulet would protect him. But no dark magic attacked him.

The sound of the word drifted through the air and sparked the amulet to life. The emerald charm throbbed with intensity and turned fetid green. The room darkened into a blackish-verdant hue.

+The connection has been made! The Chaos Gate shall open! Aetenos' greatest gift to the mortals has now sealed their doom.+

Kasai heard her words pounding in his head. The amulet's power dug deeply into his essence. It grabbed hold of something that was formless yet found a way to contain it and imprison it. Kasai somehow felt a new bond become established between him and Aetenos. Not one of the mind or heart, but of the soul. And it was horrible and wicked.

The amulet flared with green fire as it burned through the fabric of his robe and into his skin. Kasai tore it from his chest and threw it to the ground.

The stone shattered on the floor. From each piece, a demonic sigil rose into the air and then faded from sight. The stone floor melted where the pieces lay as if burned by an alchemist's acid. The smaller holes grew until they connected together, forming one singular hole. The outer edges burned with green fire and continued to grow in diameter.

Sekka stomped over to the edge. Kasai knew by her twisted smiled that whatever was coming would be worse than anything he had faced up until now.

+My Chaos Gate lives!+

Sekka grabbed the broken body of Maugris and tossed him onto the portal's surface. The charred body sank until it was gone. Sekka stepped away from the growing edge and transformed back into her human form. Her naked body was slick with wetness and reflected different shades of ugly green. Pungent vapor bubbled like a boiling cauldron from the portal.

Kasai tried to block his ears from the screams of tormented souls and nightmarish creatures coming from the portal.

"The amulet…" Kasai hung his head in shame.

"Yes! The amulet. It took your soul and connected it to another on Gathos. Now the bridge is complete."

"Gathos … another soul," Kasai stammered. "Whose soul?"

Sekka gave Kasai a sly grin. "Oh, I think you must know by now."

"Whose soul?" Kasai shouted. "Whose soul?"

"Isn't it obvious? Where do you think Aetenos has been all this time?"

"No, no, no," Kasai fell to his knees, sobbing.

Sekka chuckled before turning to Sess'thra, "Time is short, and there is much to do. Stay by Shiverrig's side. Entice him to take the demon seed. I will need a capable warlord to lead my legions until I can revive Oziax and Narthoth."

"What of the monk and his friends?" Sess'thra asked with a lascivious grin.

"They cannot harm me now. Let them stay and witness the arrival of my Frost Legion. It is a fitting reward for all they have done."

"Yes, my Mistress." Sess'thra bowed in deference. The air crackled, and she was gone. Sekka stepped over the edge of the portal and walked across its surface. Its diameter had already tripled in size. When she reached the center, she slowly descended out of sight.

Kasai crawled to Des and raised her head to his leg. She was still unconscious, and blood ran freely from the wound in her back. Kasai pleaded to Aetenos for the strength to heal her. When no help came, he tapped into his water xindu and placed his palms over the knife wound.

"Take everything. Just make her well."

The Boundless responded when Aetenos did not. The gash closed. Kasai rocked her slowly for what seemed like hours. Kasai tried to figure out what to do next. It didn't matter. Nothing mattered now.

Desdemonia finally opened her eyes as she regained consciousness.

"Is it over? Are we safe?"

Kasai smiled sadly at her then looked over at the growing Chaos Gate. A cold reek billowed from the portal in anticipation of foul things to come.

"No, Des, things are worse."

EPILOGUE

Jarei Ch'ou sent one last thought to his wife, hoping it would pierce the fire and smoke ravaging their home to touch her heart. Life had been so simple in the frontier village. Now, everything was lost.

Jarei had read the signs. The last three years of poor harvests were just the beginning. The fish in the river were washing up on the shore, bloated and dead. Pine trees lost their needles and turned black. Barn animals walked in a stupor before dropping to the ground, legs splayed behind them. A sickness had infected the land. The Frozen Dark had returned.

Jarei and his wife, Marquia, had spoken of this dreadful day many times. He knew he would be a target. The minions of evil were drawn to healers, especially those blessed by the benevolent demigod, Aetenos. His wife and their son, Kasai, would also be in mortal danger.

"When, not if, the time is upon us, you must be the one to save our son, Marquia. Find the Masters. Kasai is important. Aetenos watches over him. I believe the Great Monk has a special purpose for our son."

Marquia shook her head, no.

"Marquia, I have heard Aetenos's song. The monks will take you in. You will be safe," Jarei implored his wife.

She resisted, of course. "We shall go together. We are a family and shall remain a family."

"The creatures will be drawn to me. They will think I am the One. We can use this to our advantage."

Jarei returned his focus to the aegis of light that separated him from the *things* on the other side. His barrier wavered as fell creatures threw dark magic against it. The foul beasts were pale, gangly creatures standing on thin legs. Their dissected torsos and arms wavered back and forth as they sent spells fishtailing into the barrier. They screeched obscene curses when their magic exploded harmlessly against the wall of Light. Yet, Jarei's strength had its limits.

The heads of the creatures tapered slightly to blunt, rounded cones. They possessed no eyes, only deep slits for nostrils. Their oversized mouths were set with sawblade like teeth that were frozen in a permanent, wicked smile.

Jarei knew these creatures from ancient texts and scrolls. They were hunter fiends. Trackers from the frigid Abyss dredged up from the frozen plains of Gathos. The abominable hounds could smell and taste the use of magic in all its wondrous forms. They had finally found him.

He looked to the window where he knew his wife watched in fear. Their eyes met through a brief clearing of smoke and debris. Marquia's expression pleaded with him to stay with her and Kasai. Her eyes said they could make it there together. Jarei knew it was not to be so.

They had been together since childhood. Jarei knew everything there was to know about his wife, each expression, and bodily gesture. He knew what her heart was saying even though she could not send the message back to him. 'We can make it together.'

+No, we cannot. They want me most of all. They will follow me far enough for you to escape. It must be this way.+ Jarei sent.

She nodded slowly. No more words needed to be spoken. Her eyes said enough. 'I love you.'

+I love you, too. Now go!+

Jarei begrudgingly left her visual embrace. The fires grew higher; smoke poured out through the windows. It was everywhere. He knew he must hold the barrier for a bit longer, long enough so his wife and son could escape.

Sweat flowed freely down his forehead. He let the aegis of light collapsed. The drain on his strength was too much. He would need that strength to run. He wondered, only for a moment, how Aetenos could allow such filth to return? But Aetenos had his way, and Jarei was a devoted follower. He would not question the plan of the Great Monk. He wished he could hear the Song as loud and clear as the people of his Order once did.

Jarei heard Kasai call to him in a terrified voice. Jarei knew his son was wondering why he was not next to him, holding him, and keeping him safe. The pain was too much to bear. He spotted Kasai from across the yard, but the creatures were too close. If he ran to his son, they would both be overwhelmed.

Jarei held his son's gaze for just a moment longer. He sent him a smile that he hoped would register within such an innocent mind. His mother would explain it all to him when he was older.

Jarei turned to the fiends. Now was the time for sacrifice. He raced towards the creatures and then past them. He cast a beacon of light above his head to give the fiends an easy target to follow. Hopefully, it would also keep their attention away from his family.

Jarei fled into the dense forest. He hoped he could put up

a good enough chase. Time, his family needed more time. He ran faster.

Jarei jumped over fallen trees and thin streams. He felt like he ran for hours, but it was only minutes. He looked back in dismay to see the gangly creatures had gained on him; their thin form belied their preternatural quickness. He pressed on.

His right shoulder thrust forward on its own volition; he looked down to see a bright red shaft an arrowhead and bright red shaft jutting from his upper chest.

Jarei's breath grew shallow, legs buckling, he stumbled. The hunter fiends surrounded him. Jarei crawled forward. The pain in his shoulder slowed his movement. He put his back against a small birch tree. The arrow tormented him as it brushed against the young trunk. There was nowhere to run. Waves of pain flowed through his body.

A more human figure glided among the fiends. He handed a longbow to one of them and moved confidently towards Jarei. He then unclasped a cruel-looking dagger strapped to his thigh. His head was hidden by a dark green hood that kept most of his face in shadow.

The man approached Jarei and removed his hood. He had surprisingly handsome features that shimmered in and out of focus. The man held the dagger in one hand. He knelt by Jarei.

"They always run," the strange man said. He took out a small amulet with a bright, green center from a pocket. He dangled the small charm above Jarei's head.

Jarei looked at the amulet, then looked away with disinterest. The songs of birds in the trees brought him back to happier days with his family. He remembered a time when he and his wife and son played hide-and-seek together in these same woods.

"Another hunt ends, and alas, you are not the One," the

man said. Jarei heard the disappointment in his voice. "Once again, my talents are wasted on pursuing a misguided believer of a crazed monk.

"I ought not to question the motives of the Mistress. But still, anyone could do such a task. Why send me, the master assassin, Daxzulz Thrum?"

When Jarei laughed, blood bubbled out of his mouth. "Aetenos shall find his way to strike you down. His followers are true."

He was not afraid to die. His family would be safe.

"Your deluded fantasies have failed you. Look around you, priest. There is no savior. You are alone. Aetenos has abandoned this land."

Jarei slumped down against the birch and coughed up more blood. Thankfully, he could no longer feel the sting of the arrow.

"Aetenos has already answered my call. My family is safe. You will never find them."

Pure wickedness came over Dax's shimmering face. His dagger was in and out of Jarei in a flash.

"We shall see, priest. We shall see."

PLEASE LEAVE A REVIEW!

If you have enjoyed this book, it would be tremendous if you were able to leave a review on whichever eBook or print distributor you typically purchase from.

Reviews help me get noticed and they can bring my books to the attention of other readers who may enjoy them. Thank you for your support!

Jeff Pantanella

PROLOGUE TO BOOK TWO OF THE EVER HERO SAGA: THE FOE WARS

"*Your* doctrines, Lord Raguel, and *your* banishment. This was not the will of the Immortal Mother. Aetenos walked a road of salvation, not just for the mortals, but for us all!"

Zhao Houzi heard Artiya'il's melodic and passionate voice, though muffled behind closed doors. He could almost picture Lord Raguel's flawless face darkened with a frown as the crowds of spectators inside the Cloud Court's amphitheater erupted with cheers of agreement or shouts of protest.

"Quiet! I will have quiet now!" His voice thundered like a crashing wave and echoed off the pristine walls. The din of the crowd quickly diminished.

"This shouldn't be. It cannot be," Zhao Houzi mumbled to himself as he scurried up another flight of stairs leading to an upper balcony.

Today was the day the angel, Artiya'il, was to be sentenced for crimes against the Laws of Heaven. Never had a True-born been brought before Lord Raguel's Cloud Court and treated in such a manner.

A True-born! And I'm already incredibly late. This is all Titus's fault, he thought. *That great warhorse can be so stubborn in his ways and he never listens to reason, no matter how many irrefutable facts I give him.*

"This will change everything," the small monkey said and did his best to use only his short "man" legs and not all four limbs, as was proper in such an august and magnificent place. It was a challenge not to revert to his ancestral ways when he was pressed for time. Using four limbs was so much quicker than two.

"Pardon me. Pardon me, sir," Zhao Houzi said cheerfully and respectfully as he darted past a group of slow-moving celestials taking their time moving up the same stair. Each wore robes of office of intricate design and patterned with brightly colored sigils of turquoise, amber, and emerald.

Their feathered wings remained furled and tight behind their rigid backs. Thin circlets of silver and gold wrapped around their heads and were decorated with jeweled charms that dangled just above their shoulders. Zhao Houzi wondered what it would feel like to fly, to feel the air rush through the hair on your face, to soar and dive like a bird.

"Monkey! Watch your paws!" said one of the lower-born angels with obvious irritation. He twisted around with his back to the wall as Zhao Houzi scampered underfoot.

"Hands and feet, good sir," Zhao Houzi said. "Just like you."

"They will allow any riff-raff into the Cloud Court these days. The High Court should require an entry visa into Tanalum and block these unfavorable animal spirits from disturbing the peace. Keep them all in Elysian, where they belong. This is not their place," another said. His tone reeked of disgust. "Let them soil the First Level with their debauchery and unsupervised revelries."

"Block them all, I say. Elysian has become a droll nursery at best, unfit for the governance of the realms. Lord Raguel must keep all human souls away from any agendas requiring important decision making." His long slender nose pointed like a ninth finger at Zhao Houzi. "You will be named in my complaint to the Chancellor Pinnacle, Monkey."

A third celestial was quick to comment. "I cannot abide by these animal spirits. The stench of their former existence never leaves them." She was older than her companions and wore a purple sash around her waist, which complimented the light lavender hue of her robe and pink skin of her face. He thought the color combinations were quite pleasing.

Zhao Houzi would usually be disappointed to hear such intolerance, but today he was too preoccupied with getting a good seat. He dashed past the angels and followed the tight spiral stairs that wound to the upper mezzanine. The old stone walls reflected his small body, clothed in a bright crimson vest and cream-colored pants with swirling orange designs. His hairy feet and arms moved quickly, and he scampered over the remaining steps.

He wanted to see, as much as hear the Chancellor Pinnacle's verdict. This was a critical case, and depending on Raguel's decision, it could have monumental repercussions throughout the Seven Heavens.

Perhaps an unclaimed seat remains that will give me an unobstructed view of the court arena below, he thought but didn't hold out much hope as he opened the last door leading into the mostly filled, upper-deck seating.

"There!" He said and darted over the back of one row of chairs, then leaped between two seated celestials using their shoulders to support his small, hairy body.

"Monkey!" They cursed as he flew past their heads. But he barely heard their astonished gasps and harsh words of reprimand, distracted as he was with the incredible amphitheater.

Amber sunlight poured through clerestory openings above the upper mezzanines. A sphere of polished gold suspended by invisible means, spun hypnotically in the center of the arched ceiling's atmosphere.

The sphere was a perfect measurement of forty-nine meters in diameter with an additional glowing corona of thirty-three meters extending from its surface. A shimmering halo formed around the indoor sun, and no matter the viewer's vantage point, it was seen in the same way framing the golden orb. Zhao Houzi marveled at this effect but could never understand how it worked. It was a riddle for his friend, Titus, to decipher.

The surface of the ceiling was filled with geometric designs, each flowing harmoniously into the next. Cascading rays of sunlight washed over the silver inlays worked into the perfectly shaped stone blocks, causing them to sparkle and shimmer.

Today was a lucky day. Zhao Houzi found an unoccupied, front row seat between two elder celestials, most likely hailing from the second level of Heaven based on their white gowns. He gave each a warm greeting and then peered between the gleaming golden rails to the court below.

The immense chamber's inner shape was set as a perfect square with layers of circular terraces drawn down to the floor of the room. The upper mezzanines were filled with spectators and lower-level celestials jostling for a view, politely but assertively angling their way to the front railings.

The lower mezzanine and mid-level balcony seating had reached capacity hours ago with the privileged celestials that held rank and office over the mere citizens of the realm. Only the True-born, those celestials who had materialized at the beginning of all things, occupied the choice orchestra seats.

They sat in stoic silence, garbed in golden robes of silk and cashmere. Bright sigils of power spun in slow, clockwise circles above their heads resembling floating crowns. The movement of the sigils mirrored the pace of the glowing indoor sun above.

The chamber was full of boisterous laughter and commentary as if the event was more for entertainment than a pivotal moment in the history of the Seven Heavens.

Such a sad and desperate day, yet they all seem to be enjoying the spectacle, the monkey thought as he scanned the faces of his fellow celestials. He could smell the ripe aromas of change in the air, even if the others could not. Never had one of their own been tried for transgressions against the Heavenly Realm. Would that he believed the Chancellor Pinnacle would find compassion in his heart and decide upon a lenient sentence if Artiya'il was found guilty of his crimes. The monkey inwardly sighed. He knew better than to hope for such an outcome.

Far below, seven structures were raised from the floor and jutted into the center of the room like stone jetties. When seen from above, the negative space between each structure created an offset heptagram shape, an auspicious design for such an area of purity and law. Each podium rose off the floor from polished stone stairs that ended in a circular platform, capped by a small rotunda.

Raguel raised his hands to quiet the vast chamber. His wings unfurled into a great span across his back, mirroring his irritation at the disruption to his court.

A quieting hush flowed through the chamber as six heavily robed figures entered the great hall and walked to their respective stairs and made their way to the end of each podium. Radiant mandalas of swirling sigils spun above their heads, and their preened and perfect wings were folded upon their backs. These were the oldest of the celestial lords and had presided over the High Court for millennia, and their judgments were final.

Each of the six judges wore a specific color representing one of the six lower-levels of Heaven. Sage Green was draped over the first judge celebrating the innocence of a new soul's arrival to Heaven, for each soul entering the Seven Heavens began its journey of worthy progress in the land of Elysian.

Here the soul would be indoctrinated in the Ways of Heaven and enjoyed relief from all worry and despair. This was a happy place, filled with verdant trees and golden meadows, where fresh souls could play upon the lush green grass, and bath in blue lagoons of mineral water.

Ivory for the Second Level of Heaven called Eden and representing the pure of heart and the cleansing of sin. Zhao Houzi felt Eden was a dreary place, one of reflection and perhaps a touch of unwarranted guilt, as each soul released the last memories of a less than perfect life in the Mortal Realm.

He wondered why these souls desperately clung to the grief of their past. They were free now. What perplexed him more was knowing mortals possessed the same power within them to cast away the burden of past failures and bad decisions when alive, yet rarely exercised this ability. True forgiveness, especially of the self, seemed to be a difficult or impossible concept for most mortals to grasp.

The third judge took each of his steps with a proud swagger. He wore layered robes the color of bronze, which gleamed like the polished stones throughout the courtroom pavilion. The Third Level of Heaven, called Arcadia, was for the passionate, kind, and just. Those who would fight for others in times of need were gathered in this realm. Legions of champions of spear, sword, shield, and lance trained in readiness for any conflict with the evil spawn from the Abyss. They were the protectors of the realm.

The judge who wore the crimson robes with fiery specks of orange and magenta hailed from the Fourth Level of Heaven, named Erewhon. Mystical powers of divine force manifested in the souls of this realm. Gifted by the righteous might of divine soul energy, the warrior-priests of the Seven Heavens honed their magical craft. Their devotion to the Immortal Mother rewarded them with higher learning and powerful spells.

The fifth judge climbed the opposite platform from where Zhao Houzi sat in the upper mezzanine. When the judge reached his rotunda, he gazed up at the spectators in the grand chamber. Zhao Houzi's keen sight saw sadness in the elder angel's eyes. His robes were of a strong vermillion with lighter swirls of yellow interwoven into the fabric, showing that he represented the Fifth Level of Heaven called Canaan. The celestials living on Canaan were the caretakers and healers of all realms, though their influence in the Mortal Realm was less defined and non-existent in the Abyss.

Deep cerulean robes, under bright emerald overlays, clothed the judge representing the Sixth Level of Heaven. This realm was called Paradise. It was a peaceful place of rest and meditation, filled with high mountain peaks and valleys carved by winding rivers.

Yet long ago, those who dwelled here used their acquired mental prowess to assert control over the Third and Fourth Levels, marshaling for the forces of Heaven and directing them on the battlefield where they thought best.

Gold, representing the golden touch of the sun and all that fell under its glorious reign, was for the Seventh Level of Heaven. The Laws of Order were written in Tanalum and enforced by Lord Raguel's Protectorate. There was no higher office than the Chancellor Pinnacle, and Lord Raguel had held the office since its inception at the dawn of all things.

His wings were composed of feathers from a thousand different birds and he opened them with great flourish, as he surveyed the crowd from the seventh structure. Then his ageless hands motioned that the final sentencing would begin. The air became still and quiet.

The defendant, Artiya'il, stood alone in the center of the chamber. He wore a simple white tunic and modest sandals. His wings and wrists were bound in silver chains, but he still held his head high. It appeared he had been treated well and unharmed.

Nonetheless, two armed and armored Protectorates were in striking distance if necessary. Their dazzling and unblemished plate armor sparkled in the bright light of the chamber. Zhao Houzi noticed his ankles were also shackled and loosely connected by a chain.

Why would so many chains be needed? he wondered.

The angel dutifully acknowledged each of the judges in their high perches and ended with a respectful nod to Lord Raguel. He stood defiant and proud. "My Lord Raguel, Chancellor Pinnacle of the Seven Heavens. I hope this day finds you well," Artiya'il said. His voice sounded of a sweet chorus of nightingales as if nothing was amiss.

Lord Raguel moved quickly past formalities of greeting. "Artiya'il, your trial is at its end. The charges brought upon you, as written in the Book of Heavenly Laws, have been spoken, and your pleas and defense have been heard. The Six Judges have come to bear witness to your sentence."

The Chancellor Pinnacle's voice boomed throughout the chamber. "Do you have any last words you would like the court to hear before the verdict is delivered?"

Artiya'il paused for a moment before speaking,

collecting his thoughts. "We must change as the realms surely have changed through time. Our laws are fit for a time long past. The mortals are children who need our direction and encouragement, not a blind eye until their undisciplined mind falls into folly, for when it does, there is nowhere else to look than the Deep Dark for answers. They need our guidance and love, not punishment in its most severe form.

"This was Aetenos's Way. He, who was born of the realm of men, and a divine brother to us all in the Seven Heavens, knew this to be true. His message to us was clear. We have overlooked our children and left them cold and hungry in the wild, fodder for wolves."

Lord Raguel's face twitched at the mention of Aetenos. His knuckles whitened around the banister he unknowingly held so tight. A dull murmur flowed through the crowds. Many knew of the rift between the Chancellor Pinnacle and the demigod, Aetenos.

Zhao Houzi wondered how many knew it began from the unrequited love Raguel bore for Lady Illyria? It was plain to see on Lord Raguel's face that he still felt the prick of that rejection, and it stung.

"I do not deny my actions on behalf of the mortals," Artiya'il continued. "My intentions were pure of heart and well-meaning. They may have conflicted with the words written in your book, but they were right!"

A murmur of unease rippled through the upper mezzanine. Zhao Houzi was amazed at what he was hearing. He, too, felt the Heavenly Laws were too strict. There was no room for interpretation or a higher understanding of the Immortal Mother's will.

But to speak aloud such brazen disregard for the Law in the High Court was tantamount to heresy. The monkey scanned the mezzanine and lower seats. He saw others nodding in agreement. The Way of Heaven would be irrevocably changed after the outcome of this trial.

Artiya'il waited for the crowds to simmer down. "My final hope is that we will one day take the mortals into our divine embrace and guide them towards righteousness. Do not wait for the distractions of the undeveloped human mind to cast them astray before they have learned the Truth. We all shall benefit if we hold them as sons and daughters now rather than as afterthoughts to be culled and denied access to our paradise later."

Lord Raguel contemplated the angel's words. "You are correct, the mortal mind is a weak thing and prone to temptation, but it is not for us to tamper with until their time has been chosen. They must prove themselves worthy to enter the Seven Heavens with no divine intervention.

"Such is the Way of the Immortal Mother and the doctrines she set to stone from the beginning of all things. Great Balance must remain. The path of Aetenos was misguided. Your friend thought to change what was unchangeable, and therefore, the Immortal Mother sent him away. Now he is nowhere to be found. His voice is lost to the mortals.

"But we are not here to debate wayward actions of a wandering fool."

Monkey was on the edge of his seat. The silent tension in the courtroom rang in his ears like a continuous, high-pitched peal. Raguel was about to deliver his verdict.

"Artiya'il, you have committed unforgivable crimes against the Heavenly Realm and the Laws of Order that govern us. The will of the Immortal Mother was passed down to me, the first True-born of Heaven, and rightfully interpreted by this office to protect our way of life. Thus, Chaos is kept at bay.

"You took it upon yourself to change the destiny of

countless human souls and tampered with the mortality of their lives. Your actions have jeopardized the Great Balance, and therefore it is to my great sorrow that I must banish you. Henceforth, you are exiled from the Heavenly Realm, nor are you allowed to exist in the realm of men, such is your sentence."

Zhao Houzi's mouth hung open in shock. He slumped back in his chair. How could this be? Banishment from the entire Heavenly Realm and forbidden from entering the Mortal Realm? This was more than a punishment for a misguided deed. The Chancellor Pinnacle was sending a message to all.

Zhao Houzi looked back to the floor and watched Artiya'il lead away by the Protectorates. The condemned angel's head was low, and his wings slumped against his back. Then the seats before and behind him were filled with raucous excitement as the celestials stood to exit.

Where would he go now? Zhao Houzi wondered as he descended the crowded stairs, be as careful as possible not to be stepped on or kicked.

Outside the amphitheater, the sun was high in the sky over Tanalum, the seventh and highest level of the Heavenly Realm. Its golden light bathed the city of Asher in a warm, soothing glow. The sprawling metropolis sparkled in the sunlight. Fluffy clouds floated peacefully in the sky as the celestials went about their administrative affairs and duties of monitoring the fates of the frail humans during their short trial of life.

Zhao Houzi left the Heavenly Hall in a daze. He found a small, unoccupied wall niche along the shade side of a building and hopped inside the concavity. It felt like an upright coffin and just the right size for a little monkey's last resting place.

The building's shadow stole the warmth of the day as he

sat at the edge of the niche and put his wrinkle-skinned hands to his face and sobbed. He still couldn't believe what he had heard. Lord Raguel had given a True-born angel the death sentence.

There was no need to wipe away the tears that ran freely down his furry face. No one could see him, and he doubted much that anyone would care.

BOOK 2 IN THE EVER HERO SAGA

AVAILABLE NOW

Save an imprisoned demigod, kill an archdevil on her home turf, and somehow reclaim his soul. Simple, right?

Captured by the archdevil, Sekka, Kasai must defeat her archnemesis, the devil, Zizphander and his legion of fire fiends at her gate in the hopes she will honor her promise and let his companions live.

Meanwhile back in the Mortal Realm, the fate of the

Three Kingdoms is at stake, and without the power of the Ever Hero, all seems lost.

Kasai must finally accept his role as Aetenos's next Ever Hero and save the land he loves from the diabolical, Frost Legion, rampaging across the continent. But to do this, he must rely on the help from his closest companions, a witch with an identity crisis, who is torn between using her powers for good or evil, and a sentient three-sectioned staff, that may seek to possess him before his work is done.

But what does any of that matter while the devil, Sekka, holds his soul in her frosty grip?

Kasai must connect to the ethereal Boundless to tap into the powers of the Ever Hero, but without a mentor or master to guide him, his odds for success seem remote. Nonetheless, he must find the courage to crush the darkness. Afterall, he is the Chosen One, whether he wants the title or not.

This epic fantasy series will be especially enjoyed by fans of Brandon Sanderson, Robert Jordan, Michael J. Sullivan, Edward W. Robertson, Patrick Rothfuss, and Michael Wisehart.

Buy **The Foe Wars** now and continue to enjoy this exciting new story today.

BOOK 1 IN THE EVER HERO SAGA

AVAILABLE NOW

Kasai Ch'ou has the power to challenge the gods. He just doesn't know it yet.

Enter the archdevil, Sekka hellbent on conquest and lacking but one final piece to guarantee her victory; the soul of the Ever Hero. Will Kasai find his power in time and with it, the courage to defeat the legions of the Abyss?

A century has passed since the disappearance of the demigod, Aetenos, savior and protector of the Mortal Realm.

As whispers of war echo across the Three Kingdoms of Hanna, fate follows in the footsteps of two unlikely companions, a novice mystic monk on the run, and a feisty wood witch with a troubled past.

This series is packed with mysticism, magic, vengeance, and salvation. It does not disappoint with a full cast of mad sorcerers, fiery witches, corrupt dukes, weak kings, sinister devils, a succubus thrown in for good measure. Just wait until the angels arrive as the series gets on a roll.

Perfect for fans of Fans of George R.R. Martin's, A Game of Thrones, Brandon Sanderson's, Mistborn series, John Gwynne's, Bloodsworn Trilogy, Harmon Cooper's, Pilgrim series, and The Fatemarked Epic, by David Estes.

If you are looking for a propulsive, epic fantasy series opener that brings mystical martial-arts action, magic, and political intrigue to the forefront, as awkward companions come of age against the eternal forces of good and evil, then this book is for you.

Buy **The Chaos Gate** now to enjoy this exciting new series today!

Pantanella pours a dark, cinematic foundation in this first volume of his epic fantasy series as a singular hero rises to face both militaristic and demonic enemies. A propulsive fantasy that brings revenge, forbidden attraction, and heroism to the forefront.

"**They were physically wrong as if their bodies had been stuffed into human skin a size too small.**"
~ Kirkus Reviews

BOOK 2 IN THE EVER HERO SAGA

AVAILABLE NOW

Save an imprisoned demigod, kill an archdevil on her home turf, and somehow reclaim his soul. Simple, right?

Captured by the archdevil, Sekka, Kasai must defeat her archnemesis, the devil, Zizphander and his legion of fire fiends at her gate in the hopes she will honor her promise and let his companions live.

Meanwhile back in the Mortal Realm, the fate of the

Three Kingdoms is at stake, and without the power of the Ever Hero, all seems lost.

Kasai must finally accept his role as Aetenos's next Ever Hero and save the land he loves from the diabolical, Frost Legion, rampaging across the continent. But to do this, he must rely on the help from his closest companions, a witch with an identity crisis, who is torn between using her powers for good or evil, and a sentient three-sectioned staff, that may seek to possess him before his work is done.

But what does any of that matter while the devil, Sekka, holds his soul in her frosty grip?

Kasai must connect to the ethereal Boundless to tap into the powers of the Ever Hero, but without a mentor or master to guide him, his odds for success seem remote. Nonetheless, he must find the courage to crush the darkness. Afterall, he is the Chosen One, whether he wants the title or not.

This epic fantasy series will be especially enjoyed by fans of Brandon Sanderson, Robert Jordan, Michael J. Sullivan, Edward W. Robertson, Patrick Rothfuss, and Michael Wisehart.

Buy **The Foe Wars** now and continue to enjoy this exciting new story today.

BOOK 3 IN THE EVER HERO SAGA

AVAILABLE NOW

Why have the angels forsaken us when demons and devils destroy our world?

Kasai and Desdemonia escape the Abyss and travel to the Seven Heavens in hopes of salvation, only to be accused of consorting with the enemy and imprisoned for treason on their arrival. Meanwhile, a new threat from beyond time wakes, driven mad by the scent of fresh souls leaking from the Chaos Gate. The Ancients are coming, and they are hungry.

All the while, the Three Kingdoms are left defenseless to Sekka's rampaging hordes of demons. The Soul War has begun, and the Ever Hero is needed like never before. However, Kasai's fate and that of the Mortal Realm, will be decided by Raguel, the archangel with a personal vendetta against Aetenos. And how better to enact his revenge on the demigod than to destroy his progeny?

If you enjoy an engaging story, pitting the underdog against overwhelming odds, with dark powers turning would-be heroes into finger puppets, and mad ambition which throws worlds into conflict, you'll love the third installment in Jeff Pantanella's page-turning Ever Hero Saga.

A perfect fit for epic fantasy fans of Brandon Sanderson, Robert Jordan, Michael J. Sullivan, Edward W. Robertson, Patrick Rothfuss, and Michael Wisehart.

Buy **The Divine Fist** now and continue to enjoy this exciting new series today!

BOOK 4 IN THE EVER HERO SAGA

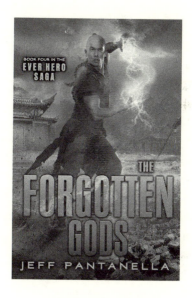

AVAILABLE NOW

What could be worse than a cosmic, world destroying, vampire hungry to drain the Mortal Realm of all life? How about two of them?

The stakes rise to cataclysmic proportions and with the Seven Heavens and Abyss preoccupied with internal war, defense of the Mortal Realm falls to the Ever Hero, a broken and recluse man.

Six years have passed since the defeat of Sekka at the

hands of the Ever Hero. The Heavenly Host has departed, leaving the lands a charred, ash-ladened dystopia. Kasai Ch'ou has returned to the ruins of Ordu, seeking solace, but finding none.

Enter Cyrus Wraith, a mysterious Master Monk of Lost Symmetu, who promises to guide the famed Ever Hero back to the elusive Boundless and help him rebuild the Four Orders of Aetenos. But Cyrus has a hidden agenda, and his obsession with the ancient staff, Ninziz-zida, quickly becomes problematic.

Kasai must rekindle the fire in his soul but in the process, starts down a path that will force him to do the unthinkable to the one person he holds most dear or watch helplessly as the Three Worlds are consumed, literally.

A perfect fit for epic fantasy fans of Brandon Sanderson, Robert Jordan, Michael J. Sullivan, Edward W. Robertson, Patrick Rothfuss, and Michael Wisehart

Buy, ***The Forgotten Gods*** now and enjoy the fourth installment in Jeff Pantanella's page-turning Ever Hero Saga.

BOOK 5 IN THE EVER HERO SAGA

AVAILABLE NOW

Kazumi was born to slay demons, until the fateful day she became one.

Kazumi is a teenaged ninja warrior eager to prove she is ready to ascend to the vaulted rank of Night Blade; an elite group of female demon slayers. Denied by her mother, the High Priestess of the Yoru Ya-iba clan to complete her training, Kazumi sets off on her own to prove her mother wrong.

But chance and fate have other plans for young Kazumi when she is attacked by a monstrous chaos beast in the forest and left for dead, or so she thinks. Soon after, Kazumi realizes the horrible truth: she has become the one thing she has spent her life training to kill.

Outcast from her home, wandering the countryside, Kazumi meets a stranger named Sunny, who joins the young ninja warrior in her quest to find an antidote. Sunny promises Kazumi answers to her unique condition but carries a dark secret of her own. Whether Sunny is friend or foe, only time will decide.

BOOK 6 IN THE EVER HERO SAGA

AVAILABLE NOW

Misfits, outcasts, loners; who could ask for better heroes?

In a world hovering on the brink of eternal darkness, Kazumi, the fearless teenaged demon slayer, and her companion, Sunny, the enigmatic fox-devil, emerge as humanity's final shield against the malevolent House D'Vross; sinister vampire lords ruling over Gethem.

Fueled by vengeance and burdened with the weight of her ancestors, Kazumi, the newly anointed High Priestess of her clan, seeks justice for her fallen family, wielding her razor-sharp katana and lightning-fast wakizashi. All the while, Lily, the demon spirit sharing her soul, offers dark bargains for freedom.

Within a city cloaked in shadows and ancient mysteries, Kazumi and Sunny join Sophia Jolla, a young noblewoman with a shattered birthright and a hidden agenda. Together, they mount a last-ditch effort to stop the D'Vross nightmare from spreading. The question lingers: who poses a greater threat, the would-be tyrants or the young maiden claiming innocence?

In this enthralling sequel, witness Kazumi and Sunny's determined resolve and unwavering friendship face the ultimate tests of betrayal and heartbreak when a haunting truth lurking beneath the surface of lies is uncovered.

"Crouching Tiger, Hidden Demon!" An anime and manga inspired action romp set within the world of the Ever Hero Saga. Buy Book Two: *KAZUMI, Wicked Fox* now and read the continuing story of a teenaged ninja warrior with a dark secret. Book Two in the Night Blades Series, an Ever Hero Saga Story.

BOOK 7 IN THE EVER HERO SAGA

AVAILABLE NOW

The hunted becomes the hunter!

Kazumi and Amos turn the tables on their pursuers and take the fight to the enemy. The quest to free Kazumi's and Lily's soul from the chaos beast connecting them encounters a deadly snare; now those professing to be healers want Kazumi's blood for their own nefarious schemes.

Meanwhile, a new threat enters the conflict, one who could cast the Mortal Realm into everlasting chaos. The Dark King has risen, and he wants Kazumi dead.

"Crouching Tiger, Hidden Demon!" An anime and manga

inspired action romp set within the world of the Ever Hero Saga. Buy Book Seven: KAZUMI, Vampire Hunter now and read the continuing story of a teenaged ninja warrior with a dark secret. Book Two in the Night Blades Mini-Series, an Ever Hero Saga Story.

GET YOUR FREE NOVELLA

JUST TELL ME WHERE TO SEND IT

THE ABYSS IS NOT FOR THE MEEK

It's a world of chaos and conflict where weakness is purged, and failure equals death. Three Supreme Devils rule with uncontested might until a young, ambitious devil sets out on a path to overthrow them all.

Sekka of Nilas refuses to wait for the centuries it will take to amass the power she craves. She is cunning, manipulative, and willing to take risks a more prudent devil would never attempt. But ambition is a double-edged sword, and now she is bleeding out troops faster than she can replace them.

Mistakes have been made, alliances broken, and she finds herself on the losing side of attrition against her enemies.

In a desperate gamble, the young devil launches a risky invasion to steal prized territory from a weakened foe, but one with ties to powerful allies. If the land grab is successful, it will catapult her over her enemies and into a higher echelon of power in the Abyss, but if she fails, she will lose everything; her land, her armies, and her eternal life.

Sekka is a novella set in the epic fantasy series The Ever Hero Saga. Download **Sekka** now and read the origin story of the devil, Sekka, and her rise to power in the Abyss.

BAND OF EVER HEROES

Join my Band of Ever Heroes to receive free or discounted books like this one as part of my Advance Reader Team.

It's completely free to sign up and you will never be spammed by me. (Because Ever Heroes respect your privacy) You can opt out easily at any time.

Click HERE or type this link into your browser window:
https://landing.mailerlite.com/webforms/landing/q6x9s8
to join my Band of Ever Heroes!

ABOUT THE AUTHOR

Jeff Pantanella is a Rhode Island School of Design (RISD) graduate, Guggenheim Fellow, fine art painter, video game maker, and fantasy novel author. He can't remember names or dates and was told there'd be no math in writing fantasy fiction, so, here we are.

"I've always been drawn to the complexities confronted by being the hero in any story. Whom do you save, and what if you can't? The "Ever Hero Saga" is my debut series into the world of dark fantasy fiction, and I explore just how challenging it can be when you are indeed that hero or you're not and think you are."

Welcome to the Three Kingdoms of Hanna and your introduction to the life and times of the Ever Hero. Follow Kasai's adventures, spanning different lands, realms, and worlds as he does his best to fight the forces of evil, that unknowingly, he lets loose on the Mortal Realm.

I hope you have as much fun reading my novels as I had writing them.

Author photo by Asian Yen

Made in the USA
Middletown, DE
08 September 2024